GHOSTING

GHOSTING

Kirby Gann

BROOKLYN, NEW YORK

GHOSTING

Printed in the United States of America.

10 9 8 7 6 5 4 3 2 1

Ig Publishing
392 Clinton Avenue
Brooklyn, NY 11238
www.igpub.com

Library of Congress Cataloging-in-Publication Data

Gann, Kirby, 1968–
Ghosting / Kirby Gann.
p. cm.
ISBN 978-1-935439-47-9
1. Drug traffic—Fiction. 2. Family secrets—Fiction. I. Title.
PS3607.A55G47 2012
813'.6—dc23
2011051470

In memory of James E. Tittle II, "Jamie"
October 10, 1965–June 19, 2007

The dead do not offer themselves up as a consoling study when we loved them so.

—Jim Harrison, *The Road Home*

All is sign. But only a piercing light or shriek will penetrate our blunted sight and hearing. . . . I've always been aware of hieroglyphs written across my path and a confused murmur of words in my ear. Till now I didn't understand them.

—Michel Tournier, *The Ogre*

The things people do don't add up to an edifying story. There aren't any morals to this confusion we're living in. I mean you can make yourself believe any sort of fable about it.

—Robert Stone, *A Flag for Sunrise*

Three shadows steal across a field of forgotten seed corn, stumbling over fallen husks rotted to the ground—three shadows bent low scurry past rough leaves that scrape the skin like cow tongues. Late November, deep night. Misting rain that once hung like fog sharpens into pin needles on great gusts of wind. The loamy mud sucks at their ankles, white breath blooms before their faces, and their bare arms burn with the cold as they surge over the sodden field, wild with trespass.

James Cole Prather comes last in line. He cannot keep pace with the healthy legs of his companions; a misshapen knee makes him list to starboard at each step, his excuse for a run an awkward pole-vaulting motion mastered from childhood. He catches up to where his friends still at the field's end, hiding out before the cracked cul-de-sac drive. Their giggles and squally hushes spring from the dark stalks, a tiny crew of the stoned and invulnerable scanning for signs of any human figure, for the infamous caretaker making his rounds, the glint of his shotgun in the meager moonlight.

The spectacular ruin of the St. Jerome seminary looms before them. It's a vast keep: five stories high, the facade as wide as a football field is long, row upon row of shattered mullioned windows gaping sightless over the broken fields. At the summit towers a stone cross; above that, clouds zoom across the moon like river rapids at full rampage.

His companions bolt across the open space and disappear behind a keeling pine. James Cole watches them go as he catches his breath, used to being left behind. He raises his face to the roiling clouds, feels the cold rain mix with the sweat slicking his cheeks. His eyes close at the simple pleasure, and he listens to the swim in his brain and the thousands of sounds that surround: wind on stalks; rain on leaves; a broken shutter attacking its hinges. Each a note sung precisely for him.

By the time he makes it around the pine his friends are gone.

He calls their names, softly; only the wind rises in answer. The basement windows nearest him are securely boarded shut. Above, on the second floor, a single window hangs open not far from the tree's sturdy center, and he envisions the scene he must have missed only a moment before, Spunk and Shady hauling themselves up the weak extended branches without speaking, sneakers grabbing for toe-holds on the brick ledge.

The rain comes down heavier, in gobs. A shiver wrings his body as three cold drops shock his neck beneath the collar. Up the tree he goes, boots scrape-sliding on the slick trunk, clumps of scratchy bark pulling off in his hands. The climb requires more effort than he had expected, but he makes it to the open window and wiggles through headfirst. The wet linoleum floor shocks when it kisses him hard on the forehead.

They've left him here as well; he can feel the absence around him. The dark is such that it swallows the weak beam of his flashlight. Rain sluices noisily in one dark corner, and somewhere there sings a plopping song, an echo as water taps into deeper water, a melody without resolution. The first purl of thunder rolls the length of the sky in a gradual motion that seems to pour far into the distance and then return. And there is a stench—the room smells of piss and rot and wet dog.

The light from his hand works like an intangible guiding rope drawing him behind its lead. He has been in this place many times before, yet at each entry feels utterly lost—even, in some way, bereft; his heart in his throat. It has always struck him as the backdrop to undesirable dreams: inexhaustible in its rooms, tangled by puzzling stairways and corridors, often presenting mystical compartments with no function he can divine. In dreams he has staggered from hall to hall with slow-thighed dogs panting unseen behind him; he has fled down stairs and stone slides; he has been swallowed altogether into the belly of the earth. As if the building masked a portal that led deep into ancient caverns, sculpted by slicked flues and hidden rivers.

Now here he is again, and, as in every dream, he is alone. But he is not dreaming. What was it the sick man had said just an hour before? *There is always something happening, you just don't know what it is.* It was a quote from somebody else.

He is twenty-three years old. He has no reason to imagine within a year he might be dead. The serrated butterfly knife folded into his hip pocket is mostly for show. Still he checks to confirm the blade is there. On such scant assurance James Cole Prather gropes forward, half-blind in the darkness, less substantial than the knife at his hip or the light in hand, an obedient and guileless spirit adrift from all familiars.

1996

The idea for the night, Cole's idea, had been to go it alone with Shady Beck, the two of them alone after much strategizing and manipulation on his part. In his heart and mind Shady Beck was an end in herself. But she needed a little party, some chemical aid she called it—*I shall be in need of chemical aid,* she cooed in exaggerated high-class over the phone, her small-toothed smile a shape in Cole's ear—as an excuse to be out with him. Or maybe she needed it just to tolerate his presence, he wasn't sure. And he did not care. For years she had been a figure in the hands-off domain of his brother Fleece, a smile and a wave walking away to her car, a sunny laugh across the room to which he always dipped his head in a kind of bow.

Chemical aid required a stop at Spunk Greuel's house, where Cole did not want to go. He *knew* Spunk, had known him most his life, and understood that once with him they might be with him all the night long. The boy was a kind of stink that got on your clothes and in your hair and was near impossible to shake off.

Cole could accept the risk for the chance at spending time with Shady Beck. And it was unavoidable anyway, so no use in lamenting. Mister Greuel was the man to see for pills and pot and any other sin on spec. He led a loose crew—got his weed direct from growers in Clay and Harlan counties, the pills from God knew what Byzantine scams, his crank from his own cooks, most of whom followed Fleece. A dark and entertaining man, Mister Greuel—always with the *Mister,* nobody called him *Lawrence*—him with his tongue swollen from some strange sickness, goggle eyes awry in a fist of a sweating head. He had a face as rutted and pocked as barnwood. His fat tongue made him spit everywhere and mucked up his words. Listening to him was like sitting witness to the creation of a new language, you had to match terms previously unknown to what you had thought you readily understood. Like Spunk's real name is William. Cole had called him Billy on the playground. But one night providing the boys with *the gifts of their destruction*—what Mister Greuel called the bottles and blunts—Billy's dad started to get on his son for not bringing any ass to giggle on his lap. It was for young ass giggling on his lap that Greuel gave freely of his gifts of destruction. Unhappy to see only skinny adolescent boys scouring his stock, Greuel started to mutter over how his own son William was a punk. Except for his fat tongue the word came out *shpunk*. Mix that moment with teenage boys baked on the bomb and Billy Greuel becomes Spunk the rest of his life.

Greuel made the kids laugh but they knew not to mess with him. It was Greuel the guy that took down three Gravy Berserkers (one of the biker gangs from Montreux city) who thought they could reap business from a hick dealer by showing up with no more than chugging fat-boy hogs and a flash of a semiautomatic Glock. Greuel swept them out with nothing but a rifle and a Bowie knife, and he strung those bodies from a town-square tree like so much deer meat left to ripen in winter.

Yet on many occasions this man told little James Cole to think on him as a friend.

The gate code had not changed since the days Cole used to ride up on his bicycle. He punched in the numbers and parked by the stables where the old man ran legit side-business boarding horses for city refugees, rich folk buying into the new bedroom communities mushrooming on either side of the interstate. Shady took his hand and the small gesture thrilled him. Together they navigated the great yard of oxidized farming implements and roadside statuary, a mazy museum of throwaway Americana. They halted at the front steps before a clutch of gar hung gape-mouthed and stinking, their eyes collapsed into folds. Cole had no explanation for the fish.

Professor Mule shouted greetings from his Adirondack chair. He looked nested alongside a column of paperback mysteries, a thermos between his thighs, his Mossberg shotgun in easy reach against the porch rail. They had not seen one another in years but Mule said he would recognize that crazy eye of Cole Prather anywheres. You staying warm, Erly? Cole asked, skipping the man's nickname, ever uneasy before his grain-sack presence and the gun, though what Cole heard was you only needed to run from Mule if you saw him with his toolbox. Mule nodded and dismissed them, falling into a singsong hum as he returned to his book, a ridiculously fragile looking object in the grip of his pork-belly hands.

"I knew you'd be out here fore too long you wall-eyed rascal!" Spunk burst out, knocking open the screen door. He torched their faces with a breath that bleached the stench of the fish. Presented with someone she recognized, Shady regained composure and was in past Spunk and at the big bowl of reefer by Mister Greuel in his rocking chair before the screen clapped shut. Feeling like a calf roped on the run, Cole felt the Greuel house upon him.

They kept off the main lights by habit, the dim room illuminated by the small blue glow of a silent TV set. That and the headlight Greuel kept at hand, wired to a car battery set on the floor. As visitors arrived he liked to blind them in the glare as he waved the headlight about. Somewhere deeper in the house a transistor radio scratched out lonesome tinny fiddles and nasal harmonies that wailed tales of warning from another day. It was a greeting impossible to get used to and Cole had walked into it a thousand times.

Not Shady; she was on a mission. She pounced into the old man's lap and had her hands in the bowl, saying, "Mister Greuel how do you do, whyn't you tell us a story while I roll us up a fat one."

The old man's laughter came sick and raspy but it had always sounded that way and he would never die.

"I like her!" he crowed as he shifted in his chair, the weight of them both wrenching complaints from the struts. "Who is she?"

As if he didn't know. As if anyone in Pirtle County had never heard of Shady Beck, youngest of the three daughters to Doctor Beck (the pediatrician who had booster-shot them all), one-time star of the volleyball and swim teams, Shady Beck the walker-away from dazzling car wrecks, subject of several profiles in the *Pirtle Notice* paper, she of the hair like vivid champagne bubbling past her shoulders, hair that seemed a celebration whenever Cole saw it freed from its usual ponytail; her gray eyes had boys whispering her name into clutched hands at night before they fell into dream.

Still she introduced herself. As she did so Mister Greuel played the headlight over Cole, the beam driving heat over his face and arms. Spunk had to remind his father twice—*That's Cole Prather, Papa, come on you know James Cole*—speaking his name louder the second time in a dance with his father's shouted *What?* and *Goddammit who?* as he shook his head and dug one finger in his ear, lips curled into a snarl. He thumped the headlight against the side table as though to squash a scuttering bug there, the metal casing casting a resonant bell tone.

"Come in here with a pretty girl and you know where my eyes're at. Been so long since I seen this boy I don't even know him on sight anymore." Greuel's smile unveiled a row of small crooked teeth the color of cooked bacon fat. "Well it's always good to have a Skaggs around," he said then, assuming the part of gracious host, "even if all you can get's the one what run off." Cole did not correct him. A rattling cough throttled the man and threatened to throw Shady to the floor. Greuel gasped and gulped furiously from a bottle of water and raised one arm; then, once he gathered himself again, he clarified that he knew Cole wasn't all Skaggs. Not that it mattered anymore in today's day and age.

"How is that mother of yours? Still splitting meds with patients at the clinic?"

Cole shook his head. "You know she's not. She quit that place first day she could."

"Why would I know that?"

It was nothing more than his game, Mister Greuel showing off before an attractive guest. He was nodding and smiling to spur Cole on to what he wanted him to say.

"You got her the job," Cole said to the floor. "It was you the one got her hooked up with that lawyer for the disability."

"Lyda Skaggs working a rehab hospital," Greuel smacking his lips at the tasty ironies, "that there's the fox guarding the henhouse if I ever heard. Now how come I never see her anymore?"

Cole raised his shoulders and held them. He didn't know what made his mother do any of the things she did.

"Must not need anything," Greuel purred into Shady's neck, as quiet and murmurous as a lover whispering.

Dishes clacked in the back of the house from the kitchen down the hallway. The radio back there had changed over to a basketball game. The front room shuddered with the changes on the silent TV screen, a general dark closing down and then pulling back. Shady, comfortable in most all situations, ignored the awkward stretch of silence; she asked and said at the same time (which was her way), "You want to talk to Miss Skaggs, why don't you just call her," and ran her tongue the length of a rolling paper. Mister Greuel patted her thigh just above the knee, his single ornament—a large gold-nugget ring set with diamonds that followed a curve into the shape of a horseshoe—glittering blue fire.

"Now I have never cared for telephones. No point in them, nobody can understand a thing I say if they don't see me say it." He wagged the mustard-gray eel of his fat tongue; Shady peered at the lighter she used to fire up the joint.

"She'll come around," he added. "You can count Lyda a loyal friend when in need. You know what I'm talking about, don't you, James Cole?"

Cole wasn't there to discuss his mother. They had argued earlier that evening and her voice still stung in his ears the way only a mother's voice can sting. She had mocked his moving in, calling him her *honored guest;* she had called him lukewarm water in the mouth of God. It stung and he could not say why, or why she would even use those last words, Lyda being nowhere near religious. Her head was so blended in roofers and goofballs that no one could explain half of what came out of it. Still the insults pricked.

Lyda had asked why he was pursuing Fleece's girl. She's not Fleece's girl anymore, Momma, they broke up years ago. She said, You can't do better than pick up where your brother left off? He's your *brother.* Cole reminded her he was only half his brother, as everyone in the county liked to remind him they knew. She said they both dropped out of her belly so that made them all brother in her eyes. Cole said the gulf between the way she saw things and the way things were was wide enough to march an army through. *A really big army,* he stressed. Some time soon after this she came up with lukewarm water and the mouth of God.

The joint made its rounds. Cole held in the smoke for as long as his lungs would allow, as if his doing so could prevent everyone else from talking.

"You seen that Fleece of late?" Mister Greuel asked.

Cole raised his shoulders again, dropped them—he was beginning to feel self-conscious about this gesture—and passed the joint. "You see Fleece more than I do."

"That may be but maybe I haven't seen him *lately,* is what I'm saying. And maybe *you* have. That's why I asked the *question.*"

Cole started to shrug his shoulders but caught himself, and turned up empty hands. He did not understand the why behind what the man was asking.

"I can spell it out. My business is such a fine-tuned machine you'd think it was designed by NASA. Fleece is my Mr. Reliable, works for me like there's no other reason for him to even *be.* Now you move back to the lake with momma. And last night I had delivery due from your fine reliable brother, but I don't hear from him. This is odd to my logic: you come home—your brother, suddenly he's nowhere to be found. I hate coincidence. Makes everybody look guilty. I hate that."

Everyone looked to Cole, even Shady, as though he should have the answer to his brother's whereabouts, as though Fleece and Cole were close confidants—which everyone in that room knew they were not. His body flushed with heat, and it felt like the skin on his face and neck exhaled, all the small veins that fed the skin rinsing themselves. His eyes watered and he pinched them shut with thumb and two fingers. He was the only person standing in this room. He had always had trouble with nervousness for no reason. Especially when attention turned to him. He said, "Well Fleece does what he wants."

"I bet he's cooling it at St. Jerome by now," came Spunk's voice, foggy as he held in his hit and passed the jay to his father, who skipped his turn.

This was certainly possible. The seminary of Saint Jerome sat far out in the northern ridge of the county, behind fields of seed corn backing all the way up to the Possler Woods. It was said to be haunted; to house the rituals of devil worshippers; to be a hideout for dangerous men on the lam from the law, family, their lives. A mad caretaker protected the place and supposedly shot trespassers on sight. Many of these stories were no more than legends created by Fleece Skaggs— except for the caretaker, a guy he had assured his younger brother was truly unhinged. Fleece sold the man reefer and crank and squatted on the top floor. They shot bottles together off the stone cemetery wall out back of the seminary grounds.

"Always been a young man I could trust, I practically raised him," Greuel frowning at the headlight, "so I worry. Anything can happen on a country road. What if he tumbled over the shoulder and he's lying there upside-down in the Cumberland?"

No one answered. Whoever was back there in the kitchen scraped a plate and turned up the radio, two broadcasters speaking with dramatic urgency over the roused crowd. Mister Greuel tilted his head as if listening, or straining to listen. In time he turned to the corridor and shouted: *Hey now. It's near ten already.*

The crowd cheered loud enough to fuzz the small speakers and the announcer's voice accelerated, hoarse with excitement. Boots shuffled on the kitchen tile and someone ran the tap briefly and then the radio shut off. The house stiffened in silence. The back screen door smacking shut clattered like a gunshot. Mister Greuel returned his attention to his guests, and began to talk again as outside a car engine revved to life, tires soon rolling over gravel.

Shady started work on another blunt, her glassy eyes narrowing to slits. She swayed her hips in Mister Greuel's lap for reasons Cole could not fathom.

"Honest truth, you can't name a place your brother might go without word to me?"

Honest truth he did not know. Spunk jumped to his feet, decided aloud they should head to the old seminary to see what turned up. His father grunted and sliced the air with his hand, said he wasn't asking him. It was a vicious gesture that cut the length behind Shady's back, and his son turned as though struck across the face, and rushed his own head into the corner of the fireplace mantel.

Seconds passed before he cried out. Like the pain needed time to alarm his brain. From above one eye blood gushed from a gash as if its entire reason for being was to be freed of his veins. Spunk clutched the wound with the hem of his T-shirt and slumped into the couch. His father shook his head and stared at the floor; Shady looked on with vague interest. Nobody moved to help him. It was like no one was sure what they had witnessed had actually happened. After a silence, he moaned.

All this transpired within seconds. Yet it seemed to take forever to Cole, and a pressure built within him, a gradual rise that swelled until it broke, setting him into the generous sniggers of the greatly stoned. He started to shake and laugh in *I'm-so-high* wiggin' giggles, an act that moved Shady and Mister Greuel from stares of blank inverted fixity to ones of mild concern, but an act too that he could not stop. And still no one moved to ask Spunk if he was all right; nobody there expected anything less of him than his smacking his head into the most convenient sharp corner. As though Spunk had survived this long, made it to twenty-two despite the parade of self-inflicted accidents and mishaps that composed his brief lifetime, the broken fingers and toes and collarbones and splintered teeth, the burns from incompetent engine work (four-wheeler, minibike, motorcycle), the concussions from irritated horses, the mishandling of knives and saws and throwing stars, the metal grinder that caught his shirt and then the rest of his torso within it—with such veteran experience behind him it was rational to assume no mantel corner could do serious damage to that head. Cole pressed his hand over his mouth and nose to cram down the laughter, it felt like his eyes were hosing streams over his cheeks, and the laughter only punched at his chest that much harder. *The hell's got into this boy?* Mister Greuel wondered aloud. Cole could not answer. All he could manage was to clamp one hand tighter over his mouth and wave away the room with the other, begging to be ignored.

"I love pot but some people it just makes stupid," Shady said. Instantly this shut him up somehow.

Mister Greuel fiddled with his headlight. He turned it one way and then another, often staring into the beam below his chin. By now Spunk had removed his shirt entirely and held it wadded against his eyes. He mumbled the word *stitches* and his father mumbled back that such could be found in a kitchen drawer. Spunk brought away the shirt and looked at the blood spattered there, pressed it to his brow again. This was not a cheap article of clothing, he complained. *I bought this at*—he couldn't remember. Then he yawned, resigned to the ruined fact of it.

"A lot of blood in the human face," Shady said.

"I thought you knew everything," Cole said to Greuel. "I thought you never let a man drive a harvest alone."

Greuel passed his headlight over the walls and ceiling. He said there had been complications with this run, his tailer had another item of business to take care of on the way back, they'd done it before in a pinch and never had any difficulties. "But you don't need to know my problems," he added. Again Spunk reasoned that Fleece was fine and probably fixed up with some tail—he excused himself to Shady from beneath the bloodied shirt—and was cooling it easy in his seminary digs.

"I'd like to think if he's in this county he would have sense enough to bring me my money or my goods or else have a damn good reason to be walking around. A man has standards to keep, a reputation to uphold."

At this Greuel appeared to fall into pensive rumination, gazing absently as the shape of the room changed with the movement of his hand. Dark veils swung opposite the wash of light and the whole room swayed; shadows dipped forward to listen in, leapt back. By now Cole's eyes felt swollen and gritty, and it seemed he could note each half-thought as it rose and floated away without his grasping it. Perhaps that was why he felt so naked and unprepared when Greuel stilled the light fully upon him.

Events have a way of fooling, the man said. You're in it and you think they're one way but turns out they were steadfastly another.

There's always what's happening below what *seems* to be happening. It's enough to drive a man batshit crazy. You have to ask questions, you have to ask *why* you ask the questions you ask, it just goes on and on. And every time, the questions take you where you don't want to go. Every freaking time.

"I have no idea what you are saying to me," admitted Cole. Greuel dismissed him from behind Shady again. He smacked his lips as though he did not like the taste in his mouth.

"You kids get out of here. Why not show some loyalty to the old man who takes such care of you? Get out to that old place and see what sign of Fleece you can rustle up before I forget him." Another raspberry cough erupted then, along with another squeeze to Shady's thigh that went unremarked by her and set Cole to cringing. "Get off me hon, I got pills to take. And son don't you take any more that reefer, I'm short in the pocket as of right this now."

Shady staggered up as Greuel struggled to rise, using the beveled edge of the table for stability. It had not been so long since Cole had seen him last but he could tell the man had much declined. Whatever illness that was at him had managed a great deal of work over the past several months.

From the hallway Mister Greuel bid farewell as though already his emissaries were a long distance off on their journey, and the bacon-fat teeth unveiled themselves again. With that simple gesture, any hope Cole had with Shady this night was effectively over. Spunk stood waiting outside the door in his bloody T-shirt, holding up a snagged dime bag he shook at Shady with glee. All three glided out and over the porch and through the littered yard, Spunk slithering, skeletal, and cackling in the lead.

The first cop to show nods at Dwayne Hardesty and stands beside him at the feet of four kids who lie spread-eagled face-down on the muddy portico steps leading to the graffiti-strewn boards that shield the seminary entrance. The wash of the cruiser's spot frescoes their captive forms in hard outline, three underfed and thin and the fourth a fat block squeezed into a Kentucky basketball sweatshirt that strains to withstand his heavy nervous breathing, the grommets in their jeans and an occasional earring flashing agleam in the white light; four pairs of white sneakers, expensive and rain-wet, shine stark and severe and unworldly. The caretaker always struggles to prevent himself from gloating too much over this aspect of his job.

"I count four," the cop says low, to Hardesty's shoulder.

"Yep, four's where I stop at too."

"Thought you called in five?"

"The one run off before I got these down. You might hear word later."

"I should check emergency rooms."

"You maybe get something out of that, yeah."

"Wish you wouldn't send these kids to the hospital, Mr. Hardesty. I understand your duty but these are just teenagers out here and you're likely to brand them for life. Kind of a hard cost for a boy out looking for kicks."

Hardesty turns from the cop and spits. The thick saliva smacks onto the pavement in a heavy gel that holds its shape until the pattering rain thins the dark phlegm and a yellow strip breaks loose, drains the wad empty. His small rangy hound scoots among the line of captives, shivering under thin brown fur soaked to a fine sheen. Her whirligig tail throws a sparkling spray in the cast of cruiser light that's fairly pretty to see.

"Get over here, Bone."

Howls erupt from on high and deep inside the building, yaps and snarls muddling together from one of the floors directly above. The dog raises from where she had her nose in the ear of one boy who dared not turn away and whines a squeaky whine. She puts her nose to him again, and again Hardesty commands her to come. This time she appears to almost nod in agreement—as though to admit her master is of course reasonable and right despite her urge to do differently—and she springs over the boy's head into the next space over, the throaty whine rising again almost to a drone. She looks up at Hardesty and then back at the kids on their bellies, and then huffs an exasperated complaint. Hardesty speaks her name again, hard. She lowers her chin to her forepaws and the tail slows in waves to a shy, low, wary swing.

"I give him a brush to think about is all. He aint going to die."

"Salt shot?"

"Gets you the bird without messing the feathers."

"Damn that has got to burn like hell."

"Wouldn't know, myself. I make it a point to be on the right end of the gun."

Hardesty chins his collarbone. He has yet to look this cop in the face, instead surveying his bounty stilled and silent on the ground, the set of each head indicating they are listening with complete and utter attention to the low voices of the two men. He has to remind himself he is performing a duty and is in his rights; usually around police Hardesty's more nervous than they are right now. This fact irritates him no end.

"Well, wish you wouldn't do it."

"You want me to walk you through this building it is my job to protect and show what these kids come here to do? There is no mercy for vandals. It is 455 in the A.D. and the sack of Rome in there. I don't like midnight work anymor'n you, my living room is warm and dry. I give them a warning shot. Sometimes a kid runs right into it."

The officer tilts his head to greet a colleague who has parked her cruiser by the empty stone fountain in the center of the circular drive, the engine running with the high beams left on. The rain flashes tinsel threads that emerge and disappear in the same instant like the very air is woven from some magical fabric.

Hardesty does not acknowledge the second cop at all. He has nothing against equality but does not believe in women in positions of physical authority. A figure of authority should be able to display some brawn. He has seen big women but none ever big enough to intimidate him into stepping carefully, and this one here's no bigger than a springtime weed. She asks what kind of fish is that they've strung across on the ground. Her voice and the bit of a mirth between the two cops snaps Bone to attention but leaves the caretaker unmoved, in no mood for hilarity that does not arise from him.

He knows they have a routine down for this kind of stop. Still he feels the same dismay once the first woman takes over proceedings and announces to the vandals' benefit how she is going to turn around and let them get rid of anything they don't want her to find when she pats them down. She'll give them thirty seconds. As she turns, Hardesty's toes flex in his boots until it pains him; the woman is staring straight at the door of his cottage. He has to remind himself that there's no reason she will ask to go in.

The fat boy lifts his head from the pavement and holds it there. He looks to his left and the other officer makes a vaudeville show of turning his back to them, too, crossing his arms as he faces the break of dead corn. The boy rolls to one side and reaches deep into his jeans, pulls up a plastic bag that shines in the cruiser lights, and tosses the bag into the scrappy boxwoods grown askew along the seminary's front. A silver spear of rain flashes directly above the bag's landing and is gone.

At the sight Hardesty's throat creates a sound that causes the first cop to ask if he's okay. Hardesty waves him off, feels his eyes burning as the woman starts to search the first of the lot. *Outrageous travesty of justice,* he mutters. A trespass charge is nothing to keep a kid from coming back. He'll look at it now like a challenge from the caretaker, a personal offense to his honor. Possession, though—a lost opportunity. The delight of the catch has already withered inside him; lately he has been wondering if he had lost his touch, having come up empty on a number of occasions while making his rounds but finding plenty of evidence that people were running riot over the place.

He recognizes the male officer, forgets his name but he knows the mustache, like two chalk lines etched into the black man's skin. He has never understood that cop culture of groomed mustaches, why they never wear beards. It's fishy to him; they try too hard.

The officer touches him high up on the back of his arm with gentle camaraderie, turning him slightly to one side.

"You put a good scare into them tonight, don't you think? Boys learned a lesson they won't forget. Especially when they hear from their buddy."

"He's still running and don't even know why," Hardesty says, the image of a boy running in total panic and spurred by the fifty points of fire in his backside leading him to amusement despite the anger growing from what he knows is coming next.

"Dwayne, listen. If I can call you Dwayne. How about you let me threaten these four here with the cold hand of the law and then we cut them loose? I would consider that a favor. A personal favor."

Again with the sound in his throat; it's a small strangled keening sound Hardesty is only half-aware of making. The cop's eyes widen in concern. Hardesty looks down at the chopped pavement, at Bone who has taken to her feet again but sticks beside him, her temple pressed against his shin. He sucks at his teeth.

"Release the mongrel hordes to the forest so they can return, you're saying. Y'know, they don't even *try* to hide, they come slapping feet in the rain without a care."

"You won't see these kids again, I bet."

"Don't matter, there's always more to come. Only me and Bone here against every teenager who don't have nothing to do in two counties and no sense to do it somewhere else. What the church plans to do other than burn this place to the ground I can't imagine."

The cop exhales a series of short noiseless puffs Hardesty interprets as blithe showmanship from a man who wants to exhibit how streetwise and seen-it-all he is. He has a lean narrow face with squared cheekbones that press the tight skin, a thin strip of mustache that meets in a sharp sculpted column leading to his nostrils. Hardesty doesn't understand why a man would put so much effort into the upkeep a mustache like that must require. He just does not understand the desire to put that much labor into your face.

"I have no use for you," he admits. Ever come to aid a crime victim and heard *that?* he wants to ask.

"Let's do the right thing here. What do you say? Let me put fear to these kids and we'll call the parents and send them home to their whippings and every one of us can get out of this rain. What do you say to that?"

"I say these jacklegs broke the law. I say your whole attitude disturbs me and these kids are my opportunity to set an example for vandals everywhere. My apologies if that sucks time away from your work on that fancy mustache but this is your job, aint it?"

Unperturbed, the officer broadens his smile. He strokes the mustache with the back of two fingers.

"Pressing charges isn't going to make an example of these kids to anybody, Mister Hardesty."

He appears to enjoy this, his accounting of the kind of wrist-slap the boys have ahead articulated with calm objectivity and near-palpable glee: worst-case scenario, they'll be sentenced to a few hours of community service, a punishment the kids nowadays only brag about to their peers. Deferred probation, maybe; a record swept clean once the state recognizes them as adults.

Hardesty hardly listens to a bald truth he's familiar with already, studying instead the second officer performing her search. She pulls a broken broom handle from one pocket, a set of magic markers from another. She throws each item into the bushes as though they never existed, although the caretaker knows they do and will have to be gathered *by him* and eventually taken to the landfill *by him* with all the rest of the garbage that somehow accumulates around this useless place in the middle of nowhere.

He interrupts the cop's speech by brandishing his shotgun, a simple rising up and down.

"I'm pressing charges and I'll be there in court when need be. Your badge identifies you as officer number 367. I expect to be notified of a court date and if I don't I will file a complaint."

The cop sighs in that slow and deliberate way of one about to embark upon a task that requires patience and that he does not want especially to do. The four boys now sit with elbows on knees, staring in dubious incredulity as the officer explains they've no one to blame but themselves for the inconvenience and the caretaker is in his rights and they are all going to the station. Moreover, he does not expect any expressions of attitude from a one of them. The fat boy complains they should press charges against the caretaker, for all they knew they had a friend bleeding out dead in the corn. Hardesty resists his urge to fire the shotgun into the seminary wall to silence everyone, to wield the weapon like a gnarled staff and he some mad prophet returned from the wilderness to warn of imminent perdition for them all. He resists his own impulses until the two officers have the kids cuffed in their cruisers and the spotlights and roof lights are extinguished and they are gone, up the pocked drive past the corn field and onto the county road and out of his life. Then he roars back at the dogs still yapping on the floors above, acquiring the kind of silence he seeks by firing his gun straight into the night air.

Excellent quiet then. The rain has died to a weak drizzle but the wind is up, and the drops needle into the corners of his eyes.

"*Vandal hordes*, Bone. Where do I come up with this shit?" The phrase brings him genuine laughter. He waits to be certain the shotgun doesn't invite the return of either cruiser and, once satisfied he and the dog are left alone, steps over the boxwoods and picks up the baggie flung there, holding it close in the dark to examine the chalky crystals inside.

Another defeat. Every freaking day, another defeat.

"Least we come out ahead," he tells the dog, swinging the baggie playfully before her. She begins to duck and sway with the movement, and her tail spirals water into the air again. Hardesty nudges her with his boot. "Get yer coon ass back in that house, bitch. We done our duty this night."

•

An hour later lightning strikes the transformer that powers Hardesty's house. He had been comfortable and almost dozing in the small cottage that smells faintly of mold and Bone's wet fur and a heady syrup sweetness he tries to ignore—he should be used to it by now—and the hour is deep enough for the TV to be into reruns of detective shows from his childhood that Hardesty can practically recite. Bone lay curled on the wool rug beneath the set, Hardesty had his socked feet on the coffee table that lacks one leg and requires careful placement of his feet to avoid spillage of magazines and candy wrappers and half-empty mason jars, two fingers of vodka tilted on his belly rising in rhythm with his low breathing, when the transformer cracked the sky like a cannon shot. The explosion is already an echo when Hardesty realizes the vodka gone, his table has upended everything onto the floor, and he is standing in the middle of the room with an empty jar.

Through the kitchen he pulls back the threadbare curtain and wipes humidity off a pane of glass with the heel of his hand. Fog hangs heavy outside. He has to crane his neck upward to find the transformer in bright burn—quivering flame licks the steel casing and disappears into the mist, coloring a tiny fogbow; a strand of violet dances up the wooden post harnessed to the building. The flames create a strange, unfamiliar noise he can barely hear, like a radio receiver between direct signals, all crackle and burst. His nostrils tingle with a smell remembered from Army maneuvers and the cottage has fallen entirely dark.

Bone presses into his legs, her frightened whimper winging up to join the howls of Fleece's dogs in the big seminary itself. Hardesty pats at his chest pockets, not looking for anything but out of habit, and as he turns to seek one overhead cabinet for his power light—a quality instrument with a one-million candlelight beam—he trips over the dog tucked into his legs. He curses and shoves her out of the way with his ankle. In the darkness he doesn't see her skitter back to his legs again, and Hardesty hears her squeal as his heavy foot lands on what might be her foreleg and he feels her mass against his knee and then he's falling, one shoulder cracking into the corner of a chair back, his forehead shucking the edge of the refrigerator door.

He's unsure if he passed out or not. It feels like a discovery when he realizes his back against the refrigerator, Bone licking his cheek. *Get*, he says, moving his hand between her mouth and his face, but his speaking only makes the dog lick with more enthusiasm and he has to shove her away.

He doesn't rise from the floor immediately. One hand cups his knee; the other feels accumulated dirt on the peeling linoleum. Through the kitchen window the glow has turned the bluish white of moonbeams. Perhaps the fire burned itself out.

"Aw, let the old thing burn, Bone, what do you say?"

She takes it as invitation and dives at his face again with her tongue, forcing him to his feet, the nails of her paws a scramble-scratching on the withered tiles. Hardesty leaves her inside and slams the door behind him, power light in hand.

He doesn't like to exit his home without his boots and gun but he's halfway to the building before he realizes he has left with neither. Midnight lies quiet, a gentle hushing amid the crowns of trees a hundred yards away in the old cemetery. The crooked moon shines over what has turned into a cold clear night, a few clouds aglow in ghostly hues passing slow beneath the stars. Smoke blankets the rooftop with moody shifts of the wind, an odor of burned rubber and singed plastic heavy within it.

He shines the power light up to the transformer, over the scorched steel and melted cable insulation, and with a lethargic sigh drags the beam down the length of the wall to his cold feet, where he takes his finger off the button and the night surrounds him again. He'll be eating off the charcoal grill for a few days; the power company does not place a high priority on this transformer.

Hardesty digs his fingernails into the flesh just beneath his jaw-bone and starts to backstep carefully over the gravel again but then stops short: something is off about the sounds around him. He stills himself with head askew, tongue fingering small gaps in his molars, wary, senses keen, listening. The low chug of a powerful engine idles nearby, behind the seminary; a radio scratches out old country music, the high trebly kind of curdled yawps and wails that rise into the quiet and toil with the wind in the trees.

Are kids so brazen these days that they would start to tailgate back here? He keeps close to the wall and crosses the width of the east wing, socks soaked, toes numb; the unseen engine coughs out but the radio continues, and then it's the rough hinge of a car door pushed open. Hardesty flattens himself against the brick where a gap between the building's wing and center chapel forms a deep courtyard, a space for the cement island that used to be a basketball court.

The car door clicks shut softly. A groan from what must be the trunk opens then, another hinge in need of oil. Must be an old car. Hardesty presses into the brick and listens to a woman's forlorn voice sing from the radio:

> Where you've gone I'll follow
> Who you were I'll be
> I'll become your shadow
> if you no longer think of me
> no, you no longer think of me

and a man (for it could be only a man, to Hardesty's mind) whistles a counterpoint that doesn't agree with her melody. Beneath the whistling comes a slosh from liquid poured, a heavy gushing that splashes loud over the flex and gulp from some pliable container. Hardesty looks back toward home, weighing the cost and opportunity to retrieve his gun, his boots. But he does not go. Instead he chances a glimpse past the corner to see.

A man there, looking nothing more than a humanoid shadow. He works the length of the vehicle, emptying two large jugs over the cowl and hood. It doesn't take long, and once he finishes he steps back and looks over the car, continuing to whistle as he tosses the jugs into high grass Hardesty never gets around to mowing. The man begins to fiddle in his pockets as the singer's voice fades to silence, a brief quiet enduring until the opening guitar strum of another song begins.

Hardesty is about to shine his power light on the scene when the man strikes a match. It's a sudden firefly in the air and then a soft *whup* like a great gas oven firing overcomes the music. Blue flame washes over the chassis. Behind that ethereal blue, a color found in flame only that has fascinated him since childhood, high capes of yellow and gold race to catch up, and in another instant the entire car is rapidly burning, a single coal visible through the flames. The gentle lament of a song can still be heard beneath the crackle of fire. The man shades his face from the heat as he begins to walk a distant perimeter, admiring the success of his handiwork. In that light Hardesty can make out a dark sport coat and tie, a shuffling thin body moving like a boxer. The flames start to eat at the interior. One tire detonates from the heat—sparks spiral into the dark—and Hardesty can't see the man on the far side of the flames. It gives him the courage to step from his hiding place, and as he does he catches sight of the man again, tail-turned and flatfoot running toward the distant Possler Woods, the gated cemetery.

Only then does the caretaker find his voice: "Hey! Hey you there!" he calls, directing his light over the great lawn behind the looming building. But even a million candlelights cannot sight the figure fleeing the scene. Like that, he has vanished.

Hardesty jumps at the touch of something live against his leg and he drops the power light—Bone has managed to open the unlocked back door. She cowers from him, expecting a kick. But Hardesty reaches to pet her gently as he looks back toward the cemetery and the Possler Woods and the moonlight that etches the outlines of forms. All he can discern now is the refuse abandoned back there, old refrigerators with the doors still connected, rusted bedsprings and engine blocks, piles of bottles and cans.

"What kind of guard dog are you?" he asks, toeing her ribs, her fur as soaked as his sock. "I mean really. What you good for?"

Bone glances at him with apparent wariness. She sits back on her haunches, and peers into the same direction as Hardesty as he strains to descry any movement within the moonlight shadows there.

Another soft detonation as another tire blows out; Hardesty scratches at the flesh under his jaw again and watches the flames curl through the windows and thrive on the seats and dash. Transmission fluid boils on the cracked cement court.

"Neither one of us did all that good tonight," he tells Bone. "Damn if sometimes I don't believe we can't make a caretaker worth the name between the both of us."

They had fled a pack of dogs on one floor and then before they had caught their breaths behind the stairwell door, slammed shut behind them and still echoing through the corridors, they were sent into flight again at the blast from the caretaker's shotgun outside. This took them as high in the building as they could go, which also happened to be where Fleece kept what he called his penthouse. It had been a suite of offices at one time but he had made a home there and now as they stumbled into it they found the rooms nearly barren again, no different from any of the others falling apart throughout the building. A pleather desk chair faced one corner, an arm rest torn off. A few books were stacked spines-out on a windowsill—mostly Catholic theology texts that he must have found somewhere in the building, but a few mystery novels as well—and they were warped from water and stank when opened. Beside them on the sill paper clips burned to a copper shine stood posed in models of twisted disfigurement. Through a second door slumped on its highest hinge they discovered bed sheets wadded in the corner and a pair of mismatched socks. Spunk asked if Cole was sure they had the right place and Cole told him angrily that sure he was sure and the three followed the two flashlights illuminating empty corners.

"Well by the evidence I'd judge he is not here now," Spunk said.

It took a moment for his words to sink in to start their snorts of laughter at his stating the obvious. He put his flashlight on the floor and pulled out the baggie he'd stolen from his father and they all three sat down while he made his preparations and they could smoke up again in the dark, waiting until the police lights flashing outside had disappeared before moving on.

•

Somehow they end up on the roof. The seminary's shaped like a capital E with the facade stacked one floor higher than the two wings that extend out either end, the chapel in the building's center. Spunk has wandered off on his own. Alone for the first time, Shady and Cole follow a gray glow that wavers within a long passageway—a passage, he thinks, like what people are said to see when they die, an obscure light at the end of the darkness. In this case the light turns out to be the night visible through the window in a steel door. The door wings open with a retch onto the rooftop, and the cool fresh wind feels as necessary then as longed-for water. Shady squeals in stoned delight; she jumps down two wooden steps and skips the length of the roof some fifty feet, her shoes scattering wet gravel over tarpaper to the far ledge, her white top glowing phosphor beneath silent lightning flares.

Thunder follows the lightning and lingers in such a continuous roll it could be a jet circling overhead. Cole doesn't join her until she motions to him. The drugs in his body, his success in tracking down his friends after they had abandoned him, have instilled a weird confidence in him tonight and he wraps his arms around her waist from behind, rests his chin on her shoulder. Wind shushes the trees in the distant Possler Woods, and it is good wind, wind as God must imagine it, pure and singing.

"What are you doing," Shady says. Softly. He can hear the smile in her voice as she leans into him, presses one hand into the back of his head to keep him there.

The smell of her up close jumps in his blood like another heavy and wondrous drug; he could pass out in it, his nose against her neck, inhaling the moist heat off her skin. His hand moves toward her breast, drawn there by the arch in her back—but then his eyes part, and the view stops him still. He has been in this very spot before. Yes, he had been here with his brother. When? They had sat with their legs dangling over the edge on a bright afternoon, taking in the old cemetery and its crumbling stone perimeter, listening for the gravel they tossed into the air to hit the asphalt court below. This would have been before their mother sent Cole to live with his dead father's family. He remembered it had been maybe the third or fourth time he had ever smoked weed and he was still cataloging the effects it made in his body, trying to note the difference between stoned and not-stoned, between cottonmouth and thirst, and he was smiling stupidly when Fleece declared that in that cemetery stood headstones so old they had been rained blank and smooth.

No names or dates, nothing left, he said. *Nothing but an old stone to mark somebody down there that nobody remembers.*

He gestured again as if directing Cole toward specific headstones even though they were too far away to see more than the suggestion of stones, winking white beneath the dense trees' dipping limbs. He said something about how the bodies lying buried there, how the lives those bodies had once led, which must have seemed very important to them in their time, may as well have never happened at all. *Know what I mean?* he asked.

No, Cole did not know. He had been eleven or twelve. Fleece always seemed to be on to things Cole was too young or too dull to come upon on his own.

That's pretty sad, Cole said.

What is?

Being forgotten like that. Being so forgotten it's like you never even lived here.

Fleece turned from the cemetery toward the horizon of trees that, at that time, appeared to go on forever, before old man Possler sold to developers who began to carve out the woods into bedroom communities and condos and office parks. *Naw, it's not sad, that's not what I mean,* Fleece said. *It's beautiful. It's only sad because life is kind of sad. And still beautiful.*

I'll remember you.

You do that, puppy. But then one day you'll be gone too, won't you?

A sound like a pigeon's coo rises in Shady's throat. She asks what's on his mind.

"Do you miss him?"

Power lines lift to the rooftop from a pole in the meadow; a rusty transformer hums hanging at one corner. It seems strange that live power connects to this empty place, and again Cole can only shrug at what he doesn't understand, which appears to be many many things as his head glides off to imagine electrical grids covering these acres and this land and off to the townships and county after county, stretching over the entire nation and all of it connected, all of it coordinated by hands and minds he will never see and leading to this small forgotten cylinder to throb with it.

"Fleece never needed me. That's no fun for any girl I know," Shady says.

"Still, you miss him?"

"Sure I miss him, sometimes. Not always. Sometimes I miss being a little kid, too. Doesn't mean I want to be five again." She turns in his arms and politely breaks their embrace. She moves to the inside of the roof over the campus interior, where a basketball court crumbles surrounded and broken by high grass, leaving Cole to stare at the trees where the cemetery would be.

What could Fleece have got up to? It's odd that Greuel would confess so much of his trouble to Cole unless he was genuinely perplexed by the situation, honestly at a loss as to what has happened, a parent unsure whether to be angry or worried at a child yet to come home. That seems hard to imagine; Greuel always knows what he's doing, and who could guess what he's thinking? Could Fleece vanish and leave no sign behind? Is that even possible? That day with his brother on this same ledge they held in one of their casual drawn-out silences—when he thinks of time with his brother there is a typical silence attached to it, so much time passed with neither of them speaking a word, just staring out at fields or the car window, listening to music or to the Nova's engine—Fleece had stood on the raised ledge near where Shady stands now, arms raised at his sides, eyes closed, his face contorted in this combination of grin and grimace as he leaned back as far as his strength allowed. The breeze that day feathered his smooth dark hair as if he were already falling, and he waved his hands dramatically.

Stop it! Cole yelled. *Stop it!* and he kept yelling until his brother stepped from the edge.

Relax, pup, nothing's going to happen to me.

The picture of Fleece swaying on the ledge near Shady hovers in his eyes like a ghost image, the afterglow of a camera flash. The transformer hums nearby—it's almost like a fizz—and the cemetery stands out only as a heavier darkness within the night's ambient dark, and there is nothing more to see. He asks if Shady wants to go back inside. She responds with a slight shake of her torso he takes to mean no, her hands clasping either shoulder and her back to him. Cole watches her for a moment from the steps of the doorway. A sad feeling suffuses his gut and his chest and neck and he feels very alone, and wishes he knew how to make something happen, to force the world closer to how he wants it to be, to act with the momentum of certainty behind him. And as if the world were listening to his head the wind and rain starts again with new urgency, the sweep of it loud in the trees. Shady sprints back to join him under the rusted awning, laughing and extravagant. Within seconds lightning is peeling seams through the sky again, the thunder coming in giant claps.

Like something out of a movie, they decide. And romantic, thinks Cole. But every dulled insulated nerve in him understands she does not want to be touched. He tells her they should leave soon now that the police lights out front are gone. She wants to stay a little longer and watch the storm.

"Find your buddy if you can," she says, and he turns to go. "Don't get shot," she adds, and that her concern for him is enough to speak of it buoys his mood.

•

He finds Spunk not far behind them, a spidery shadow standing outside the glow of his flashlight propped on the floor. Despite the fresh air flowing in from behind, the humidity in the corridor closes in and Cole's skin bursts with sweat all over. This room must have been intended for prayer or meditation of some kind; a gallery of statues is set into the wall along one side with knee-wide benches before them. Spunk has torn one statue from its base and is trying to stand the thing up but it won't stay put—to extract it he had broken off the feet. In his grasp the saint shines a milky blue, one hand clasping its robe, the other extended in blessing.

"You get on that?" he asks. Cole shakes his head even though his friend isn't looking at him. "Figured you all wanted some privacy. Since we didn't find your brother I figured I'd take this back to Daddy. Put it in the yard." He releases the statue and it tips forward and he grabs it again before it falls. He twists his hand over the head and spins the saint like a top.

"What you think you'll tell him?"

"Fleece don't live here no more. Dude I do *not* believe Fleece Skaggs would ever try to rip off my daddy. *I do not believe that.* And if he did then there's a whole shit-hurricane going to happen. My daddy is going to want to know."

A deep intuition makes itself felt in Cole with surprising conviction. "He already knows," he says. As he says it he realizes it must be true.

"Yeah? He knows so much then how come he sends us out here?"

Cole watches the bony hands batting the saint back and forth, a sculpted metronome. It's hard to breathe in here after the time outside. Spunk begins to speak of other things, as he does when he doesn't want to delve deeper into a matter, and Cole falls into his own thoughts, hypnotized by the movement of the footless statue ticking side to side. He cannot choose why Spunk would not tell him that his father knew plenty, that they are out here because the old man wants Cole to see for himself. He cannot put a why to this but again he feels convinced nevertheless.

"I don't know what it is but something bad is happening, right here now as we stand doing nothing," Spunk says.

The room fills with light. Cole hears no sound, it's like he is a piece of film cut out of time and reinserted moments later, with his back sore on the floor and his head aching. An awful ring clangs in his ears, and when he moves his head it sloshes with crushed glass. His elbow is soaking in a puddle of rainwater and some of the pain seems to originate there. Several feet away, Spunk lies flat near the statue, the white saint spinning silent on the grimy floor.

Suddenly Spunk shoots to his feet. Cole can see his mouth moving rapidly but cannot quite dial in the frequency of his voice: the mouth moves but the words cannot get past the klaxon ringing in his ears. Spunk nears him and then retreats; dips near again but seems suddenly fascinated with his widespread hands. When his words eventually become clear Cole hears *lightning*, Spunk is chanting *light-end-ing*. He starts to dance in the room's faint illumination, a dusky glow about them that Cole is unsure is hallucinated or actually in the world. Again Spunk holds out his hands, turning them back and forth and marveling at the fact of them. His face wrenches, his mouth curls into a mad scream, his feet hop as if over hot coals—until Cole's hearing returns in a great wash and he recognizes Spunk laughing, laughing a feral laughter of the thunderstruck.

It takes time for him to regain his feet, his balance is skewed, but in time he rises with the help of a windowsill. Spunk kicks the head of his saint and sends it spinning faster, screeching laughter, when Cole thinks of Shady alone outside. And then, just as he starts out to find her, her high giggling squeal comes scurrying down the corridor in the dark. He can *see* her coming, too, her silhouette defined by a throbbing glow that confuses him, where could it come from, we are in the middle of the night, it's as if some basic element of darkness has changed in a way he cannot identify. She skids to a playful stop and stands herself before him, her body haloed by pulses of light.

Come see, she says.

Of a Sunday morning Lawrence Greuel finds himself, somewhat to his own dismay and great amusement, seated in church—a renovated warehouse he remembers housing tobacco auctions when he was a kid—among over a thousand worshipful nabobs. And this is just the day's first of three services, he understands, each near to standing-room-only. Above the stage, where a conventional church would have its proscenium, a video screen hangs for the benefit of those sitting in the back rows. A light show commences in garish primary colors: laser-bright pillars of choleric red, fertile green, and shucked-corn yellow track over faces and into the rafters as the band starts a boogie-woogie rhythm, grooving on a bass-driven blues riff and deep conga drums unlike any hymn Greuel has ever heard. Not that he remembers many. He has come partly out of malicious nostalgia; he has come to silently mock; most of all he has come for the tingle of a deal, the opportunity to make money, at the urging of his associate Arley Noe. Because Lawrence Greuel is on the downward curve of life—no, it's more of a wild plummet from the high-dive—and he has a son who disappoints and embarrasses him. Yet he feels it incumbent upon him as a father to do what he can for the boy's future once he, Lawrence Greuel, has become ashes.

He knew there was money in these new churches, but to see it on display . . . Arley Noe can spot an opportunity. Plenty of business still to be done on a Sunday.

The horn section joins in and the crowd starts to stamp and holler; the overhead pots dim; a white spotlight draws still on a corner of the stage constructed from carpeted risers. Then a stringy man springs into the light with arms raised high and open hands waving, a featherweight boxer entering the stadium for a championship bout. *Welcome!* he shouts joyfully, his voice through the headset microphone too loud for the speakers, booming with fuzz. *I welcome—YOU!* he shouts again, one finger drawing over the audience, the arm ramrod straight and sweeping across space, legs braced as though to keep him from stage-diving into the aisles. *I welcome you, Christ welcomes you! Christ World Emergent welcomes you all to the prosperity promised in His name, amen!*

The atmosphere is more like a midnight roadhouse than a ten AM worship service. The attendees are going nuts as the lights spiral and wheel with the magic of God's miracles, and the musicians, Greuel must admit, jam like pros. The fulsome energy of Brother Gil Ponder is familiar to listeners of his weekly radio show, his face recognizable by the towering billboards that grace the interstates in three counties (*Are You Thriving as God Promised His Children? Visit Christ World Emergent and Embrace the Abundant Life*), but to see the man in the flesh stirs even Lawrence Greuel's indifferent heart. Ponder bounds past a podium and snatches a leather-bound book that he shakes above his head, then tucks beneath one arm as he makes the stairs to the first floor rows, not far from Greuel's wheelchair, and where Noe and Grady Creed remain conspicuously seated. The preacher jogs across the front row, slapping hands and pumping his fist, stopping suddenly to cheers as he embraces an elderly woman on whom he bestows a kiss to the forehead, and she clutches his shoulders as if to hold on for all that life has left behind her. From this close vantage Greuel can discern the ex-junkie he knows Ponder to be and that no manner of good living can make up for; his eyes may sparkle blue in the spotlight but they are set deep in shadowed sockets and betray to Greuel's experienced eye that indefatigable hunger that draws from the addict's insides, that fanatical madness begging to be consoled. Ponder's skull is a map set in relief beneath its lean skin, and he looks well older, up close, than his forty-two years.

Greuel vaguely recognizes the elderly woman's escort though he can't recall why—which he finds bothersome, as he's the kind of man who prides himself on his ability to remember names and faces. It's all the medications they've got him on, his brain's turned to grated cheese. With careful indulgence the man rests a tan and manicured hand on the woman's shoulder; in the next instant he is helping Brother Gil extricate himself from her grasp.

"Tell me who that man is," Greuel tells Arley Noe.

"Well hell, that's the preacher. That's Gil Ponder."

"I'm not talking about him, you blueskin hick bastard. The guy next to him."

Noe follows Greuel's nod to spot the man standing formal with his hand again on the woman's shoulder. He's tall, and completely bald in the hip urban fashion of the day, immaculately presented. Noe elbows Grady Creed beside him, who sits slumped low with his legs extended into the aisle, eyes half-shut and ankles crossed. The preacher moves into another aisle between sections, saluting some, handshakes or kisses to others, and Greuel is impressed by the stamina of the crowd's gusto. He wonders if this preacher plans to greet each individual on the floor—in which case he's out of here, he isn't going to sit through *that*.

"Creed says he's with some morning show, the funny one."

"They bring out the celebrities, huh?"

"Like I told you," Noe says.

"Like *Creed* told *you*," snorts Greuel.

"We are here and it's all happening," he answers, the thing about him being that Arley Noe can't be surprised or offended.

Greuel smiles. His scanning eyes alight on yet another recognized face, the young woman who had been in his home a week before: her bright hair, like a pat of apricot jam in sunlight, is impossible to miss. How girlish and pretty she looks now, with her hair down. Why would she ever sport a ponytail if she could look like that any time she wants to? A grievous shame, Greuel decides. She probably doesn't realize how beautiful she is. His wife had been like that; her disavowal of her own beauty had made him sad. But why doll up? When you get down to it, is church the place for a woman to look her sexy best? Her name comes to him now: Beck. Something Beck, a friend of his son's. He remembers her saying she was down with *Hay-seuss*, and he had been charmed. He smiles to see this wasn't a put-on. Then he frowns. That's the problem with kids—they believe in things.

Ponder quits the hands-on approach and waves to the seats in back as he returns to the stage, and Greuel has not heard this kind of bleacher stomping since a state-final basketball game. The musicians watch Ponder raise his arms again, Bible in one hand, fingers splayed in the other. With a nod to the band he turns back to the audience, and when his arms fall the music stops and the house lights come up. The applause continues in a great surge, then begins to teeter and fall, a stream trickling over many rocks, as Ponder pats the air with his hands, repeating that they should get this party started. He thanks them all for being there, for just *being*. The crowd doesn't quiet until he announces, *Let us pray*, and begins the invocation.

"Dear God look at these beautiful people. Look at these folks in their finest come to honor Your name and Your Word on this beautiful Sunday morning with which You have blessed us. We ask You to watch over our congregation and to guide us in Your name and show us the way. Lead us to Your promised prosperity. Let me hear you say Amen."

The audience complies as one. Greuel and Noe snigger as Grady Creed, surprising even himself, chimes in.

"What?" Creed shrugs them off, pouting, "Caint hurt can it?" He leans forward in his foldout chair as though wanting to hear the preacher better.

"The Lord guides us, friends. Even at those times we don't think we can feel Him, He's there looking over us all. I don't know about you but I can feel His benevolent gaze right now, His all-seeing eyes on this house of worship. You know what He wants us to know? He wants us to know He's there, guiding. He wants us to know that each one of us is precious to Him. I've been contemplating this for some time now, after meetings with so many of our members, good people who find themselves in a bind they didn't ask for. A *financial* bind. Who here can't relate to that business?"

Affirmative murmurs wave through the audience.

"People ask me about bankruptcy. That's a spirit-killer right there, I don't have to tell you. Bankruptcy. I listened to one gentleman the other day, a good man you can be sure, works two or three jobs, he could be sitting next to you just now. He was talking about his debts, the difficulties of making ends meet, balloon payments on too much house and the kids going to good schools—we all know if you want a child educated right you can't chance that public school might send home some day some indoctrinated stranger who's there to tell you everything you believe and been guided by is wrong. Am I right? And those private schools aren't cheap, are they? Big government is happy to take our tax money and put it in every cause you don't believe in, but you're on your own if you want to give your child the best education money can buy, some place where you have a *say* in what he learns. I *am* right."

Hurrahs scatter through the congregation, patches of applause flare and flutter about. Greuel's attention is wandering already. On the altar up there, beside an untouched, empty chalice and what looks like a cross bound in leather, sets of car keys hang from a small stand, the logos of luxury manufacturers recognizable even from this distance: Acura, BMW, Audi, Mercedes-Benz. He understands none of it but likes the spirit of the place.

"It hurt my heart to see this good man," Ponder continues. "We prayed together, went over his options—how do we do that? Come on, you know already. *We opened our hearts together to the Lord.* You know what happened then? God came into my heart. He spoke to me as He often does, and I'm not the only one. He said, 'Hey there Brother Gil' (that's what He calls me, Brother Gil, He never says Mr. Ponder or anything formal like that), He says, 'Why are you so concerned for this man and his situation? *Sans souci,* my child. I've got it taken care of.' I said to him, 'God I don't doubt that, you know I don't, but could you show me how to bring this man some peace so he can sleep at night?' And then God points out that He addressed just this same issue a long time ago. He told me to check out Psalm sixty-six twelve."

The preacher hoists his book aloft and sifts the pages. Around Greuel various attendees sift pages through their own bibles. When

Ponder finds the desired verse he raises his free hand and signals to the audience with splayed fingers again.

"*Thou hast caused men to ride over our heads; we went through fire and through water: but thou broughtest us out into a wealthy place.* 'How's that strike you,' God asked. I told Him He was the Man. He reminded me: God's Will never leads you where God's Grace will not protect you. And He reminded me again, 'Check Deuteronomy eight-eighteen.' *But remember the Lord your God, for it is He who gives you the ability to produce wealth.*"

Brother Ponder snaps his book shut and drops it on the podium with a resounding thud, satisfied to have argued an airtight case. His hands settle on each hip, elbows akimbo, and he bends toward his congregation. Stretched in this way, a spiking dark blue tattoo stripe creeps over his collar from beneath a swath of makeup. Greuel snorts.

"Doesn't that make you feel a little bit better? Think about it: God made each of us—that's a given. He doesn't create us just to watch us flail and fail. That's what mice and all His other little creatures are for. He made *us* in *His* image. What God wants for those in His image is a successful—no, not just successful, but *victorious*—course in this life. He's always reminding His dim creations that if we would *listen to Him,* we are going to be all right. We're going to be just fine, He's already got it all figured out *for* us. 'Faith is the substance of things hoped for'—that was said by a man I think a few of you here have heard of. His name was Jesus and he's saying: Sow your faith in Him. What's that mean? It means: Don't go hoping you're going to change your situation overnight, buying lottery tickets with the chance you'll score. Lottery winners, that's just poor people with money. They get it only a while before it's gone, because they're not wealthy in the Holy Spirit. *You* have to be smarter than that.

"*I want to get results.*" He points his finger at the audience, allowing his words to ring around the open auditorium. Then he continues. "Isn't that what we're asking? Well God's got the answer. He's been telling us since Adam and Eve: 'You want results? Come to Me.' He's saying, plant a little mustard seed—come on, folks, we all know the parable—*plant a little mustard seed of faith.* Sow your faith and reap great rewards. . . ."

The sermon lasts longer than Greuel had expected; his eyelids flutter as he drowses, and in his drowse he pictures the coffee and brunch coming after, the pleasures of food, medicine-sour stomach willing. Since he's been sentenced to the wheelchair again he no longer cares about dietary concerns or his weight. How's that for my reward, preacher? Still there is common ground to be found here. He's guessing this Ponder has an interesting take on that rich man in heaven, camels through the needle's eye, however that parable went. Common ground. His eyes open again and Greuel leans over to Noe.

"This boy know anything about horses? He should be on his elbows at the rail."

Noe's mirth is mechanical, functional, and silent. His yellow teeth bare and remain bared. He still betrays marks of the true morphine fiend himself, though he kicked it near twelve years ago and it's hard to detect due to the blue pallor of his skin. Greuel hopes dope isn't the link that brought Arley Noe to the preacher. He dismisses the notion as soon as it arises; Noe has too much of the unfeeling night about him, Greuel doesn't think he feels hunger for anything but the fun of crime anymore. Now Brother Ponder is speaking of laboring to rest, and to sleep without worry because a person's faith was enough to pluck them from debt, their little mustard seed was going to score them the house of their dreams one day.

"I like him," Greuel murmurs, "but I don't trust the type as a rule. True believers worry. He won't back out on us?"

"We get the right signature on the right paper and him and his board can worry all they want, they won't have a say to back out of," says Arley.

"I've noticed you're a big supporter of the law when it's on your side."

"It's our game; we make the rules. The preacher stays quiet."

"It's *your* game when I'm no longer around to play. Do we even have a claim on this land?"

"I am not a believer. By your logic, I am not worried."

"Of course you're not. I'm worried. I put up most the money and get to handle all the worry. We make a donation yet?"

Noe nods, taps his knee. Brother Gil is still going at it from the stage, having broadened his sermon—is that what stands for worship nowadays, boogie jams and a sermon?—from the individual needs of the congregants to the enveloping needs of his ministry; specifically, the need to build their own Galilee and the fundraising required to make such a move possible. Again with mustard seeds. Greuel peers at his watch, scowling.

"Thought you said this'd be over by noon."

"What the adverts say. Think I been here before?"

Greuel snorts again, and the coat of flab that is his torso quakes at the precision of the absurd image his mind presents. "Not your style."

"I have no style. It's a conscious decision."

Brother Gil stops in the midst of speaking as though he has overheard them, and glances at his own watch. It's a gleaming timepiece over which Greuel furrows his brow with a curate's informed inspection—the preacher wears a platinum Bulova encrusted with diamonds. Preaching must pay better than he gave it credit for. He marks a mental note to update his own watch even as he wonders whether later he'll remember making the note at all. The preacher announces that his sermon needs to stop here.

"We'll pick this up another time. I could talk all day, most of you know that already, but you have lives to get back to. Come on, let's bow these heads."

Quickly he runs through the invocation and benediction. Then the band starts up again and Ponder waves as he makes his way beneath the spotlight to the back of the stage, where he disappears. The applause is shortened by the number of people heading to the exits, the wheelchair sailing forth in the lead, Creed pushing from behind, Noe lagging off on his own. It bothers him how easily Noe can abandon him, but this afternoon Greuel has other things on his mind. He has made a decision, and it requires that he figure where he's going to find the money to make some things happen now that Fleece Skaggs has disappeared with a season's worth of reefer.

It's not like he was raised by wolves but Cole thinks himself half-feral, not exactly raised by anyone, a handful of aphorisms to guide his way. *Do not cause waves. Don't try to get famous. Never knock how a man makes his living. Never start a fight you can't finish standing up. Never call a man a liar anywhere but to his face.* The maxims carry the weight of eternal law. *Keep your head to yourself and don't go around with a greasy eye; there's always someone slicker than you.* Rules of conduct handed down by Fleece; navigating codes for Pirtle County and Lake Holloway; life advice for the little brother from the elder who warned he wouldn't be around forever.

Never corner something meaner than you.

Fleece said: *Anyone asks you live on the lake you best investigate why they asking. You may be Prather on paper but you're still a Skaggs to lots of people here with long memories. Ol' Bethel didn't make friends. I haven't rolled out the red carpet for you here either, come to think of it.*

And where are you now, big brother? What carpet have you rolled out for yourself, where did it lead?

•

Already the rumors have started. Fleece Skaggs burned up his own car to throw off the scent. He's kicking it easy with Mister Greuel's run in the Panhandle somewhere. California. Fleece Skaggs saw his opening and took it, he's the one who got away.

Or: Mister Greuel had someone disappear that upstart and that is one body, man, nobody will ever find.

His brother used to tease him that just because Cole was half-fool didn't mean he couldn't use the little sense he had. But when he was kneeling with Shady and Spunk looking over from the seminary rooftop at the sight of a Chevy Nova burning in the middle of the night he didn't know what to make of its meaning. He knew only it was his brother's car and that it meant nothing well.

Cole says he's from Lake Holloway but he spent only his first twelve years there. In Montreux, the city where he passed through high school as a guest in his uncle's family, to say *I grew up on the lake* meant nothing; anything outside town is hicksville to the people there. In Pirtle County, though, lakers had earned a reputation nobody born to the fact could speak against. You either wrapped yourself in its dirty flag or moved away.

It was the kind of place people often disappeared from. The manmade lake was originally part of a spa retreat built early in the century for wealthy families, but the spa failed before the Depression. A suspicious fire destroyed the resort hotel in time to help the original investors; then the forest overtook the walks and bungalows over the years, until scavenger types began to sneak in and lay claim, people Cole's mother Lyda described simply as: *us*. Men with one pair of cracked leather boots and a duffel bag of laundry, who belt-chained their wallets and could never wash the dirt from their fingernails—the kind of men who fell in love with country whores and brought them back to play house, where the mattress on the floor became a kind of factory production line for bodies that would fill military uniforms or carry cargo or sleep in prison beds. They were the kinds of men that punched clocks at three in the afternoon or seven in the morning and already had some scorched distillation in hand as their tires peeled off factory lots headed far from howling babies and angry wives in dry Pirtle. Those woods rang riot after dark, the night rent by yelps of laughter and cries of pain, gunshot cracks celebrating or warning or something worse. A single bad road winds off Route 9 around the lake and through the hills in total darkness beneath old oaks and conifers, and men roamed from house to hill to hollow looking for something to happen, passing a strummed guitar here to a banjo and fiddle-strangled duet there to a boom box screaming Aerosmith elsewhere, onward to where there might be no music at all, only the low scrapes of boots on planks and the murmur of a bet seen, bet raised, bet called in full.

For a while Cole had Fleece and Fleece, as much as he needed anyone, had his little half-brother. Childhood was fraught.

•

There is what happens, and there's all that seems to be happening.

Cole's earliest memory is of murder. A stale summer day with sky blanched white, the alder and cottonwoods wilted weary beneath the heat. Even the birds held still. Fleece would have been nine or ten then. They were playing in the shallows of the dingy lake. When they wanted to swim Lyda would come out with two steel buckets of bleach and walk up to her calves in the water, Fleece always begged to let him do it but she snatched at him, *No,* she barked, *you stay put till I tell you.* She slopped a wide berth in the water with the bleach and told them to wait. She told them to wait until she said *Yes,* it always took forever. When forever arrived Fleece and Cole dove with bellies smacking into the bathtub-warm water, and in play Fleece forced Cole down into the soft mud and held him there, in play he would always do whatever it would take to make his little brother cry. Cole's cheeks tingled if he let the mud stick for long. His nostrils burned, the smell like the kitchen sink where Lyda washed their hair.

Somebody's garage radio screeched *Jet—woohoohoo wooo-hoohoo wooo-hoohoo—Jet* and Fleece sang along with the guitar parts, not the lyrics. The boys were floating low on their backs so the greasy water framed their faces, listening within that strange pressure their voices made with their ears below the surface, both still sweating in the heat. From under the water the gunshot sounded like sharp thunder off a faraway storm. They sat up to neighbors hurrying toward the back of their home.

Lyda stood on the square of poured concrete outside their back door, what she called a patio though it was too small to hold anything but the charcoal grill. She held motionless, one fist on her hip and the other at her mouth, crooked at the waist with her chin tucked down. To little Cole she looked no more substantial than a small bird dead, all dried out and ready to be taken by the wind.

A crowd blocked the view. Cole rushed through the high dry grass and slid on his knees between the sprawled legs of the blond giant Morton Fifer, a neighbor he feared without specific reason but under whose legs he felt safe now, Fifer in his yellow wife-beater undershirt and blue sweats spotted with oil, cuffs tucked into heavy black boots left untied; the leather sagged and gray varicose cracks ran to the heel. He pressed Cole with the inside of his leg as a man might shoo a dog. *Git.* But Cole didn't move and Fifer paid him no more attention.

The yard sloped sharply to a creek. At its bank two men formed a scene no one would enter. One, thick and stumpy with shoulders wide as Cole was tall, stood with his back to the crowd, peering past the end of a shotgun at the other, who stretched writhing on the ground with his hands at his throat. A wet noise escaped between his fingers, an unfamiliar noise, and his boot heels dug deep ruts into the mud as though he believed he could push himself away to safety. His mouth worked at every shape of rage and curse but not a word escaped; his dark eyes drew to the man who did this to him, standing silent, and the eyes admitted he did not believe a moment of it.

His boot leather looked like tender skin of a soft and pliant cognac; everyone in Lake Holloway knew who owned those boots. Bethel Skaggs took great care to show off his boots to anyone who would look, bragging on how he won them in a card game although Lyda told the boys he had paid a fortune she'd never see for them.

His murderer did not give the boots a glance. He reloaded with calm study, his brown curly hair thinned enough at the crown that the scalp shined, the short curls limp with wet. A straw hat lay upside-down behind him, black-banded and with a frayed hole in the brim open like a dead sparrow's beak. And then the crowd turned to the shriek of a woman—a woman unknown to Cole—running up the creek. *What have you done my god what have you done?* she cried, clutching the hem of her skirt above her knees, her other hand out for balance as she worked barefoot against the slick mud. The gunman did not respond. It was as though her arrival didn't register with him. Instead he clacked the barrel shut again and raised the gun once more, and he did not seem to see her collapse over Bethel Skaggs, whose fingers dug into the earth, and he did not appear to hear her moans and sobs as she placed her palms over the gushing wound in that angry throat. It was more like he was waiting for her to notice *him*, her to come to *him* as he stood ready to fire his gun again.

She would have none of it. *You've done enough here*, she said. *You won't touch this man again do you understand me?*

The man kept his gun on them for a time, a long time, the barrel waving slightly with each breath. He shifted his weight and waited and nobody who was watching moved. And then after a time some thought or feeling must have clicked into place inside him. Maybe he saw the fancy boots had stopped moving, and had locked into the heel-scraped ruts, or that the bloody hands had stilled in the grass. The man lowered the gun and gazed over the scene of his creation. It seemed to Cole he was lightly swaying. He gave a brief nod, the kind of nod a man gives from his porch to passing strangers, to this woman still covering the dead man's body with her own. The watching crowd held fast and spoke not a word.

Only the woman's cries remained. If they registered in the man's ears he did not show it. He picked up the hat and turned from the spectacle—never acknowledging the gathered crowd—and stepped carefully along the slick bank of the creek, going back the way he must have come, the gun yoked across his shoulders.

In the woods on the creek's far side, birds began their meek day songs again. The gunman whistled back to them, out of sight now behind willows and ditchweed, and the sun pushed through the white wash of clouds and bathed again all the people huddled along the slope in ruthless heat.

Fleece appeared as the crowd disassembled. He closed in on the mourning woman, who seemed confused by what to do with Bethel's hands: she kept repositioning them, placing them together on his belly, then at his sides, then again on his belly, the hands holding the form of that final clutch made against his wound. Fleece placed his own small hand on her bare shoulder, Fleece not a full head taller than the woman on her knees. He patted her shoulder, tapping his palm against her freckled skin.

Morton Fifer made a sound like he expected to sneeze and then stifled it. His face tilted from above the massive forearms folded over one another, looking at Cole between his feet. From that angle his features puckered and mashed together to make him unrecognizable save for the straw-straight blond of his hair. He made a face as though ready to spit but thought better, swallowed it down as he turned, and nodded at Cole's mother.

Good luck to you, Lyda, he said, and with his going most of the others followed.

The woman remained atop the body beside the creek. Fleece remained beside her, still patting her shoulder with the flat of his palm as they stared at the mess made of Bethel's throat, and Lyda still had not moved from where she had watched the entire event unfold. And little Cole did not understand. Who was this woman so full of sorrow? Why wasn't Lyda in her place? His mother squatted with her skirt tucked between her thighs, elbows resting on bared knees, and fixed herself a cigarette she worked on and off in hotbox puffs before tossing it aside unfinished. Standing then, and without looking at either of her sons but at the kneeling woman, she ordered her boys inside the house, claiming there was no more good for them to see here.

This happened when he had been so young that often Cole wondered if he had dreamed it, or seen it on TV, or read it somewhere and then had the event sink deep enough into him to believe he owned it. But Fleece remembered the day as well. When Cole would ask their mother about it, she would tell him only that it was a bad story not worth the dwelling on. And besides, it did not matter, it had happened such a very long time ago.

•

Lyda sleeps in the bedroom next to his. They share a wall, their heads at rest in proximity. She has her philosophies, too. Lyda says people arrive in the world with a unique part of it readied to welcome them into its limits and expectations—that is why we have to be ripped screaming from a mother's womb.

She grew up poor when Pirtle Country was horse farms and lease lots seeded to sharecroppers for tobacco, alfalfa, hay, and corn, the county seat of Renfro Station nothing but a few developed blocks around the rail line, its city hall reconstructed from the burned remains of a Baptist church. Her father kept a dry goods store that had folded inexplicably during the boom years after the Second World War, when most businesses could not help but thrive. Not even boom years could bring fortune to a man as difficult as Ernst Newcome, Cole's grandfather. He preferred horses to people, though no one could tell if the horses returned the feeling. He scraped by via sharp jockey-ship and boarding the beasts on rented land, in flush times exercising a handful for wealthy farm owners who traveled too often to give them steady runouts. The way he told it to Lyda, he was doing right well again before she came along—screaming into her part of the world in 1951—though her mother told her this was not true, their kitchen had had the same dirt floor before Lyda was even thought of.

That dirt floor was the stuff of family legend. Lyda believed the fact of it led directly to Fleece getting born. Each morning she had to sweep the floor in one direction to her mother's satisfaction, and then sweep it again the opposite direction after supper. If it became too dry and powdery she had to sweep the plumes of it out the door before dampening the floor with a rag. Ernst had himself a radio and then a TV he'd managed to find *on a fantastic deal* before ever setting a floor to Eudora's kitchen. He worked less once they plugged in the TV. Not long after buying the thing they watched Kennedy's funeral and Ernst was hooked—calling the assassination of that Catholic impostor one of the best moves the country had made since VE day. Lyda didn't know what to say about Kennedy, and she didn't know even if her father might be wrong. By then she'd learned to assume he was.

She had not been farther than Montreux and Cincinnati except for one foiled family trip to D.C. in October 1967—the city writhing, its avenues clogged with protesters intending to levitate the Pentagon. Her father gave up on finding a hotel and in a rage swung the station wagon around on the beltway, crossing the grass divide as if it were county fairgrounds. They camped in freezing cold in the Shenandoah and shivered miserably as Ernst proclaimed his new conviction that, after the mess of the capital and the mindless inferno engulfing it, he no longer saw sense in ever leaving home.

Bethel Skaggs lifted into Lyda's view as the worldly traveler who enjoyed the outright disapproval of her father. He had been everywhere, seen the globe, Bethel said, drinking from a pewter flask in dry Pirtle, twenty-five years old and talking up a teenage girl at a dance in a high school gym. Stationed for a year in Berlin during the missile crisis—he said—and got out the second they let him; raised blue-eye huskies in Nebraska until wolves cleared out his stock; painted barns in Georgia, and then took a chance on his fiddle skills, which allowed him to see every inch of this country to help him decide where he didn't want to be. Her father suspected a man couldn't play fiddle worth a damn without deceit and immoral leanings in him and that was enough to confirm Bethel as a person of interest for her.

She was sick of sweeping that kitchen floor twice a day and she was ready for a new pair of shoes. And the only thing anyone could agree on about Bethel Skaggs was that he certainly took the strain off a girl's eyes.

He never did tell her why he came to Pirtle County or Lake Holloway; he had no people there. His littered the mountains in the eastern towns of Tomahawk, Inez, Watergap—places he swore he would never step foot in again. He had a solid job at the fertilizer plant and so she got the new shoes and moved into the small house in the woods behind the lake—where first thing she did on entering was stamp her heels on the kitchen's linoleum floor tiles—and before their first anniversary Fleece slid screaming into his part of the world. And for two or three months Lyda thought her life exhausting but happy. And then Bethel announced he was leaving. Service rung up, he said, mentioning he still had commitments to the Army Reserves for the first time. In days he was gone, and no one except himself ever learned where he got up to; she knew only the man never served in Vietnam. She checked with the Army herself out of curiosity years after any of this mattered. Her father believed Bethel wanted away from a wife and squalling baby, damned if it be boy or no, and who could blame a man for that, *I raised her myself* (she could recall Ernst speaking this to young Cole, eyes dancing beneath white brows long enough to braid). Bethel disappeared and sent no word, not a phone call or note, for well over five years. The next time he rounded the lake and walked back up the hill, he found little Cole Prather.

Lyda wished she had a picture of Bethel's face the day he found her holding the toddler—stricken, she said; sincere confusion scattering his eyes. As though he could not understand how his son had not grown a tat since he left. Then Fleece ran in through the back door (Fleece ran everywhere then, never walked, his feet scamperwild from the day he discovered them) and the argument began. She thought, *He thinks it's no different than if he stepped out moments ago, like my life could be stuffed in a footlocker for him to pull out whenever he wants.*

She dared her husband to explain her wrong. Five years without word—it wasn't like she moved to Whore Holler after he left (though she could have, she reminded him, for all he left her with; no one who knew her story would have blamed her). Lyda had been a teenage mother trying to do right, one who went to church on Sundays like any girl trying to do right would. Despite the nature of her effort she still met Mack Prather there, at First Pirtle Baptist. Now he was a man everybody liked, once they noticed him; quiet at first, he didn't jump into conversation but stood ready with a grin and some funny comment to prove he had been listening close. He was not rascal-handsome like Bethel but he wasn't ugly, either, though his thin hair, a dun brown like crispy leaves, was already moving to a combover at twenty-four. His eyes were nothing to cry over and his jaw was soft, but he did like to talk once he felt comfortable, and more importantly he liked to listen to Lyda talk. They first started talking and listening to one another at an after-service brunch, he made her laugh on a day she was feeling blue, they were looking over the table spread with bacon and eggs and Mack said from just behind her shoulder, *Well I see the chicken made a contribution, but it looks like the pig gave us his full commitment.* Then he tumbled her coffee while reaching for cream.

Bethel had been gone two years by then and she was lonely. She wasn't looking to park her shoes under anyone's bed; she was trying to be good. Sex had got her into this tough spot and she wanted a future with fewer spots as tough as this. But it helped to have a man around the house whether one lay with him or not. Mack could frame a door; he connected PVC pipe from the house to the county water system instead of the lake's, which did not use filters and made the sink smell dingy. He played ball with Fleece as well, setting him up with the basketball goal where the hill flattened out near the road until some laker boys stole it away or threw it into the lake, they never knew which.

Mack called himself a developer but that was only ambition talking. Truth was he did construction, a carpenter willing to take on more than he could handle, certain he stood only a loan or two away from drastic and enviable success. Sometimes he helped Lyda by picking up Fleece from her parents' house before she finished her shift at the clinic. Sometimes he picked her up, too. Her mother Eudora was a practical woman and did not blame her girl when she finally landed in bed with Mack after so long with a wandered-away husband—no, Eudora got upset only when Lyda got knocked up again so quickly. Eudora did not take gossip unless it covered somebody else's family, and Lyda getting pregnant with her husband gone gave everyone at First Pirtle Baptist much to chew on happy. Her own mama asking if she didn't know how to keep from getting pregnant! Lyda told her it was a little late to discuss it now.

Mack, sweet, welcomed the news. He told her: We roll with what comes. They did not talk about what they might do if Bethel returned. Lyda tried hard to believe he was gone forever. As her belly grew she admonished herself to stop looking out the front of the house for any unwanted sign of him. Superstitiously she wondered if by ceasing to keep an eye out she was somehow encouraging Bethel to show up. Mack told her she was too young for such old-woman silliness; maybe she lied about her age? She slapped his shoulder. They never had one sign of his coming back, no hint of any homecoming until Bethel was already home.

•

He arrived to find Lyda as he had left her: alone, carrying a toddler at her shoulder. The front door stood open to invite the breeze. She had finished setting the washed breakfast dishes on the dry rack. Bethel walked in without a hello standing in the doorway as he waited for her to notice him. When she did, his eyes were on the baby—and then Fleece ran in through the back door, calling her to come see a kill he'd made with his bare hand. He stilled at the sight of Bethel, too. Didn't know who the man could be.

Bethel, Lyda said.

Well Lyda Skaggs, Bethel said. He tossed his small bindle bag and cardboard suitcase onto the couch.

He said he could not accept such outright betrayal. He had come *all this way,* he said, through near-starvation and miles on his feet, only to find himself obliged to kill the bastard who give her that baby? Lyda assured him he didn't have to kill anyone, Mack was already dead. *I'll kill his brother then,* Bethel said. But the hard smile on his creased face suggested maybe he wouldn't if she told him he did not have to.

•

With Cole on the way Mack had redoubled his efforts to realize his ambitions and gone in with his younger brother Ronnie on a rental property in downtown Montreux, a shotgun that required renovations before listing. They ripped out soiled carpets and refinished the floors, only to have a rainstorm reveal the roof needed repair. Ronnie held the ladder while Mack climbed with a bucket of tar pitch and neither noticed the worn lining on the wire connecting the house to powerlines overhead. A small misstep with the bucket, and the ladder shifted; Ronnie flew back against the house next door where the wind blew out of him. By the time he recovered and reached to where Mack had fallen, his brother's skin looked like an overripe plum.

The insurance went to his brother. Ronnie did not particularly care for Lyda; he had no trouble (he made clear) telling her as much, but he promised to do right by his brother's child. And eventually he did; he did try. Years later when a twelve-going-on-thirteen James

Cole got himself arrested (chasing after Fleece in his way), Ronnie discovered Lyda harrowing deep into her own pitched spiral, and his own wife agreed they were honor-bound to get young impressionable Cole off the lake. Lyda thought they did try to do right; they all did. But they succeeded only in making the boy a stranger to both houses.

Morning blues the cheap thin valance in Cole's bedroom window. By habit he stays still as long as he can, refusing even the smallest move despite knowing he's not asleep anymore. It's dawn early, he can tell by the modesty in the twitters and calls of the birds outside, like they're struggling to wake up after a rough night. Cole remains in the cool cotton safety of the bed, eyes and ears open in a room still cloudy from his cloudy dreams. Over long minutes he watches the outlines of his few pieces of furniture begin to form in the steepening light—a dresser with one drawer missing, a footlocker stood on end—bringing with their growing shadows a strange dread. Sleep: so far and hard to come from, a good place.

He listens to the house. Lyda's one to always have her ear to the rails; she knows what train is coming in and whether it's on time.

He listens to the house, his ear exploring the short hallway past Lyda's room and into the kitchen (the refrigerator humming), through the kitchen and into the living room. There the TV sits silent. He backtracks to her bedroom and listens for any sound in the sheets, a rustle, snore, or sigh, or even the murmured complaint he often catches through the wall separating their heads, Lyda ready to set straight some imagined or remembered companion even in her dreams. Nothing there.

On his feet then for a sweatshirt from the drawer, he peeks out the window. She still drives the old Country Sedan, proudly displaying its historic plates even as rust claims the fenders, duct-taped cardboard replaces one rear window, and the suspension angles high on one side. She doesn't have money for a newer car and insists she doesn't need one, the Country starts every time she turns the key and she hardly drives anywhere anyways. The Country sits parked behind his truck in the driveway. He sock-foots through the house and does not see her as he rinses his mouth in the bathroom sink—not bothering to brush his teeth, he'll be gulping gas-mart coffee and cake in a few minutes—and runs icy tap water over his hands and through his short hair and into his eyes.

On the concrete porch with boots in hand Cole's spacey fatigue carries him through morning ritual. It's Saturday, he has horses to feed and turn out at the Spackler farm, and then he'll work a handful of hours in the city with Uncle Ron-Ron's crew. He sets to lacing the leather boots, malleable cowhide and once his father's, boots Fleece wore briefly before bequeathing them to Cole once box-toes came into fashion and his brother splurged on a beautiful black pair from Johnston & Murphy. Cole resoled his father's boots with tire-tread rubber and by now the leather has conformed to his feet, sinking outward for the bulge of his ankle bones and following the outward spread to his calves, not quite erasing the material's memory of his father's form, undecided between the two. There are moments when he believes he cannot love anything as much as these boots—moments such as this one, alone, on the front porch of his mother's house, starting another day.

It is winter-morning cold but not so cold he needs to complain about it.

He feels her standing behind him; she must have slunk into his wake when he wasn't paying attention. He feels her staring into the back of his head, into his shoulders tight beneath the hooded gray sweatshirt still smelling of the dryer sheet, a scent he likes.

He double-knots the laces of his left boot and asks what's on her mind.

"You know my burden, pup," she says, her voice worn. She clears her throat. "Your big brother. You and your big brother." Her tone implies exasperation and lassitude, as though she could have launched into a list of numerous instances in which Fleece and Cole have disappointed her, perhaps even hurt her deeply, but there are so many known between the three of them already she saw no point in listing them yet again.

"What about us?"

"You only come back for yourself? I mean who's looking out for who here?" The wire mesh of the screen door sings a faint song against her scratching nails. "I raised you boys better than to have to wonder. Blood is blood. You got to have each other's back."

"I never had to have Fleece's back. He didn't need me to. I was just a kid."

"You would have if he asked. How I raised you both."

Cole ties the right boot in the same double-knot; he needs to get on the road. He plants both feet square together and looks over them, at how small they seem compared to the rest of his body. Just like his father, Lyda used to say.

"Not sure how you'd say you raised us, Ma."

He sits facing away from the house, appearing to anyone who happened to notice as a strange young man debating aloud to himself. The hinges on the screen squeal and as the door smacks back into its frame his mother's bare foot taps his hip for Cole to scoot over, the dark burgundy polish on her big toe chipped white along the inside edge. He makes room.

"Now I tried my best, hon. You'll see, you ever get a child in this world. Only so much you can do, they end up how they end up anyways."

It's not a conversation he wants to have—or, it's a conversation he would like to have some other time, the opportunity for such conversations being a great reason for his return to the lake—but not now, not with the fatigue of four hours of sleep, no soda in his belly, a day of work he dislikes ahead of him. Cole stands and jangles his keys from a pocket and looks down at his mother on the step, her choppy, saloned hair exposing a little gray at the roots.

"Guess I don't know what to tell you."

"Tell me you got your brother's back."

"Is he asking?"

"He's not here to ask. I am. I'm your mother and I am asking you. Make it right."

"Jesus, make *what* right?"

Lyda doesn't answer. She reaches forward, plucks dry petals from the hydrangea and grinds them into confetti falling brightly from her fingers.

"Make what right, Lyda? Tell me, 'cause I don't know."

"That man don't own us. He might act like he does but he owes me, he owes me and he knows it."

Cole watches the show and refuses to be pulled in. His mother grinds her teeth and wires of muscle braid and weave along her jaw; she clamps shut her eyes, snaps them open, says in a rawboned, hard pioneer-type voice: "I don't get out like I used to but I still hear what goes on out there—"

"Maybe I should be asking you the questions. You know something I don't, tell me. All I know's Fleece aint around. That's no different from life as I know it. What do you want me to do?"

"You shouldn't need me to tell you. You're all grown up. You'll do right."

She makes a display of relenting. She repeats to the grass edging the walk that she thought she raised her boys to know better. She pulls more dry petals from the hydrangea, grinding them in her fingers and catching the crumbs in her palm and staring at the pile as though a fortune could be divined there.

"That boy just is as he does," Cole says, and mother and son share nostalgic smiles at the line, a family saying coined by Lyda one night telling police at the door how sorry she was for what Fleece had done, twelve years old, brought home for egging the cop's car miles away. *I'm trying to raise him officer but the boy just is as he does,* she had said.

"You see your brother you tell him I want to talk to him. He don't just take off on me like that."

From over one shoulder he tells her he will though he doesn't expect gossip from Spackler's horses, and this gets a laugh from Lyda. Sometimes—when he was much younger and when his mother had more energy and clarity—they used to take long walks through the woods, not quite losing themselves in its hidden cavities and hollows, occasionally happening upon a secluded sward of grass that appeared to have no reason to be empty of trees. They would circle Lake Holloway and his mother might step out of her shoes and roll up her cuffs to tramp into the sheltered corners overgrown with rushes and shush the croaking psalms chanted by frogs, where she might laugh like a woman without a care, striking out at the water's surface with an elegantly curved foot, the ruby polish fresh on her nails. Once she had been a woman renowned for dancing on rooftops. So Cole had heard.

He leaves her sitting on the two short steps to the little house, where dark green moss sprouts beneath curling shingles and the brick needs tuck-pointing in many places. She looks frail, barefoot in Fleece's old high-school football jersey and baggy flannel pajama pants, a figure he feels sorry for as much as she enrages him—even, he would admit, disgusts him at times and on a variety of levels along some murky inner scale. He backs out the narrow gravel drive. His compassion turns to mild surprise as he sees too the figure of a man in the doorway behind her, Lyda half-turned and smiling as she mouths words, her posture suddenly charged, different, astounding Cole with her ability to still be charming and flirtatious as required.

•

After the horses he hits Montreux. The city isn't forty minutes away, and even though the counties are connected by interstate, rail, and road, the drive from Lake Holloway feels like a passage from one distinct time to another. Passing through the lake again his small truck thumps over a road that's more pothole than pavement, passing swampy lawns, rust-streaked muscle cars on concrete blocks, an engine block that has dangled from its tree chain at least three weeks, houses walled in tar paper and concrete and asphalt shingles. A mile along 29 and a strip of shops appears on the right. He never has been able to figure the original purpose of the place, a series of small one-story structures connected in a line, each slightly taller than the next until the corner building, which is two stories. Like a square-moduled retractable telescope fully extended. The two-story used to be a garage and motor oil still stains the lot about it; now a man called Boonie Ed keeps a handful of jalopies there for sale. The other storefronts are inhabited on and off—nail salons and short-loan offices—but otherwise house "For Lease" signs with the name and phone number of the father of a kid Cole knew in grade school. A miscellany of shotgun churches with diverse long names bursts from the woody roadsides at uneven intervals. Then he hits the modern era of gas marts and fast-food hovels with NOW FRYING neon signs, and a small strip of upscale boutiques along Main Street in Renfro, where the rails still divide the road.

Speed up the rising onramp and the landscape turns to Interstate Anyplace USA, Southeast version. Traffic increases the closer he gets to the city and the FM classic rock radio stations come in clearer and soon he's passing identical suburban plans and waterfront and then the houses grow closer and begin to betray their ages. Cole enters downtown Montreux only as necessary—he doesn't know the layout well, and the city center creeps him out a little because he knows, by his uncle, his father died here.

The Spackler horses had been stubborn and slow and kind of mean when he turned them out and he's late pulling in. Everyone's standing by their trucks, eyeing him as they finish cigarettes.

"Young men don't care for Saturday work, do they?"

Orval's the oldest on the crew, older than Ron-Ron and ever ready to sass. His fine white hair is trimmed so short that his five-day beard wanders into it seamlessly, a soft white moss taking over his skull.

"Nobody cares for Saturday work," says his skinny companion, CD Cooter. "We like Saturday pay, though, aint that right Cole?"

"Truth be told, I don't even care for the pay that much," Cole smiling at the banter, relieved they haven't started the usual ride of him being the boss's nephew. He's the youngest of the regulars by almost half and his lack of skill outside of welding is evident and happily acknowledged. He wouldn't be employed here if not for his status as family relation and though Orval in particular likes to tease him for that Cole can tell he doesn't hold it against him, Orval himself once admitting a man can't be held liable for the family he's born to.

He asks to bum a smoke but the old man shakes his head and starts in. "Boss is already in and we don't need him to start handling that shit himself"—the joke being that his uncle has lost his touch with carpentry, better with the clipboard these days.

It's a job and Cole doesn't really care that it's Saturday, though he looks forward to the time when he will be welding exclusively and a master at it, unionized and career-bound. Ron-Ron finds him things to weld and farms Cole out for MIG welding when he can, but they have finished all opportunities here, an old firehouse they've renovated into a duplex. Mostly he's been carrying greenboard and plasterboard and hauling debris. His uncle was there then not there, zipping off in his light Japanese truck—another instance of hilarity to the crew—from this job to another and then home again, a boss content to tour sites with sleeves rolled up and hands on hips as he argues sports and politics with radio hosts on the small transistor dangling from his belt. He rarely pays much attention to Cole onsite and today's no different, Cole ducking his boss for fear his cousin Sheldon (Ron-Ron's son) had complained about money Cole owes. But his uncle says nothing about it, and he imagines Sheldon, supposedly a college student, doesn't want his father asking where he found three hundred dollars to lend toward Cole's scuba training. Cole needs the license to meet his goal of attending a commercial diving school. Swimming with fins is the one thing he's found where his locked knee is a help and not a hindrance. He foresees a future on oceans he's never yet seen, living on rigs and welding beneath the waters.

After the second time Ron-Ron checks in and escapes, the men take a break. It's a bright late autumn day and Cole sidles around the back of the building with CD—a slide guitarist and, in his deep night hours, self-styled composer of advertising jingles who would never admit he is bound forever to a career as laborer—to share a spliff. They burn one down while sharing little in speech, Cooter grunting and humming in appreciation of the herb, both lost in their heads and staring at the high brick wall of the cemetery that backs against the firehouse, and at the clacking bamboo stalks that crane over the edge as though to peer at them.

"You don't need me to tell you," CD holds up the jay in one hand and points to it with the other like he's shilling in some commercial, "but this shit here is money if you want it. You get this off your brother? Wait, no. What am I thinking, man."

Cole shuffles his feet, smiles. CD's eyes are bloated into pillows like a soft change purse slit down the middle.

"I used to get my stuff off him all the time back in the day," he says. "Sorry he aint around no more. Bet you're sick of hearing people telling you that."

"Only thing I'm sick of is people asking if I know where he's off to. I don't."

"'Where he's off to?'" CD pinches two keys together to clamp the roach, head shaking and lips at work on silent words.

"What."

"What nothing. But I mean where're you seeing the question here? He tried to rob Mister Greuel is what I hear. Don't tell me I'm thinking different from what everybody else's saying already."

Above them, the bamboo stalks clack and shush in a breeze they cannot feel in the narrow space between the walls. The movement is sudden enough that Cole's eyes dart up to see if some creature has landed there, something wild come to inspect them, but there's nothing but greenery. "People talk just to talk," Cole says.

"This is true. Suit yourself, little man. I wouldn't want that ton of shit on my shoulders, neither. Must be awful on your momma, though."

A shoe scuffs pavement around the corner. Cooter pops the smoldering roach into his mouth and winces as he swallows, both of them turning to see Orval beaming, snapping his suspenders over his great belly as he berates CD as a slacker not worth half the bad pay he gets. "Man I thought I'd gone crazy and was seeing things but I just checked with the measure and CD, you got crown molding set where the chair rail's supposed to be, you useless teahead."

"Nah, that can *not* be the case," CD says, grabbing the tape measure Orval holds out. "Bull-ee-she-*ite*," he says again, backing away to Orval's laughs with head nodding with emphasis.

"Baby, I shit you not. You may commence taking that crap down, I aint cutting again till the room's ready."

"Who made you straw boss?"

"Who told you that you're a carpenter?"

His merry eyes follow CD as he approaches, waiting for the man's eyes to meet his own, but Cooter thumps him shoulder to shoulder to knock him out of his way, lips working in disbelief. It's not Cole's fault; he hands up what CD asks for. He keeps still, listening to the breezy brattle in the bamboo, like the tick of an irregular clock.

"Don't listen to that yahoo," Orval says. "He's just pissed to be knocked back down to quarry buys without your bro around."

"How's an old guy like you know about the quarry?"

He picks two smokes from his pack and offers one, lighting it for him. They lean against opposite walls, sharing the same view of red brick not three feet before their faces. "Well James Cole, I guess when I fell off the truck yesterday my people were already talking about it."

"You think CD's speaking true?"

"I don't believe CD himself knows he's speaking truth or not half the time. I've made it this long believing only half of what I see and none of what I hear. Greuel and Arley aint the worst. One time I was so deep into Arley on bad bets, I thought for certain my days were few. But those boys think. They know you can't pay money back from Hades."

"Yeah, well. My brother's in a different business."

"I know your brother's business and I'll tell you it don't matter, all business is money business. You go your own way, James Cole. The bone truth is Fleece Skaggs took off or he's under the river. Either way it's not on you. Remember that."

•

He had asked his brother: *You ever wonder at how lakers seem like they're in on one big secret? I walk these woods and wave hello to people and I wonder, What's the story there? How'd they end up here instead of somewhere else? You got the Akins place, and Boyle Akins went nuts and killed his wife and even all the dogs. Only time I ever seen police lights in Lake Holloway. What happened in that house, why'd he go nuts like that? Or you pass the Kelso's and there's the old man with his glass eye out, turning the thing over in his one hand because the left hand's gone, and the side of his face looks melted. How did he lose his eye and his hand? What happened to his face? You can't ask, and no one ever tells you.*

Fleece said he didn't know but he could guess. Then he said he didn't care. Later he added he'd heard Boyle Akins ran too long on his own crank. But to most of Cole's questions he said, *It's their story, not mine.*

So why did Bethel get shot? Cole asked. *That's your story, isn't it?*

Fleece rolled his eyes over his brother as he would an empty room he was about to exit. His hands played with his butterfly knife, an all-metal Spiderco Spiderfly, flipping it open in the air and then catching it again, creating a fine percussive rhythm with the repetition.

You think too much, pup.

Don't you want to know? Don't you care?

I care enough not to go look for any more trouble than what already finds me.

He lost interest in the knife and flipped it shut and tapped it down into his shirt pocket. He kept his hand over the pocket, palm flat like a shield to cover his heart, looking as though he were swearing an oath if not for the fact that Fleece never pledged allegiance to anything but his own desires.

Sure I'd like to know, sometimes. But what's the knowing worth? Bethel Skaggs was a hard mean skinny little fucker, a real son of a bitch. Look at Momma—you think she got that way on her own? Hell no, that's my so-called dad still giving it to her every day.

His palm slid from his heart to his thigh, sliding further to the knee and back, uncertain where to go without the knife to trick.

Not sure it even matters much, who exactly did the deed, he said. *Knowing who wouldn't explain* why. *Could've been the last thing his killer wanted to do.*

Or he could have loved every second of it, Cole said. *He was whistling, after. I remember.*

You got the way you feel, and you got what you want people to think you feel, Fleece said.

Now his hands found their purpose, searching his jeans for the one-hitter box. It was in the breast pocket of his jacket, and he fixed a pinch into the pipe. *Say he loved every second of it. Say he sits alone and gloats over each detail of that day and how he got away with killing Bethel Skaggs. What's changed now? Would we be better off with Bethel alive?*

Cole thought, I would have grown up with you, but he knew these words were nothing his brother wanted to hear. He watched the tendril of a flat cloud break away and dissipate into empty sky before admitting he didn't know if they'd be better off with Bethel alive or no.

The thing is this, Fleece said. *The only way to know the truth of a story is you got to go through the whole story yourself. You have to be in Bethel's shoes and you have to be in the shoes of the guy that shot him. It's the only way to understand for sure, and nobody can do that. The rest is just the law.*

What would you do if you did *know for sure,* asked Cole.

Fleece handed him the one-hitter and the fixed angle of his eyes indicated he was thinking it over. Cole went through the ritual of pinch, plant, and flame and then took tiny hits off the heated brass, the metal hot on his lips and the raw smoke too harsh, scalding a passage down his young throat to a hot blossom in his chest. Fleece could kill the hit in one deep inhalation; Cole nursed it. His brother, amused, yet not going so far as to tease, watched him baby the cylinder until he finished.

What am I going to do, Fleece said then. *Kill him back? I'm off the lake, so I'm supposed to kill him back. Maybe I would if I knew the story ended there, but it wouldn't, the story just changes, and in that one I'm hiding the rest of my life from any sons or brothers the guy had.*

It's just not right to kill somebody like it cost nothing.

We don't know what it cost him. He might be paying for it to this day.

You sound like you're defending him, Cole said. *The guy who killed your father, you defend him like you're his lawyer.*

I was just a kid then, Fleece said, no more than sixteen, seventeen himself at the time. *I want to believe tomorrow might be just a little bit better than today, and even better the day after that, and on and on. And forget what I come from. Shoot. If it came out right I might even go work for the man.*

Fleece smiled at the thought. He drew a moist hand over his face, and then drove a frank stare into Cole that implied how well he knew his brother, that he understood his thoughts and wonder because he himself had been through them already as separate items and as a constellation of issues for a much longer time, wrestling, and had reached some equanimity with the matter that Cole could not yet make. *You know, lots of times a story doesn't have an end, it just changes shape,* he said. Then abruptly he stood and stepped one pace away, and by doing so finished the conversation right there, wherever they were, wherever they found themselves together that day; Cole remembers only his brother, their words, the blue sky presenting ropes of snaking clouds in perpetual motion.

I'll catch up with you later, Fleece had said, exchanging the little wooden box in his pocket for the butterfly knife again, the end of which he stabbed unopened against his thigh as he walked away, leaving little Cole holding the corner of yet another question he assumed he could never resolve on his own.

The statement *I'll catch up with you* winds through Cole's head like a carousel of thought tracing the inside of his skull as he drives the interstate north to Pirtle County. The words scroll across the screen of his mind, turn briefly illegible as they follow one another in a circle and turn backward, as AMBULANCE appears on the hood of one so that it can be read in a rearview mirror, then passing clear before his eyes again. *I'll catch up with you.* Cole has always seen it the other way around: catching up with Fleece had been practically his life's work, all he longed for. To catch up on seventeen, to catch up to his brother, whose way of being was like a pattern Cole had hoped to slip into, to be so much like him as to *be* him. Sometimes he felt—even then, a young boy—hardly more than a ghost, trailing after his brother's full incarnation, seeking to be conjured into actual flesh by this brother who understood what Cole needed to be. Yet he knew they were inescapably different as well; Cole was Cole and Fleece was Fleece and no matter how much he might wish otherwise, this fact would remain forever the case. A recognition underscored by Cole's floating eye and stiff leg, his gimp knee a throbbing alarm in changing weather like any hill-bound geezer, while his brother rioted the night, humming guitar lines as he hot-footed that Nova reckless over bad roads, suffering no doubt or dread, to whatever destination he had in mind.

By the time he hits Lake Holloway the sun has retreated enough to make headlights necessary in the woods, and the shine off the black Audi cabriolet parked behind his mother's car appears to leap at him from the dusk. The sight strikes a great chord of emotions: first, hopeful expectancy—Shady Beck has come to see him. Or she has already turned up Fleece and wants them to know. Then it's the realization that Shady Beck is alone with his mother, and he doesn't know for how long, and his hopefulness withers into anxiety. She won't have news; she wouldn't know how to turn up any. He imagines Shady describing abandoned seminary rooms and packs of starving dogs, and his brother's famous car set afire before their eyes looking down from a rooftop, Lyda grousing how Cole cares nothing for family honor.

He expects the heads of both women to turn as he enters the house, their faces craning to greet him over the half-wall partition that divides the kitchen from the front room, the oak-doored cabinets (pine within, handmade by his father, Mack) blurred behind the haze of Lyda's cigarettes, a radio playing Lite FM hits of the seventies from where it balances atop the clothes washer; he expects to walk in, perhaps, on their laughter at some shared comment he will not quite hear. He finds he is wrong. The house sits silent, the kitchen table empty, one wooden chair pulled back before a tin cup, speckled green like a leaf under siege by aphids. Three lemon cookies sit on a ceramic plate among crumbs. Cole puts one in his mouth and lets the tart fruit sizzle on his tongue. The women are out back, on the slope facing the woods across the creek. Through the kitchen window he sees his mother amid the recounting of some tale, her hands active, tracing forms through the air. Shady stands attentively in gray cotton sweatpants, her name in purple-and-gold high-school lettering visible from the kitchen light in an arc across the rise of her ass—old warmups he recalls eyeing from the risers years before as the girls did wind sprints on the track, Cole braving this same November cold beside Spunk, their behinds clenched on the aluminum, sharing weed and inventing conquests as they watched.

She turns with Lyda at the high squeak of the back door opening. As he smiles hello he pursues her face, inspects her gray eyes, the corners of her mouth, the tilt of her head, for any hint of why she's there or what she and Lyda have been talking about, but her face reflects only bland and friendly welcome. Opening his mouth feels like plunging face-first into dark water of uncertain depth.

Shady beats him to it. "We thought you'd be home an hour ago," she says, pressing to her sternum a blue tin cup speckled to match the one in the kitchen, above her breasts lost in the baggy, hooded sweatshirt.

"That was a long day, sugar, you do it all yourself?" Lyda's voice is slow, soft over consonants.

"All by myself," Cole says. "Any coffee left?"

Together the women announce, as if in celebration, that they are drinking tea. As she starts up the slope his mother says she'll make coffee if he wants some. Her hair, colored mahogany (she calls it "strawberry jam") but grown out to show dark roots with bands of gray, froths in a wild flurry about her head, perhaps originally styled as a kind of bun or twist but since harassed beyond recognition. He can tell she has massaged the day past concern in a blend of pills on the couch with her Doral Golds and daytime TV, with long breaks before the bathroom mirror examining her look. A day off from her life of days off. She stabs out her smoke in the matted grass by her bare foot and throws the filter into the plastic bucket by the door, the bowl yellowed and soiled by rain and sand mixing weeks' worth of spent butts. She brushes past him with a kiss to his cheek and he smells the tobacco over sweaty perfume. He asks if she's going out tonight.

"Not tonight, I'm plumb wore out—my back's up again, and my neck," she says, reciting symptoms gleaned from her *Merck Manual* used to pull prescriptions, manifestations practiced to the point that they have become a kind of truth. "I can only do so much," she adds from behind the closing door.

A lot of work goes into scoring meds. No one would describe Lyda as a nervous busybody, but she does possess abundant physical energy, a drive that, without an outlet, easily transforms to anxiety and paranoia; she needs to keep her hands busy. Oxy, Nembutal, Flexeril, Dilaudid if she can get it, keep her steady—so she tells Cole. Who takes most statements at face value and wishes he didn't. But when the pills wear off, the skittish edge trills apparent about her. Sober, his mother trembles as though some inner engine has broken its mount. She complains of spinal bursitis, bulging discs, a pinched nerve; she moans at random. Yet tonight is liquid calm, moving smooth and deliberate as the gentle creek running below the yard's slope. She has been more or less smooth and deliberate since he learned to talk—and often as inscrutable as that creek's voice tumbling over mute stones.

He can't get anything from Shady's face. He nears her and asks, furtive and quiet, masking indifference, what brings her to Lake Holloway early on a Saturday night. Shady ignores his conspiratorial air, and answers in a voice that hails Lyda already in the house: "Dad says I can't sit around the house just 'cause I'm between schools, I got to find a job. So I'm out looking for one, far as he knows."

"You told me that already," Lyda calls from behind the open door. "Now what you going to do with that fancy degree, Miss Prettier-Than-I-Am?"

His mother has always liked Shady. She had held hopes the girl might turn Fleece around, making her son into the man he was not. Mothers live on wishes and hope, she would say.

"Your momma's in a new dress," Shady whispers on their way up the yard. "She said you wouldn't notice but you might surprise her if you did." She answers Lyda once they are in the kitchen. "I don't know. Sit around and deal some solitaire? Stare out the window? Whatever a girl in crisis is supposed to do. Go to church?"

Lyda snorts derision. And then quickly apologizes, as though her mockery had burst out as unexpectedly as a belch. "Never had much use for church myself. All they wanted was me to sing His praises and keep these knees squeezed tight. You can see how *that* worked out."

They laugh, but the entire scene feels false to Cole, a performance he is expected to play along with without question.

"It's not like that where I go," Shady says. "Brother Ponder at CWE, he's about the positives God wants us to nourish in ourselves. God didn't put us here to fail. It's a good message, good to be reminded of sometimes."

"If you say so, hon."

Lyda sets a pot of water on the stove and the topic dies. The three awaiting the burner to light is like the commencement of some other deep ritual, each silent and respectful of the abeyant silence. It's Lyda who breaks it, telling Shady she should check the rehab clinic if she's serious about picking up a job. "I still have friends there"—now it's Cole's turn to snort, but she ignores him—"they're always hiring clerks and orderlies. Turnover's high, you can imagine."

Cole does imagine, or more precisely, remembers. He had visited the clinic many times as a kid. He remembers blood on tile floors, trembling hands and grinding jaws, zombie-shuffles down antiseptic hallways. A population of strange adults somehow absent from themselves, their feet wrapped in paper. Slow-healing, self-inflicted wounds on skin the color of lime pulp.

"Didn't you say you were studying pre-med, anyway?"

"Biology. But yeah, med school's in the Beck family plan. More and more school as far as a girl can see."

"Better than being out there on minimum wage far as you can see. You're too young to understand how important opportunities are. How rare they are."

"Cole seems fine without it, without school I mean," Shady answers in a way that betrays the effort to keep her voice playful.

"Oh honey we don't want to go *there*, do we, Cole?"

"What?" Cole says. He hadn't been paying attention, lost on the shivers of blue flame trembling from the stove jets.

Lyda sighs. "I wish you boys would've took a chance at college. Your daddy's brother could've helped there. Not that either of you was any good at school. All I could do to get them to even go."

The thought amuses her and her smile predicts a laugh that does not quite arrive while she dumps out spoonfuls of coffee into the filter taken from the broken percolator. She sets it above the mouth of a teapot made of the same speckled tin as the cups. It's not a memory Cole can find, Lyda hurrying the boys off to any school bus.

"That a new dress, Momma?"

The laugh breaks forth, then. She dismisses him with a wave. "This little thing? A gift from my new suitor! The girls look pretty good in this, don't they?"

She sways her hips back and forth, a move she calls 'ringing the bell.' *"Ding, ding. Ring a ding ding."* She laughs again and Shady joins her. "I'm not so far gone I don't know my son, you two. She already telling you what to say, sugar?"

Shady denies advising anything even as Cole insists it's still a nice dress. Lyda flicks at the hem above her knee, slumps one hip against the stove.

"Oh, he'll do for now. They always mean well at first." She pours the rest of the boiled water into the filter and sets down the pot. "Honestly I'd rather hear me a story. What's this adventure you all got into the other night? Shady was telling me."

His mouth falls open; blood heats his neck. He turns at Shady in dismay, smacking into what rushes off her tongue before he can find words of his own: *The transformer,* she says.

"Oh. Yeah," Cole says. He slumps into the table and sets a foot on a chair. He presses hand to forehead, gathers warm sweat in his palm. "Yeah, that was something to see."

"What is it with you two?" Lyda asks, squinting at both.

"What?" Cole asks.

"Nothing," Shady says at the same time.

His mother studies their faces with sporting suspicion, a rusty streak of hair falling from its nest and framing the curve of her jaw.

She tucks the lock behind her ear. "Don't either of you think I don't know when something's up. You two are acting tighter than a cat in a bread basket. You're up to something."

"What are we up to?"

"Running around like vandals tearing up statues, from what I hear. Lawrence Greuel, that man must be near sixty and you'd think he'd have bigger things to do than make delinquents out of good kids."

"That was Spunk. You know Spunk. Mister Greuel wanted us to scare up Fleece."

"I could've saved you both the trouble and told you you wouldn't have found him. Lawrence Greuel could've told you the same."

She gets a new cigarette going and makes a show of looking for an ashtray. Not finding one, she ashes into her hand, and then her tin cup, as her eyes sweep her son's.

"His dogs are running the place now," Cole speaks wearily into his hands. "Fleece was out."

"Out."

He doesn't know what to add. He joins the silence into which Shady has retreated. Faded pink and black linoleum squares make up the kitchen floor, some with rotted edges curling, one square gone completely and displaying the gray slab of the sub-floor. They sit silent until Lyda breaks to serve Cole the coffee, telling him he can add milk himself. But I take my coffee black, he reminds her. Her hair falls again, mostly over her face, the remnants of the bun fully collapsed. She shakes her head, slowly, handing over a cup separate from her set, some object found cheap at one of her Saturday flea markets, probably picked up from between glass candle holders and clear-plastic plates, the solid ceramic blue striking her as better quality than the flimsy surround of knickknacks she didn't need. The coffee's aroma, made from old grounds, fills the room with a sour smell.

"Shady dear, you ever have boys all I can tell you is hang on and hope for the best. The big worries don't start till they're old enough to be taking care of themselves."

"I've never met a boy who can take care of himself. Except maybe Cole here," Shady says.

"Not Cole I'm talking about," Lyda says into the trash can, emptying the dirty coffee filter. "Not that he's an angel. He could sure learn a lesson on how families look after their own. You wouldn't think he was a native of right here."

"I know where I'm from."

He brings the coffee to his mouth, feels its great heat before his lips, blows on the brew once, and then returns the cup to the table without drinking. Oil-slick patterns swirl on the coffee's surface, his face distorted in their purple mirrors.

"You know something on Fleece I don't, James Cole Prather."

He raises his eyes to find hers look ready to gouge. It's like this with her sometimes—a shadow self from an array of possible selves shifts to center, like a card snapped from the bottom of the deck of an entirely different set, a self suddenly before you and wildly far from the one you were speaking to just before.

"What's it today, Ma? Tranqs? Sopes? You seem anxious."

Her eyes slip to Shady, who flinches as if anticipating a slap to the face. Something's coming.

"Let me ask you, little girl. What would you do if somebody killed, let's just say, *your father*. And you knew who it was what done it. What would you do?"

"Well that's not even a question. You go to the police. I mean what else would you?"

She has hardly caught up to her thoughts before Lyda is waving her answer away, those smooth-skinned hands, small marvels of a girl a third her age, fluttering in the air as she makes a face of ridiculous hyper-disbelief.

"No no now, square law has no dog in a laker fight."

"Oh," Shady says. The challenge of trying to keep step with whatever Lyda wants works at her face. "I don't think I understand what you're asking, then."

"I'm not asking, I'm telling. I am a old lady teaching history. This is how the world works in real life. You take care of what you need to take care of. When you got history, two families, one thinks they own the other, it's an old story. You weren't even a tadpole swimming in your daddy's balls yet."

Cole watches Shady try and fail to recover, aswim in this turn his mother has taken—yet he keeps himself from interrupting, perversely enjoying the hint of Shady's discomfort.

"I don't know about that," she ventures.

"Y'all can say what kind of mother I been, but I'm all either one of these boys got. And Fleece, he *knows* this, he would never up and abandon me, abandon *us*—"

Her chair screeches against the floor and she's on her feet now, spinning from them with nimble hands clawing at the air, her ropy arms tense in imaginary struggle. And then just as suddenly the fit passes, and her arms collapse to her sides. She turns back to Cole.

"Lawrence Greuel owes this family. He owes me!"

"He was asking about you the other night," Shady says. "He asked how you were doing."

"Greuel was? Well. He wants to know how I'm doing? Well now. I don't like the sound of that right there. For starters."

"I told him if he wanted to know he should just call you himself," Shady says, warming to information she has a handle on, as if detailing an accomplishment she had surprised herself by getting right.

"Little girl I don't want that man calling my house. You don't even know what we're talking about. You come from another world."

"I grew up ten minutes from here, Lyda!"

"Honey you grew up in Hindustan where we're concerned. You don't know that, what business do you have even talking?"

Shady retreats into herself like a small child rebuked. Her face at that instant—blots of color bursting to her soft cheeks, brow pale, her mouth a round *O* of concession—moves Cole desperately, his perverse satisfaction in her discomfort forgotten, replaced now by a noble urge to defend her from an opponent she has no chance against. It *is* true; she doesn't understand.

"Hell, Ma, *I* don't even know what we're talking about."

"We are talking about your brother. And Mister Lawrence Greuel. We are talking about a man who believes he has the run of this family ever since that blue lackey Arley Noe walked in and scooped up my first-born like Abraham taking Isaac down from the mountain. How you think your brother got into that life? You think Greuel just took a liking to him? Honey I may love my forget-me pills but I didn't raise you stupid. I'd remember *that*."

"What about Fleece and Mister Greuel?" Shady asks, determined to find footing here.

Lyda has eyes only for Cole. "He said he was going to quit. He told me, he said it like it was done already."

"He never said that." This is most likely true. For Lyda, however, that's not enough from him. "I don't know what else to tell you. I'm as clueless as you are," he adds. This feels close enough to the truth to count. "If he said it to you then maybe he did get out, and that's why no one knows where he is. It's not like you turn in two weeks' notice and then hail farewell."

Lyda repeats that Fleece had *told* her, she was *sure* of it, he said he was *out* and she was proud of him—and a little scared for herself, too, truth-be-told, she didn't like to keep hunting up doctors who might fall for her each and every ailment, there's a lot of information to memorize, prepare, express—and but yet *no way* her boy would *abandon* her without word, no word near five weeks now not even a phone call? All this recited to the burning cigarette turned inward over her palm. She looks up. She says Lawrence Greuel thinks of her firstborn as an investment he would be unhappy to lose. She says she doesn't see the sense in what she's saying anymore. She balances the cigarette across the mouth of her cup, pushes from the table, swivels to the counter, and fans the gathered smoke with a single hand. "Neither of you understand a goddamn thing. Neither one of you. Go dig up Bethel Skaggs. Ask *him* what Lawrence Greuel can get his mind to, James Cole."

A great weariness wrings him. He clutches the back of his neck in one hand and gently rolls his head. He had begun to check out on Lyda, his mind turning already to other concerns as she declaimed her familiar litany of grievances, such as how he might get his cousin Sheldon off his back for the three hundred he owes. Now his mother's words fix into place the memory of that childhood summer day, and the blur of faces on the slope locks into faces of adults he can remember. Had it been Greuel with the gun, Greuel's sweat-shined crown gleaming bald among that wispy hair? And the woman bent over

Bethel's body, who had ministered to his unfeeling hands—could that have been Greuel's sainted wife (to hear him speak of her), Spunk's mother? She'd died of lupus when they were teenagers. He wants Lyda to confirm as much, but he won't ask. His family embarrasses him; its history feels shameful against the charmed family he believes Shady comes from. Or maybe he feels this information is knowledge he has possessed always, or at least suspected.

"Why am I always the last one to know what's going on?" he asks.

"Who says you know what's going on," Lyda says, her voice taking a sullen turn. "My own son. You shouldn't have come back. You're not from around here anymore."

She's at the counter with her back to them now, presenting the full mess of her hair, its lower tresses reaching the deep curve at the small of her back. Cole knows by the assertion of her shoulders, as though they have reset themselves for preparation of an entirely separate endeavor, his mother has closed this conversation and he had missed his chance. If he pushed now she would be happy to continue talking but would circle and parry the subject without ever diving to the heart of it.

From a cabinet overhead Lyda takes down a ziplock and a cloudy souvenir Derby shot glass. From the bag she selects two large pills, one blue, the other white. From the freezer she pulls a tray and places a single ice cube atop the shot glass—the cube too large to fit inside—and then makes a slow pour of a little more than a mouthful of mulled applejack over the ice until it shrinks and settles into the warm tones of the liquor. She returns to the table with the pills in one hand and the drink in the other and waits for the ice to disappear completely, warming the pills in her fist like a gambler wishing luck on her dice.

Once she's ready, they watch Lyda wash down the pills with no grimace at the alcohol's bite as she swallows, eyes closed. Finished, she sets the glass down and gazes into it, slumped forward on slender forearms, her lips baring her bottom teeth, staring into the empty glass as if all anyone needed to know could be uncoded there and she sits alone before the promise of it. After another moment a shiver slithers its way from the base of her spine up to her skull and she straightens, pulls back from the table, relaxing into the chair with a satisfied smile.

"Hell, yeah," she murmurs, and closes her eyes. Then she appears almost about to ask them when they got there.

Instead, she stands up again, and, very slowly, starts to sway down the hallway toward her bedroom, her left hand raising a slow-motion goodbye until it stills upright, held stupidly in the air.

"You two get out awhile," she says. "Whyn't you stay out late or something? I might have my suitor over and I won't want to share the TV or worry about the noise."

His mother glides on into her room without waiting for an answer. When Cole looks to Shady, he finds her eyes in an expression mixed of wonder and perplexed appeal. He can see she will not speak one more word in this house tonight. With a tilt of his head he indicates the front door. Shady does not hesitate—her body fairly leaps from its chair and she is out before Cole can finish a final pull from his cold cup.

She's at odds with herself, with the whole situation. She's not even certain she understands her own motivations. *I am a girl at odds with my self and my situation,* she thinks. *Yes indeedy.* Did she have an honest reason for looking up Cole at home tonight? And has she not been hoping to discover a little of Fleece in his younger brother? Or even, tonight—miraculously—Fleece himself?

She doesn't question what Cole wants from her. Shady digs being around boys a little harder, a little wilder, than the boys she knew from school in Sewanee. The lives in Lake Holloway seem more real, more authentic, than the prudent and secure life planned for her by her loving pediatrician/gentleman-farmer dad and self-anointed Super Mom. And yet after an hour alone with Lyda, she's not certain how real she wants life to be. Harsh reality, she thinks: okay for short visits.

On the road they lurch and toss due to a tricky clutch in Cole's truck until they hit a flat stretch and he doesn't have to change gears for a spell. With the smoother ride she feels a relative calm settle over her. It's nice to have some quiet after Lyda. It's nice to have a moment to think. One of the things she likes about this boy is the calm around him, a quiet in reserve, a hint of reflection she might describe to girlfriends as *brooding* to make him sound more impressive. His brother had been similar but from Fleece she felt it more like indifference; part of her teenage-girl attraction to Fleece had sprung from his air of unconcern, his inscrutable code, his heedlessness toward what anyone thought of him—like nectar on a sweet tooth to a fifteen-year-old Shady Beck. She thinks of herself as much more mature nowadays.

"I have questions," she says.

Cole's response could be counted, possibly, as a nod; he inclines his head, and his chin—his jawline makes him almost handsome, from certain angles—closes over his throat as though he's trying to swallow something difficult.

"Bethel Skaggs. That's Fleece's father, am I right?"

"So I hear."

"And she's saying Mister Greuel . . . ?"

He prefaces the story with a wince, saying he doesn't know whether she should believe his mother or whether this was one of those stories they could only talk around without getting to the truth of the matter, but here is what he remembers, and he had been such a little kid then. And then she learns about Bethel Skaggs being shot down in the same back yard she had been standing in with Lyda just hours before. Which she finds impossible to get her head around— Cole a child witnessing murder in his own back yard among a crowd doing nothing to stop it. And what's truly weird is *that's* the part of the story that nearly makes sense to her. The rest sounds like a story from long ago, before cars or telephones or maybe even jurisprudence, in another country or on the frontier, maybe. Or in the Bible. So Cole instructs her in a bizarre matter-of-fact tone on how money and rendered service can offset crimes of passion around the lake, if a man's willing to own up to what he's done. He sounds unsurprised but she can see him trying to make sense of the concept himself, describing the day Arley Noe arrived on Lake Holloway months after Bethel's death. They'd nicknamed him Blue Note for the blue tinge of his skin, some kind of blood disorder. His body moved with the stiff precision of those paper dolls with hinges for joints. He showed up and announced he was going to be Fleece's new friend. Cole told of how after that day his brother had a job of sorts running gopher around Greuel's bookie offices, an innocent lookout for the card games and free-flow liquor Greuel and Noe hosted in a bunker-like shack off the river. Later he drove horse trailers (once old enough) from one owner to another and assisted in breeding sessions. Then he was keeping the workers at those horse farms sedated and happy, and the kids at school happy too—even a few of the teachers, according to Fleece—but Shady already knew this part, she'd lived through it.

"I had no idea how profoundly fucked up your family really is," Shady tells the windshield.

He shrugs, keeps his eyes on the road. He appears to hold his breath as if about to speak and she feels sad for him, sorry for him. She feels blunted and dulled and obligated to help—it's her nature, a part of her she likes and dislikes at once, and which often gets her into jams that often require entire personal-eras of concentration, composure, and headaches to extricate herself from. Such as the time she tried to be friendly with a younger teammate struggling to find her place on the track team, only to be the last to discover that the girl was obsessed with her to the point of hospitalization. Or the time she recognized her biology professor's special encouragements, an interest she parlayed into better lab times and research projects, only to learn she couldn't string along a tenured professor the way one strung along boys her age. She had only been seeking advantage in her already pre-advantaged life; as one of her older sisters put it to her, she has trouble understanding consequences if the consequence isn't square in her face at the time. Hence her large credit card debt, for example.

Her difficulties seem so strangely separate from those she's observed with Lyda's boys. Here on the road beside Cole, headed nowhere specific as far as she knows, she thinks on his brother, whom she did once love, desperately, that kind of love possible only a girl sixteen-going-on-seventeen can give to a boy already out of high school. With Fleece it had always been adventure, many times no further than the confines of a single hotel room as he introduced her to rush and X and acid, and there had always been a great deal of laughter, not all of it encouraged by drugs. But he was never someone she could talk to whenever she felt sad, or lost, or lonely (which is, admittedly, often); whenever she tried to she could see the irritation draw over his face as he struggled and failed to understand, advising in each instance that she shouldn't waste her time worrying over whatever issue currently worried her. He was the kind of boyfriend that a girl would be proud to go to prom with, because not only was he handsome and older, but he pissed off her father and got her mother drinking double martinis. And then he was the kind who would conspire to never make the actual dance—unavoidable obstacles ensued, missed connections. Early on she thought she understood him; over time she thought she *could* understand him, if he would help her. By the end, however, she had become a person who tried his patience. He never needed her until the moment he needed her.

She has no idea where they are going. They seem to be exploring Pirtle County by headlight.

"I figured we could run by the quarry," Cole says. "Isn't that why you came to the house? You wanted me to hook you up?"

"That is *so* not the case, James Cole. I can't believe you would even *think* that, I came to see *you*. I was around, thought I'd come to see *you*."

He grins, his chin tucked down again. Was she right to have said this? A pang of guilt wings through her belly—he was mostly right and, worse, he recognized as much. It's true she had been hoping to bring some pot to a party off-campus in Montreux, where a couple of high-school girlfriends were going before they started their Christmas break.

"I came to see you," she repeats, and again feels at odds with why she does the things she does, says the things she says—she's unsure how much of a door she wants to open here.

"You got money? I'm not sure how much the quarry costs now."

"Yes, I have money," Shady replies. This she can usually supply, and without guilt.

•

Off Parker Highway they follow a dual-track road through fields of grass and horseweed she recalls as thick with alfalfa and soybeans before she left for freshman year at Sewanee. They roll into the settling dust of another vehicle far enough ahead that the brake lights appear like sudden brush fires, Shady gone silent and listening to the crunch of the tires, radio off as they climb a steady incline and then down again. Over the crest the land stretches for bare acres on either side save for random plates of limestone and feeble stands of buck-shot trees, until the wooded break that shields the interstate on the other side. The moon is up, looming huge over limestone cliffs, but the fallen sun isn't entirely finished and the sky scans in grades of blue, the quarry water a warm green that contradicts the December chill. Cole slows to a stop at the base of a white weather-beaten tree; she doesn't see the man sitting atop a stool there until Cole rolls down his window.

The vision of him strikes her as important as a marker, placed at the gateway to some progressing revelation she had not known they sought. He appears as sudden and as unexpected as in a dream: one hand over the heel of a choked shotgun, the other tapping a walkie-talkie against a coveralled thigh. His face looks familiar—a face from high school or even earlier maybe, someone she would have forgotten until coming across his picture in a yearbook, remember-ing then a certain walk in school hallways, something offensive he might have yelled to the girls. Yet he looks too old to have attended school with her, with dark lines as prominent as scars weeping from his eyes and bracketing his mouth. He peers into the truck and Cole leans back to give a view.

"Shady Beck in the quarry with little Prather? Honey you can't get enough of them laker boys, can ye? What's your daddy say to that?"

"We need two quarters, Lucas," Cole says. "Can you help us out?"

"How you doing tonight, sugar?"

Shady waves hello as she speaks it, but she cannot place the name *Lucas* or the face. That he recognizes her elicits a chagrin she would not have expected. She would have preferred to get through this anon-ymously, feeling something like a first-time john cruising hookers and hearing one call him by name, and he turns to recognize a girl he had a crush on in fourth grade (this story comes from her father, Shady listening in on a party downstairs years ago). . . . She sinks back into the corner of her seat against the door.

"Two quarters," Cole says again. "And maybe a dime. How much is that here?"

"All we gots is quarters tonight. Hundred per."

Cole balks at the price and says so.

"Steep, aint it. We had to reach deep to get stuff here. You prolly heard. It is good, though, shit you not."

Cole leans over to confer with Shady and they try to quickly figure how much money they have between them; a bit more than two hundred dollars, nearly all of it hers.

"You can't break a bag for us?"

Lucas taps the bottom of his walkie-talkie on the roof. "Prather, you know this here aint no opportunity to haggle. Hundred per or I send you back out the same rut road you come in on."

"We're just trying to help out some friends of mine," Shady says, offended that this Lucas-Whoever might send them away with nothing.

"Find yourself friends who give money up front, then."

Cole tells him they'll take the two quarters. Lucas raps the cab roof with his knuckles in agreement with the deal done.

"Now that's all I'm talking about, easy-sleazy. You got to show me you got the money, though. You got it? You know where to go?"

Cole nods as Shady holds up the folded bills. Lucas tells her that's not how to do it, she needs to show the actual bills so he sees exactly how much is there but he'll let it go tonight since he knows them and always thought she was something to see in her track shorts back in the day. Again she tries to place him and for the life of her cannot. Maybe it's the shotgun, which she notes he keeps angled to the ground, hand light on the stock as he speaks into his radio, which is rather friendly of him to do. He waves them on.

They descend almost level with the water and the high quarry walls blot out the moon, Cole's headlights giving the only light down here. They pass stacks of junked cars in a makeshift lot, hood-dented and fender-smashed and windowless, forlorn frames set at haphazard angles she can imagine falling over without warning, and as she thinks this they pass a stack where exactly such had happened, the cars in a distended row on their sides and with wheels up. Past here the road splits. Cole stops.

"Does that lead down to the water?" she asks.

He nods, indicates the money. "Count two hundred from that."

"Two hundred's all there is."

"No, I put some in, you don't need to front it all."

He watches out his window as she counts the money out in twenties and tens, and he doesn't look at her when she places the cash in his hand, and he doesn't look as he folds the cash and slips it under his right thigh. They wait with the engine gently rocking, long enough that the fan kicks on. Cole cuts his lights as well, in case they are causing a delay. He doesn't laugh when Shady mentions in a playful high voice how creepy the whole scene is, like in a movie where she would expect the two of them to be killed at any moment now. She's about to admit she has never seen an actual quarry before, how it's weird to think a quarry is one of those things you just know what it is. "Down there's where I got my scuba license," he tells her. "They've got an old police car at the bottom, you have to dive down and bring things up out of it, it's weird, swimming in all that deep water and not a living thing to see." He quiets at the hint of a shadow emerging from the deeper shadows. A quiver slithers up the inside of her chest at the surprise of it. Her mother would be truly appalled to see her here. So would her two older sisters. Their disapproval helps legitimize the entire enterprise, her mother and sisters and their unknowing dismay.

He's a slow walker, this shadow, moving with a rigid, straight-shouldered stride, the left arm snapping at the elbow across the belly in precise rhythm with each step as though the arm works as a kind of metronome. Reaching them, he sets his hands over the threshold of the open window, clenching the door with long burled fingers as he positions himself with his back remaining inordinately erect, keeping his eyes high enough to look down into the cab while keeping in view the hands of both passengers. A large horseshoe ring flashes brightly off the finger of his right hand in the dark; he says nothing, his face relaxed, mouth at rest.

"Well now," Cole speaks with a forced heartiness Shady has never seen from him before, "Arley Noe. I wouldn't have expected you down here. Kind of slumming, aren't you?"

If Noe recognizes Cole she cannot detect it in his face. The hands squeeze and relax, squeeze again as though the door helps him with his balance. He shifts his weight from foot to foot, casual and smooth and serene.

"James . . . *Cole* . . . Prather." The name rolls in his lipless mouth like he's trying the sound of it for the first time. His voice hints at faint disappointment. "Not one I expect to find quarry diving of a Saturday night."

"I'm light. Got a friend in need here, looking for some smiles."

A grunt pulls from Noe's throat like a pop of air, a strange tic in his breathing. His lean face sinks pitted over concave cheekbones— emphasized in the frame of the window—his white eyebrows so thin on the orbital ridge as to be invisible, Shady can make out the individual hairs, and his black eyes are set deep with grainy circles of heavy blue beneath them. His skin radiates a pale teal tinge, a pallor accentuated by the dashboard light.

Noe turns his head and brings up something from deep in his chest and spits.

"I know your friend. That there's Shady Beck out buying wicked weed with James Cole Prather. How about that. I wake up thinking there's not one more thing in this world to surprise me and I end up surprised near ever-day still. How you doing there Miss Shady?"

She sits pressed entirely against her door, lips parted, consciously willing her eyes not to saucer in fearful freak-out—why do all these men know her name? She feels like a little girl caught trying to pass off as an adult, her hands clutched into a ball between her knees, shoulders bowed even as she reminds herself there's no reason to be afraid, people come to buy in this quarry all the time.

"I said how you doing there Miss Shady Beck. Lovely night out, wouldn't you say."

"It sure is pretty," she says, except the words feel lost spinning in her throat.

"Going to get real cold soon. Hope I'm not down here taking money then. Can give a man my age the bad aches, that kind of cold around this water."

"You have to check up on your crew," Cole offers.

"We got difficulties, you could say. Need three men here, I got only two. You probably heard about that."

"You could've got Spunk out here to handle for you."

Arley Noe's features fall apart and then reassemble themselves slowly, lines and planes of flesh contracting into the semblance of a laugh, though there would be no way to recognize that if she couldn't hear the dry hissing in his throat. He diddles his wretched fingers on the roof, pushes back from the window to hawk again, then plunges his face deep into the cab, close enough that Cole pulls back to keep their faces from colliding.

"Well now," Noe says. "I wouldn't say times are as desperate as all that. I'm looking for two hundred from you. Or you kids come down just to say hello?"

Cole scoops the money from beneath his thigh and displays it, the bill three-folded in a narrow rectangle, and the man's head withdraws from the window as if drawn by a pulley. His hand swoops down from above like a raptor bird snatching small prey from the ground and into the air without a beat of its wings. He steps back and counts the money in the same hand, the other plunged deep in a coat pocket. It's enough to curdle anxious doubt in her belly, that hand in that pocket, and she breathes great relief when Noe pulls out a radio like the man before and speaks into it, too quiet to hear over the engine chug. Noe waves them on. Cole hits his lights again and shifts into first and then blurts the simple question:

"Arley, do you know where Fleece might be at?"

Noe has turned his back on them already, he's walking off in a direction from where he had appeared earlier, toward the water he said he disliked, the left arm marking off each step. Cole calls his name again: *Arley?* He gets no response.

"What, is he deaf?" Shady asks, leaning forward to see. The creeping night has enveloped the man entirely; he's gone.

A sour look from Cole gets her to sit back again. She brushes her hair from her eyes and wipes her nose with the back of her hand, meaningless gestures that only prove her loss of what to do with herself.

"So where's the pot?"

"One more stop."

They leave the gully over heavily pocked road, Cole easing over pits deep enough to scrape the truck's bottom, and as the land crests again they come upon another stool-bound figure, this one illuminated by electric lamp. He, too, carries a shotgun, the same (she thinks) as the one held by that Lucas guy lost to her memory, but he keeps away from the truck and calls out over the loud generator powering his light, *Quarter-bag, yeah?* and Cole answers *Two yeah* and the man tosses the bags through the window. "Supposed to tell you," he says, stepping closer, "you didn't get this here. In case anyone asks."

"Since when did you guys turn away business?"

"I'm told we're not selling any more to you."

"What's Mister Greuel got against me that he wouldn't tell me first?"

"I never said Mister Greuel," the man says, backing away and waving them on. "I got no truck with you, James Cole. Just saying what I's told to. You didn't buy this here."

With that he kills the generator and flashes into silhouette, the sudden silence striking Shady as something like a distant explosion; it has a palpable impact. She watches him merge into the general dark, unsure at first if he's walking toward them or away. Enough time passes without Cole moving off that she notices.

"What is that about?" she asks. At the sound of her voice he begins to pull off, but he does not answer.

•

Shady regains her footing once they hit fraternity row. Here is a world she recognizes. Here all the trees are dying; bits of trash scatter, strewn in the street from an upturned bin at rest over the wet hood of someone's Pontiac Fiero. The party has spilled onto the street, and on either side of the truck buckle groups of students reluctant to clear a way for Cole to park. More students sit on the porch roof of the DKE house in front of its billboard Greek letters, their cups held aloft in a kind of triumph—the end of term before the holidays—and already she is seized by the surprising remove she feels from this scene. Only six months out of school and her life has moved on from this, from the hulking boys finished with athletics on the field now committed to lifetimes of fandom, strutting among themselves on thick gusts of obscenities; the house rooms shining open through bare windows;

the bass beat of hip-hop clomping in battle against the southern rock chugging from a higher floor. Can six months make such a difference?

They had burned one down on the way and though she doused her eyes with drops she can feel how swollen they've become and assumes anyone who cares to look can judge her as brightly lit. She calls Denise on her cell, hoping her friend's installed in a somewhat quieter place inside, and Denise navigates her through the packed living room and its face-level haze and up the stairs to a door covered by a life-size poster of a voluptuous model in bikini bottoms soaked in the spray of a hose, her dark hair caught in mid-toss, eyes closed and heavy lips pursed in a luxurious expression of release. Someone has written with a Sharpie a single word on a pink post-it stuck to her crotch: *aspire*. Shady raps her knuckles on the model's face, hard, and when Denise opens the door pulls a lingering Cole from the poster and into the room.

"James Cole!" a boy shouts. That would be Sheldon, his cousin, who Shady doesn't know but has heard about from both brothers, in muted asides that seemed to share information she was not privy to, and which indicated bemused indifference. He reclines on the far side of the bed with big, bare feet crossed at the ankles atop a small desk cramped into the corner. A 24-ounce gas-mart cup with the scarlet-and-heather school colors tips precariously on his lap as he shouts immediate introductions to the three other girls in the room, announcing this guy here is his cousin James Cole and can y'all believe that, his cousin's here on campus tonight? Sheldon says he could have come up with twenty different names he might have met up with at this party but his cousin would not have been one of them, no sir, not one. He jumps to give up a high-five to his cousin, holding Cole's hand in the air a moment longer than seems necessary.

"People sure get scarce when they owe money. You don't want to see somebody again, loan them cash," Sheldon laughs. "You bring mine?"

Shady's talking already to Denise and Tina and turns at the question. It's the first she's heard of the debt. Cole had given up some thirty dollars at the quarry, and she was just beginning to tell her friends the story of that, eager to detail the adventure now that she was safely out of it. Cole's face draws down and reddens; he's embarrassed not to have contributed more to their buy and is now caught before her; she's prepared to be irritated to learn he held out money for his cousin—but Cole confesses he doesn't have any on him. His truck needs a new clutch.

"You need a new clutch. I need another tattoo to go with this one"—he points to his shoulder bared by the sweatshirt with sleeves torn off, some kind of Norse design Shady can't imagine wanting forever on her body—"What about my needs?" He flexes both arms like he's about to attack in a sudden rage—but to see Cole flinch makes him laugh out loud in his cousin's face. He mocks Cole's hangdog demeanor, ruffles his hair indelicately, and then pushes him away hard enough to toe the edge between play and real anger.

"Three hundred dollars to help out a brother and this is what I get. We got to work this out, buddy."

Cole leans his back into the door and turns up his hands. "You know I'm good for it. I didn't think it would take this long."

"No good deed goes unpunished, my old man says. Fortunately I am capable of drumming up a little cash on my own."

Shady takes a closer look at the tattoo. It's composed of three interlocking horns but the lines vary in thickness, like they were drawn in by magic marker held by a nervous hand. And yet at the sight of Cole's embarrassment Shady finds herself on the verge of yet another move she will later question, curious as to her own motivations. It's precisely the kind of behavior her older sisters would chide her for, she's too unselfish and magnanimous, they say, stressing that even though these are laudable qualities in a person she has to learn not to stretch herself so far, not to obligate herself to such degrees that inevitably lead her to being in great and disappointed need herself (it's always a mistake to rely on others for help or care). At what point does a helpful, useful person stop being helpful? Where's the demarcation line between helping enough and helping so much it hurts you?

Sheldon's one of a dozen campus dealers. He farms out Tina's Ritalin prescription for top dollar to his fraternity, and Tina says he gets pot and X and a little blow when he can. Never having met him before she still knew Sheldon dealt, because Fleece wouldn't sell to him; he believed Cole's cousin would only get busted and was the type who would talk quickly if it promised to get him out of a jam. But reefer can be found from other sources, it's only the quality that differs. And though she paid good money for her weed this evening, money that wasn't really even hers but her father's . . . maybe because of her father's generosity (she knows he spoils her, continuing her weekly allowance, at her age!) she can be so generous herself, for what does it cost her in the end?

This is how she thinks, seeing the present situation and its ramifications and the motivations of herself and the people who have molded her into the person she is, all at once, even as she acts. The whole routine is exhausting.

"We come bearing gifts," she announces, mentally thanking her father and apologizing to him for being so irresponsible with his money as she pulls the two quarter-bags from her purse.

"Shady," says Cole.

"You can't pay me cash but you can get me weed? How thoughtful."

"That's not mine to give, Sheldon."

"It's okay," Shady says, and thinks: *It is*. Doing this pleases her. "How much does he owe? I'll bet you clear near three hundred selling this stuff. It's fantastic. And I speak from experience."

Sheldon holds up a bag and shakes it, examining the contents with the air of a jeweler evaluating a precious but unpolished stone. "The key here is can I sell this off before I smoke it all myself," he says.

"You'll have to be disciplined, Shel," from Tina.

Cole retreats to the desk chair by the bed. His reaction to her sudden offer is not quite what she would have expected—although he doesn't surprise her, either. It's like he chose one of the ways this could go and he chose wrong (to her mind). He sits with his forehead in his hand, turning away from where Sheldon begins to pack a clay pipe, saying he'll try it first before he agrees to this arrangement—and that he's not saying these two bags are enough to erase Cole's debt—but his cousin does not appear to be listening. Cole is staring at a ceramic plate on which two white pills sit by a small pile of powder and a metal spoon. He draws his finger through the powder absently, touches the finger to his tongue. And as his cousin lights up and the girls begin to talk, Shady believes she can hear what he's thinking, and she wants to send him a message to break up those dark thoughts—you owe me nothing for this, it's perfectly okay, this hasn't cost me a thing—even as she wonders where the impulse to have made the offer at all comes from. More importantly she feels the strong desire to let Cole know she believes in her heart everything *is* okay, Fleece is out there somewhere and he's okay, and Cole does not have to worry: the way the world works in the end is with everything coming out all right when you believe you can make it so.

•

Later she tries to reiterate this line of reasoning as they sit in Cole's truck in a park halfway between Montreux and home. It's a remote place at night, abandoned on the bank of the Ohio River, several acres of rutted athletic fields with a single gravel road and lot by the shoreline, separated from a cement plant by swaybacked junk trees lassoed in thick vines. Before them, at the river's edge, humps of alluvial deadwood shiver with garbage, remnants of recent flooding. A coal barge pushes upstream, unseen but somehow felt, or heard, sifting long roods of water to collapse on the muddy bank, whispering what sounds to her as *please . . . please . . . please.* She's not certain why they've stopped.

"You should drop the med school idea and go in for business, maybe. You're half in business already," Cole says. His wrists are crossed over the steering wheel, two fingers extended onto the edge of the dash; his fingernails scrape softly at the gray plastic there, a sound like the small waves against the graveled bank.

"I'm trying to help you get what you want. You know how to go about these things, I know you do. But maybe you need a little push."

"I get plenty of pushing."

"Sheldon, guys like him, they just want some fun. You can make tuition off that and the people you know. Get to that Jersey diving school you talk about."

"Actually Louisiana's probably better. They got oil rigs right there in the Gulf, so." He runs a finger over the dust gathered on the ledge before the gauges. "Listen, I appreciate what you're doing, don't get me wrong. What you did."

"It's what friends do for one another."

"I'm going to pay you back," he says, repeating it over her as she tells him he doesn't have to. After the pause, she changes the subject.

"How long will it take to come up with the money for a diving school?"

Cole shrugs with a distinct indifference she has learned to identify as a defensive pose, his way of indicating what he doesn't want to think about.

"There's the issue of them saying they won't sell to me anymore."

"The quarry isn't the only place to make a buy. The guy even said it wasn't Mister Greuel who told him to tell you. What about Spunk?"

Cole guffaws, snorts it back. "I'm not so desperate to put myself in the position of imminent arrest, now."

Shady's hands move to the drawstrings of her sweatpants. She extends the strings to full length, untying the bow and letting them fall again. She starts a burl knot into the end of one and speaks to it: "You're the careful type. You'll do just fine. You don't want to live on the lake forever, do you?"

She peers out at the dark water, at a white form lifting near the bank. At first she doesn't know what to make of it, thinking the white came from the top furl of a wave, but it's too high to be of the river. A bird of some kind, then; a blanket. Then she realizes it's only a plastic bag caught in the branches of a fallen tree. The dull ordinariness of that—garbage on the riverbank, as common as bird shit on a car—returns her eyes to her lap. She wishes something extraordinary would happen to her, if only she could decide on what kind of extraordinary it should be.

"Fleece got off the lake," Cole says.

"Do you think Greuel would do something to him?"

"Fleece bolted and they're pissed. That's why they won't sell to me at the quarry. One more thing my brother has left me to sort out. Kind of puts a damper on your plans for financing my education."

"That's not what your mama thinks."

"Lyda doesn't think so much as free-associate, know what I mean? If she had her way I'd have already been over at Greuel's with a shotgun and a noose."

"You wouldn't do that."

"A laker would."

Lakers. Lake Holloway isn't three miles from Laurel Estates where she grew up. She thinks it strange to have grown up in the county, a place to her so wide open and peaceful with its farms and traffic slowed by tractors, the Episcopal church she grew up in and the youth group activities in which she took part; sleepovers and riding lessons and athletic camps every summer—that was Pirtle County to her, that is her home, it's where she comes from. She used to bristle any time she heard her mother and friends gossiping over the latest newsworthy arrest, always some laker running riot where he wasn't supposed to be, and her mother might say the place should be burned so that it could start over, or else bought out and its inhabitants evicted to somewhere else. . . . Shady would tell her mother, *You don't get to choose where you're born, just because you live on the lake doesn't mean you're a bad person,* and her mother would smile with her masterful condescension and tell her daughter of course she might be right, you can believe anything if you want to hard enough.

"What are you thinking?" she asks.

His response is not quite laughter, but more a flurry of rapid exhalations through his nostrils. He tilts his head toward the riverbank, says, "Speaking honest, right now I'm just wondering where the plastic sheet on that tree there came from."

Her eyes follow his to the white sheet, or bag (she's unsure), modulating its shape on the river breeze. She twines a drawstring tight over her finger as she laughs: "Boy, you are high."

"I'm not so bad, not after Tina's Ritalin. *You're* high."

Her laughter comes harder now, full from her belly. "I am high, so. What time is it? Why did you bring me down here, anyway?"

Cole studies his hands on the steering wheel; she detects tremors in his fingers. As though he realized her noticing, he moves his hands and clutches the steering wheel as if they're driving 100 miles an hour over gully roads.

"I guess I was kind of thinking we might make out or something."

"'Or something?' That old cement factory got you feeling all romantic?"

"Well now, there's the river. . . ."

Her laughter is loud and she knows this isn't the best response but she's feeling good, she's comfortable around Cole, he understands how awkward the moment is and so she just lets go, has her laugh. Still she's aware he's waiting until the fit subsides, and he isn't joining in; he is staring through the windshield at the river again. Suddenly she touches his arm.

"Oh honey, I'm sorry. You're serious, aren't you?"

"Would it be so fucking bad? Why are you hanging around me so much if you're not interested?"

"Well."

"Well what?"

"Well you have to admit the whole idea is kind of weird."

And it is, *it is weird*. She gave her virginity to his brother. She won't deny she likes Cole, though she's still uncertain how close she wants to be with him. Why can't she come out and say this as clearly as she feels it?

The bag or sheet or whatever it is out there starts to flutter and quake, shuddering on spasms of wind. It folds over the branches of the dead tree as though presenting a neat bow, a diver moving into pike position, and its underside catches the air and the entire sheet lifts with a loud complaint. Sailing above the water it turns silent and rises, flexing and expanding, and then stills like a kite capable of choosing its direction, until another gust whips the thing from sight. Cole starts the truck and throws it into reverse.

"Hey," Shady says, softly.

"I should get you home before it gets too weird in here. Fleece probably wouldn't approve anyway, would he."

"Hey, that's not fair, that's not what I meant at all."

"What is it then? You think *I'm* weird? Is it my eyes? My knee?"

She shakes her head no, ignoring the fields they pass on the way out, tending to the neat bow she ties with the strings of her sweatpants, and recalling that her choice of underwear tonight is comfortable but not flattering. "I like you, Cole," she says, and means it—she does like him, she feels drawn to the boy, and speaking so only makes it the more evident to her. Yet she doesn't feel like doing anything with him. Not yet; not here.

They're out of the park and Cole pops the clutch shifting gears, and the engine dies in the middle of the road. They coast as he tries to restart with the clutch in neutral, headlights dimming as the engine sputters; the steering wheel locks and they are headed slow toward the low side of the road. Shady says his name again, softly at first, then with more urgency and volume as the truck reaches the shoulder and the wheels on her side dip into the roadside ditch. But by then Cole has the truck started and they're on their way, the unlit passage covered by trees at either side. She thinks to speak but holds her tongue, preferring this uncomfortable silence to speaking and opening doors to emotions she doesn't feel up to dealing with tonight.

When he leaves her at her family's gate she pats his thigh and kisses him quickly on the cheek and says not a word. She forces herself to walk up the drive as without a care in the world, and feels Cole in his truck lingering, watching after her as she steps into the dark toward home, and bed, and she's grateful for the courtesy of that, for his concern for her safety even though nobody is going to be out here waiting in the great yard before the house. And I'm looking out for you too, Cole Prather, she thinks. He needs looking out for far more than she does.

Mister Greuel informs Arley Noe he wants to walk. Noe has brought him reams of documents to study and sign, to get his son to sign since he's moving everything into Spunk's name (William Estes Greuel), real estate info, deed history and title, insurance demands, enough small print to make the eyes of any healthy man cross and glaze, and healthy Greuel is not. The house canters with noise—he hates being alone but there's a cost to that, a flipside to when he might want peace and quiet to get work done. His son's on the Sega with a couple of rowdy cronies trying to annihilate one another, one of whom strikes Greuel true as an eye-catching minx (he's old enough to look at any woman younger than twenty-five, with any reasonable figure, as such), and a couple of his runners aren't even running, they're playing at cards with their radio blasting classic rock, and the phone keeps ringing for his punk son on top of it all.

Over the time it has taken his various ailments and illnesses to set up permanent residence in his body, the dining room table has substituted for his office, and it has become the center of a lazy and loud chaos. A walk would be good.

Before, he would retreat upstairs for privacy. Or down to the basement where the humid air stayed cool among the wood panels and carpeted floor and fluorescent light. Nowadays he does not like to mount or descend stairs unless he knows he won't have to traverse them again until the next day. His swollen legs and puffy feet ache.

Pain stabs where the doctors removed two toes—to prevent infection, they said, showing him how the toes were dead already (his body, dying in pieces). You need to walk more, they said, get the circulation going.

He stands with care, using the table for balance, testing his weight. Arley Blue Note does him the service of turning to watch the video game before the kids, the one with the blond Axel and brunette Blaze fighting hand to hand through the streets of Blackpool— *the once peaceful city fallen into the hands of a secret criminal syndicate.* The storyline has always pleased him, though the one time he tried to share a father-son moment and play he ended up throwing the hand console against the TV screen hard enough to crack it. Now Greuel's feet pulse with an alarm, not quite piercing pain; in fact he kind of likes this degree of pain, it has become familiar enough that he feels friendly with it, sometimes he presses his surgical wounds against the floor to sharpen the pain's edge, doubly enjoying the relief when he eases off. He stares a moment at his fat hands splayed on the papers.

"Want your walker, Daddy?" Spunk asks without looking from the set, game controller raised high, thumb and fingers working it like a mini drum kit in an extended solo.

"Goddamn it no, I don't want the goddamn walker," Greuel breathes out. He eyes the girl beside his son, who glances at him with a face of sympathy he refuses to accept could be directed his way. "I'm no invalid yet." He winks at her and she smiles, turns back to his son.

He takes the cane instead. It's a quad cane with rubber stoppers but he has added a hand-carved ivory stallion's head to give the object a glimpse at dignity. The walker doesn't imply anything other than a desperate cry for mercy. He heads for the door with as much gimping speed as he can muster in hopes he can exit before the girl sees him hobbling. Vanity, he knows, yet vanity can keep a man going when all else has fled him.

Fortunately Blue Note moves slow by inclination. They ignore Mule's offer of assistance—the three steps from the porch intimidate him but without word Arley clasps his arm, helps him down. Once on the ground Greuel's fine, he's moving, nothing to it, one foot before the other.

Full winter feels excellent after the stuffy heat of the house, the teenage hormones a greasy musk in the warmth of the fire. He welcomes the cold burn to his lungs. The sun shines a hard diamond up there, set in the sky's blue swirl—a bright crisp winter day. Bric-a-brac and gewgaws glint and throb in the light and he likes how they crowd the yard; Greuel thinks himself a country boy at heart but he has never liked open spaces, he likes to fill them up. His gaze alights upon a dull and unfamiliar statue fallen across his path.

"The hell is this thing?" he asks. He pokes the figure with a corner foot of his cane. Some footless saint in sealed plaster missing a hand. "Where did this come from?" He stabs at it again but the thing feels frozen to the mud.

"I don't keep your yard," says Arley Noe.

"I wasn't asking you. That was me *thinking*, me thinking my thoughts out loud."

He inspects the saint's muddy face, wonders which hallowed soul this one was supposed to be. At one time he had been interested in such information. Then one day it had occurred to him all the saints were dead. So why bother? Like the saints had existed to give names to places, and to holidays no one recognized anymore but were still listed on calendars. These new saints the Vatican keeps coming up with don't count; there *are* no more saints or angels, he's certain of that. He had helped to make it that way in his world.

They approach the paddock closest to the horse barn. Mule turns them out every morning now. Only five horses left, and only two of those are his own. The paint, Sadie Dame, had been his wife Clara's. She's an old mare he knows would not bring much more than lunch money at sale. His bay Arabian, Cosmo, however, has been stalwart for breeding and he's only nine, Greuel could grab some good cash for him. He hates the idea of selling Cosmo even if he knows he will never get up to ride him again. It pleases him still to watch the horse in the next paddock, all to himself, sniffing clover and shaking out his mane.

To gaze at a powerful horse in his glory stirs dreamy and romantic notions. Greuel looks away. Some forty yards off, three turkey vultures line a fence and he wishes for his rifle, from here he could drop them like it's a carny game. One of the birds lurches side to side, lifting a pendulous claw and flexing its talons. Then the one beside it does the same. Ridiculous creatures, bulbous and clumsy and ugly with their wizened withered faces, a blight on the planet despite their usefulness.

And damn if I don't look just the same, he thinks.

"I am a man with burdens, Arl. It wears me out, carrying them."

What faint sound escapes from Noe Greuel takes for empathic affirmation.

"Can I trust you in this?"

"Thirty-four years and you still ask me that?"

Greuel chuckles. His own laugh makes him uneasy, he doesn't know the sounds from his own body anymore, he doesn't recognize a one of them.

"Thirty-six almost, truth be told. Which gets me wondering why you got money and I don't. You've ripped me off before—nothing outrageous, but still. How come?"

He speaks without facing his accomplice, his supposed right-hand man, the second-in-command to the big hillbilly gangster *Mistah Greuel,* but that was all for rumor, they've been partners for decades. Half of Greuel's killings would never have worked out if it not for the blue-skin from Hindman, Arley Blue Note so indifferent to stress and nerves as to seem Vulcan, a *Star Trek* alien arrived to exploit the yokel race. The vultures sit absolute and still upon the top plank of the far fence, they seem to have become one with the boards. Do they sleep like that, he wonders.

"I don't buy into horses, for one," Arley Noe says. "Leave my bet at the booth. The other stuff"—he lifts and turns out his hand as though throwing feed to pigs—"that was a long time ago, never enough to mention. Surprised you'd mention it now."

It's true Greuel has spent a fortune on horses in his lifetime—on shares with trainers, on feed, veterinary care, farrier fees, delivery fees, stakes fees. And it has been a thrill to lose it all. Arley Noe isn't hard-boot horse people; you couldn't expect him to understand. But that isn't what Greuel is asking.

"'Cause *now* is what I'm talking about. Fleece in the wind with Crutchfield's load and me with nothing to sell. I got this little voice in my head, and this voice, it keeps pointing out you're not around so much. Maybe you're not around due to me being sick and so you have to pull for two. But that aint it. You got shit to move."

"I keep busy. As any man has a right to. You want me to apologize for that?"

Greuel leans his weight against the fence and sighs with the relief off his legs. Sadie Dame stands not ten feet away, belly sagging, eyeing the two men. Arley Noe touches nothing, he keeps his hands in his pockets, eyes on the mud caking his expensive shoes. He hates everything about a farm; this was one of the reasons Greuel wanted to walk with him.

"I am tired and unwell and I'm not accusing you of anything. I don't get why our boy would steal so much from me, that's all. After everything we done for him. He was like a son to me. Really, Blue Note, he was."

"Not so much that you'd put him in your will though, huh."

"What's that supposed to mean?"

"Word's out you're sick. Ever-body's trying to figure what'll change after, how they going to take care of themselves."

"You'll take everything of mine once I'm gone, won't you."

Noe makes an ugly pop in his throat, an unconscious habit (Greuel believes) that has annoyed Greuel since two hours after they first met. Like he's part turkey vulture himself, getting ready to throw up on his food, preparing himself a nasty feast.

"I don't plan to fall out of business. Don't plan on getting so sick I'll die, neither."

Greuel snorts at that. Like the great misfortune that has befallen him is his own fault, a lifetime of fantastic appetites returned to wreak havoc on this body that had pursued all that pleased him. And maybe it is. So what. Or just maybe, if one were to step back and see the big picture, one could say Lawrence Greuel is simply unlucky.

"I only ask you keep my boy on. He's no good for anything else."

"He's no good at what we do, either," Noe says. Greuel smiles tightly at the truth of this. "Creed will keep an eye on him. He'll get something."

Already Greuel has moved the farm into his son's name; all two hundred and forty acres are his though the boy doesn't know it and he shudders to think what Spunk will make of the property over the years, yet this is the best Greuel can do for his only child. Lifelong, his goal has been to die comfortably, in wealth, while owing much to the IRS, and in that he appears to have succeeded. But there's not a lot of cash for his son after Greuel is gone, and Noe has the line on a wonder of a land deal, the kind of deal it is beyond Greuel's nature to resist—Arley has always had a wet finger raised to the air not only for making money, but for tweaking the noses of the world's squares in the process. Such impudent gall inspires Greuel's admiration.

He tells Noe to sell off his shares in the few racehorses he still holds an interest in; Greuel himself will sell Cosmo and Sadie Dame (some young girl can learn to ride on her, he thinks) and his Cadillac; he will agree to the terms of Arley's personal loan and sign off on that.

"Forgive me invoking here our thirty-plus years as partners and one might even say friendship," Greuel says. "This is serious shit I'm talking. You will not fuck me on this, Arley. You will not, all right?"

Noe raises one foot and scrapes the mud off his shoe against the bottom rail of the paddock fence, maintaining a delicate balance with his hands still plunged deep into his trouser pockets.

"Not so it'll hurt, I'd say."

Greuel seeks his face to find him smiling, the blue bruise of his skin darkening in the folds. *Get out of here,* Greuel dismisses him, and Arley bows slightly, mockingly, his uncommon laugh beating out in chippy breaths, low and quiet. Always has been business with that guy, thirty-six years and still Greuel knows any question between them will be decided by the bottom line.

He doesn't watch Arley step off or fire up his own Caddy. Instead, Greuel rests his chin on the pillow of his hand against the fence. Two of the turkey vultures remain out there as still as before. Hadn't there been three? He studies the sky, squinting against the sharp winter light, and spots half a dozen in the air above the far fields, the birds circling over something there, something weak and dying or, for all Greuel knows, some poor beast already dead.

Fleece had told him he got along with the caretaker just fine. He said the key was to accept the man was unhinged. As long as you understood Hardesty was capable of saying or doing whatever came to him, and Hardesty understood you did as well, then you had no problem. Like a scrap with a wild dog—*don't let him feel you're afraid or it's going to hurt.*

Full winter these days, sunlight angled at the eyes. He guides the truck between withered corn stalks at either side, objects cast in hard outline, shadows engraved as by a scriber. He parks in full view of the caretaker's cottage and then picks his way over scrims of ice, walking into plumes of his own breath, dragging his feet on the stones so that the man can note his coming. The ice and remnant snow brighten the world into a balloon-headed clarity, all nature seemingly polished to the finest detail by some great and unseen hand.

Howls razor high over a wind heard but unfelt on the ground. How do the dogs survive in that building without Fleece to feed them? His brother claimed to have named them all. Have they turned on one another, or is the caretaker feeding them? It's a question to ask Hardesty, whose own dog launches into pitched yelps as Cole nears the door, her claws rasping frantic below two rows of small paned glass.

He stops short with his hand about to knock the frame of a flimsy screen, surprised by the impassive face gazing through the highest of the tiered windows. Its wide and prominent bones look carved of driftwood, the eyes set deep beneath a heavy brow being near all the face he can make out within the mess of burled beard and coppery hair. The dog's scratching turns more insistent against the door, intense in bursts as its throat explores an entire range of hullabaloo alarm.

"I need to talk to you," Cole says.

At his voice the dog vaults into overdrive and sounds about to tear clear through the wood and screen and be at him. The face, however, does not move—the eyes remain open and unblinking long enough for Cole to wonder if it is in fact a live man he is looking at after all.

He tries again. He explains that he's brother to Fleece Skaggs and wants nothing here but to scare his brother up. And yet still the caretaker remains impassive and unreadable, he doesn't even allow for the slightest narrowing of curious eyes. Cole shuts up and waits, uncertain of the next step. He returns the man's stare. Eventually the absurdity of the scene overcomes him, two men staring at one another while a dog yaps wild at their feet. He tosses his hands into the air, suddenly furious, and starts around the corner of the house to see, in hard daylight, what he assumes remains hidden behind the bulk of the empty seminary.

On the walk he spots a small gray stone encased in white ice and with his boot sends it skidding. From deep in the building the dogs clamor to new heights of outrage and he wonders if they know a way out, if he should he worry. They harrow the high broken windows as if packed into a single room up there beneath the gleaming new transformer. Passing the cottage, he hears the suction of plastic against frame as the back door opens. When he turns, the weasel-bodied hound is almost on him, leaping in long strides across the slush, clumped bola balls of saliva spinning from its mouth. Just as Cole braces for the attack the dog halts, stands tall on her hind legs, and wails a single long note of indignation.

"Shut it Bone, you coward, I see him," the caretaker says, shrugging on a canvas jacket torn at the shoulder, flannel plaid winking from underneath.

Bone spins circles and rises again on her hind legs, the soft black of her muzzle tightening like a human about to whistle, and she bays long and righteously again. But she doesn't creep any closer; her tail

flings side to side and her ears are up. As the caretaker nears he gives
the hound a stamping kick to her hindquarters, sending her into a
tailspin that shushes her howling instantly.

"What am I supposed to do with you now?"

He is a large and heavy man, his hair and beard long overgrown
and drastically unkempt. His eyes shine very blue, swaddled in a field
of pink that suggests a history of difficulties past routine understanding, a history seconded by a nose well-formed and broad that could
be called handsome save for the web of fine violet lines that run his
cheeks from the russet undergrowth—a beard so dense it could be
inhabited—and the flared nostrils wide enough to pocket marbles.
The size of the man seems to intensify the act of breathing, which he
does through his mouth, gliding on a faint wheeze after an offhand,
unusually productive cough.

"Like what I said, we need to talk."

"A man makes an oath, forsakes the world and all it offers, and
damned if the world don't just come right in after with its hat and ass
a-floppin."

He doesn't appear to be addressing Cole—his eyes jump from the
seminary to the dog and to somewhere near Cole's chest, and then
squint off into the sky.

"I wanted to get a look at that car you got back here. What's left
of it."

The caretaker makes no signal that suggests he is listening. "Used
to be we never got much even in the way of mail. Nowadays anyone
with a notion grants himself a visitor pass. Me and Bone, whole reason
we come here's to get away from people, used to be nobody but punk
kids at night, like *you* and your kind snooping around. . . ."

His voice drifts off as though he lost his train of thought as his
eyes settle on Cole. And then the caretaker's flat expression claims
finality, and maybe threat, and he's a tall one, at least six-foot-four and
an easy 125 pounds over Cole as well. Cole holds his gaze until the
caretaker seems taken by another thought, squinting up to where the
dogs inside the seminary continue to bark and holler.

"I'm not looking for trouble. You know my brother. Nobody
knows where he is. That's his car."

He rounds the building without waiting for a response, and there it is: the sooty husk half-draped by the seminary's shadow. It's easy to identify as a Nova, but the car has lost all color save for a chrome-blue arc flaking over the rear fender. The rest is a spectrum of oily grays that fracture along ornate chemical designs. He cannot tell if the car is raked like Fleece's, or if this car once sported his beautiful mag wheels; even the tires have melted into clotted mounds. The trunk gapes at them as if the car itself is in shock over what's become of it.

"You don't look much a Skaggs to me," the caretaker says.

"You know what a Skaggs looks like, do you?"

"Might know a bit about those Pirtle County Skaggs, yeah, you could say."

Cole inspects the open trunk with hands clasped behind his back and is hit by a deeply offensive mephitic odor, strong enough that he turns away with eyes burning. He covers his nose and mouth with the collar of his sweatshirt and bends to it again, examining the interior as objectively as he can think to, but the trunk has no secrets to declare. He's not even sure what exactly *is* in there—the molding appears to have softened like putty, and it surprises him when he ventures a touch to find it's cold and firm. A tire iron lies angled behind the signal light, carbonized to oyster shell.

"It's a long story. I'm not all Skaggs," Cole says, and explains all. "Me and Fleece, we have the same mother."

"Fleece Skaggs never said word one to me about a little brother. How about that."

The cab stinks worse than the trunk, a reek like bacon left too long on the burner and stewed with some synthetic chemical compound—still, after two-plus months exposed to the elements. Breaches in the floorboard reveal soft earth gone to hard clay. He pulls back to blink away tears stinging from the interior's smell, and takes in a great gulp of cleaner air.

"Listen man, he's my brother and he's gone. You know him, right? Do I look like the cops?"

He continues to inspect the Nova though he understands he would have to be like the FBI with a full investigative team of forensic scientists to glean anything from this scalded shell.

"Well he aint in this car, I can tell you that much. Boy covers himself pretty well."

"Covers himself?"

"He's your brother and honest truth, you don't know where he's at, do you?" Hardesty says, and hucks up a laugh from deep in his chest. His eyes turn merry and his bottom lip lifts over the top to suck in the copper strands of the mustache. "Never told me nothing about no brother, now aint that the devil. What I liked about Fleece, he didn't eat up the air, told you what you needed to know and let you keep your ears on. Get away from that, Bone."

The hound had been sniffing at the open passenger door but jumps at the sound of her name; her paws toss the surrounding calx into tiny clouds about Cole's feet. Atop the dash parts of the windshield have collapsed and congealed into tobacco-spit pools. The glove compartment hangs open but whatever papers Fleece kept there are part of the weather now.

"There's nothing for you in that car. I done looked it over and there's nothing to do but let the raccoons move in."

"It's Fleece's Nova, isn't it."

"Makes you sore to look at that bit of spent charcoal and think how that thing could just shit and get."

"You say he took off. You don't think something bad got to him?"

Hardesty tilts his head to one side and gives a look much like a dog spoken to, that look of curious speculation like the dog can almost understand what's being said to it. He breaks the image by turning his mouth into a thoughtful frown. "I didn't say. He could've took off like you said and then had something bad happen. I mean, as an example of concerns you might not be entertaining already. Bad shit you don't see coming happens all the time. Hard to figure he'd torch that jewel after the money he sunk into her." He pulls one hand from deep in a coat pocket and rubs the crown of his head, dipping his chin to do so and exposing the bald area there as smooth-bordered as a tonsure, the pink skin flecked with light earthy spots. "But naw, I'm playing on your worries. Seems he was leaving, to me. This here being me thinking. Giving out gifts and all, cleaning up his place upstairs."

"Gifts?"

The throaty laugh erupts again, roupy and kind of sick.

"You and your brother aint all that close."

Above them the seminary dogs have stopped barking. A heavy thump sounds against a boarded window and Cole can almost see it, the dog's front paws smacking the barrier, frustrated to get out, to see. Hardesty speaks to the sky again: "Can't say I care for his leaving them beasts behind. That does surprise me, Fleece Skaggs should've been man above that. Leaving them to me, he knows what I'll have to do before they cut my rope."

"What gifts you talking about, Mister Hardesty?"

The caretaker's eyes snap narrow and intent to Cole's face.

"I aint much for sharing."

Cole returns to the car again. He can feel the man inspecting him, considering some point Cole cannot fathom, turning it over in the rusty pinwheels of his mind—pinwheels reflected in the eyes Cole returns to, eyes he notes now are of two distinct colors: the left a pale, washed-out blue, the right a deep chestnut. He would have sworn the moment before both eyes had been blue. Yet in the steep angle of sun the chestnut iris beams flecks of yet other colors: luminous gold streaks and greenish spatter.

"Aw hell. You're cool, right? Little brother to Fleece Skaggs? Come on."

He whistles out the corners of his mouth and the hound is on her feet and past them both, leading the way to the back door of the small outbuilding the two call home. In the cramped kitchen Hardesty mumbles that he has already pardoned the mess so he hopes Cole will as well—the counters browned with coffee and splotches of dried food, cabinets splatched with the tracks of spills; a junkyard tower of crusty dishes tilts in the sink. Magazines, newspapers, books cover every surface. They cover the front room as well; the TV sags on its particleboard stand with the extra weight and the room stinks of musty paper. Hardesty checks the fields through the windows, scans left and right up the drive and the frozen corn at either side. Cole looks over the magazine covers: *Popular Mechanics, Nature, National Geographic,* most dated twenty years or more before.

"You read a lot," he tells the wide back bent deeply inside a stand-alone closet, the canvas jacket large enough to be a tent for a solitary camper. Inside the closet magazines tumble and Hardesty curses the mother of god. He digs around in crinkling plastic. With a long groan and then tight grunt of final effort, Hardesty pulls back and the magazines inside shift like tectonic plates, a loud crash there sending Bone tuck-tailed scurrying briefly back to the kitchen.

Instantly Cole recognizes the heavy, sweet-as-syrup odor that overtakes the musty paper.

"I read to impress the girls," Hardesty says, nodding at the spread of cover photos on the coffee table: *Leg Fetish, Juggs, Cheri.* "Let me be the one to tell you, good women can't refuse a learnéd man."

He holds up, straight-armed with the same sense of triumph as a warrior hoisting the enemy's head, a weighted and bulbous black trash bag that twists and sheds fine green dust. "Your brother's generosity. Got any zig-zags on you?"

Cole does not. He left his one-hitter in the door pocket of his truck, but he doesn't mention this out of a weird telling sense that if he were to leave the house then Hardesty would make it difficult for him to come back in. The big man shrugs, rips a page of old newspaper, and kicks himself some room at the table. The reefer-stink blossoms so sweet and heavy that Cole's head swims with it.

"When did this happen? Him giving you the bag I mean."

"Couple months ago. What are we now, January? Would've been November then."

"So he did make with Greuel's run."

Hardesty lifts his shoulders, turns down the corners of his mouth theatrically, and holds the pose. A moment later he sighs that anything's possible, either one of them could keel over and die in the next minute for all he knows. "I don't make claims. If this here was Mister Greuel's property it wouldn't make sense for me to have it. So it aint his property then, is it."

Hardesty's chapped hands and brute fingers are the opposite of nimble yet he knows what he's doing. Before long he presents Cole with an expertly-wound spliff the size of a rich man's cigar. They get it going and pass it back and forth, the smoke a ruminative ghost silent between them. Soon the caretaker turns talkative.

"The shit is fancy good, isn't it," he says, and Cole feels the intense and familiar waves roll through his skull and down his neck and over his shoulders, seeping slowly the length of his spine; briefly he envisions a precise image of his nervous system singing with the drug before the rest of his body brightens into a happy and welcome softness. He nods, slowly, and it is all he feels capable of doing, and the doing seems to require an extraordinary amount of time.

"Don't know what to do with it all, to be honest," Hardesty continues. "Thoughtful of Fleece of course, but it's too much for one man alone. Keep all this I'll end up crazier than I is already. Just the other night had me talking to gnomes and shit. Poor Bone there could read my mind. She hasn't been right since."

"Fleece drops a trash bag on you—what is that, six, seven pounds? Can I?" Cole asks, indicating the bag even as Hardesty nods him on. "That's got to be fifteen, twenty thousand dollars there and I mean if you don't even bother with shake. What did he say?"

"Said 'Enjoy, brother, and thanks.' He owed me a few favors. Goes to show you never can suspect another man's generosity. He always talked about Carolina's outer banks, you know. Said one day he'd decide eight hours driving was too long to get him to the beach. Two tokes of this shit and I knew I did not want to advertise what he give me. But like I said, it's too much for one man alone."

Cole considers the wildfire pace of the dry newspaper's burning. He *knows* this pot; he knows you only get this sitting with Mister Greuel in his own house. And then it occurs to him that no, this stuff is stronger than he's ever had: his stomach lurches on queasy tides, and bright streaks of light race across his eyes. "You said he cleaned out his rooms upstairs?" His voice seems to emanate from the wall opposite.

"I did say. You've been up there, I'm sure. They're empty, aint they? I didn't do it." Hardesty indicates the bag again with his head. "Hell I know what that's worth. But I can't move reefer, wouldn't know where to go. Can't even figure how to get it out of the house with me when I leave."

"You're going to leave?" Cole asks.

"Boy you are nothing like your brother at all, are you? Don't listen well. They told me not two days ago. Greuel's blue man shows up with a couple of suits, they've got the deed in hand and they're walking around pointing to this and that, we'll build here, the sewer line must run there. . . . They stepped around that Nova like it was nothing but a tree and didn't blink an eye. My services here 'are no longer warranted,' as they say."

"What's Greuel and Arley Noe want with the St. Jerome Seminary?"

"Fixing to sell it again, I gather. I hear Greuel's too sick to do much else with it."

For once Cole wishes not to be as stoned as he finds himself currently. It's some powerful weed and he cannot think clearly with it in him; it makes him want to close his eyes, ease his head against the wall (the surface there looks welcome, and pliant); the room feels too warm. A swipe of his hand across his forehead brings back a palmful of sweat, and his heart beats in his temples. "How do you know these guys," he asks.

Hardesty's face is in his beard but his eyes look to be scanning the dirty webs drifting high in the ceiling's corners. "You ever tear into an old haystack? Possums, coons, one time for real I opened up on a timber rattler really unhappy to lose his home. You never can know what you'll find when you go in not even imagining what you should be ready for."

Did he not ask this man a question? What was he talking about only a few seconds before? Cole feels like a wanderer on the edge of somebody else's story, a story that does not include him and may have already passed by. The story he wants is his brother's; his brother's story *has* to include him. And this caretaker sits there with his eyes, one pale and the other that queer autumn gold, like some mystic in a creepy fairy tale, speaking riddles.

"Me and Bone, we'll find something farther from the crowd. Been talking about doing that for a while. It's getting hard to find someplace not run over by people trying to get away from other people. Pirtle's come to be—man, I can get nostalgic for five years ago. I remember when the whole county didn't have a single street light and I'm not that old. Used to be deer all around the cemetery walking out the Possler woods. Now it's no deer and lots of suits."

As though to press the point there comes the distant hammering of a neighbor on a rooftop. Cole stands and stretches languorously. It feels good to move his muscles, to feel his body. The room briefly wobbles and then rights itself, a subtle echo pulling at his eyes. He shuts them to stop the sensation. When he opens them again the caretaker appears to be sculpted into place.

"I could probably move some of the weed for you. I know some people."

"Don't take it personal if I want to think on that."

He says he won't and means it, it's hard to be offended by the man who just got him this high. He holds out his hand but Hardesty does not appear to notice. The dog gets animated again with her tail wagging, her breaths rushing faster and harder over a squeaking whine as she lopes toward the front door. Hardesty appears to have switched off—his mismatched eyes have locked in space, he sits on his knees with lips parted and jowls slack, one hand splayed flat on a girlie mag. As though in meditation, or in midst of a coronary. As Cole begins to pull back his hand, however, the caretaker's snaps up and their fingers touch.

"You okay?" Cole asks.

"I have more in my mind than you will ever fathom. Options, opportunities missed and to come. Women and dogs. The information trapped in these walls"—he gestures at the papers and books, then taps his skull with two fingers—"is nothing compared to the info in here. How you feeling about now?"

"Aw, you know. Wondering who it was made the sky so high."

It's a good answer and Hardesty cackles in agreement. He tells Cole this reefer is worth serious philosophy. And then he pronounces: "May you find safe shelter under an angel's eyelid."

The caretaker cackles again at Cole's inability to respond to that. "Listen, I am not one to give advice. But I wouldn't chase hard after your brother. If he wanted you to know what he's up to, then you'd know. You got no need to get up under Mister Greuel. Frankly I never thought much of him, it's his partner the one to watch with your hand on the holster, hear me?"

"Blue Note? You're talking about Arley Noe."

"Well, now, I did not say that. I'm not talking about anyone. I might not even be talking about anyone either of us knows."

•

The visit to the caretaker provokes a response more quickly than Cole would have imagined. At least he thinks it's a response; possibly he is imagining links where there are none: Greuel's illness and his brother disappearing; Cole's banishment from quarry buys and Arley Noe ignoring his questions—there could be connections and there might not be any at all. When he drives home from work the next night he decides to take the long way, following snaking roads and avoiding traffic where he can, thinking the while of what Hardesty had told him and coming to no conclusions. What would Greuel and Noe want with that old place, and what did it have to do with Fleece? He stops for gas-mart coffee and then wanders past Shady Beck's house, slowing to check for her Audi. Only a Jeep Cherokee and her father's Mercedes in the two-car garage. He doesn't feel like looking up Spunk.

Up the gravel hillside drive to home he smiles, pleased to discover Shady's car again at rest behind his mother's. For a girl who doesn't seem sure what she wants of him she certainly comes around a lot. He pulls to a stop behind the cabriolet and blocks her in, feeling crafty. He's halfway up the yard when he hears a gruff voice deadpan from the dark.

"There he is."

Cole spins at the sound. Barely perceptible against the dense woods, outside the reach of the porch light dim behind cobwebbed glass, the faint outline of a man approaching takes shape. His palms are turned out, level with his chest, making a show of threat's absence.

"Hell James Cole, it's a witch's tit out here, I was about to give up on you. I been waiting near an hour and was getting to wonder the fuck my own self was up to."

The hands fall as Cole recognizes Grady Creed. In the muted light his pale face appears yellow, pocked with shadow due to his bad skin. They each reach forward and tap knuckles gently in greeting.

"What up, Grady."

"Nobody running me to ground, can't complain. Been thinking of you is all, thought I might check in on Cole Prather, see how he's doing."

He hardly knows Grady Creed save for memories of exceptional cruelty and humiliation to a preteen Spunk back in the day. He's eager to see Shady and doesn't have the patience to dodge his own impulses.

"Cole Prather's just fine. Why? Grady I could count on a hand without its thumb how many times I've seen you in this yard."

"Maybe you should be more sociable. Let a man know he's got friends."

Cole pinches the coffee cup's soft Styrofoam between his teeth, feeling the give without biting through. He stares over the lip at Creed, who used to run with Fleece and even touted for his brother before Fleece started working Greuel's dope channels on his own. The ropey man's eyelashes are heavy and long and shadowed, the porch light making it appear his eyes are lined with mascara. Creed smiles his best chummy smile, which isn't his easiest charm, revealing good straight teeth save for one high canine that twists over the tooth beside it.

"Okay I know you aint for small talk any more than Fleece so I'll get to it. Listen, I came here to tell you one thing: *I am on your side.* That's all. In case you wasn't sure. I been running with Fleece since we was kids and I love him like a brother too."

Cole doesn't nod so much as dip his head, turning the cup to pinch down elsewhere on the Styrofoam. He keeps his quiet, hoping to prompt Creed to continue.

"Okay what you need to know, man, it aint right what's happened, but you want to play it safe. Let it go. I know it's near impossible to swallow but there I said it. Just, like, don't go there."

"What are you talking about?" Cole's voice sounds hollow in the coffee cup still pinched between his teeth.

Creed steps back and ducks his head; he looks about them in a show of caution, like others might be hidden behind the trees, in the night shadows listening in. He leans closer to Cole and his voice falls into low register, eyes flitting side to side, never resting on Cole's own—amped, probably, Creed has a taste for rippers.

"Don't play me like that, Cole, you don't need to, I got ears like anybody else. You seen his car burned up. It's hard to swallow but what else you need to know asides that? Fleece is gone. That's how it is. I'm telling you don't go after him. You're the only son your momma's got left. Understand?"

"You know my mother, Creed?"

"I aint never *been* with her if that's what you're asking. One of the few."

Cole drops the cup from his mouth and talks to the ground. "What I hear is Fleece ripped off Greuel and awayed with half the Clay County harvest."

"Believe that if it makes you feel better. It's a good story. I say he fucked up. And you said Greuel's name, not me. Remember that."

"Hell I've known Mister Greuel my whole life, I can go ask him."

"Damn it all and snowballs, Cole, I just told you not to do that. Said it with my mouth!" Creed stomps hard on the hillside; he jabs a finger toward the earth as if his mouth had been speaking from there and he wants to shut it. His face betrays either frustration or rage, and he is about to speak again, his face suddenly inches from Cole's own, when his skittering eyes slide past Cole's shoulder and he ducks his head deep again, turns his back on the house and faces the darkness over the lake. "Shit," he mutters, crossing his arms.

Cole turns to see. In the double window by the door his mother stands between parted curtains. Another face—a curve of forehead and clean shining hair he takes for Shady—peers out from behind her. He grants a casual wave despite the quickening churn Creed has stoked in him, and forces a grin of assurance. When he turns back, he has to search briefly; Creed has moved further from the light.

"And I should trust you why, Grade?"

"You got to trust somebody. Maybe you don't get how close you are to real trouble. Maybe my life don't need any more dead friends in it."

"When did you start to care what happens to me? You used to shoot bottle rockets at me when I was a kid."

"That was me being a teenager without whatever, without direction. A stage. Think on what I said. This aint a joke, Cole. Your brother's a ghost."

Creed stuffs his hands deep into frayed jean pockets and bows his shoulders, a sudden portrait of complete indifference, looking like he has just been rebuffed after asking for a smoke and nothing more as he starts to shuffle down the hill, navigating by hesitations in the dark.

"Hey Grady. How come you know all this? Maybe I have more questions."

"I don't know where you plan asking them, I was never even here," Creed says without a look back. His shadow melts into the deeper shadows, into the thick growth of trees, a presence known only by his hastening steps upsetting layers of dry dead leaves.

•

Inside the front room Shady stands with palms pressed together, aligned over lips and nose in a sign of prayer, thumbs against her throat. Cole would not have guessed her eyes could stretch so wide, they've become a huge part of her face. He tosses his keys atop the old TV and stops, asking what's wrong—yet knows already, like his body comprehends before his brain the quick fury in his mother's steps down the hallway, her closet door slung hard against the plaster wall.

"I didn't say a word, Cole," Shady says, "it's like she knew already."

Her hands break apart and frame her face for an instant before falling, folding again into a knot below her belly. Lyda's footsteps clamor again once they leave the carpet of her bedroom to clack on the hardwood and into the kitchen.

"Momma," Cole says, mustering strength into his voice. "Momma I'm on this. I'm doing what I can."

Lyda stops him with a single palm raised. "I *asked* you, Cole. I asked and you told me you didn't know a thing!"

It's not true and yet he lowers his gaze to the chipped paint of the baseboard, a repulsive feeling of betrayal surging over him even though he knows himself to be guiltless, suddenly ten years old again and ashamed, chastened for some wrong he hardly understood.

"Have to learn my firstborn's gone for good from a girl who isn't even family—no insult to you, Shady—the one thing, *the one thing* I ever asked my boys is to keep it all at home but look here everyone knows more about my own son than I do."

She's all smoke and motion within the kitchen's narrow confines, snapping open her leather purse and rummaging through its many pockets as she moves into the front room, cracking her hip against the partition with an exclamation and then smacking the wall to punish it for being in her way. An empty glass teeters from the ledge and shatters into the kitchen but she ignores it, surging forward and inspecting every surface in the room (the coffee table of *TV Guide*s and *People* magazines, the particle board credenza where Fleece's name remains inscribed by a pocket knife in his six-year-old hand); her eyes alight on Cole's keys atop the Zenith. The word *don't* barely escapes his lips even as the keys ring out in the room's erstwhile silence as she snatches them up and opens the door.

"The man does not own us, James Cole. I'm not afraid of him and I'll be hellbound to sit here at home while you taddle around with your tail between your legs. Lawrence Greuel *owes* us, you understand?"

Cole doesn't understand. He follows her out onto the dead-grass path to his truck, Shady stalling behind, standing uncertain at the open door.

"Ma, you can't just go over there, you don't know what you're getting into, you don't know those people anymore."

"Don't tell your mother what she can't do."

There's a pause before she gets the engine going, ramping through rpms as she gasses the thing in neutral. She shouts through the windshield for Cole to watch his feet but does not wait for him before releasing the brake to roll down the hill—Cole falls as he jumps back. He waits there, hands in the cold grass, watching. The engine will die when she tries to find first gear. His battered transmission will frustrate her to quitting before she even makes it off the lake.

The truck lurches as the tires grab the rough macadam; he winces at the grind in the gears. The truck sputters when Lyda forces second through a dip of the road but then she's climbing again. At the sloped curve behind a row of black alder the tires squeal, and then he can find her in the dark only once she flips the headlights at the main intersection. He listens through the cranky process again, the lurch and grind, and somehow his truck keeps on going. Soon even the engine's noise is gone.

"I thought you were the only one who could drive that thing," Shady says from the porch.

Alone in the yard, Cole looks at her, backlit by the foggy light bulb in a near radiant glow around her hair. He realizes he still holds the champed Styrofoam cup and he crushes the thing, throws it aside with the other trash that gathers against the woods, and then lies back into the crunchy cold grass to stare into the night sky.

This could be real. There's no *seeming* to happen here, it's all happening in real time.

"Cole I'm sorry but she saw you talking to that guy, and who was that anyway? Because seeing you two out here it was like she knew everything at once and she turned on me and—"

He stops her speaking with a swipe of his hand through the air between them as he gets to his feet, and tells her to give him her keys, they've got to get moving.

As early evening gave way to late, pinkening *(would that be a word?) cloud tissues drifted eastward, retaining a sandstone pallor even once the sun had absconded from heaven.* That's how Erly Diddle would describe it in a book if he were ever to write one. *Pinkening?* Maybe pinkened. Pinked?

The job requires long hours doing nothing. He's suited for it. He likes the nighttime quiet on Greuel's farm, and even if his can clenches cold against the Adirondack chair in these winter months he has the thermos of whisky coffee to keep his belly warm. Seventeen years he's been sitting here. Seventeen years of humid night-sweat summers or boot-stamping come winter, piss breaks over the patio rail peering out over the fields and random statuary and historic farm equipment—the place looks like an absurd miniature golf course—feeling himself royalty gazing upon his works, eyes hungry for any headlights across 6220, Parker's Highway, his mind trying to focus on the possibilities of confrontations that never come.

His tricked-out Mossberg is the best firearm he has ever owned, as dear to him as a true friend, though Erly has used it only to splatter squirrels and turkeys. Not much call for shootouts these days.

The shotgun sits across the Adirondack's armrests like the safety bar on a thrill ride, the barrel anchoring his elbow to steady his hands (clothed in fingerless gloves) as he reads. Spillane and MacDonald novels, mostly, but he'll take whatever mysteries they got at the secondhand shop in Foster, even the occasional Western. He especially likes accounts of the gangster heyday before the war, the stories of Capone, the Barker-Karpis gang, Pretty Boy Floyd (who was nowhere near pretty, Erly has seen pictures). Stoned or sober he reads deep into the night while Greuel and guests curse and joke over cards and business inside. He reads and then drifts into daydream—wonders if daydream is still the word for it when it occurs after dark—and considers how he might invent a better story than many of the authors he has read. If he were to ever recount on paper the things he has seen! In fact he *has* composed eventful beginnings, harrowing scenes of suspense, chases that lay waste to entire towns; designed foul murders and extortion schemes and methods of blackmail that would land him lauded in Hollywood if he could set them down, lay them out (what would Greuel and his illiterate cronies have to say to *Professor Mule*—that odious nickname—then?). But then with sunrise comes sleep. When he awakens his mind is a clear slate, empty of the scenarios conceived the night before. On the rare occasion that he can recall a snatch of story or a line of dialogue it never seems as thrilling as it had in *the throes of creation*. Characters never seem to get their due. Mule conceives a failure to all the murder mysteries he kills time with in that they center on one person only, an investigator who uncovers clues by clever wit and judicious brawn, and in real life no story works like that. In real life a story occurs among legions; to understand the story you have to know all the people it touches too. The disappointment he feels after finishing a novel is that there's nothing more than a problem solved, and everyone in it except for the main guy exists to tweak the problem one way or another, they're either bad or good or torn between the two and have no life outside their brief appearance on the page. These authors narrow the scope too far; even a murderer with the coldest blood has his hopes and dreams.

"Your lips move whenever you're thinking, you know that?" asks Grady Creed, surprising Erly from the doorway. His knees start up, knocking the Mossberg to the porch boards.

"Dammit Creed, you think I don't know when I'm being looked at? Maybe I'm putting on a show for your entertainment."

Creed's lips part but the teeth keep closed, air hissing out between them. A gesture of sardonic amusement emulated from Arley Noe. These young kids are nothing but footnotes to the originals.

"You guys are sure quiet tonight, what's going on in there, church?"

"Nothing you need to know, Mule."

"Watch your tone with me, boy. I'm feeling cranky tonight and I got my toolbox full in the truck."

Creed whistles in alarm as he shuts the door (more firmly than necessary, Erly decides). It has been some time since the boys coming up were impressed and awed by the legend of Professor Mule and his toolbox and what he could do to a punk strapped to a chair. These kids have had it too easy; they'll have a hard time of it when competition comes to Pirtle County again, as it undoubtedly will, stuff coming up from Mexico in search of a home.

Creed doesn't matter; he wants to stay well with Arley Blue Note. Mule's skills are not widely sought, and Greuel's going to go some time. "'Once in the racket you're always in the racket': *Capone!*" he tells the statue of some saint Greuel's son brought home months ago. The blessing hand is broken at the wrist and he thinks it an unlucky sign.

Twenty-two paces cross the front porch—fourteen if he strides. He's pissing over the rail when night breaks on the blare of a car horn, his spine snapping erect and left hand soaked at the surprise of it. Headlights at the front gate glare down the drive; how could he have missed that? He stuffs himself into his pants without making it through the fly of his boxers, cursing *wait a minute* as he forgets to zip up. Because of the headlights he can't see the make or model but by the set of them he guesses it's a pickup. Misguided teenagers who have their purchase arrangements wrong. He fingers the mouth of the Mossberg absently, squinting into the light. The horn blasts again and he curses back even as he takes the porch steps sideways for his aching hips and tight back, not bothering with the gun. At the booth he hits the intercom even as the horn lets fly three more long blasts in defiance of any courtesy.

The sight of Creed and Spunk in the front window add a level of stress he could do without and under his breath he curses them, too. Patience has fled the world.

"*What*," he spits into the small speaker above a thumbnail gone white with his mass leaned into it.

Releasing the button he expects the giggled apologies of drunk sixteen-year-olds. Instead he encounters only empty air, a static punctuated by the jerky chug of an idling, unwell engine. Four-cylinder at that. Four-cylinder pickups are for children and women. He thumbs the button again.

"State your business," he says, not three inches from the speaker. People respond to formality, the snap of authority.

No answer? He turns back to the silhouettes in the front window, shrugs—it's not a long walk, Mister Greuel used to complain the farm's one drawback was how close the home sat to the road. Erly groans, having accepted long ago that he is not a fast man; he has the aching hips and a cumbersome body with which he has been at odds the entirety of his forty-eight years. Plus that reliable Mossy sits on the porch, and he has to retrieve that before starting up the drive to see what there is about the what.

He's hardly out of the booth when an angry voice hurls profanities at his lazy ways and declares that he is as *reliable as useless* and *put that thing away* and *where the hell is that man*. The fact of her startles him into a full stop, a beat passes before he thinks to lumber into her path, raising his hands, he's saying *Whoa now Lyda hold on there* but his girth and the dark and Greuel's penchant for eccentric lawn decorations connive against him, he smacks his shin against the rusty metal of some ancient wheeled farm implement he never has been able to identify in all those long hours of porch-bound contemplation, and it's mayday mayday man going down with sharp pain screaming up his leg, and the ground practically jumps into his face. He lifts his head, belly and exposed penis shocked by the cold wet grass, and reaches for her ankle as she passes, noting a chain of small silver seashells tinkling there, but she is small and spry and dances off. *Erly Diddle you are not worth a minute of my day,* Lyda says. Another fact he accepted long, long before.

•

Now Brother Gil Ponder strives to defy convention. It's what he expects of God and what his God expects of him, and so fundamental to his mission that he totes the claim prominently on his business card: *Brother Gil Ponder, Pastor Unorthodox, Christ World Emergent Ministries.* He sees nothing wrong with gambling, for instance, so long as it's played in the proper spirit. To the congregants that inquire (it staggers him how many focus on this issue as if it were the ultimate scourge) he counsels that Christ raged over the gaming tables for their being practiced *at temple;* games in themselves hold no value to the soul's pilgrimage through this world. As a spiritual risk gambling's no different from any other worldly endeavor—its sinful nature lies in whether it compromises one's duty to Christ.

If he's wrong, he argues in his short sermons, then capitalism condemns them all. And Ponder stridently believes God's Will is for His children to succeed. Thus capital is kind of holy. Without the opportunity of credit, wealth becomes attainable to a very elect few—a close metaphor to Calvin's view that souls are judged before arriving in this world.

Ponder doesn't think Calvin far off the mark. Nobody can free themselves completely from the culture that formed them, and if—as Luke asserts—the world is under demonic control, then none can free themselves from that nefarious influence. The Gospel of John identifies the devil as "the ruler of the world" as well. Therefore to live in Christ one must exist alongside the demonic and not shrink from it. Gambling-as-sin withers under this kind of examination. A game of poker with hard felonious types like Greuel and associates is no different from Daniel's night with the lions.

He's fortunate however that no one here is playing break-me stakes; even at his most lost, before Christ entered his heart, Ponder could not play a card game to save his life. Poker and eight-balls don't mix, and he had long preferred the eight-balls. Only seven years before, he could have been holding up this entire room for its cash and whatever else they had secreted here that could be carried away and sold. He assumes they know his story and don't care—which makes him all the more curious to understand their willingness to work so patiently with CWE and its cautiously indecisive (and funding-hungry) board of elders.

Lawrence Greuel, more sallow and gray than Ponder had ever been when copping, still manages to come across as cheerful as he deals the next round. Ponder's assistant Carolyn Dell cringes in an upholstered chair with her small purse on her knees and hands folded over its wooden handles, spine carefully arched, every bit the high-collared church lady their hosts undoubtedly expected. She bites down upon her bottom lip with small and delicate front teeth. Ponder beams great warmth and holds up his empty bottle of water.

"We got purified water in the fridge," Greuel says as he places the deck at the table's center.

"Brother Gil prefers his own brand," Carolyn says. She reaches into a knit sack for another bottle of Kentucky Sweet Springs, a CWE sponsor. Ponder has invested church funds there and allows them to advertise in the greeting room, leave flyers in the seats.

"You should try a bottle," he tells the room. "Purify it several times over. No hint of chlorine or fluoride, just good water a body needs."

"You a salesman for a water company too?" Arley Noe's lips hardly move.

Ponder broadcasts his best unchallenging laugh to the room. "Not at all! I'll cheer on any deserving product. I'm a big believer in supporting local economies."

Noe's eyes narrow. "So are we, preacher, so are we." His buddies chuckle into their cards. Greuel orders them to play the goddamn hand—and quickly apologizes to Carolyn for the language.

She has an appreciable way about her that inclines even hard men to politeness. On the drive over Carolyn had asked the point of meeting at Greuel's home, and after hours. Wouldn't a law office in the afternoon be more appropriate? She said she did not like nor did she trust these gentlemen, which Brother Gil already knew, because he knew Carolyn. Only her confidence in his vision could pull her from the three boys and the husband and her chicken tetrazzini and into the smoky night with a body-pierced tattooed reformed junkie thief to a den of malfea-sant highbinders cradling cards beneath a heavy tobacco fog; only her faith in Ponder's ability to steer their congregation could convince her to go against her sacrosanct beliefs in the core responsibilities of Wife and Mother and follow him into that part of the night she mostly read about, cowered before, or watched on the TV with the repeating self-reprimand *Judge the sin, not the sinner* winding through her mind.

Sometimes you have to be willing to get dirty to do the Lord's business. Ponder is perfectly willing to do whatever's required to fulfill his vision of founding a new community thriving with nourished minds, righteous *doers* celebrating the marvelous gift of LIFE, practicing daily what God will call them to do for eternity after their allotted earthly spans. One day CWE Ministries will break from the conventional Sunday School sessions and after-worship brunches into its own suburban village—maybe even a legally incorporated city, an intentional community with deeds restricted to Christian-based practices, if he can figure language that won't raise a church/state thing. They will transform the seminary grounds into a complex of basketball courts, movie theater, conference center, primary school, along with a chapel arena of proper size. Ponder foresees a flowering of God in the heart of wild Pirtle County.

Yet there are misgivings: he's unclear on the logistics of a land trust, for one, and knows nothing of what Noe called an "Illinois-type," or how this affects CWE's ambitions. He would like to know. It is important to come away from this deal with the church untainted. Right now he would settle to just get things started.

"Friends, I am enjoying this game," he begins, "and excuse me if this sounds rude, because I don't mean it to. But at what point tonight do we start discussing that property?"

Over his cards, Arley tightens his mouth into a V—something of a wild boar to his face like that. "Yeah, when do we," he murmurs more to himself than anyone else. There must be a customary rhythm to these negotiations Ponder is unaware of. He wonders if Noe realizes treatments exist for the problem in his blood that makes his skin blue like that.

Arley raises his free hand—a graceful object despite the blue pallor, narrow and elegant, a pianist's hands, he would guess, except for the spectacular gold nugget and diamond horseshoe ring—and brushes through the haze with an air of trying to dispel more than smoke.

"Paper's're worked out. Even went the extra mile of notarizing."

"I'm a notary public, Rev, bet you didn't know *that*."

"I didn't, Lawrence. You surprise me every time we meet."

"Ah," Greuel says, "Ah well. I prefer Mister Greuel. The whole thing's a peach of a deal: our group's the trustee, you folks the beneficiary. It's yours in some twenty years but we're all aware I won't be here to see that. So I congratulate you now—a lucky man leading a lucky church, I reckon."

Ponder wants to tell him that God's Will is not luck. Carolyn saves him by speaking up: "We thank you and yes, we are lucky—lucky to have the Lord on our side, wouldn't you say?—but we do have questions." She opens a notebook to a page marked by a magenta post-it strip, hesitates as she searches for the item she wants. Greuel stares after her with the same expression of slack-jawed surprise as if she had fallen through the ceiling.

"What she means is, we'll have our own legal advisors look it over first, and then I have to run it by my board, et cetera et cetera before we sign and return. Obviously."

"Certainly you do. A man wants to be sure he's not getting blistered," Arley says. "But understand, we want the deal committed legal on a fairly swift timeline."

"I want this deal done before I croak!" announces Greuel.

"We understand," Ponder says. He does feel a degree of compassion for the man so clearly suffering before him; feels equally the irrelevance his compassion probably means to him. "I'll do my best to speed up the process. Owner financing has some of our members feeling . . . *reluctant,* let's say. No one wants to be surprised by something like balloon payments down the line."

"Gimme their names, they won't give you any more trouble," Greuel squawks. Ponder joins him in the laughter following and keeps it going longer than feels comfortable, his mouth molded into that false hilarity of a ventriloquist's dummy. He is surprised by how self-conscious he feels here; perhaps he's thrown by the queer glow of that bizarre headlight illuminating floor to ceiling behind Greuel.

"If your board feels they can muster bank financing," Noe offers, "more power to them. We get paid that much faster. Our impression is the congregation isn't so well-endowed as that."

"You wouldn't believe how many audits we undergo," laments Carolyn.

Greuel nods into his cards, saying that it's partial land trust, eleven acres bought outright where the values are only headed up. Noe levels his inexpressive and unnerving stare above the fan of his own cards at Ponder, whose eyes remain steady despite the flux he feels inside. Arley Noe's grin, when it spreads enough to show his teeth, reminds him of a possum's mouth. He has noticed this in previous meetings and wondered if his curiosity was too obvious—a curiosity confounded by his inability to decide if the smile is endearing in a homespun, salt-of-the-earth kind of way, or chilling to the spine. The other players fall into their own habits, lighting smokes as they frown over their hands, drinking liquor or else refilling glasses, gazing over at the TV basketball game simmering low. *No doubt they've got their work cut out for them now,* the announcer is saying. *The Cats dug themselves a deep hole in that first half.*

Ponder clears his throat for the delicate question. "What did you decide as the percentage of your donation?"

The possum teeth disappear into a seriousness Ponder would have reserved for cursing the dead. The man waits an entire moment in silence, and then laughs in Ponder's face. It's not a particularly scabrous laugh, but the insult is there, the contempt. He lights a cigarette from the end of one Greuel has let burn to a coil. "You want to tell him?"

"You tell him. I feel awful. Where's my dope?"

"Beside you, boss," Grady Creed says from where he hovers outside the table. "Though it aint time yet, you got another hour."

Greuel says he doesn't give his balls what time it is, his legs throb and last time he pissed (pardoning himself to Carolyn again) he must have been passing sand for what it did to him. Noe shakes out three large white tablets and sets them on a paper napkin and tells Greuel he'll get him water. "I'm coming back," he adds, nodding to the others as he scrapes his cards into his palm.

"You leave those here you cheating fraud bastard," Greuel wheezes—and throws up his hands in exasperation at his language before Carolyn and *the man of the cloth.* Ponder finds it difficult to dislike him, though instinct points to a con here somewhere, one he believes in the old days he would have figured already, those skills for self-preservation having dulled over his recent years of plenty.

Arley's flat eyes sweep the table and he orders everybody to turn in their cards, too. "Deal another hand when I get back."

"Why don't you get one of the boys to go?" from Greuel.

"I'm already up, my cards are in."

"This is a twenty-dollar pot, for the love of your shameless whore mother."

"Twenty dollars of mine in a few minutes," Arley says. He backs toward the kitchen keen to show no credence given his companions, keeping eye until everyone tosses in their cards. Ponder cannot quite pinpoint exactly what it is about how odd the man moves; his steps look locked into slots on the floor, and there's that weird, geometric precision to his gait, like there's no give to his spine or shoulders. He's never seen its like before.

Greuel broadcasts a harmless show of smile to Carolyn. "Bastard could buy this farm and your seminary in cash right now and he worries over twenty bucks." He's no longer apologizing for his language. At his wink to the preacher, Ponder sees his opening, yet he hardly has his mouth parted before Greuel speaks again: "All on the mantel, rev. Donation's like a third of total. My tax genius says that's the best we can do if I'm to leave my no-count boy a pot to piss in." He seems to deflate to have the deal so easily summarized, as if its simplicity proved a great anticlimax to the evening.

"May I get it for you, Brother Gil?" Carolyn asks, standing, coat folded over arm.

"Creed there can get it for you, my ma'am," says Greuel, shuffling the cards in tremulous hands.

But Creed is not paying attention to them. He is leaning both arms at either side of the double-window at the front of the room, peering through the thin muslin curtain. As Greuel repeats, *Creed there will be happy to get that for you,* Ponder starts at a woman's angry voice raised and cursing, a sound that has everyone at the table turning toward the door. They hear a tumbling clatter, a grizzled cry—and then it's the complaint of plank and joist beneath the vigor of spirited feet.

Creed's a step from the door when it flies open and nearly slaps him in the face. Carolyn reels three steps back and falls with a song into Ponder's lap, while Greuel stills his hands atop the deck of cards and stares frog-mouthed, greasy eyes wide. Claiming the room is a small, sturdy woman, her face caught in a wrestling between indignation and outright wrath, her head haloed by a wild bushel of hair writhed from the wind, from sleep, from sleeplessness—it looks like the wind itself made material and stuck upon her as a warning.

"Where is he?" she asks. "What have you done with my boy?"

"Lyda," Greuel says, stretching out the name in a long slow song of three syllables, *la-EYE-dah*, "lovely Lyda Skaggs. Now here's a woman what always did know how to make an entrance."

She juts forward a delicate jaw. The muscles in her neck bulge and twist, wrenching furrows of shadow into her skin within the room's queer light. "Lawrence Greuel do you mean to take my first-born from me too?"

Grady Creed shuts the door with care. She wheels at the sound. Only now does she seem to notice the others in the room, and with a self-consciousness sinking over her features, she circles slowly and takes in each face, some seven in all before Arley Noe returns from the kitchen. As she moves, her arms begin to wrap about her body, hands sliding up to clasp herself above the elbows, and her eyes dart from figure to face, landing briefly on Brother Gil—and then holding upon Carolyn with confused inquiry, as if she cannot make sense of the straight-world dress and careful makeup, the hair finely styled, the sensible shoes. In return Ponder can hardly make sense of her: she is like a figure returned from his own itinerant past. Or no, her face goes further back, to grandparents in youth staring fierce and unbowed from photographs commemorating one proud moment in their hills-and-holler lives of hardship. And yet the delicate jaw, a sensuousness about her eyes; she is hard but pretty.

Ponder lurches to his feet and helps Carolyn into her coat. He mentions only the lateness of the hour, aware that no one is paying him any mind.

"Well, there you go," rasps Greuel. His eyes stray to Ponder for an instant. "She calls that boy her first-born only when she wants something from me. I don't know what you're on about, Lyda, I should be asking for what your boy took that's mine."

The joker charm has faded, overtaken by the kind of gravity Ponder wished he could muster in himself. Greuel leans forward, intent on this woman wavering alone in the room's center. His chest spills over the table edge, and his shirt shifts with his sagging flesh, yet he appears ready to launch from the wheelchair and overturn the table if need be. She shrinks visibly before the man's gaze; Ponder can see it happening in stages. Her fingers hover over the cheap and inappropriately light jacket for such a cold night, and her eyes ferret from faces to floor without settling. Whatever thread of outrage that had brought her here is lost.

"I'll just get those papers off the mantel there," Carolyn says. "It was so nice to meet with you in your lovely home!" She crosses the rolled-wool rug and returns with the file tucked beneath one arm, ignoring the woman at each turn as she professes thanks on behalf of CWE Ministries to everyone for their time and how positive this was now that they finally got the chance to get familiarized with one another before the launch of this life-changing project. Already Greuel is inviting the now-irresolute woman to sit with him, to come, sit, and telling the card players to clear out. And Ponder is setting the name he heard into his mind: Skaggs, Lyda Skaggs.

•

Cole sweeps the Audi in close beside his pickup and parks. An accident on 53 between a minivan and a tractor put them a good forty minutes behind his mother and now he's frantic, mistyping the gate code twice before he gets it right. He tells Shady to go on home, knowing she will refuse, knowing they'll argue as he tries to assert his rightness in the matter, and knowing he will lose yet more time and the argument anyway. He asks her to stay in the car at least. She won't listen. "I'm in this too," she insists; but how could she be? How is that even possible?

He finds his mother at the table in the front room, folded forward in her chair as if in recovery from a blow to the stomach, slim-shouldered in worn denim with the old cable-knit sweater loose over her hips, her back to him. Arley Noe and Mister Greuel sit within arm's length of her on opposite sides, completing two points of a triangle over the round tabletop. Cole had expected for find her calmed by now—Lyda's rages pass like summer thunderstorms, all flash and volume that leaves behind a refreshed and peaceable kingdom—but from here she looks near collapse. She turns, her distressingly slender arm bared as she reaches to him, the tender skin inside her wrist slightly blue in Greuel's headlight. "Son, come here," she murmurs, "you sit with me." At his hesitation, her fingers begin to draw in rhythmic waves, the gentle motion of stroking the throat of something small and vulnerable. "Come on, I need you," she says. Shady nudges him from behind. He turns a chair backward against the table edge and sits.

"Need anything?" from Noe.

He shakes his head. On the table before Lyda is a collapsed shaving kit, its black leather dulled with age yet brilliantly veined. Sidewise he tries to study her; she is cast in a numb slump and her eyelids appear to be losing resistance beneath a great weight. The hand that invited him holds above the table, palm now turned down and fingers stretched stiffly as to gauge their steadiness. Her fingers twitch with tiny quakes, and now it's her son reaching to her, clasping, covering her hand with his own.

"We have a problem needs resolving," Arley Noe says. "Now. Tonight."

"Let me handle this, blue boy." Greuel's hand slices the air with unlikely speed. His words come forth blurred around the edges but clear enough to understand, and his sacklike face quickly fills the compass of Cole's sight, his voice a blunt grinding stone. "You have a beef with me motherfucker now's the time to lay it down."

Cole's palms turn moist. "You've always been right by me, Mister Greuel." He doesn't know what else to say. He never does, not when it matters. The old man glares, mouth stuck in a wretched twist. Cole knows more is expected out of him. "I've known you all my life. You, Spunk. Miss Clara. I don't remember anything before I remember her being in my life, you know?"

"Only reason we are talking. Why you are *here* and we are *talking*. Anybody else—" his hand rises again, slices the air again, a slower chop this time.

"What do you want from us?"

"Your mother—she's got these ideas. Spend time alone like her and thoughts get into your head, you don't know where they come from. I know because hell, I never leave this house. Lyda here, I don't like her ideas. I don't like what they hint at, and sure as fuckin' Christ don't like the idea of her mouthing off with these ideas somewhere else. I doubt you're too enthusiastic about this, either. Young buck like you doesn't need this shit, your head should be on what that doctor's daughter got in her jeans, not with this here, am I right? It's awkward."

At *awkward* Greuel's throat seizes. His entire torso bolts forward, chest thumping the table as a coughing fit crackles behind his clenched fist. His eyes distend, redden, they glisten more with each successive spasm as his other hand seeks the bottle of water nearby. Despite the fit his eyes never leave Cole's face. His head rears back and he nearly swallows the bottle plunged deep into his mouth and the water pools and overruns his lips. Arley Noe starts to rise but Greuel grabs his wrist, sits him down again.

"I don't look well and I don't sound well but I assure you I am perfectly fine."

"Sure you are. I'm glad you are."

"Don't give me that. Nobody's glad I'm alive, including me." He belches into the back of his hand, checks to see if anything had come up. "I've spent the last sixteen months readying things for after I'm gone and your brother's been a big part of that, Lyda has it all wrong. I find any hand in this room touched Fleece Skaggs then that is one hand I will see nailed to a post in my front yard for all the world to consider. That boy was like a son"—here he glances at Spunk and Cole follows; Shady is pressed as far against the end of the couch as she can go while Spunk plays, grinning, whispering into her ear—"the kind of son I deserved."

He gathers himself, chews his lips and stares deeply at Cole, waiting as though a moment is needed to allow such pronouncements their intended gravity. In turn Cole watches the tics in the wild ham-gravy eyebrows, the capillary webs spidering the dark oysters below Greuel's eyes.

"I am only going to ask you once. Do *you* know where your brother's at?"

His mother touches his arm, and then withdraws. Behind him he hears the smack of a hand and Shady's intense whisper—*Quit it, Spunk!*—against Spunk's chortles of amusement, but nobody pays this any attention. The entire room feels intent upon him. But he has no answer, he has no answer to any worthwhile question he has ever thought, and he fights the urge to either stand and shout as much or else crumple into a ball beneath the table. Why would Greuel ask him like this? Doesn't he have the answers already? His eyes seek the older man's, briefly, before sliding into focus on his shiny, unshaven chin.

"No, Mister Greuel. I sure don't and I wish I did."

Greuel slaps the table again and rolls back. He turns to Noe, whose own eyes narrow at Cole as if having trouble deciding which part of him to eat first. "I told you," Greuel says. "Can you admit I told you that much?"

"I hear him saying it. That don't mean nothing."

Greuel launches at Cole again. "Fact: your brother stole from me. He stole from me so it *hurt*. Go down to my stables, you see any horses there? No, it's a five-star hotel where critters keep their paws warm all winter. I sold every one of them, even Clara's Sadie Dame. This pains me in ways you will never understand. I have been denied. I want what's mine."

"The horses?"

It's a frog-steady stare he drops on Cole now. He stabs the water bottle at his mouth again but gulps mostly air, the plastic breathing with each seething slug. Without word Arley Noe rises and heads down the hallway in his smooth and strange gait, as if he itemizes every step, counting down from a finite inventory. With the break Cole checks out Shady, who has subdued Spunk's obnoxious tendencies, leaving him grinning meanly, his head and hips miming a strange dance in repose, like a party raves in his head and he wants to milk every last second of it.

When Noe returns with more water Greuel chugs it greedily, two fingers pressed against the left side of his face. Bell's Palsy is a recent affliction. Still the water trickles out, following the curve of his rusty first chin. He clears his throat again with an awful scrape.

"So tell me what you do know."

Grady Creed leans a shoulder against the hallway corner, green beer bottle in hand, and taps sturdy fingernails against the glass, a small hammer chiming a bell.

"What did you give her?" asks Cole, indicating his mother.

Lyda's smile shifts between melancholy and contentment. Her eyes study the rims of her lower lids (*What is it you see?* he wants to ask), her shoulders curved even more deeply inward. She whispers apologies—Cole can't tell if the words are directed at him or simply said aloud: she is sorry, she says, sorely sorry. In the next instant her eyes look weepy, but no tears fall.

"The lady was agitated when she got here. I give her something to ease the upset," Arley says. He regards Lyda with the dispassion of a researcher evaluating blind-tested volunteers. "I dón't know. Maybe it was too much juice, you can't always tell what somebody'll take and she's a dry reed, that one."

"She doesn't spike," Cole says.

"I'm fine, motherfucker," slurs Lyda. The words come out as *muller . . . flokker.* Creed and Greuel laugh, and even Arley Noe is stirred enough to crease the lean flesh of his cheeks.

Now a tear blossoms to full flower. The blurred mascara and bunched lashes present her eyes as dark bursts of mourning. "Don't you all laugh at me," she says. "I know this feeling don't last forever."

"Your mama's fine. If we wanted anything done it would be done to her by now," Greuel says.

Creed shifts his weight and draws heavily from his bottle, the beer sloshing audibly; despite willing against the urge Cole's gaze darts to him and discovers Creed returning a stare with intense, careful eyes.

"I don't know anything you guys don't, is my guess."

"Try me."

Cole tells about the burned-out car. *We know that,* Greuel says, palm patting the table. Cole tells of the empty rooms at the top of the seminary. *This is not news,* says Greuel, voice rising and palm smacking the tabletop harder than before.

"Yeah, but the thing is the dogs, the dogs are still there."

Greuel stares, implacable, the toad on its lily.

"You say he's a son to you, then you know he wouldn't leave those dogs behind to starve, I don't care if he planned to rob you of everything you got."

"Dogs'll find a way," says Noe. "What they got them snoopers for."

"What's a few dead dogs against the rest of your life on vacation?" asks Greuel.

"It would be a lot, to him. He wouldn't do it. He's wild but Fleece isn't cruel."

"News to me," Greuel intones, extracting a snicker from Creed. "So what am I to divine from this bit of information? Your brother takes my run, he's hiding in Pirtle County to keep them dogs fed?"

"Maybe he arranged something with that caretaker," offers Shady from across the room.

"The caretaker," Greuel repeats as though to note the detail. "We talk to him yet? What's he say?"

"You don't have to worry about him," answers Creed.

"I decide what I worry about. What about you, Cole—you ever meet this caretaker?"

"Sure. Fleece knew him. Knows him."

"He get you high?"

"Fleece?"

"Come ON!"

Cole pictures the trash bag pulled from the closet, big Hardesty hoisting it aloft, resin shining on the dark green plastic like a cola spill, light-green dust settling in the late sunlight. He shrugs, nods. Arley asks him if it was any good.

"Not as good as yours. He said he got his from a cousin up near Cincinnati."

It's his first bald lie. Speaking it he feels a tremor in his belly, the suspicion of a first step toward failure. Can these men see him? Can they tell from here he has to make it up as he goes? From the lie he offers the last bit of truth available to him.

"His mags?"

"The what?"

"His rims. He had those expensive mag wheels. They're not there, I looked."

"The boy remembered his rims." Arley Noe's bottom lip peels below yellowed teeth in amusement, the lips twisting his mouth into a kind of sickle, "I'll be damned to say it Greuel but isn't that Fleece Skaggs?—skedaddles with a whole season run but you can't leave behind mag rims you paid good money for."

"First I heard of it," mutters Greuel. He turns to Grady Creed, smacking his knuckles against one another. "You care to explain how a car perv like you missed this little detail?"

"Dang, boss, I didn't take a comb to the thing. Anybody could see it was his car and all burned up. Didn't think there was anything else to know."

Greuel returns to the matter at hand. A new sheen shimmers on his cheeks, sick-yellow and agleam. "What else?"

"He went off for you. Next thing I know, nobody's heard from him, there's his car." Beside him Lyda nods twice in measured motion, nodding in agreement or in the effort to raise her head he cannot tell. The movement requires a great deal of her concentration, endeavor, and time. She sniffs a heavy amount of mucus and swallows. "We got our questions too, you know. What've you scoundrels done to my boy?"

"Oh enough, Lyda. Sing a new song."

"How'm I to know you didn't do nothing to him?" Her voice has grown thick; it descends to a whisper at the end.

"Because I don't have my reefer! Where the hell is my reefer I want to know! I got no money and no reefer. Do you have any idea what kind of sore corner this dumps me in?"

"Whole situation's a damn mess," Arley agrees.

"Where you think your brother would get to?"

"Fleece? Hell Mister Greuel, I wouldn't know, honest to God." It comforts him a moment to speak the truth even though it's a truth he finds no comfort in.

"Guess. Free associate. You all got family in Glasgow, right?"

Lyda's head rears back with a dismissive snort. "Second cousins of mine, they're in Fountain Run, Fleece don't know them. They're not worth knowing!"

"What could he do with all that pot in Glasgow?" asks Cole.

Greuel taps his bottle back and forth before him, sliding it an inch one way, an inch the other. His teeth work his lips as though to chew the meat off, and Noe bends to Greuel's ear and whispers too quietly to be heard. Greuel's face folds at the listening. Sweat bursts upon Cole's neck once Arley Noe backs off, smiles. "What?" he asks.

"Blue Note thinks we could save time and flush out your brother if we got Mule and his toolbox in here, let him work on you some before mom. He's concerned for our reputation, I think."

"People start thinking they can get away with product without punishment, why, then what do we have?" muses Noe, rubbing the words thoughtfully as with his fingers. "You get one man asking why's he need to pay today, maybe he's short, needs credit. Next one hears that and now he wants to renegotiate terms. And on down the line and next thing you know, you can't pay money to the people *you* owe. All a sudden you're looking at the wrong end of a pistol held by some kid who seen too many movies."

"I never could abide chaos," Greuel says.

"Chaos is not conducive to business," Arley agrees.

Their faces express disbelief at the prospect, heads shaking slow and side to side in rhyming tandem. There is not a sound in the house save the hiss of smoking wood punctuated by sharp gasps in the fire—both Cole and his mother start at the crash of one log crumbling as it rolls from the grate. No one else moves, and Cole can sense them beyond the table out of his sight forcing themselves still, like small creatures who by instinct swallow breath and freeze as they await a predatory beast to pass. Creed's still leaning in the hallway with his beer; Spunk reclines on the sofa with a palm over each eye, big feet crossed at the ankles; Shady has drawn her knees to her chin and remains as far from Spunk as she can manage. It's like a spell has been cast, leaving Cole as the single being capable of animation, agency, among the still-lifes around him.

He is alone here.

A peculiar image blooms within his mind, a vision from years ago of watching Fleece parse pills from sandwich bags into separate small teacups for their mother. He had been whistling a grim mournful tune—what was it? Cole had said, I don't understand why you give her that, she's fucked up and you're helping her stay that way. Fleece had answered that she was so deeply fucked up she needed the pills as much as she needed to get straight. Supplying her was the only way he knew how to help.

"Mister Gruel," he begins, breaking the spell, "I can prove we don't know where my brother is or what he's done."

"That's a tall order, boy. How do you propose to do that."

"I'll make it up for him."

Cole!—his name slips from Shady's mouth like an expression of pain.

"You leave my mother alone. Let me take over for Fleece. You're out a driver, right? I've even got contacts none of you sell to yet."

"Hey he'll surprise you, Papa," Spunk breaks in. "I trust Cole with anything, I'll speak for him."

"Your word means squat, son. Breaks my heart but it's true." He glowers at his fat hands flat on the table. "This isn't the unemployment office. I got my own problems."

"Maybe I can help with them," Cole says.

Greuel's scowl simmers with impatience and yet also, Cole thinks he can see, legitimate consideration. He's afraid to look at Arley Noe and try to guess what could be read there, and moreover he feels he must keep going: "You said yourself you want out. Let me get some deliveries in for you, set up some deals in the city. I can do this. I can make this happy."

Greuel's face has lost the scowl and now appears drawn by fatigue and exasperation. "Whole set-up is weirder than tits on a bishop," he tells his fingernails. His eyes roll upward. "What you think, Arl, you're the one has to deal with him."

"I don't care for the kid. But you know that."

"I vouch for him," Spunk bursts again, "Cole's all right, Daddy, you know he is."

Greuel pushes the water bottle around, droplets of condensation catching the headlight on one side, the firelight on the other. He grabs the bottle in his fist and brings the fingers to the left of his mouth and gulps deeply several times, chugging the water like a frat boy downing whisky on a dare, emptying the thing. Instead of setting the bottle down he hands it to Noe.

"This here's no part-time job, kid. You don't wing this. It becomes your life, you understand? It's a long haul from this to that scuba school I hear you on about."

"I understand what I'm doing," Cole says, looking over his mother shut deep behind her own shut eyes. What do you see there, he wants to ask her again.

"This wouldn't mean either that if I turn up Fleece he's in the clear. This does not change my problem with your brother at all."

Cole doesn't answer him; he's nodding, hardly hearing what Mister Greuel has to say anymore, he can feel the discussion subsiding to its end and he has them almost out of this house. He keeps nodding, even as Greuel shakes his head again side to side at the sight.

"Tits on a bishop," he mutters. He pushes back from the table and eases himself onto his feet, grimacing with the effort. At close to full height he composes himself into the semblance of the man he used to be. The man just casts a field of unease around him—it's his gift. Cole fights the urge to drop his gaze, to let it fall to the table, his mother, anywhere else.

And then Greuel nods. He nods—but it's a nod of resignation, perhaps disappointment, even sadness. "Well, why the fuck not," he says. "Why not." He pats Arley Noe's shoulder and nods again to everyone before turning down the hallway and the far stairway there that leads to the bedrooms upstairs. Creed quickly clears way for him. They all watch as the sick man shuffles to the steps, grasps the balustrade, and painfully begins the process of climbing one at a time.

Everyone watches him leave except for Arley Noe, who remains focused upon Cole. He looks as though he's trying to startle his face into some particular expression and finds it refuses him, it won't settle on only one.

"I never claim to know another man's thinking," Noe says in his dragging sandpaper voice. "I'm not as thoughtful as our Mister Greuel. But understand: I do not owe your family one thing."

Spunk is on his feet shouting welcome. The outburst upsets Lyda's daze, and her wide eyes startle about the room and the people in it as though she has awakened from a fine sleep into a place she does not recognize. Cole undergoes his buddy's slaps and high-fives while he reassures his mother with his other hand clasped gently on her neck. Shady, though, has not moved or looked up from her hands clenched about her legs. He waits for her, silently urging her to see him even as Creed begins to usher them out—but she is stubborn in her refusal, keeping her eyes downcast while falling into step with Lyda. The door opens and February's eager wind greets them with bitter cold.

Where the creek bends behind his mother's house there lies a sinkhole pool, limited in its width but deep enough that the brothers never did locate its bottom. Not even in the times of hard drought when the creek shrank to a trickle—dried to flat warm limestone where brilliantly striped skinks of emerald and ruby flashed away at the boys' approach—and left exposed a shallow cave secreted beneath the banks, a hovel of clay and slime that stank in the heat. No matter how dry the season this sinkhole remained brim-full with a slow surface whirl spinning dry leaves, bits of dead grass strewn by the mower, specks of dust, and the insects that lived and died there. Into the water the boys would discard any object they could do without and that fired their curiosity: a bird's stale carcass, model airplanes, soda cans, several bonfires' worth of oak and linden branches, —one time even Cole's old tricycle, which he did not believe would fit and so Fleece had to prove him wrong, wrestling the bike down the pool's gullet until it plunged the rest of the way on its own. The brothers would sit and watch the bird, the airplane, the stick turn slowly on the water until it sank from the surface and disappeared just as if sucked down an enormous drain. Then they would sprint over the knob to the lake and splash about in the shallows certain the object would reappear, for they sensed that somewhere the pool must follow an underground passage that opened into the floor of the lake—they didn't know then that Holloway had been manmade. Nothing ever came back. Cole imagined the whirlpool must sink straight to the deep heart of the earth, beyond the reach of any light, and he pictures those objects still descending there over the years, still spinning, silent in that dark, obscure quiet found only in deep water, all the abandoned toys and dead animals (thready skeletons now) circling low in that pool to nowhere. A mysterious place where time had not so much ended as come to a standstill. Sometimes they joked and wondered at what some explorer might make of them one distant future day when all of Lake Holloway was gone and the whirlpool had finally dried up and everything they had left there could be rediscovered. But in his secret self Cole believed the water would stay deep and dark forever, the detritus of empty summer days, these bits of their childhood selves, preserved yet hidden away for eternity.

•

It takes time to get used to what they have him doing; takes even longer to get used to how little there is, in reality, for him to do. Lots of down time in the mule business. Creed staked him for sales in town, first to CD Cooter, an employee of his uncle's, then to Cooter's friends. Dealing didn't eat up the hours either. Over weeks Cole learns a new respect for dim Spunk Greuel because Spunk knows already how to do what Cole's just beginning to learn. Car rentals—Cole had never rented a car or room before. Navigating Kentucky's secondary and tertiary routes and figuring where these bypassed the interstates; identifying state patrols' preferred speed traps and the location of their station outposts. He works sober yet drives as though stoned to the gills, the night late, a cop trailing close in the rearview: Cole pins his hands at ten and two on the steering wheel, speed pegged at five miles faster than the limit, eyes measuring the boundary lines.

Primarily he's nothing more than a delivery boy. He rarely sees what he carries but is savvy enough to understand it's not weed. The secondary routes drag out the drives. His first run had him coupled with Spunk in a VW Rabbit picked up from Rent-a-Wreck with a Bette Midler cassette stuck halfway in the stereo and magnetic tape spilling out its mouth. Every few miles Spunk said he was hungry and they would pull over for a candy bar or chips. Twenty minutes later the two were pulling over again for sixty-ounce sodas; another half-hour and it was Spunk complaining he had to piss. "Why don't you drive, then?" asked Cole. "You can pull over any time you want."

Spunk cackled and bent to his straw to slurp among the ice left in his huge "souvenir cup." He shook his head and looked out his window, formed a pistol out of his hand and fired at cows along the road. "It don't work that way, see. I'm the face man. You, on the other hand, are the driver. You're the muscle."

Cole glanced over his mirrors, certain every car behind them had to be an unmarked state trooper. He was starting to think he should cut his hair and shave daily and work toward a generally more upright appearance that wouldn't hint at his being a roadhound skeech.

"We're fucked," he murmured, wondering what sort of *muscle* they might meet at the other end of delivery. Suddenly Spunk's enthusiasm for the martial arts began to seem less foolish.

The hatchback carried twelve sealed cardboard boxes that Grady Creed, gun tucked visibly at the front of his waistband, had instructed them *not to open* or else he would hear about it. The boxes were not labeled. All Cole knew was that they were to ask for a man named Cherokee when they got to where they were going, some place kept secret in Spunk's head.

They headed south and Spunk turned him at 357, then 224, and Cole was lost among hills and cows until they hit a field topped by an aluminum hangar announcing *The World's Biggest Open-Air Flea Market in the South*. The Rabbit ambled in gravel dust kicked up behind a pickup until Spunk motioned him toward a double-wide stall festooned with advertising insignia from the early century, Coca-Cola and Marlboro and German beers Cole had never heard of. Long tables sported bric-a-brac glasses and ceramics, iron skillets shining oiled; beneath the tables rows of cardboard boxes lay open. From the angle of the hill Cole could not see what was inside them.

Spunk, serious now, told him to get out but stay by the car. He tossed his soda cup to the floorboard and waved half-heartedly up the rise to a wiry rawboned man with long and sparse blond hair combed back and gleaming damp, a steel cane leaned against his knee. The man looked like he could be related to Spunk, perhaps a vision of Spunk ten very hard years into his future, shirtless and pink-skinned save for the green eagle's wings tattooed the width of his chest shoulder to shoulder.

Cole stood by his door and crossed his arms and tried to look the type of guy nobody would find reason to fuck with. A curious, straggling horde of shoppers began to take notice of the car, stopping to inspect the canted Rabbit as if it, too, might be had for a bargain, or maybe pieced apart and purchased item by item, even as another crowd gathered around the stall, some slack-faced and perusing the stall's goods, others seemingly listening in on the conversation Spunk was holding with his future self, a debate that appeared somewhat heated although Cole could not hear much of it. Something about time, whose was worth the most.

"Can't you identify a man busy at his work?" the man said as he rose heavily on his cane.

"I got a boss he says you make the time," from Spunk.

"And your boss, who's that now?"

"You want me to say his name out loud right here?"

"Word is he aint long for this world," angling the cane forward, looking over it as if it were not already his.

"Word's wrong," Spunk said. "Wouldn't make a difference for you anyways," but already the skinny man was limping toward Cole and the car.

"If you want I can do better on that," he told a woman speculating over a skillet as he gimped down the incline to where Cole stood sweating in the not-quite-spring's clammy air, his eyes on a number of large and meaty men who seemed to have congealed from the general crowd for the sole purpose of suggestive menace. "Open up that car and let me see what you brought."

"Your name is Cherokee?" Cole situated himself between the man and the hatchback; Spunk remained up beside the stall, watching.

"What, you need to see an ID?"

"I guess I expected somebody different," Cole said.

"Bet you did. Not every Indian wears buckskin and sells blankets, you know."

"You don't look real Cherokee-like to me, that's all."

"Boy if ever-body who says they got Cherokee blood really had it then there must've never been no Trail of Tears. My mamaw was full Cherokee. I got Norway blood from my old man's side." Cherokee spun back at Spunk, thumb cocked over his shoulder, his back tattooed with the same pair of wings. "I don't care for people with eyes like that. You don't know where to look. Makes you nervous whether you're a criminal or not." He returned to Cole and the matter at hand as though Cole could not have heard him speak. "Open up that hatchback and let me see them boxes and stop stereotyping my people. It's a form of exploitation."

Cole checked Spunk for a signal, some advisory gesture—but Spunk was no longer paying attention, holding two pint glass like binoculars over his eyes, speaking to a girl with no more clothes on than she could mop a floor with.

"Here?" he asked, nodding at the public nature of their location.

"You under the impression I got me a receiving dock?"

Cole opened the hatch and stepped back. Cherokee pulled out a penknife and unsealed the nearest box, removed the heavy paper packaging at its top, and uncovered a stack of what looked like videotapes—until he lifted one out and Cole saw how thin the box was. Movie titles on the covers. Cherokee shrugged and told him to bring them on up. To Spunk he shouted, "What can I do with a bunch of DVDs? Nary a body out here can play these things."

"You'll get players, they just haven't fallen off the truck yet," Spunk said, prompting laughter from the little girl looking through those tall glasses herself. Once Cherokee met him the two slapped hands, Cherokee nodding toward an old Advo Gold Medal coffee tin beneath his foldout chair. Cole followed him up carrying three of the boxes.

"Take that coffee on home and send your daddy my best regards. But get that wall-eyed motherfucker out of my sight before I scalp him one," Cherokee said, grinning madly and waving his cane in the air above Cole like an ax.

•

Soon he is driving on his own. Never has he seen so much of Kentucky; he's never been farther than two counties from Pirtle, and this, the traveling—exploration of lands unknown, yet close enough to fill him with sentimental feelings of home—is the part he likes best. That and driving so many different vehicles: he rents GMC passenger vans, Saturn wagons, and Toyota 4Runners that Professor Mule encouraged him to use since the company had opened a plant in Georgetown and thus, to Mule's reasoning, driving Toyotas in any fashion was good for the commonwealth.

Creed stakes him again with weed and crank for Sheldon at the college. Sheldon tells him business is excellent, but the money passes through Cole's hands and back to Creed like the bills are nothing more than secret messages the messenger is not allowed to open.

Sometimes his deliveries require cash in hand and some times they do not. Sometimes he knows what he's carrying and other times he does not. Often he makes no human contact at all, crossing the entire state to Prestonburg or Pikeville and abandoning the rental in an unpaved lot behind a dry cleaners or an antique store, after which he walks six retail doors south, finds a similar minivan waiting, and drives away north. He takes interstates when not hauling but sticks to secondaries and rural highways when laden, a state map quickly tearing along the fold lines as he maneuvers routes, hours on hours lost in his head, wrestling between the urge to gauge the precise degree of paranoia he should permit himself and trying not to speculate how many years in prison the haul might net him. He wonders if his brother ever rented these same vans, if his hands were placed on the wheel precisely where Fleece had held his, and he wonders what went through his brother's mind alone on these long drives—a woman? His seminary dogs? Did he ever think of Cole and their mother? Or was he always planning, figuring a strategy for what he would do one day that would cut him from every link to the life he had lived? Cole tries to re-imagine talks they had shared but in truth they had never talked much about more than whatever matter was at hand. After a time his mind simply blanks: he admires the deep wooded mountains, speculates how far those woods go on, or how far they reached before humanity cut them up. He tries to imagine Fleece hidden in those backwood hollers, the strip-malled towns, where it's like every other yard has the Ten Commandments posted over a tiny American flag and everyone's struggling with weight. His brother is not here. The land's worth the marveling but Cole can see it only as land to escape *from*, not to.

His drives take him past lonesome cabins, or else expansive mansions crowning hills, and the intermittent thoroughbred farms. Cattle, winter-fallow fields. At these times he thinks his brother stupid for ever wanting away, that Cole himself is stupid to dream of a future far elsewhere, sunken beneath heavy ocean and shoveling current, trapped off-land nine months a year. The sight of horses brings him both relief at being past their four a.m. mornings and stinking stalls, the sticky vitamin solution he shot down the foals' gullets with a syringe (the smell always made him think of hot urine), but also a nostalgia for the *feeling* of a horse barn, the animals' earthy sounds echoing off the brick floors, the ridiculous curiosities a young foal could get itself into. Tools secured neatly in place on the walls, hoses rolled into tight loops. And then the turning out, walking pairs by hand into the fields, banks of mist over the grass. The sight of the fields' expanse to the tree line, or the land's sweep to the river at Greuel's farm, always evoked a poignant feeling he never quite understood—as though the land was *his* and he had been a part of it for years and years.

But the land always belonged to someone else. It's his single insight into what his brother might have been thinking: none of this was his own; none of it ever would be so long as he stayed.

Cole drives and thinks of Fleece and debates his obligations, *as his brother*. What he owes Lyda as a son. Fleece would say Cole owes nothing to his name, that if he had any sense at all he would get on to what he wants to do. He thinks of that time on the seminary rooftop talking about blank headstones in the cemetery, Fleece proclaiming he wanted it like that: *Once I'm gone it'll be like I was never even here.* Yet if the situation were reversed, Cole knows without hint of doubt, his brother would wreak havoc until the world had been set as straight as he could make it again.

A sudden, powerful, strange love for his brother fills him, a deep connection beyond shared blood, a *fastening* that breaches the supernatural. So he's gone now but to Cole Fleece hasn't disappeared, he's everywhere, each step Cole takes is one his brother stepped before him. Maybe his awareness of this means Fleece did get away; if he were dead then Cole would know this somehow, in his gut—wouldn't he? He would have felt some shift in the world. It's enough to convince him that he is doing exactly as he should.

Mostly, though, on these drives Cole thinks of Shady Beck.

•

She had become scarce. The night Cole pledged himself to Mister Greuel Shady had stabbed another scare through him, scratching a fingernail across the storm screen of his bedroom window not an hour after he had put his mother to bed. He had been lying awake at the end of a night that had felt endless already, not knowing what he had got himself into or how he would get out of it, wondering too what Creed or Noe thought of him now, if they went to sleep easy as you please with thoughts that tomorrow is another day. Or did they lie awake like he was, staring into the dark without a plan?

He was surveying the stack of diving gear accumulated over the past year, each item purchased at a discount, used: the mask and exo hood, fins, the paint-chipped tank and shining compressor. He still needed another $1200 for a dry suit. And then there were the actual tools for welding underwater as well. He had planned come summer to contact the Montreux dive shop for cave and lake dives if he wasn't already in Jersey or Louisiana for commercial training—a future that once had seemed possible, attainable, a murky daydream now.

The leaves outside rustled with human steps. Cole leapt to the window, his gravity blade whirling to the bare floor in midswing and clattering there. Then her voice: *Are you going to let me in?*

The screen screeched in its moorings as he raised it. She joined him on the floor, their backs against his bed, the window left open and February air bracing their skin.

"I couldn't sleep," she confessed, softly, followed by a yawn she didn't bother to cover. "I didn't even go home. Well no, I went home and sat in our driveway and looked at our house with all its lights off except the porch, which Dad leaves on because he worries I might trip on the steps, or that some creep could be hiding in the hemlocks. And I didn't know what to do with myself. I mean because it's very sweet on his part that he thinks of things like that, and I am one lucky girl to have the family I have, but how could I go to bed after tonight? Greuel's house, your mom—I don't know what to do with this."

She looked to him for an answer he didn't have. Then she said, "I'm more than a little angry with you, you know. What do you think you're doing? I just drove around awhile. I drove nowhere and felt really paranoid that cops were going to pull me over for nothing, like they could sense it wasn't normal for me to be out alone this time of night and they'd know I was guilty of something—somehow—and pull me over and ask questions and I would end up crying to them, telling everything that happened tonight, and this made me think of myself as being a stupid girl, stupid, stupid, stupid." With each instance of *stupid* she smacked her palm against her forehead. "Were you sleeping?"

Cole had retrieved the butterfly knife—a poor excuse for a weapon, with a rusted washer and dull blade, but he liked the heft of it—and was running the flat edge along the inside seam of his knee, the gimp knee he kept extended for comfort. Shady considered the object silently.

"You're scared," she said, one hand touching the inside of his wrist, the single raised tendon there. "I'm not stupid, am I. For being freaked out."

He tried to juggle the blade's arms but the bad washer kept one from closing completely and he had to squeeze the handle shut. He set the knife on the floor beside him, Shady's thigh pressed against his own. She stole in a little closer. He felt the warmth of her, a warmth almost like fever. He didn't answer her question. She placed her head on his shoulder, and her strange heat radiated over his throat. She settled her face into his neck, nuzzled her nose in a discernible line over his collarbone, and he tried to imagine what her face must have looked like right then, that her eyes must be closed, her mouth open slightly. Her breath shipped skids of air beneath the collar of his T-shirt, and despite his great fatigue there came an upsurge in his blood, a quickening. She stilled her head again on his shoulder. Cole's entire body began to teem, as if every nerve ending or capillary web in his skin had its own song to sing—a song heightened as he tried to remain perfectly still.

"Sometimes it's really hard to know what you're supposed to do," Shady said. Her voice vibrated in his chest. Winter ladled cold over their bodies. She nestled closer and stretched one arm across him. "Listen, I'm sorry about the other night."

"For what? What other night?"

"By the river. In your truck."

His head fell back onto the bed as he remembered. He stared at the ceiling and saw the white bag flapping over the river and his clumsy advances; saw Shady playing with the drawstrings of her sweatpants, knotting them and drawing them straight again. The brutal quiet between them as he'd driven her home.

She straightened, rubbing her hands over her arms. "It's freezing in here," she said, and stood and shut the window with a loud clap, apologizing immediately and looking to his open bedroom door. But there were no stirrings from Lyda, not even snores. Shady kicked off her sneakers and wrapped the old quilt from his bed around her, sitting on the mattress. With her feet on the floor she toppled slowly to one side, raising one foot and resting it on his shoulder. They remained like that for what seemed to Cole several very long and difficult-to-interpret minutes, long enough for him to inspect her foot sidewise, to decide her feet were pretty, and to wonder if she had fallen asleep.

"Are you staying on the floor all night?"

"You going to crash here?"

"Is it okay if I do?"

"It's all right with me. You know it's all right with me."

She made room for him and opened the blanket as he got in, Cole flat on his back and suddenly aware of his sheets, quickly speculating how long it had been since he had washed them and noting they smelled of his sleep and maybe a touch of mildew, or dust, he wasn't sure, glad his wet dreams ended up in boxers and that he jerked off into socks. Shady set her head on his chest; she used some kind of floral shampoo—no, not floral, but fruitlike, the scent of berries in your mouth, fresh black raspberries plucked from a patch stumbled upon in the woods. He marveled at the firmness of her body, embarrassed by the thickening between his legs that she must have felt as she slid a leg over him. Her leg stilled there, the inside of her knee over his crotch. His jeans trapped his cock at an uncomfortable angle. Shady was aware, he could tell. She pulled his shirt from his jeans and guided her palm up his side, let it rest over his heart.

Her breathing turned heavier and evened out and they lay still, her body clutching his. He wondered if she had fallen asleep and could not believe she could, not with her ear pressed against the pounding in his chest. Finally she rose with a small moan and in the dark Cole could barely make out her face inches away, staring at him, considering him. Then she brought her mouth to his.

The moment was as he had hoped it would be, his tongue searching hers, this instant so longed for in secret and with the guilt of a brother's betrayal, but these concerns fell aside easily as his hands, his arms, came alive. It did not take long before he was naked above her. She cradled his face in her hands, casting warm smiles into his own. They wrestled one another, twined themselves in the blankets; he pressed into her and tried to slide her jeans down but she was adept at preventing him, he couldn't figure how she managed it, a twisting of her body or a flex to her legs so that, somehow, the jeans would not move. He tried everything he could, shifting his mouth from hers to her jaw and to her neck and then down, taking in the palm-sized wonder of her breasts and the smooth belly, managing to get his tongue to graze the top of her pubic line and inhaling the deep true smell of her there—but her hand grasped his jaw gently and tugged him up again. Over the next hour the bed turned on dyskinetic awkwardnesses: Shady over-ardent, almost penitent, Cole relaxing, forcing himself to a degree of calm in disappointment. The jeans stayed on. Soon the kisses shortened, died away, and he rolled onto his back, drawing the sheet over his waist, painfully aware of his full nakedness next to her half-clothed.

"I'm sorry, Cole," she whispered. "I'm not ready."

He tried to be gracious. He did. He told her it was okay in a way both sincere and respectful and yet expressive of the effort it was costing him at that moment to be honorable. He wanted to tell her there were many things he wasn't ready for in which he had to take part, thinking this bitterly even as he recognized the saying of it would ruin all.

"You kiss well," her voice hoarse and close to his ear. "I always wondered."

"I always wondered, too."

"If I kissed well? Didn't you ever ask your brother?"

"No, I wondered if *I* did. I guessed you kissed well."

This prompted a guffaw from her, Shady rising on one elbow and with her small breasts in clear view—Cole was still inexperienced enough to be thrilled by the sight of an actual girl naked and close. He was still hard. She told him not to worry, she was no tease, but did he know she drove his brother crazy?, fending him off for months once they'd started dating and this one time—

Cole covered her mouth with his hand. "Please, Shady. I don't want to hear this."

She hushed, nodded. "Of course you don't, I'm sorry," she said, and then took him in her hand and leaned in to kiss him again, her tongue slipping deep into his mouth before retreating; she bit at his lower lip, nibbled at the thickest fold and held it between her teeth. Then her mouth was on his neck, his stomach, moving down his body with quickening velocity and it did not take long for him to empty into her mouth, his hands bunching the sheet on either side. He made her laugh into her hand held over her lips as he thanked her not once but twice, and with great feeling.

"No problem," she said.

•

Weeks have passed. He keeps his bedroom window cracked open in hopes she might surprise him again, but each morning he awakes only to late-winter chill and her absence. Shady's mother answers the phone every time he calls and she doesn't appear to know who Cole is and informs him that Shady isn't available, or she's out. (A phrase he tries not to read much into.) He doesn't own an answering machine, instead he has Lyda, and with the long stretches of time on the road he has no idea if Shady ever calls back or not. Every few days he calls again, gets the mother again, and then he's gone.

When finally she does reach him she sounds preoccupied, admits she has needed some time to herself. Her father is pressuring her to get on track with her schooling, to enroll in summer courses to ease back into med-school discipline, but she feels no motivation and doesn't want to waste his money.

"What's your mother say?" Cole asks.

"She's supportive of whatever I do, she's a great mom."

"You talk to your sisters?" Shady is the youngest of three and her two sisters are significantly older, and wildly disparate in the directions their lives have taken: Laura, at thirty-two the oldest and the pride of her father, researches blood diseases at Duke as she pursues her PhD, while the middle daughter, Breyer, leads a life of breeding with three children each from different fathers, living now with a man who is father to none of them. Shady says she doesn't want to follow either direction, or maybe more precisely a little of each; she hopes to find her own middle way.

"I've talked to both of them. Laura says since I was the surprise unexpected baby of the family that I was doted upon and so have no real understanding that gratification does not come on an immediate basis. Ergo I should just shut up and realize how luxurious my situation is and embrace my opportunities and buckle down to school and create a life that will not be reliant on anyone else, in particular not any man."

Shady says things like *ergo* and he doesn't know anyone else who does and that fact alone thrills him.

"And she has a point, it's true," she continues. "I'm listening."

"What about Breyer?"

"Breyer says I should listen to my heart and prepare myself to recognize my path when it presents itself to me."

As he listens to her expand on the subject, he fingers small cakes of plaster from the hole in the living-room wall that he knows he should get around to covering one day. It has existed there since before Lyda packed him off to live with his uncle's family. He doesn't know how it got there and Lyda says she does not remember. It's possible the hole, grown with age and absent-minded picking like now, goes all the way back to Bethel Skaggs; wouldn't that be something, to have left behind as the marker of your existence in the world nothing but a hole in a wall—a hole made in anger, your violence imprinted, a house-wound no one ever bothered to fix. Not three feet away he spreads one hand on the faded hallway wallpaper covered with vines, a design he had followed many times as a child trying to discern the path of each stalk that wove in and out to blooming flowers, striving to identify the repetition in the pattern; he never did tease out the scheme of it. Somewhere beneath that decorative paper his name is inscribed beneath Fleece's in the plaster—Lyda had been infuriated to discover their carved signatures, and infuriated again at the cost of the wallpaper to cover them up.

"I've *got* to get a job," she concludes. "I need to get off my ass."

"That doesn't sound like the path your daddy wants presented to you."

"Be nice, Cole. I love my sister. Is Lyda around? Can I talk to her?"

She is and he passes the phone to her and sits at the kitchen table half-listening to the gradual arrangement for Shady to try a position at the rehab clinic where Lyda used to work. He's lost in his reverie over the various family imprints scattered about this house when he startles at Lyda replacing the receiver in its cradle.

"She didn't ask you to give the phone back to me?"

"No, she didn't, hon. You should probably get used to not hearing from her like you want. She's not a girl for you, you know that."

He doesn't know that. He knows what happened three weeks before, and what was that? He stares at the phone and waits. He stares at its gray plastic receiver standing ready beside the rusty toaster oven on the corner of the counter while his mother stirs herself a cup of instant. The small LED light indicates the phone is charging.

"Do you want some motherly advice?" she asks. Cole raises his eyes to her with a feeling of growing alarm. "I know you don't want to listen to me but I'll say it anyway. You need to be careful of yourself with a girl like that."

"Careful? With Shady?"

"A girl from her background, a boy like you. Honey I'm a woman and I know my types. Once you have her in your hands she's liable to tear you to shreds til there's nothing left."

Cole remains motionless on his feet taking this in, listening to Lyda move on down the hall, opening and shutting the bathroom door. Then she opens the door again and announces that she plans to get some tonight and so has her doing to do. "You pick up anything for me?"

The question stirs him from his thoughts and he pulls a sandwich bag containing twenty oxy-eighties from a pocket—pills bought from Grady Creed—and brings them to her. "Stretch these, will you? Don't throw a party."

She answers *Mmm-hmm* and shuts the door again. He returns to the kitchen as the shower kicks on and the lights on the phone have not changed. The hole in the wall is slightly bigger than his own fist, seismic cracks bracketing eight inches in all directions around it. That hole has been there so long it belonged there. He thinks he can be like that; he can wait. She'll call again. She will.

•

Following instructions from Arley Noe, he meets Creed in the strip-mall parking lot where CWE Ministries holds services. No rental this time; instead Creed hands him keys to a ministry van, an Econoline with bus seats. "For our purposes, the safest rig on the road has got to be a church van," Creed mumble-mouths, pushing a magenta tooth-pick from side to side. "This is a experiment. You got a seven-point-three liter V8 under the hood if you need it. Try not to get pulled over."

Behind the last row of seats a large net holds soccer balls. *These are not full of air, okay?* Creed says. Cole is to deliver the balls to Morehead. There he'll exchange vehicles and drive to Prestonburg to deliver, then over to Ashland to deliver, and then back to Morehead to pick up the ministry van again.

Looking over the van he can see Creed's point: these are not the kind of wheels anyone would pay attention to. On each side, beneath the CWE insignia, the slogan CHART A PROSPEROUS COURSE THROUGH

LIFE spans fender to fender, the two *T*'s amended into an image of the Cross. Cole looks over at the old warehouse storefront where the church continues to hold services.

"Don't think so much," Grady says. "Nobody's watching you."

"Shady goes to that church sometimes. She says I should go."

"Then you best be careful, young man. A girl gets you into church with her then it won't be long before she's either marrying or burying you in the same place."

"Well."

"Don't think too hard on it. That preacher's street-schooled sure as me and one day I'm going to figure him out. Now get a move on 'fore I decide to make this run myself just to get off this lot. What's your momma do when you're gone? She alone tonight?"

"You're a sick fuck, Grady."

"It's a sick world. Don't you worry over Lyda, I'll certify nobody hurts her any way she don't want to be hurt."

He can't think of a good comeback. He hops into the driver's seat and snaps the chew foil from Creed's shirt pocket and shuts the door before Creed can grab it back. He doesn't roll down the window until Creed has thumped it several times, the two of them staring one another down.

"Promise you'll keep your dick out of my mom. That's all I ask. She's got it rough enough as it is."

Creed's face betrays a brief interior consideration. Then he shakes his head, decided. "You keep my chew then. Don't spit on the floor less you're keen on cleaning it up, we have to return this van when you're done," and he slaps the fender twice to send Cole on his way.

•

Shady had said she'd hook up with him on Wednesday night, but when he returns on Tuesday she calls and says she can't make it tomorrow night after all. The trips leave him beleaguered and forlorn and when she calls he's already suffering a vicious dehydration headache, belly aswim from Grady's chew. He feels too unwell to analyze what she is saying. He tells her all is cool and he understands how things get in the way. I'm sorry I won't see you then but let's get together soon, he says, and she says okay.

Yet on Wednesday a sudden impulse prompts him to call. Just to see how she's doing. Her mother answers and Cole feels dirty, creepy and stalkerish. He almost hangs up when she tells him to hang on, she's unsure if Shady's still home or not and she'll have to look. He hears her call out to her daughter, and a long time passes in which he feels nakedly stupid, absurdly obvious, filled with that horrible word—NEED—and then Shady's there and short of breath like she had sprinted to the phone, asking, Yes? and he shuts his eyes: "Hey Shady. I was just calling to say hey, see if you needed a ride anywhere." As if the girl would prefer being driven in his go-cart quality pickup rather than her own fine Audi.

That's sweet Cole but you're going to make me late to work, remember?

He apologizes, already bored with the conversation and angry at himself.

Oh forget it. You all right?

Yeah of course I'm fine. I'm always fine. I'll see you soon.

Count on it.

Not real often but sometimes Shady likes to get high alone. At night, alone, not doing anything else and she's not going to call anyone or get in the car to wake up a girlfriend because she's lonesome, just some time alone in her room with the window open, preferably on cold winter air but any time of year will do, like now, nearly April and with March this year holding winter longer than usual, and with the porch light below her window lending the only light to her room. The type of light is important; smoking up in a bright room isn't the same. Her father has his martinis and her mother her Librium and Klonopin and Shady doesn't think that choosing a bowl that she doesn't even smoke every night, not even once a week unless she happens to have a whole lot on hand, which isn't often, in fact it's almost never that there's more than a dime in her underwear drawer and even less in her purse, she doesn't think it's any different from what either of her parents do to relax. She's not a wake'n'bake kind of girl. She's not high all the time nor does she allow it to run her life. She doesn't even really do any other drugs, doesn't even like to drink, particularly—the occasional pop of X on nights with her friends clubbing back at school. But that was nearly a year ago now.

But late and when she's alone and it's so quiet in her neighborhood (if it can be called a neighborhood; the properties are all so large that it feels like the middle of nowhere at night) and her parents are asleep, she likes it like nothing else. She likes how good pot, when she's alone and in this certain frame of mind that seems to come only late at night, seems to open her to certain avenues of thought she doesn't have otherwise—and somehow having the room dark except for that soft porch light outside encourages this—she likes how she kind of slides into self-conversation about her current place and moment in life, where she is and where she's going, the kind of questions she tends to avoid because they make her all anxious. She looks over the trees out front and thinks, *Where are you going, Shady Beck? What will you do, little girl?* Like the doing so allows her to almost touch on some special knowledge or insight into secrets she may be keeping even from herself. Maybe it's only that she's relaxed and it's quiet with that feeling that the world is asleep and soon she will be too but not quite yet. A sort of meditation-slash-prayer routine. And she's high. When talking about this with her girlfriends back in school they decided it's something like what Indians used to do, maybe. She calls these little sessions her dream routines, and often that's just how it feels, like she's dreaming but awake in it and it's good and as she looks through her window at the darkness out there—there are only a few distant house lights visible, mostly it's trees—she can be filled with such an overwhelming love of life and the world even as she comprehends that she doesn't understand any of it.

Something happened during her routine several weeks ago that haunts her. There's a small TV in her room and she had smoked up after watching Letterman (who she doesn't care for much but this TV doesn't have cable and there was nothing else on and even though he's kind of a dick Letterman sometimes can make her laugh). She turned off the TV before the musical guest played. She opened the window and took two deep hits off her pipe, it was this strong stuff Spunk Greuel had given her that night she had been running around with him and Cole at the abandoned seminary; she thought it special stuff and had been holding on to it, parsing out only small amounts to herself. Everything felt fine as she entered her little dream routine and there was no wind outside and she admired the single pine among the hemlocks in the yard standing straight and strong like honorable dignified sentinels sworn to protect the house. She felt fine; *excellent*, even, but soon got sleepy too and so lay back on her bed with the window open, protecting herself from the cold with the duvet wrapped around her (a luxurious thing filled with real goose down, she had missed its warmth and felt guilty for missing it the night she stayed under the threadbare quilt at Cole's house), and looked at the dim bluish rhomboid of porch light on the ceiling and part of the wall. That's the last she remembers.

Later (she's unsure how much later, unsure how long she was out) she awoke in complete terror. The room no longer felt like her room, and it was filled with this incredible dark, a dark like she had never seen or experienced before, a dark like the deepest cave at the deepest bottom of the sea, it wrapped her up in this mass of dark that light could never penetrate, and even more frightening was the realization that it was impossible to move: her arms and legs had become unresponsive, she could hardly feel them. She had never felt such an absolute fear like that moment before. What made it worse was that she couldn't understand *why* she felt so afraid—she was safe at home in her own bed. It seemed that the room had been taken over by this pure *cancellation of life*. Which what little part of her mind was working at the time interpreted as *evil*. Like evil as a pure element.

It was so dark she couldn't see the digital clock on the bedstand. She didn't know how long she had been asleep. Though she couldn't move her head, the position she woke up in allowed her to see the television set, and there the screen gave off a peculiar horrifying glow, soft and dim but perceptibly radiant. Like the glow that comes up immediately after a TV set is turned off, except this glow was the negative of that, a glowing darkness, and it did not die down but instead grew forward and unfurled into the air like the way water spills into fabric—the glow being water and the air fabric. This glow, from what she could surmise, fed the heavy darkness that kept her paralyzed. There was no more light from the porch light; no discernible air; her room had become a coffin stuffed full with this black stuff, this evil stuff that seemed to *want* her. To want to *erase her*.

Her mind raced in a panic she did not know she had the capacity to feel. On the bent antenna above the TV she had hung a necklace of charms, tokens and gifts she had added over the years as she picked them up: a heart from her mother; a broken coin from Fleece Skaggs;

a small silver cross bought for her by Brother Gil Ponder from a tiny gift shop inside the church, her "emblem of gratitude" given for attending a second Christ World Emergent service. The cross dangled above the area that was filling up with dark and she concentrated on that. The sight of it seemed to snap the entire situation into focus: she understood that this was a religious moment, having to do with her very soul—that something demonic was making a play for her soul. An idea she would later find difficult to sustain as credible, she had studied biology, she was a scientist, but at that instant it made perfect sense. Instinctively she began to pray. She started to pray manically, nothing formal to it, just started to repeat over and over that *Jesus is our savior* and *He is my savior* and *I accept him in my heart* and therefore whatever that was streaming out of that television set had no claim on her, it could not touch Shady Beck.

This did not seem to work. She became yet more terrified, terrified like she imagines she would be to find herself strapped down naked on a table with a room full of men she couldn't see except for the glint of light off their scalpels. Or more precisely like being tied down to railroad tracks and you can only watch the train's spotlight grow as it speeds nearer and nearer, your head's vibrating on the rail with the rhythm of the wheels churning closer and here comes the thundering noise. . . .

The darkness vanished the instant her ceiling light flickered on. She found her limbs and bolted upright; her feet slapped the floor; she found her mother standing in the doorway in a thick flannel nightgown, puffy and dull-faced from pill-aided sleep and half-inside the room, her hand on the light switch. *You were whimpering,* she said. *Bad dreams?* Shady didn't know how to answer her and so said nothing. She looked at the television set. With the whole room bright again it looked like a normal TV set.

Her mother was still standing there in the doorway so Shady mumbled something like *Yeah it must have been bad dreams* and after flashing one of those "I worry about my little girl but I'm exhausted" faces (a face Shady has provoked often enough to recognize easily), her mother left her alone. But in fact the state of dreaming seemed the exact opposite of the experience. It did not feel like some weird post-hypnagogic state, either (though she considered this possibility and read up on it). She does not consider herself an irrational girl prone to wild imagining. Naturally, and despite the intensity of the terror, she assumed the pot had something to do with what had happened.

She intuited, however, that the pot wasn't the only factor involved here; contact of some kind had been made. The problem was that she didn't know what it was that was contacting her, what it signified, what it was trying to say. Perhaps because the pot came from Spunk, and because of her eye falling upon the broken coin given to her by Fleece hanging next to Brother Ponder's silver cross, she connected this experience to Cole Prather. A warning to her? A warning to warn him? It all felt so mysterious and yet the more she weighed that night in her head the more certain she felt she had been opened to something that was linked to Cole.

She wanted nothing more to do with it and made a point of not thinking about it for several days. She tried to put the event behind her and stayed away from the routine for a while. Yet, after a time, once the immediacy of the terror had softened somewhat, and after she had not seen or spoken to Cole in weeks, the strangest thing began to occur—it was almost like she *wanted* to experience that night again. Like she longed to feel it again. To be tempted toward that darkness again. As a way of understanding; perhaps to hear the warning more clearly.

So she's been returning to the entire procedure with the greatest precision she can manage. She tries to set it up exactly as it had gone down that night: hung her necklace on the antenna, smoked off a bowl, endured Letterman and his buddy Paul trade jibes, turned off the TV before the musical guest appeared. But she sleeps through the night undisturbed. She has now repeated the process more times than she cares to count, trying to recapture the greatest terror she has ever experienced, practically making a ritual out of the steps she can remember, *practically inviting* that bad, evil, negative element to return to her room so that she might find what it meant, what it wanted from her and what she might find in it to bring to Cole. Yet these nights at home disappear in the peaceful sleep of the oblivious.

Paradoxically, that she doesn't seem able to make the event reoccur has led her to believe more fervently in the reality of that night, that it was not simply the strength of Greuel's homebatch weed working on her subconscious, but that Evil is real, an element as real as positive energy, at least, and it is capable of engaging a person body and soul. And it's like you can just bump into it, accidentally. Lately she discovers herself doing the most menial thing, driving alone or checking in at the new job or standing in line at the kwik-stop, and in her mind she is picturing this entire other galaxy, an entirely separate dimension encompassing this world like a vision out of some medieval fantasy, where there is a perpetual war going on, or at least a yin and yang push-pull conflagration, of Good vs. Evil, absolute energies the human mind can only conceive of as demons and warrior angels going at it in this spinning tornadic vortex for the, what?, the souls of each of us?

Admitting this makes her feel kind of ignorant, and superstitious, and plain silly, which is not how she likes to think of herself. But if she looks at it from a certain angle she can frame it as a kind of gift, too: for whatever reason she has been presented with a brief glimpse into what is *actually going on out there*, just out of sight. If she's interpreting it correctly. An acknowledgment she finds even more disconcerting and so she tries to avoid that one, too. What if the warning was for her? How would she know to heed it?

Intuitively she feels this is not the case. If it's a warning it is not for her, it's for others. The prophets in the Bible underwent such experiences that were meant only for them to share with the others who could not see what they knew. But again Shady thinks the entire notion is silly; she doesn't live in the world of the Bible. That world ended a long, long time ago, didn't it.

Cole finds himself frustrated, brought to stasis, treading water furiously and getting nowhere he wants to go, like he's caught on the far edge of a rapid current whose violence he feels only as a tug near his body, he can't tell if the pull is irrevocable or if he can still swim to safety. The sense of adventure and the kick of high-risk remains at each run but he's no longer petrified by the sight of a state trooper and he wonders if this means he is becoming careless. He's busier than he would choose to be and yet he has little cash in pocket. Half the state's on one drug or another and it's like the responsibility has fallen to Cole to insure everyone receives their allotted share.

Spunk tells Cole he's already the luckiest of couriers. The others never saw Arley Noe or Greuel himself. The other guys in the trade (Spunk says) think Arley and Greuel are voices on a phone. I'm honored, Cole says, but it's not helping him get any closer to where he needs to be.

"Oh yeah? Where's that?"

"You know what I'm after. This is your world, man. I'm a stranger here for my mother."

"If that's what you want to believe. You shouldn't blame your decisions on your momma, James Cole. I mean look at her. You're here because it's your life, man, this kind of thing is just what you were destined to do. That other stuff"—he flips one hand in the air between them—"that's all just high-talkin'."

Cole lifts his shoulders, drops them. They are standing in what Spunk calls his new *base of operations*: a self-storage garage rented as a retreat of his own, a hundred-fifty windowless square feet with a roll-up for a front door and a screened ventilator fan in the back. The bunker reeks of bong water and feet despite the ventilator fan. Spunk has outfitted the unit with rugs and an old leather battlement of a couch, one that used to reside in Greuel's basement before Spunk moved his bed down there, the leather peeling and burred in spots, stretched enormous across the wall like some prehistoric rhinoceros that once lay down against the concrete blocks and died. Opposite this sits a Zenith on a rolling stand with an eighties-era VCR—key tabs instead of buttons; atop that is a hi-watt boom box of the latest quality, with a five-disc CD changer and onboard mixer. The VCR no longer works; he uses the TV as a monitor for his Colecovision and Atari games.

A gray pit bull curls into one arm of the couch, a female Spunk rescued from the pack left behind at the seminary. The only one he could get his hands on, he says, and since she has become his property Cole can see Spunk has made up his mind she's the best of the lot, a pure breed of stellar demeanor, intimidating if he needs her to be, and though Spunk has had her for weeks he has yet to name her. He calls her "my bitch."

"Check it, I've already taught her how to shake. C'mere, bitch!"

Cole watches as the dog, which seems either tired or bored, regards Spunk as he tries to get her to raise one paw on command. Her eyes keep flicking away from him, to Cole, back to her master and then to Cole again standing near two potted plants.

"She doesn't want to play 'cause she's looking out for me. People think I'm stupid but I can do this business myself. Why I got this place. I don't know what Arley's going to do once Daddy's gone but I got to look after my own self-interests, right?"

A fine haze sifts the ceiling, adding to the ghostly hue cast by a single metal halide grow-light hanging over two small skunk seedlings stuck into gallon buckets. The plants are not thriving. Spunk admits he's not sure he did right in transplanting them. "I maybe jayed the roots or something," he says. "My first shot at it. Maybe they're still shocked from the move."

"Could be. They look hopeful still. You sure these are females?" Spunk shoves him sportingly.

"Check'em out. Step up close, don't be shy." Cole does as asked, bending closer to study the jagged leaves but they're too young to make out any resin shining there. As he nears, the pit begins a low growl deep in her throat. "Reach for one," Spunk says, grinning. Cole barely moves a hand forward when the pit is off the couch and at him, snarling until he's back into the corner. Spunk's laughing goofy hard as he grabs the dog's collar and reins her in. "See how great she is? Don't worry, she aint gonna hurt you with me here, she's all show aren't you, girl? Aren't you a mean little show?"

At the touch of Spunk's hand the dog does undergo a remarkable transformation. The violence disappears from her like a wave that has crested and crashed and now recedes from the sand. She trots back to the couch and, regaining her place, stretches on her back so that her master can rub her belly, her long tongue lolling to one side, saliva drawing to the floor.

"Look at that belly," Cole points out, "is she pregnant?"

"Hell, I don't know, I just got her a couple weeks ago. No telling what those dogs've been doing in that shithole. Grab a seedling there and see if she cares if she's pregnant or not."

Cole asks where Spunk got the plants—his father won't allow growing on their property—but his pal shrugs off the question. He backpedals to the ragged couch and collapses beside the dog. "Need to get my own thing going," he says, preparing another bowl in a funk-water bong. "You can't rely on anybody these days to come through for you, not even your own daddy." His voice turns almost mournful.

Cole studies the wallowing seedlings again. They don't look good but they might live, he can't tell. It is a hardy weed after all. Spunk's attention span scattered in every direction on awakening, but he could concentrate long enough to meet his own needs as well as anyone else.

"Doubt old Blue Note would be thrilled that you're trying to grow here, either." The water gurgles as Cole sucks in the smoke, picturing Arley Noe. Something about the man reminded him of soot—the ashy powder of it like bits of cloud discarded behind him anywhere he moved, scouring the air for long moments before it dissipated.

"I'll make my move after a while, nothing fancy. Daddy won't be around forever but I aint ever going to cross him, neither. He knows that." Saying this, Spunk's eyes clarify and focus briefly, sadly and with deep sentiment, and with also a kind of despairing lonesomeness usually experienced late at night when you had no girl and the bottle of whisky is empty and the music on the stereo hammers at everything you had that once made you joyous, though you might not have realized it at the time, and which now seems gone forever.

"He's pretty sick, isn't he."

Spunk shakes his head slow and silent in angry disbelief. "I tell you, man . . . I know nobody could ever mistake the old man for a saint, but he deserves better than this."

"He's only mean because he has to be."

"That's it, Cole! You have to be a motherfucker in our business or else you're gone forever. You'll see. You still got to learn that yourself, you're too nice, too considerate."

"Was that Fleece's problem? He was too nice?"

"Fuck you, Cole. Fuck you for even thinking I'm talking about that. I don't know where your brother is and I'd freakin' take you to his right hand and leave you there if I did. God*damn*. Shut *up*."

Spunk's transparency is one of the reasons Cole still loves him: if Spunk knew something Cole would know, too, because the secret would come out soon enough. The only other possibility is that Spunk holds lowdown facts that his brain hasn't connected to Fleece or to his father—and that's the kind of information Cole can only wait and listen for it to slip out. He's not very good at this.

"I figure he's alive at least," Spunk squeaking a straw back and forth in the Big Gulp in his lap. "If you think about it, he has to be."

"Why's that?"

"Look at the economics of the situation. We were dry three months after Fleece took off. Stretched what we could get our hands on but that wasn't near enough for the Greuel and Arley show. Even I was smoking mostly shake myself. Daddy won't buy from those Mexicans, neither. He says you let in those fuckers just once, they never go away."

Cole takes this information in his mind as though weighing it in his hand. He wishes for paper and pencil on which to write out a timeline, but there isn't any in the garage. So he thinks: If Fleece stole the harvest at the end of October, then Spunk is saying they were dry through January. Cole's been running since February and here it is ten days before April. When did he buy the two quarters with Shady? The weekend after Thanksgiving; Sheldon's fraternity was celebrating the weekend after Thanksgiving.

"Why three months? When did you pick up again?" Cole is trying to count back on his fingers without making it apparent.

"Last week of January. I rode to Harlan with Creed myself. It took a while to get set up but you should see what they got underground down there—"

"That's your mom's brother, right?"

More squeaking from the straw as Spunk nods, sucking out the last of his soda. "That's the man. You'll get to meet him someday. One cool mofo, my uncle Crutch. A weirdo, too. In a all-right way."

Cole would like that and he admits as much. For a time he had loved Clara, Spunk's mother, as if she were his own. While Lyda cleaned houses after her fall at the clinic, waiting for the disability application to go through, Cole spent after-school hours at their farm under Clara's eye. He has a vivid memory of her from when he ruined his leg. She had a piebald horse named Sadie Dame that had kicked him, shattering the patella and tearing the ligaments, and it was Clara who drove him to the hospital. He remembers her as gentle and beautiful and kind, with straight ash-blonde hair down to her waist that she often wore in a single braid, and calm mudflat-brown eyes, and even-toned skin save for the roseate butterfly pattern across her nose and cheeks—a sign of the lupus that eventually took her before he and Spunk were ten. She was a lover of the earth and held a hippie's sentimental, communal idea for the land of Kentucky; marijuana was a plant she *believed* in, part of earth's bounty. He remembers watching her roll up and smoke while she watched the boys run after her horses. Back then Spunk called the jays and pipes her medicine, a child repeating what his mother had told him.

His friend nods and his eyes appear to lose all feeling; his hands fall to a rest with the big cup in his lap. "Wonder what she'd think to see us now?"

•

Days later he awakes in early morning, before sunlight. There are horses to turn out on a farm as a favor to friends of his uncle who have left town for the weekend. He starts the pickup and turns on the defroster and it isn't until he gets out again with the scraper that he sees the black trash bag sunken against his back tire. Initially he thinks someone vandalized the truck, dumped garbage in the bed, but when he looks he finds only the usual Big Gulp cups and the aluminum crossover toolbox that had been his central perk for buying the truck, though he rarely needs his tools anymore. There's no movement around the lake in the chill sharp air, he can make out only outlines of houses under the skeletal trees. The bag slouches against the tire, not quite half-full. Cole toes it with his boot. The touch confirms what he had begun to guess already.

He undoes the tie and looks inside and the rich cloying odor assaults him despite that the thing's triple bagged. On top of the reefer sits a seven-year-old copy of *Leg Show*, but no note. "Mister Hardesty," he muses aloud. "Too much for one man alone, like you said."

He slips one red-tipped bud into the magazine and places it on the floorboards before the passenger seat. Then he reties each bag and looks over the landscape again. The sun isn't up yet but its rays are graying the sky, and frosty vapor burning off the trees seeps into the air. Not even the birds are into it yet. Cole limps to the garbage cans beside the house and drops the bag behind them. Pickup isn't for two more days, and Lyda isn't going to take out the trash anyway. He doesn't want to haul around that much pot unless he knows where he's going with it.

Back in the driver's seat the smell is already overwhelming. He rolls down the windows and turns on his heater full blast and still after two miles of driving he feels like he'll be sweating out the stink for days. Even the horses react to the stink on him, their lips curl and nostrils flare as they nudge at his chest and hair to figure him out. By the time he has their day started the morning is in full bloom. Cole stops at the first pay phone he can find and wakes up Shady. "Girl, you are not going to believe what I have for you."

She agrees, once she sees the bud for herself: she can't believe it. But the stuff's not for her (not all of it), and she insists on keeping it so. You need to learn to think more to your advantage, she tells him. So Cole gets the key to Spunk's storage shed and after her shift he brings Shady there, and she comes prepared, carrying a postage meter and more boxes of ziplock bags than would seem humanly necessary. Also a variety of mixers—oregano and Italian seasoning shakers, ditchweed yanked from the roadsides, a pouch of loose dark tobacco—but she isn't truly stepping on the product, she's adding mixers to the shake to get the weight right. Sheldon waits at school to sell all that he can.

"You're going to be in the money here," Shady says.

"With Sheldon? I doubt that. I need to turn up that caretaker to see what he wants."

"Seems to me if he wanted anything he might let you know without leaving pounds of weed in your driveway." She measures another quarter ounce of shag and bud and begins to bag it herself as Cole, slow, falls behind with the meter. "Is that really the story here, Cole? Do I get to know that much, since you've got me committing felonies?"

"To be honest, I don't know. Came out this morning and there's the bag."

"Just tell me you didn't pull a Fleece here. This isn't Greuel's, right? Am I right? I don't need those people after me." She zips shut a ziploc and pulls more out of the box to ready another stack. She had had the wherewithal to bring a deodorizer and candles, eucalyptus, cranberry—some unidentifiable fresh scent mixes with the reefer. The variety of odors makes Cole nauseous and from time to time he gets up to stretch his legs, works his knee out, and puts his face to the ventilator fan.

Shady has also brought her pipe, a glass cylinder of swirling colors. She breaks from bagging to hit, motions Cole to join in as tendrils of smoke draw waving lines above the bowl. He takes the pipe and inhales deeply, intent on the burning embers. Instead of exhaling into the room, he bends low and—one hand gently grasping the base of Shady's skull, a move that prompts from her the question, *What?*—exhales into her mouth. Her surprise allows this. Simultaneously she giggles and coughs, then mostly coughs as he pulls away.

"See, I don't understand you," she says again, reaching for a bottle of Gatorade. "Is this still about Fleece? About your brother and your Mom? Mister Greuel?" She gestures at the small piles of weed, the large trash bag, the quarters and dimes stuffed into a nylon duffel bag Cole had bought that afternoon.

He doesn't want to think about it and he tells her so. He says, Thinking is what I do for hours and hours on end and I'd rather not think tonight, I'm not driving, I just want *to do*. Fair enough, Shady agrees. He eases onto the couch in a position half-lying, half-sitting, his head resting against her arm. It's a calculated provocation he would never have the gumption to try were he not high, but hell, Shady (he thinks), how long you want to make a boy wait? There's a swagger in him tonight—already he can guess the amount of money this gift can bring him—and it pleases Cole how she does not move away or start to bag again. Instead, her free hand begins to finger a path over his scalp, playing with his hair and bringing a feeling like a grin in his belly.

"Your mother has kind of—don't get me wrong, I like Lyda and I don't know her life or anything, I'm not judging, but she kind of fucked you up."

He nods as they stare together at the loot and a life-size poster of Michael Jordan sailing forth with tongue wagging on the otherwise blank wall of concrete blocks across from them. Outside, semis pull along the nearby interstate, small explosions of air brakes punctuating the great wash of speeding cars; briefly the siren of an ambulance or fire truck veers its frantic alarm. The U-Stor-It is not particularly hidden, which causes moments of concentrated listening and an eye at the opening below the roll-top door for any shift of light there; but it's not a high-traffic location, either. Five rows of sixteen units apiece face one another within a graveled lot that dead-ends against a high fence and the woods behind it. The woods decline into a mosquito ditch and then run back up to the interstate. There's only the one way in or out.

"That's okay," Cole answers after a time. "As long as you're not judging."

She surprises him with a long, lingering kiss that fills his mouth. Her tongue is a soft and pliant pleasure to him despite the dryness.

After this brief moment passes he remains as he was, head tilted back and eyes closed, her three-beat laugh—*ha ha ha*—so close to his face he opens his eyes again.

"Maybe what this is about is you," Cole says.

"Speaking of not understanding somebody. Cole you are a good friend to me, a good friend I don't want to mess things up with, and we can be friends and have good times too, okay? But don't mistake for a second that any of this is about me. It's for you. It's all about you and your brother and Lyda. And you getting out of here. You know this. What've you learned since you dived in undercover or whatever it was you had in mind going to work for Greuel."

He tells her what he knows. Hearing himself account for such few details underscores a sinking feeling of inadequacy deep in his belly, as though he were still in school and had blown off some important project and was now trying to come up with an excuse before the teacher's disappointed and disbelieving face. He tells her of the visit with the caretaker and how supposedly Fleece had given the man this trash bag—"But there was way more in there than this," he says, indicating what's left—and of how Hardesty said he was being let go from his employment through the Archdiocese because of the property sale. And that Greuel and Noe had something to do with the sale but he doesn't get what if anything that has to do with Fleece. Otherwise, he admits, he knows nothing more about what Fleece might have done or what has become of him. Even though he feels, driving, delivering, closer to his brother. And like that's the only way he's going to get to the bottom of anything, by slipping into his life and gauging the lay of the land. And on those lonesome drives he has felt another impulse, a temptation, that he wonders if his brother struggled with also: you begin to focus so much on not being noticed, not being seen, that it seems natural to believe you can disappear.

It's an idea Cole likes even as he is uncertain of its meaning. He likes to say aloud in the empty car as he drives, *By then I will have disappeared.* As though he were concocting some diabolical plan, though he knew, in reality, he was only making it up as he went along.

"One thing sticks at me. They say Fleece got off with the October harvest. Spunk says they were dry three months because of that."

"Yeah?" says Shady. "And what's that mean?"

"Means I don't know what. But the weekend after Thanksgiving—we bought at the quarry and it was expensive, remember? And Arley Noe took our money. Arley Noe doesn't work the quarry, that's for little guys like me. And the time before that, the night at Greuel's *before* the holiday, when Greuel gave us lip and got on Spunk too not to take any more reefer out the door with him."

"They shut down the quarry is what I heard," Shady says, like a proposition meant to prompt him.

Cole is staring at the ceiling and a large water stain there. "So I guess I'm wrong, they weren't lying, Arley was there to fill in for Fleece till they dried up."

"Maybe. Unless he wanted to sell his stuff somewhere else."

It's a strange-looking stain; it warps the plasterboard in pools and humps, making a shape that could be likened to a camel. Already he's losing focus. "Dang, Shady."

"What?"

"Don't you think that's being kind of suspicious? Why sell somewhere else if you can sell all you got right here?"

Shady shrugs. "I'd say maybe you don't suspect enough. But what do I know?" She picks up the magazine that had come with the trash bag. She leafs through the limp pages, studies the pictures. "This proves this came from the caretaker guy?"

"Don't know anyone else likely to have a copy of *Leg Show* from August 1987."

There seems so little Cole can hold in his head at one time; once he snatches a detail he's already watching it dart away. He wishes he could work like the detectives in movies, identifying clues, employing logic, but he lacks the mental equipment for investigation—in fact movie mysteries baffle him, he's always surprised when the culprit is exposed at story's end. No, Cole's more comfortable moving on instinct and impression: on what *feels* correct with some inner calculus he's not even sure how he figures. Such as now, with the confluence of Shady Beck and a softcore mag and nobody else around.

He places a hand on her leg and slides it up her thigh, the denim smooth to his palm until he hits the belt loops; for all her face shows she's studying an article. He plays with her belt, flicking the tongue of it—the buckle is one of those spring-loaded types that require only a flick to pop open, and he does that, listening to the small chink of metal. Her hands don't move.

"Here?" she asks into the magazine.

"Here would be excellent."

"Did you not hear me a minute ago?" Her tone sounds irritated, but she tosses the magazine aside and draws his arm around her. "The door isn't even all the way closed."

"I can close it," he says. No sooner does he move to do so than three hard smacks from outside shake the door in brilliant noise, it hurts deep in his ear canals, it's like being trapped inside a steel drum. Cole motions to Shady to hide the stash. *Wait wait wait* she repeats in a high-whispering voice. Hoots and cackles meet the rapid skid of tires kicking up gravel, and then someone smacks the door again, the noise jarring Cole to a panicked standstill.

"Open up, damn your hides, it's the *po*-lice!"

He recognizes Spunk's hoarse, drunken drawl; the recognition calms him enough to kick the duffel bag out of the light beside the couch. "Hold on," he says, indicating to Shady again to do something with the trash bag as he pulls on a sweatshirt. Her eyes express the small unit's lack of options, and it doesn't matter in the end as the chains start to rattle and Spunk's unlaced hightops become visible, then the baggy jeans, then the topmost of his three oversized T-shirts present themselves behind the unveiling door. He's grinning happy as his eyes slur over his storage unit, a six-pack of Little Kings cream ale tucked under one arm. Behind him Grady Creed is leaning back against his tricked-out 4Runner, arms crossed to accentuate the bulge in his biceps, cowboy boots set heel to toe. The rims on his vehicle are shiny new spinners.

"Smells like y'all are having a party," Spunk says, stepping in and situating the ale in a small styrofoam cooler. "Grady you going to nab that ice?"

Clotted flesh about the eyes of both betrays deep chemical influence. Creed strides in, bedecked in the air of a victor awesomely pleased—with himself, with the scene, with the whole scenario of walking in on Cole and Shady Beck. On his greasy face is plastered a grin that marks him as an imperturbable keeper of secrets everyone wishes to know, secrets he can't help but add to, that others would offer much to insure he kept. "Shady is this a one-man show or you gonna take us all on? I been on a dry stretch." He makes a play at her ribcage and cackles at her slapping hand; already he's past her and at her pipe on the small particle-board stand beside the couch, sniffing at it like a hound set loose to hunt a man down.

Spunk spouts roundabout forms of apology as he pokes through the CDs beside the boom box. "My bad, you two. I figured y'all'ed be done by now and I couldn't stall this boy any more." He settles on a kind of funky metal noise that Cole doesn't know, guitars and drums lashing out in an assault on them all, Spunk busting ridiculous moves as he pops open a Little King and combines a high falsetto with the singer on the CD.

Creed collapses into the couch beside Shady, presenting the twisted tooth in his smile; on his lean and narrow face are two small sores puckered scarlet at the rim. He scratches one and it opens a brilliant pinhead of blood, asks, "What d'ya say?" She gets up off the couch and hits the cooler herself. Creed exhales after a hit and rolls his tongue around in his mouth, considering the taste; he eyes Cole and winks once. "I get it now," he says. "Yeah, I get it now."

"Get what?"

He points to the smoke as it plumes above his head, then holds up his hands in surrender. "We don't got to talk about it, we don't got to say nothing at all!" He sets down the pipe again and Cole sees him note the duffel bag. "Looks like y'all were planning to spend the night here or something."

"That's mine, thank you very much," Shady says, pulling it out from beneath Creed's hands as he started at the zipper. "As a matter of fact maybe I was."

"Aw man, now I feel bad. I'm a romantic at heart. I would've thought a class girl like you'd want a hotel room somewheres, something nice with a shower. Never would've figure you for a *Leg Show* kind of girl, either." He scans a few pages, finds an explicit beaver shot of a girl touching the floor in spiked heels and torn stockings and her eyes intent on the camera. "Mmm, look at that. If that don't just get the ideas going in your head." Creed presents the spread to Spunk. "Check it out, man, Cole's mom's in here."

"No way!" from Spunk as he wrenches the magazine away. He shakes his head side to side, examining the entire portfolio. "It does kind of look like her. Maybe ten years ago or something when she had more cushion. Your mom ever go for modeling?"

"Give me that," Cole says. He tosses the magazine onto the trash bag and hopes no one bothers to pick it up again and reveal what's underneath; the unit holds enough random trash that the bag doesn't look out of place or even recently added.

"No need to get offensed," Creed concedes. "Nobody has a say who they come out of."

"I take offense every time you open your mouth Grady Creed," Shady says. She shoots a meaningful glance at Cole, but he has no idea what meaning she is trying to convey. "I guess I should be heading out, let you boys get on with it."

"Yeah you probably should. Sorry," says Creed with no hint of actual apologetic feeling.

"She came with me. She's in my truck."

"Yeah, well. That part of your evening is over. We come *for you*, James Cole my young rookie friend, and our business does not concern the pretty lady here. She can drive your truck, she seems capable."

"You ever fix that clutch?" asks Spunk.

Shady gets to her feet. "I can drive it. Let me out, there's too much testosterone in here all of a sudden."

"We could all have some fun first, if you're up for it. The offer is a good one and it still stands," taunts Creed. "I swear you'll still have our respect!" But Shady is out on the gravel marching toward Cole's truck, duffel bag slung over one shoulder, one middle finger solemnly raised with no looking back.

When Cole catches up to her she says, "I should take this on to Sheldon now, am I right? Does he know it's coming?"

"He knows but he hasn't paid for it yet. Don't give him anything he doesn't pay you for."

"I can't take this stuff home with me, Cole."

Off to Sheldon she'll go, then. Typical of Shady she then rattles off a brief plan concocted while Cole's head spins and wanders like sparkling motes in a dusty light beam, thoughts mostly lamenting the loss of the two of them alone just some precious minutes before. She informs him she'll leave his truck at the front of her family property with the keys in the exhaust pipe and that he should get dropped off there; he's to rap at her window when he returns, and she expects to hear what Creed and Spunk have put him up to. "And none of this is up for negotiation," she says, "or else I go drop this bag in Grady Creed's lap and see how he likes you now."

"Okay," he agrees, too stunned to respond with anything more. "I might be out late, mom."

"Don't be like that. I care." She tiptoes and pecks him beside his mouth. "I'll be up. Don't disappoint me," and as he swallows hard she is in the cab with the engine turned over.

They watch her maneuver the truck without difficulty, dog-legging it in reverse and speeding forward with a wave of gravel breaking on the slips before the units' roll-up doors. Creed and Spunk are but bent shapes fluctuating with the candles behind them. Cole believes there's not much left in the trash bag, that Shady has most all of his morning's find. He limps back to the garage, accentuating his stiff-knee frailty even as he taps one hip as a reminder of the gravity blade tucked into his ass pocket. As he nears, their smiles transform to masks of glee.

"What's so important you had to blue my balls like that?"

Creed hands over a Little King and briefly drapes a consoling arm over his shoulders as he wags his head with compassion. "You wanted the life, this is the life," he says. "Duty calls, and she's a bitch one whole lot uglier than Shady Beck."

•

Creed teems with a savage relish, he's hopped up and jittering, he can't sit still and won't say where they're headed. He stomps the clutch, slams the gearshift, and fills the Toyota's interior with unspoken malevolence. What was it Grady had said to him that night, ghosting out of the dark woods around his mother's house? *I'm on your side.*

Yet now they ride with all the doors locked. Creed announced at the outset that he locks his doors when driving, a safety issue instilled by his parents. He announced too that he did not want to hear any teasing about his listening to the good advice of his parents. And no loud music: he prefers news from the world the three of them have only heard about. "And I don't like talk, so don't talk," he says once they hit the parkway.

They pass the latest developments and then it's fields on either side, and darkness, the road cutting through steep shelved hills and the air smells of wet leaves and rain, and he guesses where they are headed about two minutes before they arrive. As Creed slows to turn, his headlights capture the billboard sign at the edge of the drive:

FUTURE HOME OF

CHRIST WORLD EMERGENT

COMMUNITY AND FELLOWSHIP COMPLEX

BROTHER GIL PONDER, PASTOR UNORTHODOX

and it's there only an instant as Creed follows the drive between the building and the caretaker's cottage, pulling up in the back on the basketball courts. The cinder of Fleece's Nova, sopped to a darker rust in the wet, glows phosphor after Creed shuts off his headlights.

"You know all I know about that," Creed says, "so don't even start."

Arley Noe's powder-blue Cadillac and Mule's Toyota truck sit parked directly behind the cottage, half-hidden beneath heavy conifers. Creed kills a Little King with a showy flourish, the bottle held above his mouth unfurling a liquid tongue down his throat, and then he hurls the bottle to shatter up high beside one of the seminary windows. The glass explodes sharply and they listen to the shards sprinkle back to earth. The three stare of them at where the bottle hit the wall.

"Dang. I was aiming for the window."

"You got no arm left, Grady," from Spunk, in a tone of honest rue, dancing his limbs like a boxer loosening up before a fight. "I remember when you could bust midway games at the fair."

Creed shrugs his throwing shoulder, kneads the muscle with his knuckles. "Those days stopped the second I heard that pop against Metcalfe County. I didn't know it then."

Despite the noise of their arrival and the thrown bottle, the building remains silent inside. "Where are the dogs?" asks Cole.

Spunk sniggers and covers his mouth as he spins away, echoing the question—*Yeah, where them dogs, Creed?*—and Creed buddies up with him: "Ah-haw haw *haw*."

"Tough world for a dog," says Spunk.

"Tell me you didn't. Where's yours?"

"My bitch is fine, James Cole. Turns out you were right the other day—I'm gonna be a daddy. Or a step-daddy, I guess. You want a puppy when they're ready?"

"Hush up," says Creed, "Mule hears you two and there won't be nothing else to talk about." Mule is a lover of animals; a dues-paying member of Raptor Rehab and PETA, a keeper of budgies and home-finder for kittens.

They enter the back door without knocking, hesitating in the lightless kitchen. The far interior door is framed by a thin amber glow. Beneath the quiet Cole hears something soft, a low suspiration muffled and fierce.

"It's us," Creed declares, eyes toward the ceiling. "Finally."

The door clicks and glides wide. Mule towers within the frame, backlit, a hulking silhouette. He nods welcome, massaging one red, smeary fist inside the other, catching his breath as he backs up. Arley Noe stands formal and rigid in black suit and felt trilby, his blue face winched against smoke curling from the hand-rolled cigarette clamped in his mouth. He doesn't acknowledge the boys, keeping his attention instead upon a mass of angry suffering before him, a man sagging heavy against the burden of sitting up despite the duct tape strapped across his bare chest, arms, and shins. It's the caretaker Dwayne Hardesty. His thick shoulders quiver as he strains forward, but the tape holds firm. Hardesty's shiny white throat faces them; his head lies back on the chair, and in the wooly brass beard are clots of blood and torn flesh.

"You started without us," Creed says, disappointed.

"He has not been agreeable," murmurs Noe, narrow features bunching bemused as he evaluates the level of distress in the chair. "Mule got bit."

"I can't remember the last time I got a tetanus shot," Mule says, shaking the pain from his hand and tossing splats of blood on the dusty wood floor, "and dammit look at that, now I got to clean that up, too."

Noe bends forward and rests his hands on his knees, peering closely at Hardesty's face with near medical attention. "So everyone's here, then."

Hardesty's head lifts—both eyes are swollen shut, the left completely, the right with just enough crack to give view within the puckered eyelid. Something black spins in the yolk there. His head tilts, swivels side to side, taking in each of the men around him.

"That's him! You ask him," he shouts, until his voice breaks into coughing.

Noe raises to full height again. On top of two stacks of magazines and newspapers a large homemade toolbox stands open, displaying tools settled within cloth-lined pockets.

"Well," he says. "At present we're more interested in the how of things. Like how my property disappears from Harlan, say, and ends up here," his voice a level whisper, as if talking to himself alone. "In this little house." The blue fingers—deep blue, floral—tap along the tray of tools. They turn over a set of hawks-bill snips, move aside a brad driver. The diamonds in his horseshoe ring flicker and dance with bits of lamplight. He selects a rip hammer and inspects its iron claws through the smoke as he manipulates the cigarette along his lips to the opposite corner, turning the hammer in the faint light of the single table lamp as if searching for evidence of marred craftsmanship. He returns the tool to the cloth, picks up a dovetail saw. "Mule, I can't decide. You got a preference here?"

"Probably won't get much with that baby saw. I can't grip so well my good hand's all swole up. Fucker bit clean through to the knuckle, Cole, look at that"—he shows Cole the wounds on both sides of his hand following the curve of Hardesty's teeth, the skin there purpled and swollen, Mule's blood running easily down his wrist. "Could probably cast a mold of his mouth off this. Let's try those locking pliers, see what they get me."

Noe picks up the pliers and holds them out even as he continues to inspect the array, lips tight. Just as Mule reaches for the pliers Noe pulls them back, sighs, and hands him the hawks-bill snips. "Try these first. We don't need to be here all night."

Mule takes the tool and tests it, wincing at the spring's resistance in his injured hand.

"You want me to do it?" asks Creed.

Neither answer. With his free hand Mule pulls Hardesty's lolling head by the hair. The caretaker's breathing intensifies again, sucking in quick inhalations.

"I got nothing to say here. I gave you what I got last night, I got nothing to do with this, the boy just up and give it to me and he said *it was you*"—but he can't finish because Grady Creed steps forward and with pitcher's-mound intensity crunches his fist into the man's chin. Hardesty's head drops back and stays.

"Now I don't see how that was necessary," says Mule.

"Why don't you let a man do his job and wait your turn," Arley says at the same time.

Creed hops lightly on his toes, wiggling his arms. "I thought you wanted us here for help. This turd's lying already."

"Simmer down, junior." Noe stubs out his smoke in a crusty saucer. He inspects the burnt end, twists it between two fingers before depositing the butt in his jacket pocket. Then he returns to Hardesty. "Mule," he says, "I never understood why a man needs his nipples."

"It's got something to do with how we start out in the womb. Did you know a man can produce milk, get breast cancer, all that?"

"Mule. A man don't need his nipples. You understand what I'm saying?"

"I know the freaking routine, Arley."

Gently, Mule spreads Hardesty's thick chest hair away to expose a surprisingly small and pink aureole. He presses the open edge of the hawks-bill against the man's breast, steadying it in place despite the rapid heaving of Hardesty's rib cage.

"Hold on, boyo," Mule says. "This'll hurt."

"Wait, what're you asking me, you're *supposed to ask something before you hurt me*, man, what do you want to hear?" Hardesty speaks quickly, then groans deep as the snips bear down, his entire body tensing up, the chair jumping on the floor.

Where his nipple had been a small mouth snarls stark white. Creed nudges Cole and tells him, quietly, to check it out, give the body time, and even as he tells him this the white mouth quickens with pink; the blood beads up in tiny dots that gradually pool together, then starts to run freely into the hair over his belly. The nipple sits on Hardesty's thigh. His head angles in contemplation of it, his face seemingly baffled by the ease at which a piece of his body has changed location, moved from where it had existed for years without notice to there, above his knee.

Arley bends back in close to him. "There's not much from you I want to hear, honestly. I think I got the how figured out. Not so sure about the why. You steal from me, you steal from Greuel; steal from all of us in this room, in fact. Why? Try again."

Hardesty does try, as far as Cole can tell. None of what he says can satisfy Arley Noe. It almost seems as though words are not even what the blue man wants to hear, and it feels like they are there a long time, asking. Cole cannot figure exactly what Noe expects to learn from the man—everything Hardesty says appears to arise from some deep-seated honesty and the utmost desire to be released from this chair and this room, yet with each answer he loses another piece of his flesh. First Noe asks a question, and then Mule comes down with a snip from the hawks-bill, regardless of the response. As though the whole scene is a show; a kind of play-acting.

But for whose benefit would that be? Whose?

Certainly not Dwayne Hardesty. The man's chest and belly has begun to thicken with an extra skin of his own blood, like the scum that gathers on the surface of boiled milk; his ears disassemble into pieces lost from a jigsaw puzzle. Soon the white of his skull gleams from what used to be his left eyebrow. At each cut, Professor Mule places the piece of the man's flesh onto his thighs for Hardesty to view.

Helluva way to make fighting weight, Creed says to general silence.

Through it all Noe never raises his voice, never loses patience. His stare, Cole thinks, is as flat as an owl's. He sticks to a line of questioning about a man named Crutchfield—was Crutchfield in on this, too? Did Hardesty ever talk to Crutchfield? Did Fleece ever talk about Crutchfield? With the repetition of the name Cole feels an acceleration, the room spins from the house and the ground and whirls into some other dimension, a place of deeds that would fill a heart with shame if they were to occur in real life. The name *Crutchfield* rings no bells. Hardesty claims he's never heard of him, either—this even after Creed uses the brad driver to pop a bolt into the tendon below his kneecap. Cole believes him and wants to say so. Yet he shudders when Hardesty calls him out.

"Cole Skaggs," Hardesty says, "the little brother, you tell them what I told you"—the caretaker dips forward and a long strand of varied color splashes on the floor between his legs, Cole uncertain of its source—"what I tell you? I ever say anything about the Crutch?"

"You talked to this guy?" asks Spunk.

"He didn't mention anybody to me. He said Fleece gave him a few books in a trash bag. For letting him live up there."

Arley Noe casts his strange smile, a smile from stillness, as though the man had adapted human expressions while unable to understand the motives behind them. "I *know* where *my* weed's at. I don't understand why it got to be there is all." To the man on whom his gaze has not left he continues: "You say you don't know anything. How you come to calling this man 'the Crutch'?"

A roaring groan erupts then, and Hardesty's head falls back. He spits and starts again. "Motherfucker I'm from Burnside. I shipped home in seventy-three with a morphine habit and nine hundred and fifteen dollars I could spend in a week. Anybody in Pulaski County like that's going to learn him Nate Crutchfield if that's who you're asking about."

Noe straightens again, hands in his pockets; he works his thin lips silently. Mule eyeballs the caretaker as though chewing over the best way to remove a stubborn stump from his yard.

"It's James Cole," Hardesty wheezes at his thighs. "And not all Skaggs. James Cole."

Cole looks at him. He wishes Hardesty would stop bringing him into it. He wishes he could tell the man he's here because he has no say and he has no conception of what to do with himself or with the caretaker and—his head runs empty of thought, fills with a signal close to a dial tone.

"James Cole, get them off me. Get me out of here. Do I look like I need to be here?"

"I talked to Crutch," Arley continues in his quiet drone of a voice. "He described a man—well, way he described him made me think of you, caretaker. He said you drove Fleece down yourself. Some tale about Fleece with a broken hand, cast and all."

"Bone," Hardesty calls out.

"Lying to spite the nose on his face," Noe says.

"Arley I don't know how much longer we got him, he's going to black or bleed out soon, one or the other."

"Lies to spite the nose on his face. Mule. You understand what I'm saying?"

He holds out the dovetail saw.

Lawrence Greuel reclines beneath a mound of woolen blankets and one quilt of sentimental value, the real thing, passed down from the nineteenth century by his grandma. Its ratty resilience impresses him, squares of cloth thinner than paper save for the few patches he had sewn in himself over the years. He fingers the yellowed batting inside a small tear as he squints at the late-night news glowing between his fat feet, two bloated blobs exposed to the air, propped on his sofa's armrest. Those talking heads have nothing to tell that Greuel needs knowing.

He used to be the man who made things happen. Now his feet look like something inflated by a clown for the amusement of children. He hates the sight of them, but they burn radiantly even as the rest of him freezes, so he can't hide the feet beneath his blankets. The right one lacks its little toe, the left has only the first two, both feet white as fish bellies save for the puffy purple amputation scars. He doesn't even think of them any longer as parts of him: never as *my feet,* simply *the feet.* They feel encased, without pores. When he complained of the discomfort, his private nurse—a meaty thumb of Thai attitude that Greuel likes and abhors in equal measure—told him, *reassured* him, seemed like, that she could do nothing about hot feet. *That mean you been bad man, Hell get ready for you,* she said. Then she burst with a display of unforeseen hilarity and shook his big toe. "The look on you face, ha! The look on you face, ha ha ha!" until he, too, laughed, struck by this tiny woman so worked up over what she said.

He never could get the names of these nurses right despite the many times they've slowly sounded out the stacks of consonants and vowels that make up who they are—a name with six or seven syllables, his head can't hold it, hardly anyone understands what he says these days anyway. This morning he called on Gwen and she answered, *Pakpao! you call me Pakpao!* in a merry shout. Another nurse tried to coach him on *Dhipyamongko* but Greuel gave up on that one, settled for *nurse.* Was she the one to tell him that it was hell licking at his feet?

Always did have a thing for Asian babes. Blue Note had told him this was due to his never having been over there, surrounded by chest-high people everywhere you turn. He claimed he got enough of that cut in the service. But Noe—if Greuel didn't know the son of a bitch so well he might guess a guy that strange was into boys or cows or whatever, maybe not even anything living. In the end (as in all things with Noe) it came down to clarity, to clean lines. Noe likes him some whores. Back when they owned majority interest in that strip club in Lexington— in seventy-two?—his partner confided that he found "use of a woman satisfying but they's no-count otherwise." Greuel had laughed and he had understood. Pay a girl outright and you owe nothing after, don't have to care what she thinks of you or wants from you or (the real kicker) what she *hopes* for you. Things get rough, Greuel had decided long ago, once a woman decides on a man's potential.

Pay-to-play worked for a creepy crow like Arley but would never work for him. Greuel likes women. He likes the clack of their heels on his hardwood floors, their easy enthusiasms, their laughter—the real thing, not a put-on laugh but the kind that froths up when they can't help it and aren't concerned with how they sound. Because of this liking Greuel has dealt with more grief and headache and expense, he readily admits, than Arley Noe has ever had to suffer.

Does it bother him that he has to pay to be looked after now? Absolutely not. He never had met another Clara.

And still Noe got into some mess himself when he ran a few escort girls, on paper it looked good but Greuel knew going in he didn't want to muddy his hands with that shit. He still had Clara then to answer to anyway, he'd had to keep even the dance club secret from her (the name of the place escapes him now, *Saddlebreds* or something)—not because she would've been against the investment morally or ethically but because she would've ended up as friendly counsel and advisor to the dancers, and Greuel didn't need the aggravation.

What does Noe do with his money? Greuel hasn't a clue even though he has looked into it, secretly, and more than once. He knows a lot went to lawyers, because Noe's loyal escort girls turned to easy talkers when they realized the talking might help them out of a jam. The eighties hadn't been friendly to Arley Noe, he had been forced into eggshell-walking for a few years there.

That's why Greuel stuck to the reefer, the pills, more crank since the kids seem to be into it. Everybody an independent contractor who don't know more than what they have their hands in directly save for him. Save for him and Arley. It's all old Blue Note's concern now.

He looks over his burning feet again. Flexes his aching legs. The backed-up feeling from the phlebitis makes him picture clots colluding in his veins. One shakes loose and that's all she wrote, like having a bullet in you already just waiting for its moment to hit where it matters. Not the most fitting end after the life he's led, fact it's a damn shame. But isn't it always? He had watched outraged at the injustice his Clara had suffered, thirty-six and her body winding down, first the stiffness and odd aches and then after the diagnosis her determined attitude, then the demoralizing fatigue and outright pain, then the catheters and bed pans and Greuel bedside in the hospital watching her blood pressure and oxygen percentages ticking down. She was out of it by then, didn't even know he was there.

For him it's not so much a winding down as the goddamn wheels flying off. He plans to complain and curse every downward sign whether anyone listens or not.

•

His feet teem in a high sizzle. He cannot sleep and he's alone. Where the hell is everybody? Past twelve midnight at night and the phone hasn't rung and where is snakebrain Noe and where the hell is *anybody?*

He wills the phone on the low table beside him to ring. He'll stare it down until it does, he's got more heart still than any dumb insentient object. He stares at it, glaring. Then he bores with the standoff. He picks up his address book and thumbs the wrinkled and food-stained pages, careful with the ones torn loose of the binder rings. He's had this book some forty years now. He marvels at the number of entries crossed out and updated with moves or blacked out as they died. Pages and pages of associates . . . friends are those gone, *because* they are gone, cold bones in the ground or else ashes, invisible molecules floating, maybe, in the very air about his room . . . the thought of which leads him to suck several deep huffs from the oxygen mask.

These days his friends are doctors and their script pads and these Asian nurses with impossible names. In his book he does not see one name to call, one name that could expect his voice past midnight for anything other than mean business.

There's that pastor's mobile phone number. A pastor with a mobile phone—so incongruous to Greuel's sense of things that he chuckles, decides right then maybe it's best he kicks soon, this world no longer fits him. Noe's going to make a squealing pig out of that pastor and his church, stroke of genius, who's going to bust a church? and Ponder in too deep a money bind to say a word about it. He flips past the business card to the end of the book.

Not a soul worth his missing toes. From the inside cover pocket he pulls out more pages, most weathered by time to tissue, and they sprawl floating across his chest. He selects one yellowed scrap forgotten long ago. Forgotten, but on sight of the number he recognizes it perfectly, recalls *perfectly* the day he watched a half-literate boy scrawl it down for him, that would have been, what, seventy-six or seventy-seven? Is it possible the number's still good? What a shock to her. Goddamn if ever there was a woman who owed him her time and attention whether or not she accepted the fact.

I am a man who makes things happen. He pulls the phone to him, a heavy rotary thing. None of this bullshit hand-wrung wondering where people are when I crave company. The other end rings and rings, so the line's good and he's going to wake up somebody who evidently does not own an answering machine. He counts twelve rings but there may have been more, his attention keeps blanking (or feels like it does), he'll give it twenty, twenty-four if he can keep track that long. Or he could go all night—but a sleepy voice, husky as a drinking man's, answers.

"Who is this?"

"I bear untold gifts and surprises," Greuel croaks as clearly as he can, and smiles satisfied into the mouthpiece.

Her voice perks, wakes: he can see her sitting up in bed. "Is it Fleece? Did you find him, where is he?"

"What? No, it's, wait a second—"

"Cole? Have you done something to James Cole now you fucking, where is he, what's happening?"

"Lady, calm down. This is nothing to do with either your boys. I came across your number."

"What time is this?" Her voice softens, falls sleepy again. "What do you want?"

"You. I want the presence of an old friend and fellow conspirator. Get up and get yourself over, we got everything you could want for the taking, it's an open pharmacy over here."

"You wake me in the middle of the night out of the blue and think I'll jump right to it?"

Greuel chuckles, feels the front of his teeth with his thick tongue. On the TV there's a mother lion teaching its young how to tear apart a carcass.

"Yeah, Lyda, I do. In fact I know you will," he says, and hangs up.

It had not occurred to her before because she had never thought about it, but after very few moments alone with Sheldon Prather, Shady realized a dislike for him that frightened her with its depth; she loathed him with a repugnance that stabbed like shards in her gut. She didn't like how sharply he dismissed her caution on the phone, or her suggestion they meet elsewhere than his frat-house room. She didn't like his gratuitous use of the word *bitch*. Okay she could look past that, it wasn't like she had to marry him; but she did have to take him seriously on behalf of Cole. She had to deal with him seriously and she had to do it with extra caution, too; since her dream routine gave her an extra perception into the workings of the world she's felt more confident in her intuitions about others, her insights into which side they were on, knowingly or unknowingly, because what she comprehends as well as her own needs is that different sides are at work all around them. Sheldon didn't give a deuce that Cole was family. Sheldon cared only for whomever he could get to do him favors.

And she was helping *him,* too. Sheldon Prather was about to be one popular boy. As long as he did not get caught—and Shady doubted he could keep from bragging about what he had and how much. She voiced this concern from the truck-stop pay phone: "I'm telling you I have this bag wrapped tight and every window open and the stink is still making me dizzy. Trust me on this, you don't want it in your

room." Sheldon told her he would meet her out front and walk her up
and not to be such a stupid bitch.

"Do you even have the money to buy?"

"In my business this is what we call 'stupid-bitch behavior'; I
asked you to avoid that. I *asked* this," and he hung up.

She was neither stupid nor a bitch but she was used to the tire-
some wacked machismo of fraternity boys longing for street cred and
histories of economic suffering and violence they would never have to
actually undergo. She never understood why women bothered with
them. Maybe many did not, and that's why frats tended to have access
to great drugs. A Darwinian scenario: selfish jerks who don't want to
grow up have to entice girls somehow. Like rock bands and the sex
musicians allegedly get (she had discussed this with her sisters): girls
like to dance; good music feels good; naturally a girl might be interested in whoever creates this music that makes her feel good. She had
lots of theories, lots of notions. When she was high her mind raced
with them, she didn't know why.

She stuffed three quarters in her purse and left the rest in the
truck. Sheldon led her in without greeting, swatting at fruit flies that
swarmed in the parlor of the old house, past a group watching TV in
the front room (she avoided looking at the screen), Sheldon moving
shifty like in a stop-motion film—he turned several times to check
she was still following, catching her eye each time and then tittering
in a nervous, high pitch. His pale face with its scattering of dark whis-
kers sported one angry pimple on his jaw line and he was clenching
his teeth in a pulsating rhythm. In his room he had replaced the desk
lamp with a black light; it was all the light on offer.

"You must be chewing up the books in here," she said.

"I'm allowing myself a long-deserved vacation. Make money—no,
create wealth—have fun, blow off the semester and make up for it once
they drop me to probation." He broke into a fit of deep coughs and
then asked to see what she had, his white shirt aglow, teeth flashing
creepy neon. Already the fan was in the window blowing out into the
world. He stood with a hand on the back of his head and one leg jig-
gling. She placed the three quarter-bags on his desk. He did not move
from the door.

"From our phone conversation I was under the impression you had more than that."

"I do have more. I didn't know how much you wanted to buy."

"If it's as good as you said it is, I want it all. You're going to let me try it out, right?"

"Have at it," she said. "Seems like you could use a bit of bring-me-down." He laughed his nervous staccato and, with a friendly face of disbelief, admitted he was on hour fifty-six without sleep. "An experiment," he added, and then he leered at her a broad, demented smile of infinite self-assurance. Shady said she could use a bump herself for the drive home, wondering if he had any of Tina's Ritalin left, but if he heard her Sheldon let it ride without comment.

He made a show of loading a new copper pipe he was proud to have crafted from his father's leftover building materials. She asked if he had used it yet and he shook his head. She watched as he filled the bowl and then lit it, and she waited as with a child to learn for himself: the steel soon burned his lips and he dropped the pipe with a howl. Now it was Shady's turn to laugh. He pinched his lips with thumb and three fingers, purring a combination whine/hum as he waited for the pain to subside.

"A new lesson, one I will never forget," he said, fishing out a juice from the fridge beneath his desk. "Now it is inscribed into the synapses of my drug-addled brain!" In spite of herself she laughed at this, too; he held the cold can against his lips, murmuring that all this was part of his whole experiment, he was continually garnering useful information that had nothing to do with school. Shady took out her ceramic one-hitter and packed it for herself, burned it down, and then packed it again for Sheldon even as it felt as though her body was sailing away from her. She dismissed his offers of more, dizzy and light and impatient to get the transaction over with so she could go home.

Sheldon lay back on the bed, kicking off his unlaced high-tops and setting his bare bony feet crossed at the heel on Shady's knee as he exhaled, languorously, toward the ceiling.

"Fuck . . . me," he said, drawn out and solemn.

"What I'm telling you," she said. She pushed back the rolling desk chair and Sheldon's feet dropped to the carpet with a heavy thud.

On the ceiling glowed an array of stars and planets as in a child's nursery. She sat patiently, staring mostly at the fan but watching Sheldon from the corner of her eye, noting his lack of movement from where he reclined on his elbows, head thrown back. Time passed; she lost track of whether it was passing quickly or not.

"So how do you want to do this?"

On the floor above, a stereo came on so loud that the door and window buzzed in their frames.

"I'm considering a sort of partnership, you could say."

"Cole doesn't need a partner, he needs this off his hands. You're his family. Help him out."

"I am willing to move it off his hands. As any good family member should."

"You're short on cash at the moment."

"You've got money. Isn't your dad a doctor or something?"

"He's not going to invest in you dealing, if that's where you're going with this."

"Doesn't any of that doctor money trickle down to you? I bet it does. You have really nice hair."

"Look, Sheldon, how much can you buy tonight? I'm tired and it's a long drive home."

He continued to stare at the ceiling with its tiny stars and milky ways and handful of suns. If he had placed them there alone it must have taken hours, but Shady found it hard to imagine Sheldon taking up any tedious task, however small, alone. He would have had a phalanx of girls to take part, having convinced them that placing day-glo stickers of stars onto his ceiling would be their best bet of an evening.

"I am conceiving a plan even as we banter," he said.

•

This much Shady tells him up front. As agreed, she had left his truck at the front of her family property with the key in the muffler, though she worried he had already been by the house. Though she felt exhausted by the driving and the hour and the weed she felt a deep urge to see Cole, contriving a compromise with sleep and waking, positioning a rocking chair before her window from where she could view the truck past the far fence, a spoon in her hand. When she drifted and the spoon fell to her hardwood floor, she would awaken and look out front again. The truck was always there.

She's uncertain how many times she did this, her thoughts scrambling each time with doubts and motivational inquisitions and those surveys of one's life that occur only at such groggy and anxious moments in the middle of the night. When morning sun warmed her face she awoke to an awful taste in her mouth and the spoon on the bed behind her. The truck remained. She worried.

Ditching her mother's queries she changed clothes and scrubbed her face with a rough towel, olive oil soap, and water, and said she had to meet a friend before her next shift. She drove the truck to Lake Holloway with the sun beyond the hills burning the clouds from within, a crimson ember-like glow that looked like the morning-after scene of a great medieval battlefield, the entire eastern horizon on fire. Why medieval? She didn't know, and she wondered. She found Cole filthy and asleep on the front porch, flat on his back with his feet on the lower steps. She wakes him by tossing the keys onto his face.

"I forgot you had the truck until after the boys dropped me here," he says. "I sat down to figure out what to do. I fell asleep."

"You look a mess. What did they have you do?" Mud and grass streak his damp jeans from boots to thighs, a smear of mahogany-colored filth stripes him cheek to his chin, and bits of leaves mat his hair. The hand that gestures at her question is chapped and blackened. A faint odor, like sewage, wafts from his clothes.

"What time is it?"

"Are you in trouble about the pot?"

He wrings one hand as though it hurts. "What did Sheldon say?"

She relates what she feels is relevant. She hands over three hundred dollars rolled up in twenties, and before he can begin to protest—his face closes at the sight of the thin roll—she stops him with her hand in the air: "You knew he wouldn't have enough for all of it, right? He said you knew. He bought eight quarters at what he called wholesale. The rest he promises to pay as he sells. Spring Break starts in another week, it'll all be gone by then."

"What did you do with the rest?"

"Sheldon has it." That wakes him as she knew it would.

"Shady, come on! You gave him a pound of weed on his promise to pay for it later?"

"Well what would you have had me do? Three hundred is what he could get, I even went to the ATM with him and saw the receipt. Feel free to school me on what other choice I may have had. You want me driving over two counties with your drugs and a porno mag in that excuse for a truck that, by the way, Sheldon was alert enough to point out it's got expired tags? I'm not going to jail for you, Cole. You're no kingpin daddy and I'm no mule, or whatever."

She didn't mean to sound harsh but she doesn't soften the edge in her voice, either. He sits with his elbows on his knees, hands clasped behind his head; his eyes close, and such a still calm overcomes him that briefly she wonders if he has fallen asleep again. She fights a sudden urge to slap him awake. She wonders if his mother is up yet, and only then notices her car isn't in the driveway. She thought Lyda never left the house.

"Aren't you going to at least ask how I am?" Shady asks.

His face raises and his mouth opens, a dazed look. The pads beneath his eyes are swollen, the eyes themselves rimmed pink, and she feels sorry for him—but then again she's tired, too, and what is she to get out of any of this? She hasn't asked for a thing. She's only in because she cares; because his whole story seems to matter to her.

"You okay?" he says finally.

"I'm fine, just take me back home. I've got to be getting on."

"Where do you have to be?"

"I have a *job*, Cole."

Again it sounds harder than she means but else-wise is beyond her, she's exhausted and feels suddenly *done* with all this—even as she knows she is not done, knows she cares about this boy (she can't think of him as a man; men are her father's age), and there's something sweet and pathetic about him that she feels the need to protect, to aid. Positive energy (the good angels) shielding against the negative, the anti-, the evil. With his shoulders slumped forward and hands hanging limp between his legs, he looks like a beaten and abandoned dog.

Cole nods weakly as he takes in what she has said, but doesn't appear ready to say anything in response to it.

Both straighten at the rev of a car engine accelerating up the hill. She recognizes the vehicle the moment she spins to see: Grady Creed in his 4Runner. He skids to a halt behind the truck, chrome rims spinning gaily in the morning sunlight; the black paint job gleams as if newly waxed. He is clean-shaven and freshly showered; his high-top basketball shoes look new out of the box, and the expression on his face is as though he has just heard a fantastic joke.

"Morning, sunshine! I'm really beginning to think yawl should get yourselves your own place together!"

"What is he doing here at eight in the a.m. on a Sunday?"

"Meet the new boss," Cole says.

"Same as the old boss!" Creed sings, windmilling his arm across an air guitar in the trademark Townsend swing. "You got my scratch?"

Cole still holds the roll of twenties; he hasn't even counted it out yet. He raises the money on his open palm like some mendicant friar making an offering to his order. Creed swipes the cash and weighs it in his fist as he grins at Shady, his jaw exercising the same thin tendons as Sheldon's had the night before. He smells of strong aftershave, and his gray eyes seem wholesomely clear in the morning light. He squeezes the roll in his grip without looking, and to Shady he tips his chin, says, "This does not feel worth a gym bag of reefer to me. Feels like"—and here he guides a thumbnail across the paper edges—"feels like I don't have even half a grand in my hand. That can't be right. Can that be right?" He slips off the rubber band and begins to count silently.

"It's three hundred dollars," Shady tells him.

"So it is. Someone explain to me why I drove over here for three hundred. We have some fire sale I didn't know about?"

Again Shady starts into the arrangement she'd managed but Cole interrupts her and takes over the story himself, saying it was the best she could get with Sheldon and he wouldn't have done any better and so Creed should leave her out of any problems he might have with the order of things. Creed disagrees.

"Okay, first: fuck this cousin of yours. This is more work than I want on a Sunday, but whatever, you're new at this. Let's split up the bag and I'll move everything else."

Cole and Shady take turns looking at one another, at Creed; their gazes join over a similar patch of ground.

Creed clasps his head as if to hold in an exploding brain. His fingers pull at his features as he drags the hands slowly down his face. "No you did not. Tell me you did not do what I am thinking you did. You do not leave product with anybody without pay, I don't care if it's your own mother and she gets paid tomorrow. That's like, —I can't believe I am hearing this. That's like *dealing lesson number one*."

"Where do you get off, Grady Creed?" Shady says. "It's Cole's stuff, his money, right, Cole? That caretaker left the bag for you. It was a gift, right?"

Before Cole can respond Creed begins his own tired explanations, speaking slowly and with distinct enunciation as if to a dim and struggling child that he has lectured countless times before. "Shady. What you are failing to understand is that this caretaker's pot was never his, see? It was *mine*, me as a representative of a community interest much larger than me—right?—and that crazy mofo just happened to have it *on* him because of certain mistakes made along the line of supply, certain unfortunate events perpetrated by somebody we all three know. *I'm* the one what left the bag for Cole—you get me, little girl? That's on me. Trying to help the little man. See how he handles a bit of good fortune."

"Then it was Greuel's, not yours," she says, and then Shady finger-quotes the air, "'Dealing lesson number one, never leave product without getting paid.'"

Creed ducks his head and spins away. His hand clutching the money slaps against his black-jeaned thigh, and his fingernails, strangely long and scrubbed clean, scratch at the back of his neck as he turns to her again. A tremor shakes through his shoulders.

"Cole and me came to an agreement last night. So *I* thought. Jesus this is like we don't none of us speak the same language here." He steps between them and taps his leg again, looks off into the woods. The muscle on his jaw beats a fast metronome, and Shady is struck by how thin and insubstantial the skin there is before it thickens coarsely into his neck. He starts to bob on the balls of his feet. Instinctively she backs up a step.

"And this is what I get. This is what I get for helping out a kid because I like him, feel like I owe him a hand up because of his brother. And this is how you're going to do me, freak eyes?" He glares at Cole, who doesn't look up. "Why don't you say anything? You so weak you have to let your girl here do the talking for you?"

Creed lunges forward, he smacks Cole across the forehead and sends him back onto one elbow. Cole raises his other arm to defend against the next blow but already Shady cannot stop herself, she's shoving Creed with both hands, shouting *What the fuck, Grady?!* and *Back the fuck off!* It's enough to get him to stop, and he stares at Shady with complete incomprehension.

"We're not alone out here, you *ass*hole," she chokes out, and it's blessedly true: from across the gully falls the stare of a neighbor—a tall towering mountain of a man with long blond-and-gray hair past his shoulders. He stands with a tool of iron as long as her arm, beside a pendular auto engine that twists on a chain from a thick tree branch. They all three turn to look at him. He moves behind the engine, begins to look it over.

Creed wrenches his arm from where she continued to grasp it. "I don't care if he's the mayor of the friggin' holler, that old man don't mean shit to me," he says loudly, as if he wants the man to hear him. But he does step back from Cole and the porch.

Across the way, the neighbor steadies the chain and solemnly considers the tool in his hand; he appears to be actively ignoring them now, intent on whatever he expects to do to that engine block. Creed sneers as he starts to return to the 4Runner in earnest, backward stepping. "Only reason I'm not cracking heads and taking the three of us to this cousin is 'cause Fleece was my main man, little brother," he says. "Neither one of you would want to even *hear my name* if this was any different. You picking up what I'm putting down?"

Cole is getting to his feet, swiping at the debris on his jeans. "I'm down with it, Grady."

"I hope that cousin comes through for you, I really do. But you best think how your brother was solid money ever time."

"If that's so true then where is he now?" Shady asks.

"Free as a bird or dead like I don't want to be. Do you all really want to fuckin' know? 'Cause I don't."

He slams his door and revs the engine once it starts, stereo blasting at aneurysm-promotion volume. He wheels backward out of the drive without a look behind him and purees the pavement once he hits the road.

•

It's a sullen silence in the truck, Cole driving. She's embarrassed to have left the bag with his cousin, but Shady's angry at Cole as well (she would like to tell him) for not knowing how to arrange things properly—angry at him for not knowing things he has no way to know. She stews over what she could tell him: that his cousin Sheldon is no partner; that it's a result of her own pluck and perseverance to have squeezed out the money she did manage to get. "How does my wall-eyed cousin pull a sweet piece of ass like you? You're doing him, right?" Sheldon had asked her. "It isn't your business but no, we're not," she'd said, and her saying it embarrassed her for some reason. "Cole is my friend, he's your family. You should be his friend, too." Sheldon had suggested she might like to screw a man who could bend both legs and meet her eyes with both of his. When she laughed in his face he persisted, describing how attentive and generous sex with him would be, and in the pall of that black-lighted room she had taken longer than usual to realize he was serious, and that they were alone. Sheldon was big enough to make her think twice over how quickly she could get out his door; upstairs the music boomed loud enough to cover a struggle.

What I could tell you, Cole Prather.

What she doesn't tell him is the transparency with which her life had appeared to her on the long drive back to Pirtle County. Since the dream routine every experience—even the most routine—had been thrown into stark relief; every action she took, every thought she had was imbued with ramification and meaning. She had driven through the night between tears and a flat numbness that overcame her in fits,

Shady freezing with the windows down but nauseated still by the heavy stink from a bag that was no longer even there. What did she think she was doing? Two-forty in the morning alone on the highway in a junk-heap of a truck with expired tags on behalf of a boy for whom she was still unclear how she felt. And *this was it,* if she wasn't careful this could be happening to her for the rest of her life, riding the tail end of a high in a rattling old pickup in the middle of the night with nerves frazzled from bad encounters with people who wished her not ill will, not good will, but no will at all.

It was like her father's admonitions and advice had merged into the voice within her own skull. She feared she'd become caught in some dread loop; rather than growing up she moved only from inexperience to inexperience. And *Shady Beck* was better than this; the better angels expected more of *Shady Beck* than this. All winter her mother had been gathering—quietly, on her youngest's behalf—course catalogs and applications for schools close to home, keeping the books within view on the kitchen counter but never alluding to them explicitly, never adding additional pressure to a daughter who, her mother would tacitly admit, she could see was in *a delicate situation,* and at a tender age, and who should take the time she needs. Several times her mother has voiced her desire to be supportive, *within reason.*

She had not been to worship in weeks. Even though Shady never considered herself a fervent Christian she did believe, and she did miss the fellowship—missed too the feeling that overtook her in the midst of congregational song, the sweep of a thousand voices singing in unison, and that sense of being part of a spirit much larger than her own. A good church service inspired in her sincere gratitude and a wholesome solidarity with whatever it was out there beyond her own paltry self; a something she knew now was certain to exist, no matter how abstract, for she had seen and touched its opposite, and she wanted to be on the side of the good. Yet she felt, vividly, the lack of goodness within her; felt it as distinctly and with as much yearning as how Cole must feel for his vanished brother. A brother who, she would like to point out, no matter how much you idolized him, had always been ready to abandon you.

What was it Grady Creed had said? *I don't want to know. Do you?*

She glances over at Cole. She doesn't think he's made any progress in discovering clue one about Fleece's fate. Could it be he did not really want to? She had believed he was different, but here he is, now, swimming furiously in the wake of his brother's life and taking it on as his own. On his exhausted face she can already begin to discern the pathways of future fatigue and worry lines. Rather than uncovering the truth and enacting some kind of vague vengeful justice, it's like Cole's carefully building an illusion he can live with, or in.

She's aware he knows none of what she is thinking; in his eyes her silence is simply Shady being emotional and intransigent, a girl who will get over her mood with sleep and time away. Recognizing this doesn't annoy her; rather, it spurs a tenderness that surprises her with its sudden intensity. How young they both are. Both of them are only getting started, each with a future ahead. Yet today *counts* (her father's voice again), this isn't the time for mistakes, today shapes who and where they'll be twenty years from now. If he could only adjust the lens through which he sees his world. If only he would step to one side and *look*, he would realize he owes nothing to Fleece or his mother. Shady almost reaches across the gearshift to pass the back of her hand against the rusty stubble of his face, a gesture she knows would change the air between them entirely, cause him to turn and smile.

But she doesn't. She's too worn to make that small gesture. She thought to do it, and that's enough. He leans over to kiss her but she's already out. He says he'll call her later; she tells him to do what he wants. She does not look back as she hurries to the house, even though she can hear the truck's coughing idle linger in the drive, waiting expectantly for her to turn and wave goodbye. But Shady's gone already. She doesn't feel like she should have to say so.

Lyda's wagon is in the driveway when he returns home. The man she slept with must have been something special for her to stay the night—usually she gave some stranger run of the house for a weekend or two, until the inevitable blew up and she kicked him out. Whatever. All Cole wants is a long, scalding shower, and to shove the night he just lived through into some hidden and forgotten cranny in his mind. He wants the water hotter than he can stand it, so hot the ceiling's loose plaster shines with steam and the walls run amber from his mother's nicotine. The mirror so clouded he won't have to look at himself.

She's not in the kitchen and he doesn't call out. He tosses his mud-caked boots to the corner on the pile of accumulated diving gear and does not think over how long it has been since he used it. In the bathroom he flips on the shower to get the hot water going. The spray is freezing when he tests it and he pulls back to wait, takes off his sweatshirt (noting then the sticky grime on his hands) and rests his backside against the sink, the mirror out of his line of sight. He studies the mold settled in the corners of the shower stand, it looks like discarded coffee grinds, most likely something off of him—pill-head swinger ride or not, Lyda is a woman who likes her bathroom clean.

No steam yet. Sometimes it takes a while. He switches off the cold water entirely, leaves on only the hot.

He can't blame Shady; he shouldn't have sent her to Sheldon, and she shouldn't have seen Grady Creed smack him like a disobedient child while Cole sat there and took it. Everything is beginning to feel like a test he's unprepared for and fails at with each new, unforeseen level. He is learning about Fleece in ways he would prefer not to have learned; unsettling things that, however vaguely, make him feel somewhat better about himself—at some fundamental level he has a conscience. He's unsure his brother does, or did. But he knows Fleece never involved Shady in the work.

He tests the water again and the cold shocks his hand. He switches the water off and stares at the handle for a time as though he can will it to find heat. Then, opening the bathroom door, he meets his mother nearly chest to chest.

"Pilot's out," she says, already holding up a flashlight. "Do your mom a favor?"

As he reaches for the flashlight she steps back, taking him in. "Whoa, baby, let me get a look at you. What did you get into last night, weren't you with Shady? Where'd you all hide the body?"

It's like a crucial piece of rigging behind his face snaps from the strain of keeping it in place. He can't find his voice for a moment, though his mouth hangs open large enough to pop a golf ball into it.

His mother titters, pats his cheek several times. "Did you two at least put a blanket down? Don't you have a place to go?"

"I should be asking you, ma. What brings you home after morning sunlight?" It's a phrase she used to say with feigned admonishment to Fleece when he was barely a teenager, rampant on the terra with a will of his own Lyda never tried to rein in.

"Honey it is a wicked world out there and I don't have to tell you." She hands him the flashlight with a slurry smile, swaying; she leans back into the hallway wall, and by the flush in her cheeks and the rime rimming her eyes he can tell pharmaceuticals are filling her with love. "But sometimes you can almost think, maybe it's not so wicked in spots. You wouldn't believe what I've been up to. And you wouldn't approve."

"Try me," Cole says, but her eyes close and her head glides in off-measure from side to side, her coy smile making her a young girl keeping a secret she will wait to tell.

"It's a new day. Spring is here and can't you just feel it? I hardly slept. Everything might be all right after all."

"What everything? Fleece?"

She shrugs as though suddenly sleepy. A great yawn reddens her face and she doesn't cover her mouth until the yawn is finished. Her hand dismisses him from there. "You get the heat going. I'm thinking a cup of tea, myself."

Her purse sits open on the kitchen table; among the sundries he spots the black film case where she keeps pills on the go. Within the assortment of sizes, shapes, and colors, he recognizes a few oxy-eighties and swallows two with water so cold it hurts his teeth. His body feels tender from what he put it through last night, and the little sleep he caught on the concrete out front only settled the soreness deeper into his bones. He left his sweatshirt in the bathroom and he's too lazy to go for his boots. Outside he quick-steps across the wet grass in loose socks and under the thin T-shirt his skin tightens with the rude cold of the March morning.

Beneath the house the air is dank and chilly as an icebox. Cole hasn't felt properly warm since he and Shady were at it on Spunk's couch. He rubs his hands over bare arms. Here it's the same smell as by the river last night: moist, mineral, silty. A shiver runs through him. He dismisses images from his mind as they come.

He never knew Hardesty. The man had been more of a dark specter over his childhood rather than an actual person, a bogeyman he should feel relieved to have lifted from his spirit.

The pilot lighter rests on the brick ledge that gives to the crawl space accessing the pipes. Cole kills the gas and waits for the air to clear. He squats with the small of his back against the brick, then sits to ease the pressure on his frail knee, and stares into the dark. The chill against his back starts an ache in his lungs and he coughs into the damp.

The body had been heavier than he would have imagined. Hardesty was a big man, well over six feet tall and thick across the shoulders and torso, a body of hefty muscle gone slack, age-fatted into simple bulk. His head was large and wide-boned as the rest of him, great in diameter and with teeth that looked chiseled from some dense material found in deep woodside, stone or clay or live oak hewn by rough tools. It was difficult to carry him. Creed had left the task to Cole and Spunk, leading them into a field of tall saw-grasses, a spade slung over his shoulder as casual as a kid with a baseball bat. He moved in lumbering spurts, preoccupied, as though trying to divine a specific location from hints on the wind.

"Could've pulled us up closer," Spunk complained. "What four-wheel-drive's for, I thought." Silently Cole agreed; his knee burned like a tight ball of fire, and with each step Hardesty's bare heels, sticking out of the rolled tarp, thumped against his neck like clubs. "It's all grass, you could make this ground easy."

"Yeah—we could cut a nice new trail for anyone to explore, right on," Creed answered, searching. "They should put you in charge. I always slept real sound in jail."

Their shoes sank in a loamy gumbo that sucked harder at their soles the closer they got to the river; Cole smelled the Ohio before he could hear it. By the time the grass cleared around an oxbow of stagnant black water, so still its surface perfectly mirrored the bone-bright gash of moon, they were all high-stepping against the pull of the mud. Twice they dropped the body, Hardesty and the tarp taking on water and weight each time. Cole's back was shrieking.

"Smells like a sewer out here," Spunk said. "We going to sink him in the river?"

The Ohio appeared as an expanse of pure black stretching endlessly before them, and they set the body on the rocky outcropping— gently, as if now they were afraid of hurting him. Above, the naked branches of white sycamores and other trees Cole couldn't identify rose and dipped in the wind, like giant fingers conjuring spells, or curses, he couldn't guess which. The wind itself moved like a bodied presence through the grasses and it was much colder here. His sweaty skin crawled where his clothing stuck to him. Hardesty's great teeth gleamed in the moonlight beneath the cavity where his nose should have been; a sight that made him queasy each time he ventured a look at it. Yet he couldn't stop stealing glimpses of it.

Grady Creed stood on a berm with fists at his waist, facing the river as though in survey of a great victory that had occurred there, the spade angled from his hip sharp-edged and silhouetted like a dangerous tail. He set one foot on the bleached trunk of an elm weatherstripped of bark and gleaming like prehistoric bone. Cole and Spunk both clutched their thighs in each hand, bent and gasping. Creed sniggered.

"Sink him in the river? Boys," he said cheerfully, hoisting the spade, "this county sits on limestone bedrock. Now you'll find limestone bedrock is a great natural accomplice to criminal mischief. Tonight you learn the proper method of body disposal in a river environment."

He told them to pay attention because this would be quick. Sinkholes provide readymade graves, he explained, with half the work done already. "But what makes a sinkhole—either of you know?" Neither of them did. "Water erosion. Sinkholes let rainwater find its way underground. For us that means once the body's out of sight you got to worry it might still move around down there, end up on a fishhook or in some noodler's hands. We don't want to encourage this thing to float. Why's a body float?"

"Gas," Cole said.

Creed nodded as he set a foot near Hardesty's hip. "Basically we're whisky stills full of fermenting juice. I've seen it, blows you up like fuckdoll. You want to allow a place for the gas to get out, like this." He plunged the spade into Hardesty's belly. Then he widened the cut by shunting the blade back and forth, an earthy squish and suck sound that Cole knew instantly was in his head now and forever. "But shit still moves down there, we get floods and all, right? You got to make sure that if anybody ever finds this they still can't figure out who it was. How you think we do that?"

"Fingerprints?" from Spunk.

"Good. We take the fingers. And?"

He turned his attention to Cole, enjoying his personification of the attentive professor in the field, but Cole was hardly there anymore. He was hardly anywhere, he felt as empty and purposeful as anything else around them that wasn't speaking: the wind, the grass, the moving river. A rain owl hooted its strange and unique call.

"*Teeth*, good. You don't have to take everything, just mess it up enough so nobody can match this mouth with a record somewheres. Though I doubt our caretaker spent a lot of time at the dentist. Still."

He handed Spunk the spade and told him to gather the fingers, a job Spunk applied himself to with merry diligence. *Sick!* he exclaimed at the feel of the first thumb falling away. Quickly he finished one hand, and then inspected the small pile gathered beside his boot. "You know what, these would make a real fancy and powerful necklace," he said. "I should make me a necklace and hang it over my bedroom door, keep away the evil spirits."

"No, you're not. You'll give them to me, you demented fuck," Creed said, shaking out a plastic bag. "Cole, you get the teeth."

Cole snapped to at the sound of his name. "I don't think so, man."

"Sure you are. You're going to do his teeth or I send you in there after him." Creed stepped up to Cole's face, his forehead closing in near enough to press against his own. He smelled tobacco and ale over the river stench.

"C'mon, Cole," Spunk said. "Come on, man, he's dead already."

Cole remained bent at the waist with his hands clutching his knees, breathing deeply through his mouth. Breathing had become difficult for him, a deep wheeze had begun to web in the back of his lungs. He didn't move.

"See, now's when it's good to have some Little Kings in the belly," said Creed. When he spoke again, after a pause, his voice had lost its mocking tone, turning almost brotherly, almost gentle and commiserating. "First time's always a bitch. But you got to do it, every man does his share. Arley told me to make sure you do something. Specific instructions."

"Carrying the body aint enough?"

In his home Hardesty had remained with his head thrown back, lips smacking at something tasteless, his throat working noisily. He blinked at the ceiling, and Cole had watched as the blinking slowed. Nobody spoke for some time. As if for no reason save to break the silence, Hardesty murmured, "My nose."

Mule was cleaning the saw with a paper towel; he had begun to wipe down each of his tools with some kind of bleach solution that sharpened the air, returning each piece to its respective pocket. Arley Noe hovered nearby, out of Mule's way.

"Goddamn you, Arley Noe." Hardesty's voice sounded strange, flatter than before. "My very own nose."

"You don't need it no more," Arley said. He sniffed the air above the man, who continued to face the ceiling as though lost of the energy to raise his head. "Smells bad in here anyway, you're not missing a thing."

"God damn you. Arley. Just—God damn you."

His head jerked up as he coughed out a clump of what looked like blackberry compote. The jelly caught and hung pendulous from the whorls of beard even as his head fell back again. The substance rolled over itself slow and hypnotic, shifting shape as it wormed from whisker to whisker, the lamp light shifting over the surface as it wandered, wavered, until its own weight pulled it onto the floor with a dull splat. Noe patted him on the shoulder, several times, finally leaving his hand there, squeezing the shoulder in gentle rhythm, in some lost gesture of consolation.

"Don't you worry about me and God, caretaker," he said. "We damned one another a long time ago."

Beside the sinkhole Creed handed Cole the spade. He hardly felt the tool in his hands; his hands were only tangentially his anymore, as if the cold had taken all feeling from them. Creed nudged him forward and Cole obeyed. He felt for the body through the extension of the steel tool, straddled it, and located the dull and hefty teeth within the open mouth. With the spade's edge he pushed back Hardesty's hoary upper lip and settled it on his gums. He braced one foot on the back of the blade.

"Go on, Cole, we're watching," Spunk said.

In the quiet of their waiting, the single rain owl called out: *who spooks you, who spooks you-all?*

He pressed down with all his weight. The bones gave so easily that he fell forward past the body, Creed catching him with a hoot and then passing him on with a hearty smack on the back. Cole continued forward and did not turn around; he made the edge of the water and stood in the gaps between the rocks, inhaling deeply sludgy river fumes. The cold river began to seep into his boots, paining the bones in his feet. He wrapped his arms about his head like a kerchief, chinned his chest. The rain owl called again.

Who spooks you? Who spooks you-all?

It used to feel so damn *good* to breathe, Lawrence Greuel thinking how nostalgic a man can get for all the little things he took for granted once they're gone forever. Now he's no longer sure he feels gratitude to even *be* breathing. He exhales a chorus of high pitches, a swarm of distant seagulls range throughout his lungs, his chest sounds as if he's got the friggin' Gulf of Mexico trapped in there—inhale, and it's juddering waves against the shore; exhale, and the seabirds take flight, raging riot, their beaks gnashing at one another's wings. Yet he feels no pain. There is a not-unpleasant numbness, a disassociation; he's surprised, when he moves, to see his limbs respond. Like the entirety of *Lawrence Greuel* has retreated into this soft blur within his head, and only in his head does he perceive sensation: a firm and disagreeable pinch pressing his skull cap. Like it's been forced into a hat too small. That, and the constant watering of his eyes—particularly the left, which stings to boot. Who knew the eyes could be so prodigious, so productive.

He blinks, and a puddle expands against the bridge of his nose. A tissue comes into view and sops it gently; he pinches the eye shut and the tissue drags over the skin and lashes with evident care. A woman's touch.

"Was I asleep?" Honestly unsure, and the fact frightens him. Gray light fills the thin curtains over the window where he could swear it had been dark a moment before, the Tiffany lamp casting a rose blush against the beige linen there. Now it's gray light luminous behind the curtain and no lamp at all.

"Only about a day," Lyda says. She lifts his arm as though to take his pulse, but she's only turning his wrist to check his watch. "Near a day and a half, truth be."

She crosses the room to toss the tissue into the trashcan by the bureau near the window. She wears cutoffs and sandal-toed heels, a woman who always shied from sensible shoes when she bothered to wear them at all. Between her knees he sees the trashcan overfilled with tissues and Lyda bends from the waist to pull out the bag, giving Greuel a cheesecake shot of her legs and fine calves, the form-fitting shorts outlining her vulva swollen as a primate's; he'd heard tales of Lyda's fat pussy and the sight of it outlined there fills him with unfettered gratitude. How could a pill junkie still look that good, and at her age? Goddamn if God was indiscriminate in wasting great genes on useless people.

The tears stream freely past his cheek and into his ear. "I remember when you ran around without enough clothes on to wad a shotgun."

"Ha," she says, caught midstride.

"Don't look like you've found much more to wear since then."

"I wore this in high school. Any lady my age would be proud to show that off." She spins on the floor with the garbage bag held out, a swaying silent bell, then tugs at the cuffs of her shorts. "These jeans were my daddy's. He used to call me Little Old Nasty Thing."

"Clara was like that. Not nasty—we buried her in a dress she said was her favorite from high school."

"Clara wasn't forty years old, that's nothing to brag on. Maybe not nasty but she was no Virgin Mary either. And I don't care to hear about her even if I'm standing in her house."

"*My* house," Greuel coughs, and the coughs rake him over for a full minute. His body shudders and quakes and unfortunately feels all his own again. "Everything from the gate out front to the river is mine, heaven high and hell deep." He settles back, sucks for breath, listens to the seagulls deep inside. Lyda's heels clack down the hallway. "That was near twenty years ago, you still hold that against her?"

"You don't?"

•

He must have passed out again. He didn't hear her leave or return but there Lyda is, standing empty-handed and smelling of cigarettes, a silhouette haloed entirely by outside light.

"I don't like talking about your wife. I know it worked out best for me in the end, but still. You talk like she was some kind of saint and she sure was not that."

"Don't I know it!" He coughs again, once, and hesitates with his fist before his mouth, expectant—but his lungs settle. "Can't tell you how much I wished you'd wanted to balance the cheat. But nah, you were too crafty for that, you saw your way out. One wicked crafty lady."

"Don't blame me for what you wanted to do."

He looks at his watch but cannot read the face of it, his vision too blurry even if he shuts the running eye. He looks down the blanket that covers him, molded to his naked body in relief. He is very thin. His bare feet on the armrest display purple sores he hasn't seen before. He wiggles the remaining toes, sees them move, amazed he controls them somehow still.

Lyda bends again, this time shaking a smoke out of her pack by the window. "It's not the doing that bothered me. It was the acting like he wasn't, like it wasn't none of my business."

"Dumbest thing Bethel Skaggs ever did, out of a lifetime of dumb things, was take out an insurance policy."

"You silly man, you think he ever thought of insurance? Any wife knows how to sign her husband's name."

He admires this, her worldliness as matter-of-fact as weather. But talk of the past tires him—it's all over and will never change. He wonders how many days, hours, are still allotted him. Time feels like a bank account with dwindling funds and no further deposits.

"Why don't you sidle over here and drop your daddy's britches, let me get a good sniff of something other than all this medicine?"

She doesn't even turn, searching for her lighter. "Old man, you are in no shape to be thinking on snatch." She gives her hips a little one-two shake and winks at him as she heads for the door, and secretly he's relieved by her refusal, resigned to empty bravado.

"Got nothing else worth thinking about." Greuel shifts his eyes back to his covers and the tears, emotionless, emptied of any signifier save biological process, run onto his cheeks. "All my life I resented not being a thinner handsome man and now look at me, bet I could fit in one leg of my trousers and but all I can do is piss honey."

"I believe it do smell like it," Lyda laughs. She holds up her cigarette, says she's going outside.

•

The sulfur of a lit match fills his nostrils. Pakpao is speaking quick in that half-talk, half-song speech of hers. That she's here means dialysis and he's glad for it, he feels better for hours after, almost normal, like normal and just getting over the flu. It's the best he can hope for, it's what passes for normal now. He says as much to Arley Noe, though he can't locate him exactly. He recognizes the dark tobacco.

"Look at this mess," his hands waving over his body.

"I will not deny," Noe says. Greuel sniffs him out against the doorframe, spectral and dissolute, hands plunged in pockets and the hand-rolled smoke dangling from his mouth, disheveled in his shapeless suit and trilby. Looks no different from the day he sauntered into Greuel's Danville pawn shop circa 1960, dropping pilfered candlesticks, wedding china, and a TT-30 semi-automatic pistol he claimed to have brought back from Korea as he teased out the morphine habit into its eighth year. As Pakpao continues her chatter-song at him—*outside with you cigarettes, outside!*—his face and eyes feature a fantastic, bored melancholy.

"How long till you're clear?"

"You'll come back?"

The eyes shifting from Pakpao's mouth to the floor being the most he could expect. "Give me a couple of hours."

"You go outside, you going to kill your friend," says Pakpao.

Noe smiles around the cigarette and does not answer. "Nah, I don't do him no more favors."

Greuel had figured Arley would be first to go. He had looked forward to discovering what-all the older man had kept hidden during his lifetime—to discovering how many different ways his friend and partner had screwed him over. That's only one more mystery he'll never know the solution to now, just as he'll never understand why did Clara stray, or what made Fleece Skaggs, the son he should have had, steal so much as to nearly break him. Shouldn't a dying man receive some enlightenment at the end? Justice comes maybe in the next life, here all we get are guesses and the Law, Greuel's father had told him. He'd spent his life rendering his own justice to prove the old man wrong. If not justice, at least judgment. But no answers to the questions that matter to him.

•

He wakes again to raised voices outside the house. It's night, the curtains hang flat and colorless with it. Pakpao's gone, the portable dialysis machine nestles in its corner draped in opaque plastic. He hears Mule's foggy drawl out there, and a cawing laugh that could be either his son's or Grady Creed. Then the voices fall too low for him to tease out. His gummy eyes make the room look like it's behind distended glass. They've left him alone in here. He hates being alone and they know it and they've left him, sick as he is. Everyone sticking around to see what can be plucked from the carcass.

The realization hurts him. It's no surprise and he would be the same if it were one of them stinking on this couch. Still he snorts at how hurtful this is. Of all the things to be affected by . . .

A few words outside make it to his ears: *I don't care what you need to talk to him about—*. That one's Lyda, she'll stay reliable as a dog as long as his amber-bottle array supplies her reward.

"I am not dead yet," Greuel calls out as loudly as he can. The coughs wring his body like he's enclosed in some great angry fist. He pulls up further in the couch, covers his hideous feet. "Where the hell is everybody?"

The front door opens. Out there the night's black is entire. That preacher boy enters first, decked out in a light gray double-breasted suit bought off the rack, no tie, hair cut close almost in military style. At the sight of Greuel in the pullout bed Ponder hesitates, his fingertips against the doorframe as though he needs to haul himself in. Mule's long face appears above and behind him, eyebrows curled curious over what to make of the boss.

"You got him up, may as well go in, then," he says, nudging the preacher hard enough to force him right up to Greuel's feet.

Lyda slips in and shuts the door in Mule's towering face. "You want I get rid of this guy?"

"Grab yourself a chair, preacher. Grab me a bottle of water while you're at it, why don't you."

Ponder slides one from the dinner table and places it near the pullout but doesn't sit down. He hikes up a foot on the seat and sets his elbow on his knee, giving Greuel full view of loose dress socks gathered around the ankle, the shin pale and hairless, the bottom curve of a dark green tattoo snaking up under the cuff. Ponder's hands knead one another and he stares at Greuel with a strange swirling mixture of outrage and empathy, the battle of emotions apparent on his face.

"What brings the good man of faith into such a den of iniquity, Preacher? It's too late in the game to discuss the future of my soul," he laughs. "I got this Indonesian nurse comes in, she tells me I'm half to hell already. Like it's some kind of joke. Laughs like it's the funniest thing ever she heard. What you think of that?"

Ponder opens his mouth but no sound escapes. Lyda announces she'll get the water and does Ponder want some. He waves her off without looking. His eyebrows raise, hover, and then settle. The mouth stays open.

"You come to see for yourself?"

"I didn't expect to see," and he hesitates, tucks his chin into his neck as though to swallow the words before they got away from him. Yet words come. "I didn't realize you were this ill." His eyes scan the hospice equipment of IV towers and myriad prescriptions, the dialysis machine, settling finally on Greuel's naked skin as yellow as a dry gourd. His discomfort fills Greuel with a perverse pride.

"Would've thought you'd be used to sights like me, in your line of work. Don't nobody die in your church?"

"We have matters to straighten out," Ponder says. "I'm sorry to

find you like this. I am. But there are matters here. We need to renegotiate our deal."

"Renegotiate."

"Can we talk frankly?"

Lyda returns and Ponder straightens; he turns away, fiddling with
his trouser leg so that the cuff falls correctly over his loafer. She has
the bottled water and another tissue that she presses against Greuel's
seeping eye. She's wearing full jeans now, and not so tight to her
body—Greuel notices with a frown. She opens the bottle and hands
him a single tablet and he tells her to double the dose. Grab a couple
for yourself while you're at it, he says, a small tip for the service. She
thanks him and does, wily enough to not let him see how many she
throws down.

In her chair near the window Lyda starts to flip through a magazine. Ponder stares at her, silent. Soon she begins to hum a melody.

"Things change," Greuel says. "We're friends again."

"I can see."

"You can talk frank as you want, this is my house."

"I will. Listen, I appreciate your help in getting us a home for
my ministry. I do. And we're grateful for the land trust, don't get me
wrong, we fully understand—"

"You couldn't have done it without us. You'd still be preaching
how God wants us to prosper in a warehouse off some pea-gravel road
without me. I know this. Why don't you say it, too?"

"It's a worthy message that needs to be heard." He pauses. "I won't
lie, I knew who you were. You and that Arley Noe."

"Everybody does. Why don't you just say it once for me. I'd really
like to hear it. From your mouth. Where would that church of yours
be without me and my generous nature? I sold eight horses to make
that deal go through. All I had."

"I didn't ask you to sell your horses."

Greuel dismisses the thought with a gesture. "My son would've
sold them anyway. Horses scare him, they have more sense than he
does."

Ponder slips both hands into his pockets and stares at the empty
chair between them. It's a worthless wooden chair, one of four Shaker

rip-offs Clara bought early in their marriage and for that reason alone he never had them replaced. The suit's all right, not flashy like you find on silver-haired TV gospel cons, but still: a quality fabric. And yet there lingers that rat-running-off-the-street stink about the guy that Greuel cannot stand—he's a user, a fiend, someone Greuel's boys would sell to, once, and that stink never wears off. What fool gets a tattoo on his shin?

"Go on, man. Say it for the benefit of my dying ears."

"Without your generosity we would still be holding services in an old warehouse. Satisfied?"

Greuel slaps his puffy palms together and falls back into the soft comfort of his pillows. He feels as alive as he has in months. Like the weeks of corticosteroids have only now begun to kick in. As he sighs in satisfaction, even the seagulls in his chest are silent. "Used to be an auction warehouse for tobacco, you know. My own daddy sold his whisky there while he negotiated prices for his bosses. Funny place to make into a freak-show church of God."

"There's nothing freak show about it, it's a legitimate place of worship. Any place people gather to worship is legitimate."

"Wouldn't be legitimate in this house, I bet."

"Listen, my ministry is not the issue. We help people, we do good work. You are undermining this, you know you are. You mock our efforts. I'm sure you know what I've had to overcome. Many of my parishioners are fighting the same battle. It's a big part of our outreach. So imagine my feelings when I learn my church is selling the same shit I'm counseling people to relinquish." As Ponder speaks his face reveals the difficulty he is having in fathoming such information, no less an impossibility than if Christ had returned to inform him that he was going about his faith and service all wrong, that Christ was here to tell Gil Ponder that He had never known him.

"Nobody's selling my drugs at your church. Nobody I know of. I'd know."

"Our vans are used for *youth group* activities. We pick up seniors to bring them to Sunday worship. Deliver books to rural schools. Our softball teams use these vans for away games. They are not for hauling contraband all over the state."

"I thought you were into community outreach."

"Larry, please."

"Ah, that's still Mister Greuel to you. Listen. Sounds to me like you have some kind of internal trouble in that congregation of yours. What do you think I can do? Look at me. So much of me's seeped into this couch they'll have to burn it along with my body."

"I came here to talk this out. You want to make it a game, fine. What's keeping me from going to the police then? Is that what you want?"

"What I want is to breathe easy and get up and piss on my own, that's what I want. What you *don't* want is to be forever known as the ex-junkie preacher who financed his fine car and mortgage and big church complex on reefer and pills. Am I right? I've got this certainty, see, sick as I am, that this isn't what you're gonna do. 'Christ World Emergent Hauls Weed for Jesus.' I can see the headline perfect in my head."

Ponder spins to check on Lyda, to gauge her degree of attention to their discussion. Greuel smiles to see her sitting upright but with her head back, dimpling the curtain, her eyes closed. "You still with us Lyda?" he asks.

She doesn't move her head from the curtain. She has a lovely throat, he thinks.

"I'm right here, singing in the sunshine."

He reassigns his smile to Ponder. "That sinking feeling you have in your belly is what people in trade call 'buyer's remorse.' I believe the gentleman you want to speak to is Arley Noe. But good luck talking to him. He can be difficult to find."

"I'll find him." His voice dies away on a grave inflection, earnest certainty giving way to speculation, and then unease, all on three syllables spoken.

"Sure you will. I'll even help you. So you'll remember me kindly after I'm gone." He indicates the address book on the table, has Ponder bring it to him. He flips through the pages and pockets. "One last little tittie-twist from beyond the grave. Blue Note'll appreciate that." Greuel asks for a pen and tears out a scrap of paper that he hands to the preacher. "Make sure you get to him in a lot of public. I know Arley like I know the sick in my own body. Heaven may await you, preacher, but I doubt you're in any hurry to get there yourself."

Ponder's eyes sweep the paper; he slips it into his inside breast pocket and then straightens his jacket. His mouth moves from a grim tight line to lips curling as he sucks his teeth.

"We're finished here, I'm guessing. Can I do anything for you?"

"I'm past help. You're not one of them healer types, are you? Not your gig."

"I was thinking more of a prayer," Ponder says, looking over Lyda, his head bent awkward in observation. She has not quite nodded off, yet she's not quite *there*—again her eyes have closed; her lips pucker and relax, then pucker and relax again. "A blessing, that kind of thing."

"I got the TV for entertainment. More than five hundred channels there."

"You could use some mercy. If ever I saw a man who needed the gift of grace and mercy."

But still he is not looking at Greuel; evidently he is waiting for Lyda to notice him. His gaze personifies soulful concern, a gaze Greuel imagines the man practices in a mirror—as though Ponder believes if he stares long enough she'll feel it, or else will notice the conversation has died; but many minutes pass, and Lyda shows no interest. Her lips pucker, and then a brief grin forms beneath her closed eyes.

When Ponder steps out the door a warm breeze sweeps in and over Greuel huddled on the hideaway bed, country air sifting the oily strands of hair on his head and bringing a fresh smell of grass and brisk spring evening that briefly overcomes the odors of his own decay. He inhales it with the avidity of the fiend in full jones and feels an exhilarating jolt of life. The sensation does not linger. The door clacking shut nudges Lyda from her reveries and she looks toward the sound, and then, blinking, smiles at Greuel.

"How many did you take?"

"Of what?" Lyda asks, honestly curious to know.

Greuel cackles. "Goddamn but that was fun. I am really going to miss this."

On the road Ponder thrashes his palms against the steering wheel as though the wheel were hot enough to forge into some new and as-yet-to-be-envisioned form. He shifts and misses the next gear and the engine roars in neutral—and he then blesses the stick with the same violence, batting and thrusting it about until he finds a gear and the Acura lurches with a screech. The rubber catching the road nearly throws him past the curb and he composes himself for a few silent seconds. Then rage and the familiar frustration at his own gullible stupidity and arrogance and ungraspable fate get him pounding the wheel again, the dashboard, stomping against the footrest and swerving into the next empty lane. He corrects the car and drives, the pitted terrain twitching his headlights over the verdant farm hills, and launches a scream that he pushes farther than his lungs can allow, gawing until his throat feels about to herniate.

The road before him swims up a stream. He swallows air, blinks; his breathing slows to normal. Tears burn his eyes. He's in no condition to be operating this fine machine. It calms him to realize he is together enough to acknowledge as much. To damage this machine in any way, alone on a spring night, would bring yet more board scrutiny. Already he's got elders questioning his judgment with the ministry's growth and finances and general shepherding. "It's important to me that we act as careful stewards of the future of this church," he heard at the last meeting. "We cannot betray the generosity of our congregants.

We won't have Brother Gil forever." The main worship center isn't close to finished yet and already Ponder can feel the shifts, everyone jockeying for position. He's heard open whispers that on the cusp of forty their leader has never married, never fathered children. As if that's his fault?!

Ponder's initial impulse had been to lease the drool-inducing Acura NSX. The idea had thrown him into a real interior wrestling match, debating with himself the pros and cons of the message an evangelical driving that wild ride might encourage. He wanted to attract youth to CWE, especially boys—who require a *great influence* to master themselves—and boys in this corner of Kentucky love fast cars. But his accountant responded with perplexity and confessed it was difficult already to guarantee the ministry's tax-exempt status, and Brother Gil went the practical route, settling for the two-door coupe. A solid decision he credited to the Man upstairs, who tested his flock with their weaknesses but showed the way out, too, if you paid attention. And even still: the coupe has a twenty-four valve V6 engine that can surge to sixty under eight seconds, so the horses had balls beneath the sensible elegance. A decision to be proud of, thus. A reminder that he has made, in the past and therefore giving no reason to doubt his ability to continue into the future, sound decisions.

But he feels like testing factory claims that a 145-mph top speed can be reached by the time he locates a conveniently sturdy wall. He knows this is impulse; knows too that impulse is the domain of the demonic creature that enjoys dominion over this world—it had been precisely this revelation, connecting such impulses to the Gospel's demonic rulers, that had started him on his redemptive journey. *Impulse* is in the body; it seduces with its suggestion that one is not responsible for its origin: impulse comes, the body acts. That's the power of Paul's Evil One, "the god of this age." It's the powerlessness before such impulse that one gives up to Christ, to God, to manage. *Consideration* of what impulse demands sucks away its power, hinders its intensity, and in that distancing instant a soul's bodily mind can turn from the seduction of self-harm to grace.

Ponder had discovered this path—received it—while lying on a steep grass bank above an open drainage ditch, hidden from the road by cornering himself against nineteenth-century culvert limestones. It was morning, early enough that dew clung to his neck, the summer sun bright enough to erase the treetops from his eyes. He was coming down from what would turn out to be his third-to-last spike when a calm, resolute voice inside him asked: *Why are you hiding?*

He looked to see who had spoken and saw he was alone. I'm not hiding, he thought—and understood his own thoughts were lying to him. Each car that passed or pedestrian that strode by above his head, were they to look, would find him as nothing less than hiding. But he was in full morning sunlight. Yet he felt he was in hiding and too felt dread at being found—by whom? By the sun, it seemed. All this starting a message from the Holy Spirit direct to Gilly Ponder, junkie city ham, near twelve years ago.

So no high-speed kisses into sturdy walls tonight. God sends trials he expects us to overcome. Often opportunities arrive in the guise of trial. He eases off the accelerator and listens to the engine's sighing down to purring revolutions; waits for some hint from the Holy Spirit or his subconscious (sometimes he wonders what the difference between them is) as to what he should do next. And as he marks that moment of call and communion he spots the looming glow high afloat in the starry night sky, a beacon burning orange near the interstate ramp, beckoning travelers to pull in for food, fuel, showers.

Ghostly luminescence haloes the gas pumps and quik-mart entrance, that cold blue-tinted halide light that makes everyone look like they're on chemo. He winds past the pump islands toward the long skirt where semis sit dark save for amber running lights. He parks in that near-seclusion—shielded from the main building by an eighteen-wheeler carrying a bevy of makes and models and, if he's correct, even different years—and quits the engine, window down, listening to soft-pop hits of the seventies from the station's speakers warp and woof on the interstate winds.

The music stops for a bored voice to announce *Pump six ready for fillup thank you,* and then after a static clap that shivers his spine the music returns, Glenn Frey counseling them all to take it easy.

Past the semi he hears rough laughter, young boys ribbing one another over tall tales. Ponder can't see them but he hears one voice, animated, perhaps acting out a story. Then the harsh laughter again. When Ponder opens his door and the bell chimes he hesitates, uncertain what exactly he intends to do; he's neither hungry nor thirsty, doesn't need a Kentucky ball cap or T-shirt, and never made use of pep pills. Once he shuts the door with his hip, the laughter stops. From behind the semi two thin shadows and another round one appear, backlit by a hovering light, mounds of drift stone pocked with weeds and cement chunks bright behind them.

"Evening, gentlemen," says Ponder, flipping his keys around his ring finger.

"You miss the lot, mister? You can park closer to the grocery there," one says, arm aloft pointing the way, a forty-ounce bottle of malt liquor dangling half full.

Brother Ponder leans his elbow on the Acura's hood. Now these are boys he knows. Although he can't see their faces he could guess each one's life and family history with fair accuracy, homegrown roads to quiet failure as much as his own had been. "I wasn't looking for groceries," he says. "Thought I'd stretch my legs a bit. They sell forties in there now? Pirtle County's still dry isn't it?"

"We're not selling if you're asking," the boy answers.

Ponder takes the risk and walks toward them. "Anything else you might be selling, then?" He pulls out the gold money clip, the bills folded thick enough to impress any kid who lives by five and twenties. He counts out forty dollars and asks what that might get him. The boys eye the money. "Take it, finger it, there's nothing wrong with good American bills." The boys scan the lot, Ponder's car, their eyes practiced in catching any hint of authority or badge interference. A silence extends between them.

Oh, but this is what he needed; this is what he is here on this plane of reality to do. The boy shakes his head and shrugs. "You some kind of strange dude," he says, but the three of them begin moving back to the mound of cement blocks and broken concrete, Brother Gil following. He welcomes the thrill of recognition, elated—it has been ages since he got to work like this, one on one, *fishing for men* as it were. *Command them to do good, to be rich in good deeds, and to be generous and willing to share*, Timothy wrote. "Where around here you from?" one of the boys thinks to ask. It's then that Brother Gil takes out his business card and begins to tell them his story. "From the city, but it doesn't matter where I come from. What matters is the prosperity in which I'm living. I always have a pocket full of money because I've learned to live in grace with the Almighty, who wants to see his children enjoy the abundance of His creation. Wouldn't you boys like to own a car like mine? What if I told you I can prove God wants you to have one, too?"

•

She lists deep in restless dream, a dream teeming with morning light, blinding columns of honey gold embracing her body where she lies in a verdant meadow on lush grass, grass as dense as the hair of her first-born son, grass she fingers for the scratch of their parchment blades. She grips a tuft in her fist and tests the roots. Trees shush nearby, she feels their proximity but cannot seem to open her eyes enough to see them.

I got a phone call today. Sitting there eating good eggs and the phone rings. You know about that.

How would I know who calls you? Look at me.

Because of the light—that peculiar light specific to dreams, so bright it bleaches out all shadow, she cannot unfold her eyes. Spring is a smell, a lime green pixie dust in her nose, it feels like an army of tiny miners chipping away in there.

You used to be able to take a joke.

I never. Not when I'm about making money.

She cannot get her eyes open to see what's happening around her. All she can make out is light filling her half-open eyes, the grass faded beneath her hands in the bright morning of it. That, and voices. Her head swims, struggling against a current.

Look at that. The woman sleeps more than I do.

She sleeping now? She with us?

"I'm here," Lyda says. One corner of her mouth drags warm and novocaine-numb. A stiffness plagues her neck, and she wonders how long she drowsed with her head thrown back. "I was just in the nicest place. Why did you take me from there?"

Arley Noe stands over Greuel buried on the couch beneath two blankets and his heirloom quilt. Noe's hands hide in his pockets, his wide cheekbones as prominent as welts, lips a wadded purple bloom; his gray eyes scan her face with disinterest. Lyda yawns, scratches at the itch in her nose—the single effect of painkillers she does not like.

"What time is it?"

"Late enough for me to wonder the point in talking to a dead man about his troubles," Arley says. "Whyn't you make some coffee."

Her body responds automatically to the command, Lyda rising to her feet; as soon as she's up she understands something is wrong, there's a tweak in her equilibrium, and the house lurches as a boat battling storm-thrown seas—no sooner is she upright than a wave knocks her down again.

Arley Noe steps out of her fall with a grace and dexterity she would not have expected to be in him. Her shoulder takes the full impact. His blue face peering down at her displays all its crannies, the hoods of his eyes so deep from this perspective that he seems to have no eyes at all.

"Excuse me," she says. "I don't feel quite right."

A hiss fissures Noe's mouth in place of laughter. He reaches down and grabs her just beneath the injured shoulder, squeezing hard as he wrenches her up. The intensity of the pain surprises her and she cries out something, she's not sure what, she cries it again until he lets go. She massages the muscle where his hand had been, contemplating its soreness as she tries to diffuse it. There will be a bruise there tomorrow. She can handle a bruise.

"I take mine black," Arley says.

"Somehow I knew," Lyda answers. Her voice does not feel completely her own; it greets her face a few steps before her—her throat, tongue, teeth absolved of all responsibility and sensation. She hears that voice tell Greuel she'll fetch him water as well.

The two men, the couch, the IV tower slip past as though taken by conveyor belt. The journey to the kitchen is arduous and distressing and unconscionably long. It's true, there's something not quite right about her. She cannot even feel her soles on the floor. But none of this is unpleasant. How long has she been like this?

The clock on the stove shows two-nineteen. The past six hours are lost to her, aside from the meadow and bright morning dreamlight. Her own body feels at one remove, cocooned in some soft pliant substance. Scooping grounds into the coffee filter provides great amusement. It's so lovely to drift like this, to see her hands act without her willing them. Like watching yourself on the TV while you lounge beneath favorite blankets, and you don't have to question the why or the how to anything, it's on the TV and whatever happens there is already written, it's finished and composed, the show will end as it always ends, every time. Lyda starts the percolator and then goes to the back window, drawn by night wind cool through the storm window.

Nothing out there but the dark. And then from within its depths a long rasping screech serrates the air, increasing in volume and intensity before it ceases abruptly. The sudden end to the cry makes the silence after feel weighted, wary. Lyda presses her nose against the fine steel mesh, catches the scent of rust. The wires pattern a waffle imprint on her skin. That there's a barn owl, she speaks aloud, her voice towed out through the screen onto the breeze. Again the harsh screech sounds, ratcheting high and and then ceasing. This time she finds the owl's eyes reflecting copper from the kitchen light: it perches on the lowest branch of some tree not ten feet away. As her eyes adjust to the dark out there she begins to make out its placid white face shaped into a valentine, the copper eyes unequivocal and remote, mirroring her stare. The owl lifts one claw and holds it raised, talons clutched. Its head dips, and a loud hiss emanates from deep in its throat.

"Little buddy, how you going to find a nice girl with a call like that?"

Minnows surge and twist in her belly. As if he has heard and understood her, the owl extends himself to full height and splays his wings at their widest expanse, arches his back upward, his face transforming—she would swear—to the picture of righteous indignation.

Her nose tingles fierce again and she rubs it hard against the screen. But it's not the same tingle inside, it's a sting, a stench. Something is burning. Something is on fire. The coffee machine coughs clouds of gray vapor and she runs for it, yanks the cord from the wall socket unaware it is her voice saying *shit shit shit* and *no no no* in quick repeating chants. She pulls the decanter from the machine and discovers, impossibly, nothing swishing around inside, nothing's been brewed. And yet the kitchen reeks of scalded coffee. Lyda opens the top of the machine and finds no water there—apparently she's been trying to brew off condensation. The stench of old grounds seizes her face and slips one hot finger down her throat.

The minnows swim up so quickly she hardly makes the two steps to vomit into the sink. Six cruel heaves throttle her, hard enough that she grasps the counter with all she has so as not to be thrown to the floor again. The pliant tissues in her mouth burn as she holds panting over the mess she's made, drenched in a burst of warm sweat, staring into the dire expulsion from her stomach: a viscous, yellow, pancake-like substance expands slowly across the basin, streaked with pink. Floating within she sees several small, half-digested pills; foamy and soft marshmallows on the surface of a hot chocolate.

She turns on the faucet and watches the water begin to draw her mess toward the drain—and then smacks the spout aside to the next basin, unable to allow what's left of her pills to go down with the rest. She splashes her face several times and the water is good and cold. Then she tries not to think about what she is doing; she pokes among the muck with her little finger, the only nail not chewed to the quick. She scoops up four of the least-dissolved pills, creating a line on the median between the sink's two basins.

From the front of the house comes a sound like a cross between a gasp and a belch; Lyda raises her head to listen, straining to hear above the water. That owl again. Still, the sound focuses her and she feels suddenly she has been in this kitchen a long time, she's not even certain Arley Noe is still around. Quickly she forms a bowl with one hand and piles the foamy pills within and then fills the bowl with as much water as she can without allowing the pills to run away, and she does not look at what she brings to her mouth, and she swallows with a deep shudder, bile hot again on her tongue, and the minnows swim back down her throat to their home in her belly.

Lyda braces herself against the sink, ready to heave again; the smell is starting to get to her. She holds her breath and waits. Then, once she's certain she can manage, she returns the spout to pour over her vomit and leaves it running as she steps to the hallway, no longer concerned with—no longer remembering—why she had gone into the kitchen in the first place.

Beyond the hall she spies Arley Noe above the couch, leaning over where Greuel must be whispering secrets to him, Noe's head quarter-turned as if listening closely. Because of the position of the sofa she cannot see any part of Lawrence Greuel save for his bare, chopped-up feet, which tremble and jerk in violent spasms, the quilt working its way up his ballooned ankles and hairless legs.

It won't take another minute, says Arley in that matter-of-fact, side-of-the-mouth way he has, barely moving his lips.

Something thumps the back of the couch, but she cannot see what. The minnows are churning again, deep in the pit of her, and the water's rush in the kitchen fills her head as though pouring directly into her brain. I'm not supposed to be here anymore, she thinks. I am supposed to be gone. Arley Noe leans further forward, rising, his meager body pressing its full weight down on his arms. I'm supposed to leave, Lyda thinks, but she makes no move. Instead she watches Greuel's feet toss like a dog's paws as it undergoes a bad dream, the way a dog digs or claws its way through sleep, whimpering. She watches just as she would watch a show on the TV she has seen before. She watches the feet slow to a stop, the heels come to full rest on the sofa arm; and then the feet part, very slowly, the remaining toes angling outward in the shape of a final V.

Arley sits back. He checks his watch, holding it up for a long time and glancing at Lawrence Greuel and then returning to the watch as a man who counts time waiting for a result. It's not until he drops the hand, satisfied with whatever calculation he was making there, that he notices Lyda swaying in the hallway.

"You bring me that coffee?"

Lyda doesn't answer. Noe's voice snaps her from her trance with the same suddenness of an unexpected slap. She moves fully into the room, stepping around the sofa where the feet lie still on the arm-rest. Noe does not turn around; he waits for her to come up behind him to see for herself what her body has already figured out somehow: Lawrence Greuel is gone.

The whites of his eyes glisten flatly beneath the half-open eyelids, and she can make out where the pupils have frozen at two on a clock's face. A wadded hand towel protrudes from his mouth. Noting her gaze, Arley Noe retracts the towel and begins to fold it carefully, slipping it into the side pocket of his suit jacket. Greuel's tongue swells to follow the towel out, pushing forth over his bottom teeth.

"Nothing happened that nature wasn't about to do any time now," Noe says. "Only so many minutes in a day, I can't be everywhere."

He stands and his eyes search for a place to look, landing finally on her hands empty and hanging by her sides. He glances back down the hallway, appears to listen to the water pouring out into the sink back there. The lipless mouth stretches into something akin to amusement.

"I ran into a problem," Lyda says. "I didn't make the coffee."

"You shouldn't be here. There aint anything left for you to do."

Again his eyes scan the room, resting briefly—it seems to her—on each object as if making a specific inventory of the room at this precise moment. He takes a step beyond Greuel's body and stops, kneeling to the floor and raising again with the old address book. He pages through the book as he walks to the dining table and the spread of prescriptions aligned there, sets his finger within the pages to prevent losing his place, and with his other hand he turns the bottles to expose their labels, ticking each aside.

"Those are mine," Lyda says as Noe appears about to slip one into the same pocket that holds the towel. He looks at the label again.

"So it is," he says. He returns the bottle to the rows. Now is the first time since she returned that he looks fully upon her, his gray eyes aglow in that strange blue face. "Tell you what. I am going to sit down here and look at this book for ten full minutes. In that time you can take whatever you want that you can carry out. But when I stand up again, you better not be in this house. I don't want to see you again, Lyda."

She brings a hand to her face, her arm aching where he had throttled her. Lyda leaves her fingertips against her jaw, looking over the body of the man she had felt so strongly against for so many years and in so many guises—felt anger, repulsion, resentment, sometimes sympathy, often jealousy; never indifference—and realizes that even with the pathetic tongue swollen past his lip she feels only empty, numb, null. Noe sits at the table and holds up his watch. There's nothing left for her here. It's a deal she finds reasonable; Arley Noe is a businessman above all, and there are the amber bottles displayed before her with the sumptuousness of a great wedding buffet. All of it set out just for her, Lawrence Greuel finally making good on what he owed.

On four wheels it's three hours to Harlan. Halfway through the run and they're out of conversation, passing Lexington and on the far side of Richmond as sports radio drones away in the Christ World Emergent Econoline. The back burgeons with nylon nets stuffed with soccer balls, orange corner flags, a bright red gym bag stacked on top, high enough to be seen by any fellow drivers who bother to look. In front sit two young ostensible believers, tattoos hidden beneath button-down shirts; nothing about this vehicle or its passengers worth attention.

Something feels wrong in Cole's stomach and it's not simply nerves, it's an intestinal thing. Driving, he catalogues the day's meals—eggs over easy with home fries for breakfast, a black bean burrito for lunch; the queso had swum within a rim of brown grease; remembering just the image makes his belly lurch again. He tells Creed he might need to make a bathroom stop soon.

Grady Creed is involved with the radio host: no way the Cincinnati Reds will ever compete like they did in the seventies as the Big Red Machine. The large markets on both coasts have all the money, pricing out competitiveness. Take away 1990 and not even Eric Davis in his prime could bring a pennant to Cincinnati, and now he's fighting colon cancer; that Deion Sanders is something to see but no matter how good one man is he can't carry a baseball team. Creed's telling the radio host you can't do anything without near all the money in the world. Who's gonna get the hits, Pete Rose, Jr.? *Junior!?* If Creed expects Cole to second him on this, he doesn't ask for it. Cole has no opinion to offer. Baseball bores him. He prefers basketball.

"Rule one is we make no stops on this run, that's rule number one," Creed says. Creed's always citing some rule to whatever they're doing, like there's a list he should be familiar with, and yet each time Creed stops at rule number one.

The radio talk comes tinny thin in the van's poor speakers and it feels like a shield, or a warmup, before Creed starts on something real Cole will have to respond to. Why else would he assign him this drive unless he has a discussion in mind? It's not for talking baseball. Creed has never invited him anywhere, not even for work, never just the two of them. If he wanted ball-talk he could've hauled in Spunk, but he told Spunk to stay home—the guy needs to deal with his old man's death, Creed said. Cole thinks the best thing for Spunk would be to get out of the house where his father died and roll on with his partners and drugs. Maybe Creed understands that bringing Spunk along would mean extra contraband in the van, as Spunk was in a nonstop period of numbing self-medication, and he did not want the aggravation. Or because since Greuel died it seemed like all the boys did anymore was fight. "It's going to be this way for a while," Creed had said. "It just gets like this sometimes."

There are runs Cole has made routine, and then there is The Run, the delivery that speeds an interstate beeline a few miles past Harlan, that carries the kind of briefcase Cole has seen only in movies, code-locked and steel-braced, stashed beneath Grady Creed's seat. The return will take much longer and he'll be alone with a two-month supply of reefer to satisfy stoners in three counties. Creed's to follow in a tracer vehicle—a protocol begun, he said, after Fleece disappeared.

"Your big brother doing what he did, I don't know why, but what it got me was more work and more driving," Creed said. "I hate driving more than anything. I don't see how truckers do it, no wonder so many of them are tweaked. Not that I'm complaining, I mean half my money comes from them. But it's too much time in the head for me."

Seeing firsthand how The Run works complicates the questions behind what Fleece allegedly did and what is said to have happened after. If he had been interested only in theft, then why go down to Harlan at all? He was to pick up the October harvest, the largest of the year and the riskiest to grow, as it was planted outdoors, spread over several locations, and so most treacherous to reap. The amount of cash on him must have been extraordinary—Cole would guess seven- to eight-hundred-thousand dollars at the least. Could you fit that much money into a single case? The radio show ends and Cole asks what Creed thinks. Creed looks like he's chewing over the question in his mouth—but it's only him working up spit off his dip. "Your brother wasn't always the most practical man I ever dealt with. He didn't know the code to the case, I know that much."

"He didn't? How would you know that?" asks Cole. "Because none of us who make this drive ever know the numbers that open the case," says Creed. "Who does?" asks Cole. "The guy we give it to. Him and Greuel and Arley. Well, not Greuel anymore, obviously." "Who do we give it to?" asks Cole. "Is that Nate Crutchfield?"

Creed eyes him sideways. He says: "Maybe. Pay attention to your driving, I don't trust that floater eye of yours, you could roll us into Wolf Gap following that thing and I want to snooze before we bump up, it's going to be a long night." Before Cole can ask why the night will be so long Creed adds: "It's always a long night with the Crutch, you'll see."

Dusk arrives like a thin veil thrown from behind the eastern hillsides. Creed shuts down to snores with remarkable speed, light, gentle scrapes that sound like fine sandpaper against unfinished wood. The radio mentions a shootout in Mexico near the border between rival cartels; a hostage was released somewhere in the Middle East; a jury in Denver sentenced that Timothy McVeigh cunt to death. He's content to hear it but none of the news means anything to him. He checks his speed and his mirrors; traffic's heavier than he'd expected. Traffic's always heavier than he would have expected, he's regularly surprised by how many people live out between Richmond and London. Usually when he drives he likes to zone out, to daydream over which car is going where, who the people are inside, whether they're kind or maybe complete bastards moving on after ruining somebody's life.

His gut pinches, and a blade of heat slides out between his legs. They have another hour to go at least. Surely he can hold it together for another hour.

In the rearview a slash of light catches his eye; bright headlights leap from behind a semi well behind him and speed past the trailer, cutting back in with a deft swerve just behind the van, the powerful engine loud enough for Cole to hear over the radio murmur. The car lurches forward as the driver taps the brakes, and there, in that instant, the hair on Cole's neck and along his arms flare in alarm, his body startled by the recognition—it's not yet so dark that he can't see the make and he would know the familiar trim of the Nova coupe any day. Its candy-red finish gleams as new; the flip-out window stands open on the driver's side, a marker of the same year as Fleece's car. The Nova revs, slots onto the dividing line, but can't pass due to another semi, WASH ME scrawled in the film of its scum on the back door parallel to Cole's eye line, blocking the lane. Interstate lights glare on the Nova's windshield, it's impossible to see inside.

He speeds up to pass the semi as the road starts to ascend. The Nova accelerates behind him, so close that its headlights are blocked by the equipment stacked in back, the candy-red canopy all that's visible to him. "Why you got to be on my ass like that?" he mumbles.

"How fast you going?" asks Creed, not opening his eyes until a time passes without Cole answering. "How fast," he asks again. "I want to get around this semi to get this guy off my ass," Cole says. Creed checks his sideview mirror. Then he turns fully around. "Get a load of that," he says. "Tell me about it," Cole agrees.

They've barely made a car length ahead of the semi when the Nova splits the space into the next lane. Here Cole notes the yellow front fender replacement, not even primed yet, it could have come right off his brother's car before it burned. The Nova doesn't roar past; rather, it steadies next to them, the driver pulling into alignment with Cole. He fights the urge to look. He has always resisted looking at another driver directly on the highway in that awkward moment of hurtling forward together, the strange feeling of invasion that acknowledging one another in those few shared seconds invoked. But the Nova keeps pace beside them as they pass first one then another mile marker, long enough that Cole can't help but sense the other is trying to gain his attention, to communicate something—and Creed must sense this too as he leans forward, looking. And then Cole looks also. But the windows on the Nova are tinted deep purple and mirror the bluing evening light.

Cole checks the road ahead, then again the car beside him, expecting the window to drop as they careen down another long hillside curving like a flume. The window doesn't move. As the road bottoms out and begins another ascent the Nova's engine roars, accelerates, slows down, leaps forward. "What the fuck's he want?" asks Creed. And then: "Jesus, Cole, you're going over ninety."

So he is—he lifts his foot from the accelerator. It's true, they had been flying. As he watches the speedometer dial down to eighty, then seventy-five, his heartbeat clamors within his head; by the time they hit the summit of the next hill they've returned to the speed limit, and it's not until then that Cole takes a deep breath—realizing at the same time that it's his first breath in a while. The Nova races on, shooting the lane ahead and zooming past cars that brake and change lanes to allow the wild driver plenty of room to maneuver. When they reach the next downhill slope, a long lightless stretch among walls of dynamited limestone, the Nova's rear lights are so far ahead as to be indistinguishable from all the others on the road.

"I didn't realize I was driving so fast," Cole says.

"Dude's probably wondering what those church boys was trying to prove, racing him like that," muses Creed. He pinches a wad of chew from the can, pulls out his bottom lip to set it in place. His face tightens a moment with the sting of the minty tobacco and he smacks the dash with the flat of his hand. "Poor Cole boy, your face was like you just swallowed my spit cup, you must've felt like you seen a ghost. I mean, yellow fender and everything. I mean, *damn*."

He's shaking his head as he scans the radio for another station worth the listening. He switches from AM to FM and peruses the entire spectrum of the dial, finding nothing but commercials or the New Country they both despise. Eventually he gives up, shuts the radio off as he points Cole off the interstate to the Hal Rogers that crosses Boone National Forest.

"It was the wrong side," Cole says.

"Who is?"

"The fender on that Nova. It wasn't the same side. Fleece's was on the driver side."

Creed stares at the cliff walls outside his window without comment. And Cole begins to wonder at the possible connection between things, between different lives lived far apart, how you might almost meet a person at several junctures in your life and yet never do. Like someone out there's living a mirror image of your own life. That yellow fender—could it be possible that it had come from the same yellow Nova as his brother's? And if so, then what's the story behind that yellow car, who had owned it, what forced it into some junkyard to be pieced out as needed? How many candy-red '76 Nova coupes were left in Kentucky?

There must be a number of them; it was a fast car with pieces cheaply found and car nuts love their Mustangs and Novas. Still, Creed's right: it felt like he had been brushed by a ghost. He had driven alongside the thing, struggling with the van to keep pace, his head reeling with *What? What? What?* as he awaited some communication to come, to signal something important, something essential— why else the coincidence of *this* run, his brother's last? What was it trying to tell him?

Why does he feel like it was trying to give warning?

He shakes his head and runs his palm over his face. That entire time beside the Nova he had wondered—no, he had been seeking to know—what it had wanted from him; but it was only his own foot on the gas pedal keeping the two vehicles aligned. It had been Cole himself creating the connection where there was none.

•

Fleece had told him it was a stupid idea, back when Cole had called to say he was moving back to the lake. "Pirtle County's got nothing for you—I thought you were heading to the coast somewhere, diving school," Fleece said. Cole pleaded poverty. And then Fleece said: "You can't find a better job in the city?" And then he said: "Living with Lyda aint going to change a thing, puppy. You can't help someone fine with the problems they got."

The day Cole reclaimed their old bedroom in the house was the single time he saw his brother before he disappeared. Fleece watched Cole carry in his few belongings, thumb hooked to the waist of his jeans and making no offers to help, not so much as even holding a door open. With Cole installed, Lyda clapped her hands and exclaimed, "I'm one happy mother hen with a full nest right now!" standing between the boys and squeezing their shoulders. Fleece pulled off. "I still got my own place," he said.

"Either my boys can live with me long as they like," said Lyda.

Cole felt his brother was somehow disappointed and only wanted him out of there, he didn't understand why. The feeling had hurt him then. But maybe Fleece had been trying to look out for his brother in his own halfhearted way. Maybe he knew already—he *must* have known—what he was about to do.

Later that night Cole had looked over the three low shelves on the partition dividing the kitchen from the main room and found, among coil-spined cookbooks and drugstore paperbacks and the Merck Manual Lyda used to memorize symptoms she needed to present to obtain a prescription, the Pirtle County High yearbooks of Fleece's junior and senior years. The endpapers had few signatures or notes, and these only from girls whose names Cole did not recognize. Invariably they referred to how each would *always cherish* their *special times together* with Fleece, and expressed hope that they would remain close. As Cole paged through the yearbooks themselves he had to smile at his brother's ability to make it through without notice or record. He was missing from the class picture taken on the school's front steps; he hadn't joined any extracurricular groups since getting cut from the basketball team his sophomore year. The only mention of him at all was among the individual student photos, his name listed beneath an empty frame where there should have been his portrait, identified as "missing."

If his brother is dead then Cole has failed him, now with Greuel gone. If he's alive, then Cole has no reason for what he's doing, and the ground crumbles beneath his feet.

Creed directs him onto 421 toward Harlan. "Not far now," he says. It is close to full night now and the van's interior is dark, the dashboard lights dim. "Your belly all right?"

"I'm fine." At the mention of it his insides cramp, and he tightens his gut until the pain passes.

"I paid a visit to that cousin of yours," Creed says. "That kid's a bigger mess than Spunk. You sure he's kin to you and Fleece?"

"He's no kin to Fleece. His father was brother to my father. Fleece and me share our mother." He explains this quietly, knowing it doesn't matter, that Creed doesn't care one way or the other.

"That kid's a storyteller, he's a whatyoucallit—a myth-o-maniac. Right? Got big plans for himself and us and don't even know his own brain's telling him lies."

"What did you do to him?"

Creed's hands rise in innocent surrender. "I didn't touch the kid! I got a right to see where my money's going to come from, don't I? Keep an eye on that boy, though. You know that, right?"

"This why you had me make this drive with you? To tell me that?"

Again the hands surrender. "No, man, why you got to be always suspicious like that? Fleece never believed in anybody neither, not even his best pal who wanted to do a favor. I got a sweet side. You ask Lyda, she knows." He snickers at Cole's reaction to his mother's name. "Yeah, you heard me say it. She's a good woman, your mother, I aint going to do nothing to hurt her. Or you, 'less you give me reason to. Pull over, we're almost there."

He doesn't understand why they left so late, insuring they wouldn't reach Harlan until after dark, instead of first thing in the morning and thus having time to make the buy, load the van, and return home by nightfall. All done in daylight, with less time in Eastern Kentucky where the Feds operate. But he has been at this long enough to learn that a procedure exists behind every delivery run he makes, refined over time by trial and error (he guesses), and he is no one to be suggesting different modes of operation.

The radio had said tonight would show the brightest moon of the year but there's no sign of one yet. They travel a lightless two-lane road pressed upon by trees. He pulls over where Creed says, stopping on a gravel drive that appears like a natural tunnel in their head-lights, pines, oaks, elms forming a tight colonnade on either side, their branches closing off the sky; moths gleam white before the windshield and then flicker into the darkness again. "Turn off your headlights," he says. "Keep your foot off the brake."

The trees and gravel road evaporate. The darkness is as total as if the drive had been scored through a mountain, until Cole's eyes adjust and he begins to make out a distant bluing where the trees must end. He rolls down his window; the cacophony of woodland life fills the van with its noise of tiny saws, minute screams. His gut lurches again, and again he tightens his thighs to keep in whatever's going on down there.

"I've got to find a toilet here soon," Cole says.

"We don't need but a minute, we're not far." From his front pocket Creed pulls out and unfolds a small ziplock. From another pocket he pulls a small steel plate no bigger than an index card, a fancy engi-neer's pocket protector, and shakes from the bag a thick scar of powder. Then he closes the ziplock again and shoves it back into his pocket. Using a small straight razor and steadying his hand against the dash, he thins the scar into three short lines, telling Cole he'll want some of this, too, but only a little, it's pure and clean as you can get, you watch, it'll help your stomach. He sheaths the razor in its fitted cardboard and drops it into his shirt pocket, takes out a cut straw, and inhales a full line. Creed's head pops back; he winces, pinches his nose shut with the straw stuck between his middle and ring fingers. "Who?" he asks with a groan. Then he slams his hand against the dash. "*Hoo boy* but if that aint a kick."

An eighteen-wheeler rushing along the two-lane behind them rocks the van with its afterwash. The movement calls Cole's eyes to the rearview mirror, his thumbnail a different razor against his palm as he keeps watch, expecting somehow the appearance of figures, blue lights; he doesn't take his eyes away until Creed prods him with a knuckle.

"That shit is poison," Cole says.

"Yeah, well. Poison fuels our game." Creed proffers the plate near Cole's chin. "It'll dry up that gut, I promise. You don't want to see me angry on this. I claim no responsibility for my actions for the rest of this night."

With the powder this close he can see it's a only small amount. Creed's staring adds a thoughtless urgency. "Go on, now," he says. "If I was Shady Beck here you wouldn't stop a second, would you." It confounds Cole to feel Creed making sense. He snorts hard and a blade thrusts up his skull into a star directly above his right eye, and his head shoots back as if taking a blind punch. An expanding, steady burn flares the circumference of the eye and he pinches his nose. Soon then the pain starts to subside; his heart beats in his cranium, and he feels entirely new: alert, strong, the best version of Cole Prather he's likely to ever get. Each tree aligned by the gravel drive turns and acknowledges his arrival. Cole smiles; he wets his finger and wipes up the rest of the remaining powder, sucks it onto his tongue. He hands the plate back to Creed, who nods in aggressive affirmation and tells him *What I'm saying* as if they'd been discussing some grave issue and he wanted it to be clear that they were in agreement. "Awrighty James Cole," he says, "let's get to work."

•

Harlan looks like a nineteenth-century river town preserved under glass. They leave the state highway at the next exit and head toward Black Mountain. Cole has never seen Black Mountain and his skull feels carved out and he has always wanted to hike the highest mountain in the state someday. The thought launches from casual idea to committed goal, an experience he *must* have, essentially now. Better yet he should take Shady, wouldn't it be great if he turned around and sped through the night to fetch her so the two of them could enjoy Black Mountain together?

He checks the speedometer to see if he is speeding again and it's hard to reconcile the tempered needle locked on its judicious number with his certainty that they're flying but there the needle sits at 43 mph, two below the law. Maybe they're to meet on Black Mountain, he would definitely like to see Shady again, she's taken an apartment in Montreux he hasn't even seen yet; she's already started the summer's first-term semester, remedial courses in anatomy or something to get back into the swing of things before beginning med school proper in the fall and he's unsure what this means for him, for them, for the two of them together—Creed directs him to another road that winds hills and demands concentration. Every detail suddenly matters. To his left begins one of those slave-stacked stone walls (or else a fabricated one, he forgets how many actual slave-made walls are said to exist, but this one appears old enough to amaze him—and no mortar that he can see), it runs nearly a half-mile before giving to a three-plank fence working as a dam to the thick woods cascading behind. Here Creed leans forward and tells Cole to slow down, which allows him to gather that the fence isn't planked after all but crossed with hewn logs, many of which have fallen, pushed from their posts by the encroaching trees. The entry they turn into is less a gate than a gap in the woods, no postal box, two ruts of dirt road angled up to the night sky.

A constant whisper of tall grass drags against the undercarriage. On either side gleam white spiny sculptures, vaguely figural, spectral forms at the edge of the headlights stilled in fields of high fescue teetering in the wind. Atop the ridge, a white scalloped curb runs along the rutted track and another fence begins on his left, close enough for Cole to identify what swings between the planks, bleached canes forming tripods around each post. The rim of the moon far across the valley rises behind the next ridge like a sun.

"These are bones?" he asks. The road banks right to descend the hill in earnest.

"Them be the Truth's cow bones," Creed half-mutters, half-sings, without further elucidation.

Cole can make out their destination some way still ahead and below them, where vapor lights illuminate a compound of cleared land between a two-story farmhouse and a few low outbuildings rounded as Quonset huts. There's a gathering of vehicles—old battleship cars and late-model pickups—parked in a tight mass of no discernible order. The fence follows the drive along various slow serpentine curves, adorned with the chalky bones smooth and bright and swaying in Cole's headlights, lending the fence the semblance of breathing, of being alive in some way.

The lot's packed gravel grinds beneath the van, a sound that, met with the crank fueling his veins, Cole takes for his grinding teeth. Creed points between the house and the first Quonset and they pass lit windows, but see no one inside. Then they turn behind the long low building and Cole has to step hard on the brake: a lone figure stands before them, eyes set above the headlights.

Dangling from his left hand is the longest pistol Cole has ever seen. The girth of the barrel implies large caliber. The man himself is small: narrow-shouldered, lean as the parade of bones they just passed, a skinny chest naked beneath a set of denim overalls a size too large, overalls weathered to a blue wash punctuated by an explosion of white fibers where the chest pocket had been. He's small but looms bald and pale, made top-heavy by a thick and weighty brow that juts a shelf over the eyes, shading them, masking the face like one glimpsed at the edge of an inscrutable dream.

Creed makes no remark. The van idles long enough that the exhaust turns nauseating. Cole keeps his hands visible on the steering wheel even as it occurs to him that he can't be seen above the head-lights' glare. The man appears to be breathing hard, his reedy shoulders drawn back and heaving, his mouth contorted in a furious snarl.

After another moment Creed begins to cackle. He rolls down his window and leans out. "We gone do this or not you fuckin' hillbilly?" he shouts, slapping the outside of his door.

The man breaks into a smile; his teeth glisten with metal. He steps toward Creed's side of the van using the pistol against the gravel as a cane and he's cackling, too. "Did I get you or not?" he asks. "I'm a hell of a scary sight aint I?"

Creed hops out and the two embrace with the closeness of brothers separated during a protracted war, both happy to have made it through alive. With the door open, exhaust fills the van and Cole cups his hand over his mouth, and music blares from the house, some kind of cantina or mariachi tune compounded by the voices of guests joining in to sing along. It sounds like a raucous party back there, but he cannot see anyone through the windows. The van's slide door opens and the man with the pistol takes a seat in back, setting the gun across his lap, his face cheery.

"I love breaking me in new boys," he says with a wink. "Welcome to Wolf Stills, James Cole. Now get me the hell out of here."

•

The man guides them along another two-track deeper into the property, dropping into the valley until it joins a paved road that Cole follows with increasing dismay at each added turn and curve—it seems they looped back through a dense thicket of woods at one point (he believed he recognized a small bridge crossing a feeder creek)—and even with the rising moon's bright light he is soon at a complete loss for direction. Through gully and hillock and dense woods heavy with new leaves the world is sightless beyond his headlights. Meanwhile the man behind him mutters a melody about murder by the sylvan brink, a song that sounds very old. They pass twenty minutes in this way.

"What county are we in?" Cole asks. The comment fuels general sniggering but no answer.

They make another farm and a weathered barn there and park beside a rusted pickup pulled up close to the barn door. Inside, three Latinos stand before the horse stalls cooing to a few nags. A dull yellow light set high on a beam makes even the bushels of hay look sick. At the sight of them, the Latinos set to work immediately and without word, carrying packing boxes from a stall to the van. Creed and the bald man disappear with the suitcase. Already the reefer is in books, surrounded by packing material and wrapped tight in tinted cellophane. Cole bends down to pick up a box, and one of the men bursts from where he was kneeling and shoves him backward, not quite violently, but still showering him in a torrent of angry language and with a finger in his face, Cole back-stepping until stacked hay bales hit his legs and he sits. The man, small but powerfully built, glares over him to make his point; he stinks of heavy cologne. Each of the Latinos reek of it, the same cologne, a vigorous dusky smell that tickles the throat and hangs about inside the barn.

He ends up holding the van's doors open as the three workers—dressed entirely in soft blue denim—remove the athletic gear and unlatch the back bench and fill the van neatly with cargo. Once the van is full, they rearrange the gear as a covering, and then the workers return to their pickup, two squatting in the bed and the third, the one who had become so angry with him, taking the driver's seat. The man starts cigarettes and passes them on to the guys in back. Cole waits, uneasy and silent against the barn planks, not knowing what to say to these strange foreigners, who seem now with their work done to have forgotten him, content to smoke with their heads back, contemplating the dead light of spring stars above and the brightness of the huge moon hovering above the trees.

He thinks to look for a toilet in the barn even as he realizes Creed had been right, he no longer feels the need. More than anything he's thirsty, and the surge from the crank has settled as an insistent reverberation in his tricky knee, where it aches and glows in rhythm with the fireflies pulsating everywhere. He decides it's not a bad drug, except for a faint unrelenting feeling of panic.

Creed and the bald man reappear from around the barn without the suitcase. Creed's spitting a happy patter low into the other's ear, pointing emphasis with his hand before them and then giggling at what he'd said. The man swings and plants his long pistol, and as they near him Cole can feel himself grow apparent beneath the moonlight, feels himself the subject of close scrutiny even as the man appears to be ignoring him.

Creed tells him he's proud of Cole for making it halfway through the job without fucking them up. He smacks him once on the shoulder in a comradely fashion unusual in him, and then announces that he'll ride with the river-runners. "The Truth rides with you. Now you don't want to get lost with twenty-five-to-life in the van," he adds, "so stay close to these guys. I sure as hell don't know where we're at." He hops into the back of the pickup and slaps the thigh of one of the workers in welcome: "What up, Pancho?"

Already the Truth is in the van with his window down, filling a long curved pipe in his lap. And again Cole feels the scrutiny—like he is being surveyed, examined—even though the man seems focused on something else entirely, lighting the tobacco. Beside them the pickup roars into reverse; pauses; and then with a hard spin it peppers the van with gravel, its rear end veering wildly before the truck steadies and vaults forth into the night, running lights blurred by the dust behind it.

"And they ask why they don't get to make runs," the man beside Cole sighs, watching the truck by the large sideview mirror, the dust beginning to mix with the odor of burning plums.

"The Truth. Why does Creed call you that?" Cole asks. He eases the van into reverse, wary, his voice chippy from the crank and too much silence.

The man clamps his mouth onto the pipe and stares around the vicinity of Cole's right leg. "It could be because Mister Creed is what my old man, lost to this world these many years now, would have called an *im-bee-cile*"—he draws out the word with long disgust—"but I'll grant he can carry money. Or it could be that truth is what everyone gets from me. It is all I deliver."

He smiles the degree that his eyes shut and Cole is charmed, comforted by the man's steady cadence and general grandfatherly calm, a calm he feels particularly sensitive to just now as his own body thrums along the opposite end of the spectrum. The pickup's taillights disappear over a rise in the land as they pull out. "Can I ask your real name then?"

"Surely. My name is Nathan Crutchfield."

Cole touches the brakes and their momentum carries both men forward in a lurch. "You're the Crutch?"

"That is not the name my old man give me. Mostly I think of myself as Nate."

"Okay, Nate. Wow. Man do I have a lot I want to ask you. But I guess first thing is how do we get back to where we're supposed to be? It feels like we're on another planet out here."

"I bet it do. If I was you I'd do as your man Creed said and hightail it after them Mexicans. I don't know quite where we are myself."

Cole grins at what he hopes to be a joke but speeds up just the same. At the top of the ridge he can see the taillights have moved very far ahead of them.

"I try to stay home mostly," Crutchfield says. "Now if we had all day and was walking I could deliver us no trouble, I know these hills like the back of my eyelids. But we have to take roads, we're fastened to them you could say, and it is night. You might want to accelerate."

Cole presses the gas. He doesn't believe the van can go very fast over this kind of terrain—the chassis shudders and lurches with the speed over the two-track and the wheel fights him even as he despairs at the sight of the taillights turning off the farm way ahead. "Do they know I'm following them?" Cole shouts over the noise of squinched shocks and creaking steel, the soccer balls bouncing from one side to the other.

"I believe so. My Spanish is not good, and they are Mexicans with a party to get to, so it's easy to imagine I did not express myself clearly enough for them to understand."

Cole pushes the van as best he can. It's an automatic and he stamps the pedal to the floor once he makes the paved road—but he does not want to put the van in the trees, either. His heartbeat churns into a thrash-metal percussion in his head.

"I am not being fair."

"What?" The van's laments overpower Crutchfield's voice.

"I said I'm not being fair. Alfaro, the driver, he's no Mexican, he's from El Salvador. That's bad country there, you can't blame him for making his way to the bluegrass. And now I think of it, Humberto, the one with the cologne"—his shoulder bumps Cole's on a steep curve, Cole thinking it impossible that only one of the men had been wearing that powerful cologne—"Humberto's from Honduras. Only one of those scamps come from Mexico, I think. But they're all Mexicans to me. Why is that?"

They bank out of one hollow and rocket to the top of another and briefly sail over a railed bridge hardly wide enough for two vehicles. At the top of the next hill Cole slams the brakes, surprised by a T-section stop sign, and the balls surge forward in their net and clap both men on the back of the head. He hardly notices the impact in his searching: he looks left and right down the long stretch of empty country road. He cranes forward and scans both directions again, but there's no sign of any truck, no glow from fleeing taillights. He slumps back into the seat and his hands fall from the wheel. They ache from the grip he'd had them in.

"Can't say it matters much where your driver Alfaro comes from now, Mister Crutchfield. Alfaro is far, far away."

Crutchfield reenacts Cole's search in a slow-motion pantomime: he leans forward, peering left down one end of the road, peering right the other way, eyes asquint against the smoke of his stinking-plum pipe. Then he, too, eases back into his seat. He stares a moment at the windshield without speaking, and again Cole feels that odd sidelong scrutiny in which his core fiber seems to be under measure. What is he supposed to be doing here? What does the man expect of him? Crutchfield bleats a puff of disappointed air through rubbery lips.

"James Cole, you didn't think we were really going to catch that truck, did you?"

•

They ride along the country roads without a single identifier to location save a bridge, a certain sharp curve, the glomming mass of trees creating an illusory uniformity to either side of the lane. He directs Cole to turn left and at another bend the road rises and the hills part and the bright moon captures them with the clear focus of a spotlight. "I know who you are," Crutchfield says, settling back in his seat, one hand firm on the pistol. "Know your type, too. The dutiful son and brother. You're of a kind that goes all the way back to the Bible. Not that its long history helps me understand the type, though. The motivation."

Before the windshield the road unfolds on banks and angles that lift and guide the van through curves and inclines, and it feels like the road is constantly rising.

"I don't get what you're talking about."

"You don't want to be here, James Cole."

It's true. A sour rush wells within him as he realizes this—yes, it's true.

"First time I ever met your kind up close was in the service. I used to fly those C-54s, the transport planes? Wasn't much older than you are now. One time a civvie comes to recruit a few of us to take part in some scheme, CIA wanted to overthrow Cuba—they didn't tell us that then, but that's what it was for. You ever hear of the Bay of Pigs?"

Cole has heard of it. He doesn't know exactly what it was about and admits as much.

"It was a turd on a plate was what it was. And no reason for anybody to raise his hand and say 'I'm in,' but still some went. I know it is so because I watched them go. That amazed me. I had this buddy Angus, he volunteered. I didn't want any part of some *secret mission*, hell I was only there because I didn't know what else to do with myself. Got to ask him before he went off to his island training, I asked him, 'Gus'—that's what we called him, *Gus*, he hated his given name being a kind of beef—I says, 'Gus, why volunteer for a mission you don't have to do what might get you killed?' And he says to me, he looks at me like I just fell from the moon. Like we never bunked together or spoke English from our own two mouths. He says, 'Duty calls, Nate.'"

Crutchfield lifts his pistol and pokes the barrel into the dashboard, hard enough to leave small indentations in the plastic. It doesn't look like the kind of mark that will fade, and Cole wonders what softball-playing churchgoers will make of it—wonders if they'll even notice or wonder where it came from. Crutchfield feigns two shots out the windshield and sets the gun down again. The pipe swirls smoke throughout the cab; he seems hardly to pull any smoke from the pipe himself, enough only to keep it going, otherwise gesturing with it in the air, a priest swinging incense.

"Course I knew what *duty* was, and I understand *honor* and *duty* are supposed to be virtues. Especially family honor. But I never understood why anyone would die for it. Anytime I hear duty calling, that's the time I need my ears checked, you get what I'm saying? You don't ask to be born, not one of us do, and for years you don't get one say in how your family is going about making you the person you are. Then by the time you *do* have a say—suddenly everbody's got expectations on what your obligations are to them. Most people, they just go along. I don't get it. Never have. Can you explain it?"

Cole tries to grasp what the man is asking, uncertain of what he is on to. More pressingly, he doesn't know where they are—he wants to ask his own questions, and he wants to be told where to turn. He keeps driving, the van hurtling through the unknown dark. He asks, "You have family?"

"Like you, had a brother older than me. Beat the tar out of me any time I did what he didn't want me to, which was about ever other day. My daddy, too. Never held it against either of them. Never felt obliged to stick my neck out for either of them neither."

"You got kids?"

"Nope, never did. My first wife wanted some bad, too. She wanted a whole tribe, but nothing ever come of it. Doctors said I had lazy swimmers. She said she could believe that, no reason for my sperm to be any different from the rest of me. Took up with some other feller with pipes that worked and I don't blame her, she was still a looker then, any boy would've been happy to have her shoes under his bed."

He rolls down his window the rest of the way and slaps the tobacco out of his pipe against the door, then retches from deep in his chest and shoots something heavy onto the roadside. "Fair enough," he says. Cole's unsure if he's referring to his wife or to what he spat out the window. Crutchfield tells him to slow on a long curve and take the next left; once he does, they drop beneath the trees again.

"I like this road," Nate says. He tells him to turn off the headlights and Cole hesitates; Crutchfield says *Go on, turn'em off* and he does, slowing to a bicycle pace. The sound of the tires on the road become the single sound; the moonlight streaks down through the dark tree canopy in haphazard spears, luminous pillars of a cool gold that appear almost solid. "Now I will declare that is something to see," Crutchfield murmurs. And it is: the shafts are formed in such contrast to the dark that they seem to strengthen the blackness; the trees seem nearly uniform, undifferentiated backdrop; the world does not seem the same place as it was moments before.

The van nearly stalls as they lift from the gully and Cole presses the pedal again; at the top the trees clear and he flips the lights back on, although here the moonlight is enough to get along without them.

"I suppose I should admire you coming this far into this but in all honesty—no offense meant—I take you for a fool," Crutchfield says, tapping the pistol against one unlaced boot, contemplating that small movement. "I've no business telling a young man what he ought to do with his life so I won't. But I knew your brother, and I will say one look told me you're not much like him. You are not stupid enough not to know this. Fleece fit the job. You, though," and his head moves impossibly slow from side to side. He repeats the phrase: "You, though."

The van jimmies and squeaks with the rough surface of the road, and the soccer balls bobble on the boxes behind them. "Don't get me wrong," Crutchfield says. "I'm not on your side here. Not against you, either. I owe you nothing, but I figure you don't need to be stuck in your brother's life any longer than you have to."

"They call you the Truth because that's all you speak. That's what you said."

"Now you're talking."

"Can you tell me where Fleece is?"

"No I cannot. And not because I won't. Because I don't know."

Cole rubs at an ache in his jaw that stretches to his temples. He's desperately thirsty as well, and wonders how it's possible, since it feels like they've driven twice over all creation, not to have passed so much as a gas-mart. And why is it that whenever he feels he is about to receive an important revelation to why he's here and what it is he's supposed to do, he never does?

"This is what I'm getting at, this right here," Crutchfield says. "I know some about you. I know your kin. You want one of them four-dollar words of virtue—retribution, atonement. But you don't know what your brother did or if there's anything to revenge him for. If Greuel put him down, then now what? There's no more Lawrence Greuel. And even if he was still here, you have to agree that Fleece knew the risks and Greuel would've been justified in his judgment. That truth leaves you going through motions you think you owe your family, to Fleece, a man I'm sorry to tell you but you didn't even know." His face slackens and a melancholy gentleness softens his eyes. "You feel some obligation to him because you was kids together a long time ago. Some might hear that story and think you're an honorable lad. I say it's sadly misguided affairs."

"I've never seen you before. How come you think you know me so well?"

"Would a man in my position let anyone on his property this time of night without knowing where they live and who's their kin? Fleece never even talked about you, son."

They are high above another steep valley lit as bright as dawn. As he drives Cole tries to fit such few details to his brother as he remembers him—the silver chain of his wallet, the unstyled hair always "a cut away from nice-looking," as Lyda called it, the thick forearms and wrists Cole envied. Snakeskin boots dyed to the warm dun of sand. The way he said *you know it* whenever he agreed with you. How he looked as natural to the water in the lake when he swam that he could have been just another part of the same water. That was it; that was the key to Fleece: he was natural and expected as a fish in water, perfectly attuned to his environment, he had carried himself with that most natural and yet rarest of gifts—how to be in the world.

"Let me ask you this. Did you have any clue he was going to steal that run?"

"No I did not. Well in retrospect maybe so. It's hard to think what you really knew before something went down you didn't expect. Understand what I'm saying? I wasn't looking for a problem, we'd played this gig a thousand times. But after Greuel and Noe got after me I thought well hell, I'm not surprised, of course that's what Fleece did."

"Why did you think that? What was so different?"

"For one, he come down with a ghost from my younger days, guy by name of Hardesty used to help with a still and had himself a bad morphine habit back then. I understand you know him."

"Knew him. Not well."

"Knew him, right. That is so. Funny—sometimes you cross paths with another person and you just know, know it in your gut without thinking, that this person is not going to make a ripe old age and that the manner of their ending will be ignoble."

"Why did he bring Hardesty?"

"Said he couldn't drive with his arm broke. He had a cast that covered his fingers, I didn't inspect it or anything. Arms get broke."

He didn't have a broken arm when Cole saw him. And if Hardesty had any plans designed against Greuel or Noe he never suggested that when they were alone in his front room; a little paranoid, maybe, but as far as he could tell all the man wanted was to be left alone. Cole figures he must have that situation all wrong or else Hardesty would not have come to the *ignoble end*—as Crutchfield described it—as he had. Unless all order and form has fled the world. Arley Noe and Mule were murderers but they didn't go killing people for the fun of it. *The fun of it:* this phrase brings unsought images of Hardesty's face in death, how within minutes after he died the color of his face transformed to a cold white closing in on green. The hole above his mustache, the crunch of the shovel against his teeth.

"There's this other thing sticks in my head," says Crutchfield. "Your brother shows up and gives me my money, and then he announces like it's a decree that this reefer is no longer mine and so therefore I have nothing more to do with it. Sounded like a joke at the time, Hardesty got a big laugh out of it and he said it wasn't Arley Noe's neither. But I wonder maybe Fleece was making the situation clear to me. Like he wanted to ease my conscience after it went down, he didn't want me beating myself up wondering if I'd taken part in something I didn't want to take part in. Which would've been thoughtful of Fleece. I upheld my end of the deal, even Greuel admitted that."

"If Fleece was going to steal from Greuel, why bother with the run at all? Didn't he come down here with the cash to pay for it?"

"He did. I got paid." Crutchfield's heavy brow thickens, and he tucks his chin to his chest and frowns. He remains silent for a full minute or more. "Fleece was always square with me, we were almost friends—you don't really have friends in this show, you've learned that by now. But Fleece, maybe he wanted to stay square, I can see him thinking it out that way. It was Greuel and Arley he wanted hurt. He doesn't bring me that money, all three of us get hurt. I got paid."

"I don't know why Fleece would want to punish either of them."

Crutchfield screws up his lips and nods as though Cole has unwittingly confirmed an assumption. Rather than answering immediately, the man digs around in the good pocket of his overalls, and it's peculiar that he uses only his right hand for everything he needs to do and never lets go of the pistol in his left, as if he's fused to this ancient gun, or physically reliant upon it in some way. When his fingers grasp what he's looking for he holds the object before his face close in the dark, his screwed-up lips broadening into a knifelike grin. *Yes,* he says to himself, and tosses the object onto the dash. It clinks against the windshield and tumbles about, and then rolls to a stop against an air vent.

"Go ahead," Crutchfield tells him. "It might be nothing but that right there."

Cole picks it up even as he already recognizes the thick gold nugget ring set with a constellation of tiny diamonds bedded into the shape of a horseshoe.

His face must show his bemusement, because when the Crutch looks at him now, he chuckles.

"I know," the man says, "you can walk into any jeweler in Kentucky with a couple grand and come out with that ring or one close to it. It's not the hunk of jewelry that matters, see, it's what it signifies. Only three of us got to wear that particular design, with that specific number of diamonds, and it means doors will open and phones will pick up in five states from here to Minnesota. It means silence and safety from the fuckers who want to keep a man from what grows natural in God's green earth. Fleece wanted one for his finger and I don't blame him, it's normal to want to move on up. When you work for Greuel and Arley, you're never nothing but a mule. Unless you have that ring."

Cole studies the band again. Headlights from an oncoming semi wash the van and flash the diamonds into dazzle. It's pretty to look at, but Cole has never been much interested in precious stones. He would not think it possible that Fleece's motivation could be so simple. There is nothing Cole can do with *that*.

He tosses the ring onto the dashboard. Crutchfield leaves it there, and the ring rolls with the curves of the road, the diamonds winking in small bursts of florid light.

"People've killed for less," Crutchfield offers.

A silence descends. Without knowing why, Cole thinks of Fleece as he had known him in childhood; he sees Fleece tossing bleach into the lake shallows so they could swim; sees him placing a blanket over their mother on the couch as she slept; sees him handing Cole a fifty-dollar bill when he was twelve. In each image he cannot picture his brother's face exactly; it is like Fleece has receded into shadows, somehow avoided the camera in Cole's eye as he had avoided the cameras at high school.

Beside him Crutchfield begins to sing another of his old mountain songs. *Lord, the water done rushed all over, down old Jackson road. Boy it starched my clothes. I'm goin' back to the hilly country, won't be worried no more.* He interrupts to give Cole directions, holding the melodic note as he tells Cole to turn, then muttering into the lyrics again. Soon they are among the cow bones at Crutchfield's property.

"I do like a long ride of a clear evening," he says along the rise up the two-track drive. Cole asks why he has the cow bones everywhere and he says that clean bones are beautiful and, even better, bare bones keep superstitious people in line. "All Mexicans are superstitious," he says, satisfied with the statement as though he has accessed an undeniable truth. "At least all mine are. Doesn't matter what country they come from. Lay out your farm with bones and nobody fucks with you."

•

The Truth leaves him with the other vehicles parked by the Quonset hut, driving off in the manner of the old man that he is, babying the old pickup at little more than a walking pace among the roadside bones agleam beneath the moon, riding the brakes. The tic of the van's cooling engine clicks time with the music faintly audible from inside the farmhouse. He stands at the outskirt of the lamps' wash on the gravel lot and looks to the sky scrubbed of stars by the powerful radiance of the moon that hovers over the land, following him, tracking him like some cosmic spotlight he could not escape if he tried.

"Brightest moon of the year, they say," he says for the sake of saying.

He enters the kitchen through a screen door lost of its screens. Inside, his body reacts in a peculiar fashion—the hair on his neck stands on end. The kitchen is a nasty sight and feels heavy with menace, as though something bad happened there recently and the fumes of the act still linger. Crusty skillets and pans sprawl sideways in a collapsed stack; the sink teems with dishes, filled with a water that glitters oil and brown grease. A dark fungus arcs along the wall between the counter and open cabinets above. On the counter itself stand a number of empty bottles—tequila and rum and beer—and scattered salt lies thick over everything, free munchies for the roaches that flee at his approach.

Cole opens the refrigerator door; he selects the only brand of beer available, a green bottle of something called Cerveza Hatuey with the profile of an angry Indian warrior on its label. He checks a few drawers for a bottle opener but doesn't find one, and clacks off the cap with the end of his lighter, not bothering to note where the cap falls to the floor of shaky tiles.

In the next room he discovers the origins of the music: an out-of-date stereo straddles two large speakers set upon a wide wooden box, the kind of box used for carrying loads of fruit. The room is crowded, but no one is singing anymore. They seem to have fallen under some hypnosis, or sedation, their bodies collapsed unmoving across ramshackle furniture shoved together so tightly it's tough to maneuver from the doorway. Grady Creed is not among them. Nobody acknowledges or even notices Cole's entrance. A large TV against the opposite wall flashes skewed images between bursts of white noise and holds everyone's attention.

Cigarette and marijuana smoke wafts in great clouds. He glances over the different faces, several men and a trio of women, everyone foreign and the men dressed in similar dungaree outfits that are not quite uniforms, like those who had loaded the van earlier—but he doesn't recognize anyone. One woman lounges across the laps of two men on the couch, sipping at a lime green drink she holds just below her chin. He feels distinctly exposed and out of place. A general sense of degeneracy and hazard permeates the entire floor. Where else would Creed be?

Cole sucks a heavy swallow from his beer as one lengthy, thin man, reclined in a La-Z-Boy chair and heavily mustached, gestures at him with his head, smiling a broad smile that lacks one front tooth. The man nods in a way that suggests they share a joke or a familiarity—or maybe he's only indicating welcome, Cole cannot tell.

"Grady here?"

The faces in the room turn. Each appears a mix of melancholy and anger, like they have recently received terrible news for which they are also culpable, their eyes swollen red and faces shining. Or it's like they are all resting after a fierce brawl and no one's happy with how the fight ended. Nobody answers his question, either; soon Cole is uncertain he even asked the question aloud. The others return their attention to the flickering TV. One of the women leans forward and sets her drink on the coffee table heavy with bottles and cans and TV Guides and magazines; then she leans further and her long black hair falls to one side of her face as she draws a line of powder from a compact mirror up her nose. She turns to the man beside her and offers the mirror but he does not look from the screen, holds his hand up in refusal.

Cole looks again at the man in the La-Z-Boy, who continues to nod and smile, leading with his chin, encouraging Cole to something he doesn't understand. "Any of you people speak English? Grady Creed? White guy about yay tall?" He makes a motion with his hand to indicate Creed's height.

The guy with the missing tooth has nothing to add but that inscrutable smile, a weird combination of warmth and mockery. The music ends and the speakers fill with the turntable's needle dragging at the LP. Nobody gets up to take the needle off the record.

"If that shit's supposed to be cocaine then you all got ripped off," Cole tells the man in the recliner. He merely nods and presents the single-gap smile again.

The rest of the first floor is empty, hardwood floors beneath scattered trash, discarded boxes (one for the large JVC television set) stuffed with takeout food bags and empty paper cups; unlaced work boots line the base of the wall by the front door. A stall-like bathroom houses a filthy toilet beneath a bowed and stained ceiling.

Mounting the carpeted stairs he catches sight of the tall man from the La-Z-Boy following him. "I'm looking for my buddy, he up here?" Cole motions to the second floor with his hand. The man glances at him as he passes the stairs. He slips his feet into a pair of boots and heads out the front door. From the TV room, a small cheer and a lone set of hands clapping.

The carpet on the stairs has a path worn to fibers, but once on the second floor it's like another house entire, cream walls freshly painted, framed pictures of bucolic farm scenes, a long clean houndstooth rug running to the single door at the hallway's end. Four other doors, each closed, line the hall on either side. The scent of that cologne from earlier at the barn hangs heavy, an invisible fog of it. The door at the far end opens suddenly and the man who had pushed him in the barn comes out, perhaps it's Alfaro—yet before Cole can speak he perceives the look of unbridled fury, the man in a quick march, shoulders pulled back, like he is about to launch into a tackle and send them both toppling down the stairs.

Cole surrenders, hands up and palms out as he presses his back against a wall. Alfaro sweeps past—the broad fireplug of a man strides down the stairs without so much as a glance or nod. It's like Cole is not really here, invisible to the people in this house. A strange floating sense of unreality overrides everything here, the little bump of crank left still pulsing in his body like a star about to explode yet he's a star within a vacuum, he's the proverbial tree falling in the forest with no one to hear it. Downstairs it seems a full melee has broken out. A woman's voice cries out and another screeches into a quick and sustained patter that increases in volume until something happens, unheard by Cole, that silences them all. Heavy furniture groans across the bare floor and ends with some grave impact that shakes the very walls. Beside him, a small framed needlepoint of yellow flowers tilts askew above the light switch.

Cole moves. He lists his ear against the first door he comes upon, taps it twice with a knuckle, hears nothing, and tries the knob. A small bedroom furnished with a single metal-framed bed, the floor covered by sleeping bags, two rows of them set out neatly, they must sleep here on the floor side by side; which one gets the bed?

Now there is laughter swelling from downstairs after the lengthy silence, too loud and not quite believable; canned television laughter, TV volume turned way up. Otherwise it sounds as though everyone has left, the slushy drone of the turntable still audible beneath the TV.

At another door Cole hears sheets shifting and a woman's throaty groan, or maybe she's speaking something, an almost familiar chant. He knocks and the woman quiets. He can picture her head in the room on the other side, chin raised, listening. He taps the door again.

"Fuck off. *Vete al carajo.*" A male voice.

"Grady, it's Cole."

"Fuck off, Cole. I'm busy here."

"Grady. Let's go." He looks back down the hallway at the door where the man he took to be Alfaro had come from. "I want to split. Let's go."

"You'll go when I say we go."

The door is painted white but has cracked in the grooves of the wood, revealing a pale pea green beneath. He scrapes a flake from the white with his thumbnail. When he tries the knob it turns and the door opens easily.

Creed voices rage. He's out of the bed and at the door as Cole steps in, blinded by the room's darkness after the light in the hallway, and now it's Creed pushing him back and across the hall to the opposite wall, pinning him there with surprising force, a forearm beneath his chin and the other hand at Cole's belt, lifting him.

"The fuck you think you're doing? Why you always got to act like I'm playing?"

His forearm presses into Cole's throat hard enough that he can't speak. Liquor and cigarettes swoon across his face on Creed's breath, the pungent smell of a woman on his hand. Creed's gray eyes search his and Cole recognizes the familiar struggle, Creed does not know where to look to meet his gaze. The man's pupils are as small as pencil points. He shoves him against the wall again, harder. "I said I's busy. I meant what I said." He shoves Cole again and a picture frame falls off the wall nearby. "You wait for me till we go."

He smacks Cole twice across the face—forehand and backhand— but the blow isn't hard enough to mean anything more than a shaming. Creed is bare-ass naked. A few cheap blue tattoos have blurred with time over his neck, collarbone, and arms. Three diagonal striped wounds sit precisely apart on the inside of his left pectoral, parting the dark patch of hair over his heart, some kind of intended scarring that looks like the logo for Adidas, Cole has no idea what it might mean. Creed half-turns back to the bedroom; his erection bobs and shifts, shining in the hall light, and on the bed inside Cole now sees two dark-haired women, one holding a sheet over herself and the other naked without care and lighting a cigarette as she watches the two men as indifferently as a commercial break on the television, waiting for her program to begin again.

"Crutchfield left," Cole says.

"Course he did, you think he lives here in a house full of Mexicans?" Creed dismisses him with his hand and slams the door shut. "Go find your own fun," he says, and pushes the door hard into its frame, the lock on the knob slipping into place. One of the women inside giggles, lightly.

•

Downstairs in the filthy bathroom Cole runs cold water over his hands and splashes his face and looks at himself in the mirror: his hair is wet and matted, skin pale as paper except for the purplish raccoon mask circling his eye-flesh, his jaw drawn down with the first reddish stubble of beard. He rubs his teeth together and they squeak and he shivers at the sound. He cannot tell from his eyes what he is thinking.

When he enters the first room he notes the TV reception has improved, blaring late-night infomercials to nobody; the people that were here are gone. Someone must have moved the furniture back into place, though he had heard nothing, and he sees no sign of the fight. Again he has the feeling of having wandered into a story that has nothing to do with him, or at least one in which he was supposed to have stayed upon the farthest periphery and has now broken its form by leaving his ascribed role—or like he has stepped onto a movie set in the middle of a shoot but the actors and the cameras have already moved onto the next scene; the house, the entire farm, seem to insist to him that they are not quite *real*. The bottles and drinking glasses remain upright and cramped together and small plates have been overrun in their use as ashtrays. On the far wall he's drawn to a small crushed imprint the size of a softball, level with his face, but he can't tell if this is new or if it had been there forever.

The stereo needle still scratches at the end of the record. He picks it up and returns the needle to its clasp. Yet the sound continues. He stares at the slowing LP, dumbfounded—then he realizes the sound is not tied to the stereo, it's a scouring noise from behind him, in the kitchen. At the table there the man he has named Alfaro sits among rags and bright brass bullets, cleaning the cylinder of a revolver with a bore brush. He is intent on the procedure and working hard, and does not look up until Cole nears. Alfaro stops in his work and glares first at the table before him, and then at Cole. Cole forces a friendly smile. Alfaro smiles in return but with no friendliness attached; his is a smile iced in cruelty. He points the gun at Cole's face and spins the open cylinder. They stare at one another through the rapid whirl of empty chambers. When the cylinder stops, Alfaro leaves the gun pointed at him. Now his smile seems genuine with merriment. He sets the gun back on the table and shrugs, squeezing a few drops of solvent onto the stained bristle brush. Cole stays for what feels like a long time, watching the man at his task; he wants to show that a gun pointed in his face means nothing to him.

Then he's outside. Only the church van and a battered Buick he assumes must belong to Alfaro remain in the lot. How did he miss the noise of all those vehicles leaving? The dull lamps are extinguished and the moon holds him under its great eye again, the metal roof of the Quonset hut glowing silver. The moon's brightness is such that when he looks he cannot make out its features, the face of the moon looks bleached to near white, an incandescent bulb. Bright enough to drive without headlights, like Nate Crutchfield said.

Shady lies asleep in her bed. He pictures her in the same position from that night he had watched her sleep in his room: one arm slung high framing her head, the other clutching the sheet to her chin. Her face never serene but animated in dream. He imagines pale pink sheets, a lush floral comforter; rooms buoyant with clean smells, potpourri and scented candles in the student-housing apartment she has yet to invite him to. Her feet, which she complained got cold at night, nestled within fresh socks.

You don't want to be here, Crutchfield had said. Cole hears his voice in the way Crutch had said it. Did he really think moving back to his mother's house would help anything? Fleece had sniggered at the idea. And then Fleece disappears and near a year later Cole has learned nothing of use, nothing he can bring Lyda to ease her mind or even his own. You don't need to be stuck in your brother's life any longer than you have to, Crutchfield had said. There is what happens, set against what you think has happened. Greuel had told him that.

He will never know what happened to his brother. He can know only what happens to *him*. To himself, to James Cole Prather.

Keys in hand, he hurries across the lot and checks that everything in the van is where it should be. He pushes the soccer balls back onto the packing boxes, closes the side door softly, and then hops around to start the engine, leaving his door open. At the same time he ponders the Buick nearby. He looks at the house, all the lights out on the second floor. He slides back out and pulls the knife from his pocket and flips open the handles, and with a single thoughtless lunge plunges the blade up to the choil into the Buick's front tire, pausing only to listen to the tire exhale a long breath like a pent-up sigh.

He stands a moment looking at the gravity blade in his hand. After years of carrying it in his hip pocket it's the first time he has ever used it for anything other than parlor tricks.

The screen door smacks against the house. Over the Buick's hood Cole sees a moonlit Alfaro rushing toward him. He is running with the gun in hand. Cole begins to backpedal, watching for Alfaro to ready and aim—as if he could duck and avoid the shot in time. But the man does not stop, he's not carrying the gun by the grip, he's clutching the entire weapon instead as if afraid he'll drop it. Once he reaches the car he vaults over the hood and dives, tackling Cole so that they both crash into the van's side. The gravel gives from beneath Cole's feet and they fall, grappling, Cole thinking only to get the gun away, find the gun and get it away.

To his surprise, though, the whole melee seems to be over before it even began. They are hardly on the ground when already Alfaro's grip is loosening. His breaths have turned to a high, plaintive panting: *Aye*, he cries, *aye*. He half-rolls off of Cole and lies back, lungs heaving. The gun is nowhere to be seen. Had he imagined it? A frantic moment passes in searching. The Mexican's hand cradles his shoulder, and it's another surprise to Cole to see the knife sticking out between his fingers. He had not felt himself doing it but there it is, his cheap knife plunged into the man's body to the choil, its unlocked handles bent in the air.

There's blood on Alfaro's shirt but it isn't gushing out, he hasn't cut anything important. Alfaro holds the knife in place, touching one handle and then the other, and then holding the wound again as he murmurs in pain. He can't seem to decide what to do with this knife in his shoulder.

There's the gun, then, radiant beneath the van's open door. The dumb weight of the thing in Cole's hand suddenly infuriates him—this little guy came rushing at him with a freaking gun!—and in his anger he sets all his weight behind his good knee on Alfaro's chest; he makes quiet noises to calm the man, to indicate he's willing to help now; he taps the man's hand to get him to move it. Alfaro comes to understand, and he brings the bloody hand to his forehead to cover his eyes. At first Cole grips the knife gently. Then he shifts it back and forth, working the blade out of the man's shoulder the way he would work an axe from a deep cut of wood. The howl this produces is satisfying in its way, an unfamiliar satisfaction further strengthened by Alfaro's feet kicking in agony, his free hand gripping Cole in a gesture begging mercy, his tongue delivering words that have never fallen on Cole's ears before.

•

All roads lead somewhere. He drives as calmly as the vibrations in his body will allow him to drive. He wants to head west and north. He'll be fine going west or north. Soon he spots signs for US 119 and drives east, not another soul out, now he's glad for the crank Creed forced in him, he feels awake and thriving, now he is going to be fine. 119 hits 25 at Pineville; from there he knows the route—he should hit Corbin and I-75 by dawn.

There's a pinch in his gut and he leans into it but this worsens the pain, sharpens it, and when he touches his belly he feels the hard steel there and remembers he stuffed the gun in his waistband as he got off of Alfaro to leave.

He does not want a gun. Merely holding it, a thirty-eight revolver, seems to summon bad tidings—as though by having the gun he only invites the need to use it. He checks the rearview and sees only the moon's ghost-lit night behind him and leans across the passenger seat to roll down the window there, a wall of National Forest trees beckoning from across the roadside ditch. Once he gets the window down without crashing the van, he spits on the gun and uses his shirt to wipe it down as best he can, no reason not to be as careful as he can think to be. Again he checks the mirror and the road ahead, and, seeing no headlights in either direction, hurls the gun out of his life.

With the gun gone he feels more settled, his mind piercing a clear and hallowed space that allows him to think. As though his doubts and uncertainties and fears, the confusions of what he is doing, followed the thirty-eight out the window and into the night behind. Now it's all thrills. Cole knows what he is doing, and it thrills him. He knows what he is doing but does not know what he's going to do next. Was this how it was for you, brother? Maybe you didn't know what you were about to do until you did it. Maybe you felt like this was the only thing you could do that was entirely yours.

He's going to have to be fast, and he's going to need help. Shady will have ideas. When he makes Corbin the first thing he'll do is call her. She won't believe him and then she will. He'll get her to run by Lyda's for his diving gear, get him a map to Louisiana or Jersey or one of the Carolinas, whichever one. Hell he can hit them all.

A trucker blasts by in the opposite direction and in its high headlights a glinting flashes from somewhere deep on the dashboard, up by the vents. Cole reaches over, feeling for it with eyes readjusting to the darkness of the road, until his fingers clasp Nate Crutchfield's ring. How could he leave this behind, after all he said to me? Cole wonders. Yet there it is. The ring fits the middle finger of his right hand, the stronger of the two. He leaves it on but makes a note to pocket it any time he exits the van. Until then he admires the dancing fire within the stones, moving his hand this way and that, the diamonds alive beneath this strangely bright moonlight.

He cranes forward to get another look at the moon. It's strange—all night he thought of the moon as following him, eyeing his every move, a spotlight he could not escape. It floats lower now, yet still bright enough to blot out the stars. The face of it remains blank and brilliant. As though the night is solid, total, except for this one clean hole bored through its armor and revealing what lies behind: radiant, golden, perfect light.

There is a number, a random number in the amount of coffee consumed in a day—and it's never the same cup, say, cup numero cinco or six each afternoon—when the caffeine not only loses its effect but rather even reverses it; instead of charging his blood, this random gulp hits the stomach and his exhaustion feels complete and irreversible. Such point Brother Gil Ponder has reached tonight. He wants to believe it's the fault of this weak coffee, not fatigue from a day stretching into hours thirteen and fourteen that has him ready to shut his eyes and lean his forehead against a convenient, quiet wall. His assistant Carolyn is a genius in the species of assistants; in the Platonic realm of assistants he envisions Carolyn Hightower and her sensible outfits and the pencil staved through her ponytail and the small Dayrunner tucked under her arm, save for her inability to make a good pot of joe.

The thing is she thinks in terms of quantity—an entirely forgivable offense; in the end it helps his standing with the congregation when he gets up from the wealth-building seminar in the basement cafeteria and heads into the kitchen to make a pot of his own: look there, busy Brother Gil ministers to us all and still he starts a pot of coffee for anyone who needs a boost. Carolyn has left for home (her family having already stepped away from the defeated life, not in need of the workshop's information on subprime mortgages and the uses of home equity), and she won't see or mind this small undercut to her general excellence.

The kitchen opens onto the cafeteria. He hears the guest speaker wind it up by thanking everyone for their time, and a brief silence ensues while the group waits for Ponder to return and give a benediction to the workshop and its attendees and their goals. He likes this speaker, Bobby Howell; he's a believer and fair businessman, too, and it was Howell's idea to set up the bank's generous agreement to donate $300 to the church for each contract loan taken out by a parishioner. Ponder keeps the supplication short, giving thanks for God's abundant creation and the inheritance of silver and gold He has left all His children. He then asks everyone to recite with him the fundamental verse from Third John: *Beloved, I pray that in all respects you may prosper and be in good health, just as your soul prospers.*

The attendees applaud one another and begin to scoop up their handouts and folders and head to the exits at Ponder's urging, for the space is needed—Carolyn keeps a tight schedule, no meeting can run over its allotted time save the last. Already behind the double doorway a crowd waits to start the Recovery seminar. Outside of Sunday services, the weekly Recovery assemblies bring in the largest number to the new building, many of whom are not regular members of CWE, and so he strives to be on top of his game.

Not all of the construction is complete as of yet (the future cafeteria exit is covered in plywood sheathing) and so there's a traffic problem between meetings, an awkward confusion grabbing the reins as the two groups mingle and bump and try to be polite with one another. The situation requires patience. Still he puts on his best face and greets each arrival with effortful warmth, his gracious-host act undermined by a newly sour stomach as he moves into the hallway himself and joins the horde. Then, there, the lift he sought arrives—his hopes met—at the sight of two women near the back of the line, just in sight against the iron railing at the top of the stairs. Ponder strides down the procession to meet them as they make the landing, gratefully awake now as he squeezes Shady Beck's shoulder before taking Lyda's hand in both of his.

"You *did* come," he says, "good for you." A blush rises in the woman's pale cheeks; a tremor shakes her soft upper lip. "This is brave, Lyda. It feels impossible, I know."

"I'm here. I almost wasn't. Little girl here helped me out."

"You're here. You *are* here," he says. He drapes his arms around both women to lead them in, barking welcome again to the crowd hovering about the seats; he darts to one side of the cafeteria to secure two chairs. Lyda declines coffee; another drop might send her through the walls, she says. Ponder fetches bottled water from the kitchen and adds to the stock sitting on the table by the lectern. His appearance there encourages the attendees to find their seats, and at this he brings the meeting to order.

"For anyone here for the first time, my name is Brother Gil Ponder, pastor of Christ World Emergent, and I am an addict. I have been sober nine years and four months and seventeen days, and for this I serve the Lord and the Holy Spirit joyfully and gladly. The way to serve is through *hard work,* the hard work each of you know by simply being here. Thanks for coming. I like to begin these meetings with a bit of verse for us to meditate upon, to set the tone of our gathering. For anyone who would like to stay after, we can discuss its implications until dawn if you want. I can make coffee all night."

He waits a beat for the expected laughter and then quotes the evening's meditation, a favorite he falls back on often: Proverbs 14.23. *All hard work brings a profit, but mere talk leads only to poverty.* Ponder allows himself a few minutes to expand the statement, sculpting a context— experience has taught him that people often need a springboard to start their own thoughts—and then he opens the lectern. He takes his seat, ready to listen to the story of anyone willing to speak. But tonight is Lyda's night; her story is the one he truly wants to hear. He's hoping for revelations, epiphanies—for some hint of solace to be made from what he has done. Perhaps even news, or clarification. The anticipation her confession stirs in him blurs the tales of the first two speakers, their stories familiar recountings of bad choices and woe which echo his own, which he has plumbed and pondered and recounted ad infinitum so many times it bores him—he struggles to recognize the person he used to be. Still, he listens.

After the second speaker finishes, a long pause fills the room with coughs, a sneeze, the crinkle and squeak of styrofoam cups. The group waits, politely. And then Lyda stands, her hand dragging from

Shady's with reluctance as she takes the first step toward the front of the audience, her eyes upon her small-stepping feet.

•

"I'm not sure what-all I'm allowed to say up here," she begins, her voice soft as a girl's. She points out she's been to a few meetings now and listened to what she must guess is a hundred stories and she's struck by how few details are on offer, the true ins-and-outs of what people've done, how they managed to justify what their addictions demanded of them. "The mama in me wants to hear the whole story, you know?" and with this she gets some appreciative murmur from her audience and this settles her, visibly, her eyes rising from the lectern for the first time. Ponder knows the hardness about her, the angular features and sharp lines that frame her uncharacteristically soft mouth—the signs of a person who has held a lifetime of hurt and anger—but in that instant of acknowledging the people listening he feels he caught a glimpse of a hidden softness within her (that's the only word he can find, *soft*), her soft mouth seeming then like a portal to another Lyda, the deeper one, the armor shed and the kind, if lost, soul that is hers alone peeking out to the world through the plush softness of her mouth.

She straightens her spine, says: "I have been owned by pills and painkillers near all my adult life. Name a drug and I bet you I've swallowed handfuls at a time. And I've done a lot of terrible things. Pretty much all out of the love of dope."

At this last line the armor is retrieved and the softness evaporates and Ponder despairs that they will hear nothing other than the boiler-plate narrative of bottoming out. He knows the basic outline of Lyda's version already, how she began her slow ascent from the bottom weeks ago when Shady Beck had invited him to meet at Lyda's house and he did and he spoke to her about where her life choices had brought her, and at what cost. And he had counseled her that if she wanted to she could make a change, she could—she could count on his help, and on the help of the Holy Spirit, and on the help of all who strove to work within the Spirit. Something about the woman fascinates him, he can't put his finger on it, exactly. She's like his shadow, what his life may have been. Maybe it's just that his life has become inextricably bound to hers, in ways he hopes she will never know. There's extra meaning for him beneath what she feels comfortable to speak here; a meaning or coded message he hopes will give him a degree of respite, if not absolution.

"What's strange about this terrible stuff I done is that when I look back, and I've been looking at it long and hard a while now, when I look back with my head clearer than it's been for the last, oh, twenty-three years or so"—Lyda smiles at the few chuckles from the group—"I'm stuck thinking all these things were done out of the fire of true love. Does that make sense to you all? When you have true love, the *real thing,* you'll do whatever you have to do to keep it, won't you? You'll lie for it, steal for it, kill for it if it means you and your true love can be safe together. Maybe you ladies out there especially can relate to what I'm trying to say."

She doesn't get the laughter this time, only a few closed eyes and solemn nods, melancholy smiles. The men around Ponder are frowning at their loose hands dangling between their knees. How many different ways are there to fuck up a life? Everyone here knows.

"But I'm not talking about the love you get from a man. I had plenty of that before I was even seventeen and had a little boy of my own to prove it! No, what I'm talking about is love like what angels must feel from God. I remember hearing as a little girl stories of how much suffering saints endured for the love they knew was true, the love God filled them up with. I never got how someone could feel so certain in that love and, I don't know, so *righteous* in it that they took being burned alive or stuck with arrows or any of those ways they used to torture and kill saints with—that they'd accept that suffering rather than part from this love they felt with God.

"Don't get me wrong, it wasn't like I thought about this every day. I chalked it up to being another one of life's little mysteries. But this one time my husband broke my wrist in a fight we was having. He didn't mean to. He felt bad enough about it to take me to the ER and we told them I fell down steps holding the baby. They set the bones and give me some pills, I don't even know what. But my wrist, it didn't heal right. Once I got out of my cast—sometimes, it could be any old thing, I'd turn my hand a certain way and it felt like bits of glass were tearing at the little muscles, setting down a cup of coffee felt like someone stabbed me sharp. You can guess the messes this brought on. Which made Bethel mad—Bethel was my husband—I'd spill coffee all over him and he was not a kind man and this meant, sometimes, another trip to the doctor. But the pain in my wrist was the worst part; that never left. We tried tylox and vicodin and by the time we got to demerol I'd come to understand the sort of love a saint must feel for God because I wasn't feeling no pain anywhere anymore, my body, my heart in my body, was glowing like jewels in the sun. It wasn't long before I knew I would do anything to keep hold of that kind of love.

"But I wasn't no saint. I was more selfish than that—I didn't care what happened to anyone else if it meant I could get my hands on my demerol or the oxy reds or greens, percodans in a pinch, you name it. It didn't take long for me to figure there was the dose the doctor prescribed and then there was the dose that helped me the way I wanted help. When you get that first great wave, like you've been waiting all your life to find *just this*, I remember thinking, 'lordy me I have been waiting for you so long and didn't even know it and now here you are.' I didn't have to worry about a damn thing anymore, never again. So long as I had me my pills.

"There was this man I won't name here. I bet more than a bunch of you here knew him, too. This man had a big problem with my husband—everybody had a problem with Bethel, but this man had a special problem with my husband and his wife and he planned to put an end to that problem. And he came to me with this, he wanted me to know. I was humming high when he told me. I told him I didn't care what Bethel did, but by this time there were two mouths to feed. My husband wasn't good for much but he did keep a job. And this other man, he understood. He made promises. We sealed the deal, as they say, with a big bottle of pills he knew how to get, and with him swearing that Bethel's son wouldn't starve. My boys have different fathers but that's another story.

"It sounded rosy to think about it. My bad husband was gone, and we weren't ever close to rich but we got by. Most important to me was that I got to glow holy every day. I wasn't much more than a girl myself and so long as this man kept his word we'd be safe. And he kept his word, in his way. What I learned was that in this part of the world you can cut a decent life for yourself if you know how to turn your face a certain direction and keep your mouth shut."

She angles her face away from the audience as if to show what she means; and then she pauses, biting her bottom lip. Everyone here can relate to this turning of the face, closing the mouth, Ponder thinks; isn't that the way for each of us, all the fallen who merely wake up one day to find ourselves in the world? Every soul in this room has traded on the opportunity to look aside, to gaze upon some dream while they tried not to notice their lives burning down around them. He's grateful now to have the faith to approach his life full-on, to know what he is doing and why. It pleases him to help people in need, to see them uncurl from dried shells to full-flowering humanity. He could not do this with any meaningful scope without his ministry. Or, now that it's in progress, this new building complex. He is willing to do anything required to grow his ministry further, and has proven this willingness over and over—a fact these meetings force him to reflect upon. How similar the impetus is to the addict enthralled by her addiction. Similar impulses, but with a crucial difference, the salient difference that saves him, saves them: the addict will do anything for herself, to feed her hunger; Ponder will do anything for a ministry whose mission is to save others.

Doesn't that make even the most grave offense forgivable? At least potentially? How many sacrifices have been made throughout history to make such ministries possible? The list of the dead stretches back farther than the death of Christ Himself.

Lyda palms a tear as she speaks of times she came to realize her need for dope was greater than her will to do anything else. That the love it filled her with was not love for anyone else, but for herself. Which as a mother she knew was not the right way to love, but she was helpless within it. Sometimes she cut back; she managed to go cold turkey for days. "But then I wouldn't recognize who I was," she says. "My body didn't feel like mine anymore, it was a mean friend who hurt me all the time. So I'd get out the medical manual this man give me to memorize the symptoms I needed to show. Later I got too lazy to do even that much, and got my oldest to cop for me. On my medicine I could be myself again, glimmering inside. I stopped thinking of the pills as drugs, they were more like vitamins, stuff my body needed. *Drugs* meant weed, blow, that stuff. Twenty-three years like that. I never thought one day I'd be alone without even my boys to talk to. But that's where it led me. I'm the mother who doesn't know where her boys are, or if I'll see them again, or if they are even alive. That's what my medicine cost me. My health? I've been lucky, my health isn't bad. My life? I'm still here, though often I wish I wasn't. But my boys—only you that's mothers yourselves can understand what I lost. My boys are grown and left me and neither a one said so much as goodbye. Why should they? What have I ever been to them? In my head I was Mom, but all they got to see was a junkie they had to take care of. I thought dope filled me with true love, a mother's love, God's love, but that was a lie. Left me alone not feeling a thing for anybody. But knowing that and doing something about it are two totally different things. If it wasn't for that little miss prettier-than-I-am over there, a good friend to my boys, I wouldn't even be here."

Her voice softens to a whisper.

"Not that I know for certain if my being here is even right to do. Here I am telling all you strangers my story and who knows why. Isn't that just how the world is? We do things we're ashamed of, and then we look somewhere else hoping we'll be told it's all right."

Ponder stares at the brassy ponytail hanging over her seat-back as Shady tilts up her head. He has always thought so highly of her—a bright kid with a good head on her shoulders, helpful to a fault, an example to younger girls; the confusions for which she sought his counsel were standard for anybody her age. Except for the singular phone call she made five weeks ago. He would like to see how she turns out, confident it will be something good. He's obligated to her as well: it was this doctor's daughter who gave him the opportunity to regain full rein of his ministry, though she'll never know that. Isn't it strange and true that empty saying of how the Lord works in mysterious ways. Ways more mysterious than a man simple as himself could imagine on his own. He wonders if God has written out every story already and then sits back and watches his creation unfold, and this is what we call Fate. Or does He make it up as he goes along, dropping hints and guesses to those willing to listen, curious to see what they will do.

Shady had been the one to contact him; it was nearly four in the morning and he hardly recognized her, hearing the nervousness in her voice as it underscored each apology; he had to tell her several times that she had done the best thing for her friend in calling him and of course he would help.

"He needs a safe place to stay until we get a few things together," she had said. "He doesn't want to steal your van."

"That's honest. I appreciate acts of honesty. What kind of trouble are we talking about? He's running from, —he's what? What am I supposed to do for this young man?"

Ponder apprehended before she asked that the idea was for him to harbor the young man in his home. She was vague on the details and at first—before he realized the ramifications went beyond the boy, beyond Shady, and conceivably could immerse Ponder himself and the CWE ministry—he advised she go to the police. Then he apprehended it would be best for no one else to know. For the sake of propriety and uncomfortable speculation. He tried to position his sense of obligation away from legal and moral concerns, and to set it under the purview of his calling: shelter to those in need is a fundamental responsibility he *believes* in, not only as a pastor but as a man. He stopped with the questions and took the reins, instructing her on how best to get the church van into the parking garage beneath his condo high-rise. Then he got on the phone with Carolyn to see what in the schedule could be put off to another day.

An emergency counsel session, he explained, trying not to resent her request for explanation.

And when the boy showed up and Ponder recognized him, his nerves briefly shattered.

He tried to look past the fact, but the unavoidable truth was that he had not expected to know this boy, yet when the boy arrived, Ponder did. He did not *want* to know him. His name and his family was a cup he would have preferred to have pass from his lips. For Ponder to pull off the plan he was barely aware of even strategizing yet he would have preferred an absolute stranger, not the young face with the floating eye, the lank rusty hair tousled from sleep or from being wind-blasted over an all-night drive, the limp to his gait that looked like he had a crutch in place of one leg. Nothing more substantial about him than a garden rake. Ponder remembered him from that surreal and gloomy night at Greuel's house, and in a sudden inner dawning he understood what the boy had done and why he needed help. He was a runner for Arley Noe. Here was the thief of his church vans, and now he was a thief to Arley Noe.

Sometimes you have to be ready to recognize the moment God cracks open a locked door and leaves it for you to decide whether to walk through.

Ponder welcomed his guest somberly. You look like you could use a rest, he said, and the boy said yes, he was tired, but what he wanted more than anything else was a cold glass of water and a hot shower. Ponder told him to get himself a bottle out of the refrigerator and went in search of clean towels. Once he had readied the bathroom he came out to find the boy standing in the center of the main room, circling in place as he took in the condo's spacious design: two levels, the bedrooms upstairs along a balcony that overlooks the main floor, the exterior wall composed of high vaulting windows that give over the wooded land cut by roadways and punctuated by water towers, steel globes at that moment rising above the morning mist and glistening in the sharp light—a wonder-view of Pirtle County.

"What is it?"

"This place. I guess I imagined a preacher living somewhere different."

"It's not mine. I just live here. Even preachers have to live somewhere."

"I always wondered what these condos looked like. My brother worked this job when it got started."

"Oh yeah? Your brother's a builder?"

The boy didn't answer. He pressed his forehead against the window as he tested how far in either direction he could see. When he stepped back again he stretched his sleeve over one hand to wipe at the oil on the glass where his forehead had been. He had emptied the water bottle already and looked for where to put it. Ponder took the bottle from him, asked if he wanted another.

"I really appreciate you letting me come here," the boy said. "If Shady comes through I'll be out of your hair before the day's out."

"What are you going to do?"

The boy said he didn't know, but he expected to do it very far away from here.

"Stay as long as you want," Ponder said, once assured his guest would not be with him long.

After his shower he accepted the clean shirt Ponder offered, a twill button-down that fell nearly to the boy's thighs, the sleeves running past his hands; he was too small for Ponder to offer trousers, so he got back into the jeans that appeared to have been lived and sweated in for days. He tried to hold a conversation for some time but the struggle was obvious and Ponder told him to sleep. He said he had errands to do, a meeting he couldn't miss. Not quite a lie. Ponder asked if anyone besides Shady knew where he was, and the boy shook his head.

He crashed on the guest bed, his bare feet still on the floor. He hardly stirred when Ponder bent to move him fully onto the mattress and then covered him with a sheet. In sleep the boy's eyebrows arched and settled, arched and settled, as though he were dreaming questions for which he awaited answer.

After this point Ponder's own behavior mystifies him. He half-shut the bedroom door and took the van's keys and left for the garage. He located the van, opened the rear doors, found the church's soccer equipment and rows of boxes stacked underneath. He shoved the balls out of the way and used the teeth of his door key to slice the packing tape of one box, and he was neither surprised or moved by what he discovered there.

Quickly he counted the number of boxes he could see, made rough calculations in his head. When he came up with the number, he whistled in disbelief. Once there was a time when such a find would have meant the world; now his concerns were of a much larger, sweeping view. Still, the boxes and the boy could make a world of difference—not to Ponder, who told himself he wanted only to do good, but to Christ World Emergent, to his ministry. There were things much larger and more important at stake here than Gil Ponder.

He drove to a public phone despite having a cell at the ready in his suit pocket. He dug in his wallet to find the folded note and the number there that Greuel had given him the last time Ponder visited. He sat with himself for long minutes, impassive in the comfort of his leather seat, warmed by the growing summer heat as it began to bake through the windows, waiting silently for a line of verse or that familiar still voice to persuade him one way or the other. A line from Timothy came: *Command them to do good, to be rich in good deeds, and to be generous and willing to share.* It was a truth he understood, one he went to often, but of no help now and hardly even relevant. He pictured the boy exhausted in his guest bed. Ponder's mind then revealed a dose of Deuteronomy: *Because you did not serve the Lord your God joyfully and gladly . . . therefore in hunger and thirst, in nakedness and dire poverty, you will serve the enemies the Lord sends against you.*

Deuteronomy was tough. No doubt about that. There the Lord showed where the rubber met the road. He dialed the number through his open window and was surprised to have the voice on the other end of the line before the second ring. Ponder examined his watch.

"It's eight-oh-four in the a.m.," he said. "Do you know where your run is?"

It pleased Ponder greatly, the length of the hesitation before Arley Noe spoke. He imagined him sitting in a furious stew, staring at the phone with those flat unwavering eyes, and the image filled Ponder with a great swell of confidence, an enormous sense of well-being and peace mirrored by the sublime sunlight rising above the gas station and saturating his face, blinding his eyes. "I can help you find something you've lost or I can make certain it's lost forever. Totally up to you."

The demonic holds dominion over this world, Luke wrote. A man has to work within those confines to effect any change or progression toward the better. What he wanted to tell Arley Noe was that it was unfruitful to mess in the service of the Lord and Holy Spirit, that God in His grace looked after his own. But the meaning and power of such words would be lost on Arley Noe; he would grasp only the immediate situation, balancing his need against what Ponder held.

They negotiated. No more use of church vans for running dope. Nothing but honest financial debt between CWE and the holding company Greuel had set up before he died. Finally, he demanded Noe's word that he wouldn't hurt the boy, or else the world would know it all, straight from Ponder himself. You have to give me your word, he insisted.

"I will not touch the kid," Noe said. It took time, long enough that he had to add coins to the payphone—Ponder understood the idea of renegotiation was foreign and not easy for Noe to engage in—yet he was equally surprised by how quickly the man agreed to his terms. "He isn't going to be around Pirtle County anymore, though," Arley said. "We can't have that."

It was the best settlement Ponder could arrange. He gave the information and hung up, and then waited with a gas-station cappuccino in his building's garage while he played tricks in his mind to force away doubt. He hadn't drunk half the cup before he recognized the man they called Mule driving a small Toyota truck, his body so large it took up half the windshield. Ponder followed the truck as it wound through the garage from floor to floor until it located and parked beside the CWE van. He watched the big man work his way out of the driver's seat, wondering why such a large person would drive such a small truck, thinking to himself that these guys, tough as they liked to act, used not half the sense their mothers gave them.

He did not wait around for more; he did not want to see. He left as Mule brought out a toolbox in the truck bed—probably wanting to appear to any onlookers that he was there merely to work on somebody's condo. Ponder spent the day distracted at the few meetings he made, the prayer luncheon, anxious at what he would find at his home, what he would say to Shady Beck, a member of his congregation, when she arrived later with the boy's things.

In the end the story he told was false in only small parts. He returned home to find the van gone, his furniture straight, his kitchen gleaming and clean with a new faintly orange-scented cleaning solution. There were no signs of struggle; the boy must have been surprised and gone willingly. Even the guest bed had been made. When Shady showed up with a duffel bag and a back seat brimming with scuba gear, Ponder told her the boy had moved on after a shower and a long nap, telling Ponder that he didn't feel he could waste any more time. When she asked why he would leave without clothes or his truck or the gear, Ponder could only shrug.

"But I didn't even get to say goodbye," she said. For a moment he thought she might burst into tears, or screech that he was a liar, a murderer, or threaten to call the police—and yet it did not surprise him when she did none of these things; she was a strong young woman, with a good head on her shoulders. "He must have been pretty desperate," she said. Ponder agreed that this had been his impression. It comforted him somewhat to note this part of his story was true.

1998

Summer again and hot as you please and there is no wind on after-noons in July. Like the wind just got burned out of the sky. You keep thinking the wind is going to come, the air turns so weighted, humid, you'd swear there's a fog over everything, molecules of visible moisture reflecting the sun's light in fluid floating diamonds, and you think any time now a storm will come to renew the earth; the weatherman says tonight's the night, we're due a big howler, there's one on the way and better make sure you're up on candles and batteries. Not in July. The storms clear out the valley in May, and June, and August, but in July it's like an enormous glass bell has been placed over the county and nothing can cloud the sun or budge the motionless air, you can feel it press on your skin and sour in your clothes.

Unlike her mother, who retreats deep into their cavernous home and explores the pleasures to be found in a tumbler, Shady loves this time of year. She loves the full-bore Kentucky heat and when she does not have to be anywhere looking proper she doesn't bother with her car's air-conditioning, she just rolls down all the windows and lets her hair rip, the wilder strands sticking to her sweaty face as she sings along with the radio. She keeps a large-toothed brush and a spray bot-tle of water to make herself halfway presentable again, wetting down the mess and combing it back into her signature pony—but there's no point in the effort today. She has all the water she needs waiting for her, all she has to do is dive right in.

The place looks a whole lot different in daylight. A better vibe, peaceable, everything painted in pastels. No chugging generators or buzzing walkie-talkie radios or visible shotguns.

She's the first to arrive, it's not yet two o'clock, and she feels a touch wary at how cold the quarry water might be despite the long weeks of hot days and no rain. She hauls the gear out of her trunk, one of the few students to have already bought most of the necessities rather than renting them from the shop, carrying the large duffel containing her fins, snorkel and mask, the weight belt and buoyancy compensator that were once Cole's, down to a spot of cut stone near the shore. The car door's open with the radio on—it's not turned up loud enough to be called obnoxious but in the cove-like shape of the quarry the music pings back off the limestone shelves in a queer echo and seems to assault what would otherwise be perfect silence. When she retrieves the air tank and slams the trunk, it sounds like successive claps from three directions.

She turns off the radio and shuts her door with more care, the quiet draping the day like a shroud. Not even the trill of birds or the lap of water; the light green surface as she looks over it appears solid as glass. She throws her keys onto the duffel bag and strips to her swimsuit and dumps her clothes in a pile, kicking off her flip-flops as she trots to the water's edge. It's warm on her toes, but then the water is shallow there, barely to her ankles. Shady's ready to swim. She's supposed to wait for the instructor and the rest of the class but she just wants to go for a swim. Dr. Beck had made it a point of pride that each of his daughters were strong swimmers from childhood.

The road that once guided trucks hauling stone from the bottom is ground smooth as sand and disappears into the lake. Shady skips out on the steep grade, diving once the water crashes into her thighs. Her eyes close as she's engulfed in the sultry mix of warmth and cold, exultant in the clamor of water as it fans and then slicks her thick hair down her back on the currents of her momentum, bubbles of air rolling the length of her body, nearly kneading her skin, one of her favorite sensations in the world. She doesn't open her eyes until she surfaces, turns her head for breath, and then begins a languorous crawl, the entirety of her vision beneath the water encompassed by a lime green made ecstatic by the ruthless sun, the heat of which still roasts her exposed skin. She swims some 300 meters to the far side without thought, immersed in the pure physical effort of her body, her ears getting nothing but the noise of her churning limbs and the air bulling out her nose and mouth. Which is more difficult: to think or not to think? She's found the only time her mind empties completely is during physical exercise. When she pushes off the stone wall again she turns into the backstroke, eyes agaze on the gradations of blue and white in the cloudless continuum of summer sky that posts no markers. A falcon, or hawk, rides the thermal currents up there; a pleasing silty smell in the water flushes her face and feels extra clean, almost like soap. She swims on her back until the bird passes from sight. A few further strokes and it starts to feel like she's been swimming a long time, and she starts to wonder how far she has gone, begins to doubt she's traveling in a straight line and has fallen into some pointless zigzag pattern—for a moment she likes the strange lost sensation this doubt brings, and then she doesn't like it and turns over.

She's been on a long diagonal headed away from the drop road where she dove in. Her instructor Theo stands ankle-deep there with hands on hips giving her the affectless sunglassed stare of a lifeguard. The rest of her class has arrived as well, spilling from their vehicles, the men pulling equipment out of Theo's truck while the women wait and chat and look around. From Shady's position in the water their voices sound both near behind and far before her. She waves hello to Theo; he keeps his hands on his hips, jerks his fine chin in return. Shady titters and then starts a crawl in earnest, meticulous with her form since she is being watched, she doesn't know why she should care what any of them think of her freestyle swimming ability but there she goes just the same, she wants anyone who sees to know Shady Beck can swim really well.

"You got here early," Theo says, unflinching as she smacks a bit of spray at him.

"I did," she says. She rises fully out of the water and snaps her thumbs beneath her suit to pop the Lycra from where it has sucked up onto her breasts. Theo turns to the others; he has that kind of husky voice that makes her think of football coaches who yell so much they've ground their throats to sandpaper.

"It doesn't matter how good of a swimmer you are, people, if you've learned one thing this week I hope it's to never swim alone," he announces for the benefit of all. Then, to Shady as she opens her bag: "What if you'd cramped out there? You're alone, the water's cold. . . ."

"Theo, please. At my age, fit as I am, if I'd've cramped up out there then I was supposed to die."

She's pleased the comment garners smiles from the students close enough to hear; they're all either slipping on wetsuits or getting tanks filled. Theo's only being half-serious anyway, one of the reasons he makes a good instructor is that he isn't a fascist about rules for rules' sake. Besides that he wants to sleep with her and Shady is pretty sure she's going to let him, maybe even tonight after the cookout to follow the day's final open-water certification dives. She's up for a summer fling; she's moving on soon.

Med school did not pan out. She finished the first semester and made it through half of the second before deciding to take a bow. It wasn't the difficulty of the courses that discouraged her. Biochem, Histology, General Anatomy—the demands were fine (she likes studying). Basic Doctoring 1 raised the initial red flag. Over the past year she had learned something about herself (it seemed she was learning about herself all the time, like she was on some kind of three-month cycle of self-enlightenment, every ninety days or so came a series of revelations she couldn't avoid if she were to remain truthful to herself, a phenomenon she figured was probably normal for everyone in their early twenties; yet in Shady it felt accentuated, she suspected the cycles were especially pronounced in her for some reason—her father and oldest sister agreed, though this hardly helped; she thinks despite all her gestures at living widely and open and willing to experience life outside her given social circle as a successful doctor's youngest daughter, that somehow in spite of such willfulness she had lived a kind of naïve and sheltered existence so far). Okay—Shady likes people, she likes helping people in need, but what she learned last fall was that she did not like to examine the bodies of random strangers, especially strangers in pain or suffering from sickness. And these people weren't even the real thing, they were acting out symptoms for the first-years' benefit. The result being another recall to the drawing board, another reassessment of the blueprints for the ongoing project of being Shady Elizabeth Beck.

Cole had disappeared on her as peremptorily and conclusively as his brother had disappeared on everyone before. She had arrived at Ponder's condo on time, as agreed, and found him gone forever—leaving her with an Audi cabriolet full of diving gear she'd believed he would never leave behind; equipment he needed. Lyda said she didn't want any of that stuff around if Cole wasn't there for her to bitch about it being in her way. The problem with being sober, Lyda had told her later (Shady had tried again to return Cole's belongings over the holiday break), was that it allowed you plenty of time to feel the sadness you were putting off by getting high. *I'm supposed to be making amends to people who aren't here for me to make amends to,* Lyda said. *I don't need more reminders telling me my boy isn't here.*

Shady had piled all the gear into the bedroom closet in her apartment, thinking vaguely that if he did ever come back he would want these things. It wasn't too much in the way but there was enough stuff still to be a constant presence each time she slid back the two folding doors to debate what to wear. For a while school kept her too busy for the gear to be anything other than a nuisance. Then it became a conversation piece, her roommate bringing up the mystery of Shady's stowed scuba equipment among fellow white-coats in the cafeteria, apropos of nothing, Shady's roommate being the type who didn't shy from borrowing clothes without asking. By semester's end, the tank especially—its chipped and dinged red paint revealing the chrome beneath, suggesting one-time heavy use in a sea somewhere—had subtly turned into a kind of lure, a signal she felt forced to decipher, an invitation to adventure and a freedom she wasn't getting from textbooks and lab appointments and brutal exams and running about with a stethoscope in her pocket.

Shady on her own, not feeling particularly happy; a rare snow day in winter, two inches of ice on the roads: she began to consider the confining nature of medicine, as opposed to the wider peripheries inherent to oceanography, marine biology—something down south directly on or at least very close to the beach.

•

At school, from time to time, she still got high alone. Less often than as an undergrad; too much studying to be done. And never again did the fabric of the moment break apart and display for her the secret workings of the world. Still, on nights when her roommate slept over at her boyfriend's place, or was hitting the books with the group at the library until closing (Shady preferred to study at home on her own bed, in solitude, testing herself on flashcards of her own devising), she would open a window and smoke a bowl. Her routines had lost the feel of ritual there, they felt different in the heart of the city where you could never escape the feeling of enclosure, of being corralled. In her apartment the routines slanted more often to melancholy, Shady a ship heeling leeward, hollowed out by an absence she had not felt or recognized before. Sometimes to alleviate the symptoms she would carry out Cole's things and arrange them as best she could into a human form on her floor. Two fins, a weight belt, the tank and regulator and buoyancy compensator (she didn't know what it was called yet then), the hood and mask and snorkel. Gloves made of some material like mesh and neoprene simultaneously that she set at either side of the tank. Set out like that, the empty gear felt as a kind of connection to a dream of a friend she once had, or believed she'd had, a boy she had once liked without ever feeling certain exactly of how or why. Which was strange and uncharacteristic of her. . . . She would stare at these assorted objects, stoned, and wonder what had become of the person who was supposed to use them. She would wonder and come up with extravagant fantasies for his fate, futures entirely opposite of what Arley Noe or Grady Creed could do had Brother Ponder not helped him escape: Cole making a killing on the coast somewhere with all that weed, he fitted himself with the latest equipment you could buy and was on his way underneath the ocean seeing every day a different world from the one he'd seen the day before. That's how she liked to imagine the ocean: protean, under perpetual transformation, the landscape and creatures living there changing almost perceptibly by the hour.

She thought up other lives for him, too. She thought of him taking another name, and wondered what he might choose. Something normal and standard: Bill, Jeff, Sean. She imagined him becoming an entirely different person, someone she would not immediately recognize—Cole fattened up and in a suit swinging a briefcase, Cole tattooed and lean in swampy Florida shooting alligators, Cole bushy-bearded and long-haired taking tickets at a traveling carnival ride. All of it was possible; she believes that. Endless possibility, hardcore transformation—it's what she believes it means to be young and American. Take off whenever and wherever you like, start over as somebody new, someone even *you* won't recognize for a while. The essential right of a person is *to be* whatever she believes herself to be. The question is how you do it; how often you get the chance.

•

The class—nine of them, not including the instructor—make a day of it. The water is very clean for a quarry, visibility around thirty feet. She doesn't wear her wet suit even though below twenty feet they hit a thermocline and the temperature drops dramatically. Their fifth and final dive is constructed like a scavenger hunt, requiring the divers to explore a number of items scattered around the bottom, sixty-five feet down, and retrieve from them a weighted tag. There's the police car she remembered Cole mentioning as they waited to pay Arley Noe; a number of small sunken boats; a bathtub and commode behind an old school bus with a fake skeleton placed at the wheel. There are fish, too, bass and bluegill and supposedly carp who are fearless of the divers; she makes a note to ask Theo once they return to shore where the fish came from. They dive until their tanks are nearly empty while at the bottom, a task they must prove they know how to negotiate. Everyone manages to meet the NAUI certification, as expected (it seemed to her impossible to fail, as long as one showed up), and once on shore the mood turns celebratory. The coolers come out, the beer smokes with ice, Theo has burgers and chicken breasts to cook up on the portable grill. The quarry has been annexed in a way that keeps it closed from the general public, and the local dive shops pay the county for the privilege to use it. The group has the place to themselves.

Shady has not had the opportunity to get to know her fellow students well; she's the only one there, aside from Theo, not part of a couple. She passes among them, studying their smiling and laughing faces. Everyone is good-looking or nearly so, and all are fit, tanned, white-teethed. She was surprised to find, when the course started, that she was the youngest by several years; in her mind, taking up diving would be the domain of people her own age or younger. Not that the others could be considered old: as the sun descends and a bonfire catches light, she feels like she's taking part in a beer commercial. Or she has walked into a catalog shoot for J. Crew or the Gap. James is a graphic designer who specializes in logos; his fiancée Marilynne manages an upscale women's shoe store and they're going to get married soon and honeymoon in the Antilles. An older couple (older to Shady; they're probably in their mid-thirties) tells her they wanted licenses because they'd become bored with the usual vacations, hotels in Europe, cruises in the Bahamas, and now wanted a theme to focus their future destinations, something to get them out of the clubs and pools and into the world. "Now we have this test, there has to be diving available as a feature," says Esme, who is beautiful in a way that makes Shady wonder about herself, beautiful in a way she would like to be, although it looks very expensive.

She drifts in and out of the gathering, keeping her eye on and distance from Theo. A minute ago she'd seen him standing before the grill near his truck, bragging about the marinade he'd soaked the chicken in for twenty-four hours. Now he's barefoot and shirtless embracing his knees, a bottle of some craft beer loose in hand against his blond-flecked shins, regaling listeners with tales of underwater adventures, the sharks seen, turtles ridden, the vicious aggression of the Moray eel. To Elaine, the woman closest to Shady's age and who already runs her own business—a popular vintage clothing store where Shady had often shopped before meeting her here—he explains the difference between jellyfish and the man-of-war, something to do with nematocysts and the pain of the venom. He shows off a spandrel scar that wraps his shoulder and part of one fine bicep. Off the coast of Australia he swam right into a man-of-war and nearly died from an allergic reaction. What does it feel like, Elaine wants to know, how much does it hurt? No more than being whipped and salted, Theo says. It's a strange turn of phrase to use. It isn't apparent why he would make a reference like that or how serious he means it. Elaine admits she doesn't know what that would feel like and she calls to her boyfriend down by the water, "Hey Bobby, what's it feels like to be whipped?" No one else knows what she is talking about and the comment provokes a great deal of laughter.

Shady catches Theo's eye, allowing hers to linger on his long enough that he'll notice she's walking up the graded road alone. She's surprised by the impact the alcohol is having on her after only two beers; it must be due to the full day in the sun—maybe the mix of gases from diving, too. She's looking over the abandoned cars where the ramp to the water meets the curving two-track road that touches the edge of the quarry and then leads back out across the field, the sky in twilight pulling long shadows from the stacks. She feels him arrive somewhere behind her before she hears his sandals kicking up the ground. He has taken off his sunglasses and thrown a shirt back on and she's glad for that, there's something about being outdoors near a man without his shirt that makes her feel even younger than she is, kind of grossed out and stupid at the same time, and she greets him with a smile. "What are you doing up here?" he asks. "Don't you want to celebrate with the others?"

"I just felt like a walk," she says, and she does. Feel like it. "I used to know this place. I've never been here in the day, though, it was always night."

"I've heard stories of what this place used to be like at night. I wouldn't have guessed you for that kind of crowd."

She smiles again and they walk. She's trying to place where she must have been in the truck with Cole—where they stopped and waited; where Arley Noe had appeared like an apparition in the dark. The area looks much larger in light than how she remembers it; in her mind they were practically traveling through tunnels until they rose back up onto the old alfalfa field. And it had been cold then. Now the junked cars look smaller—many of them are crushed, compacted—and the sandy terrain is still lit up with the day's sun, vibrant and glowing. She can't decide where Noe had come from; he was there and then he wasn't. She would swear he had walked down the graded road toward the water but where would he have gone to then? It's all broken rocks and slab-like platforms and sheer cliffs.

"What about you?" she asks.

"I'm not from the county," he says. As if that meant anything. When the dead space between them extends over several slow steps he adds, "I rode through with a coupla buddies in high school, I think. We picked up some weed once or twice. I was never big into it, that stuff makes me sleepy more than anything else. You smoke?"

"Sure. Sometimes, when it's around." She smiles at this touch of self-censorship, thinks: *You can invent who you are any time you want; that doesn't make you any less true.* Today—maybe for the time being— she's the kind of girl who smokes pot if it's around.

They don't follow the road but stick instead to the edge of the quarry, climbing over stone where necessary (Shady first, glad to have pulled on a pair of gym shorts over her swimsuit), following the lip up to the highest point and settling there, allowing their legs to dangle over the edge. It's brighter up here, the day clinging more tenaciously than below; she hadn't realized how much of the setting sun was blocked by the cliffs. Where the rest of her class moves about the small bonfire, dancing, it looks like they've already gone under night.

"You don't strike me as the type to be running around here buying weed," Theo says. "I have a hard time picturing that."

She would have expected a magnificent prospect from this vantage, a sense of grandeur with views in every direction; it had not occurred to her that they were merely returning to the surface from what's essentially a big deep hole. Behind her is weed-riven field (it will be ragweed season soon); the vista below her feet returns the pathway she'd followed up, and, farther, the bright lights of a distant strip mall and gas station.

"We all get into our own little messes," she says.

"Still. My understanding is this place was pretty rough for a while. Guys with guns."

She asks him if he remembered whether he had a student once named Cole Prather; Theo's eyes blank as he thinks. Eventually he says he doesn't remember the name. Shady begins to describe the boy she knew, his pole-vault gait, the eye aslant. Theo blanks as he thinks again, then shakes his head. "You sure he got his license through us?" he asks. She doesn't know; she was guessing. Her eye traces back to the still water below.

Theo's leg rests against hers; she likes how the hair on his legs catches the sunlight streaming low from behind them. She looks at him straight-on for the first time since they left the others. He's a convincingly good-looking man, she knew this already, he had stood in as her dive partner to even out the numbers in class. He's handsome in a conventional and friendly way: tall and broad-shouldered, muscular without seeming desperately so, not a gym rat but someone active, who tasks his limbs. His blue eyes are friendly and reflect a slight glow from this angle of sunlight, and in close he appears older than she would have guessed, a scratch of crow's feet around the eyes that his tan diminishes from farther away.

"You talk about this guy in the past tense," he says. "Was he a boyfriend or something?"

"I'm not sure what you'd call him," she says. "I don't talk about him in the past tense, though. I don't mean to talk about him." She looks at the stubble of his beard, blond and fibrous like the rest of him, and again, maybe it's the beer in her, but she thinks again of how handsome this guy is, he has a jaw for heroes, it's like he's not even real— half-surprising her own fool self, she lurches forward and kisses him.

His first reaction is a laugh that she fills with her tongue, and his skin smells of warmth and salt and very lightly the taste of beer. He allows her to kiss him, one arm taking the weight of them both. But then it does not take long for her to notice his response is not as passionate as she would have liked, or even, to be honest, expected. With his free hand he touches her bare shoulder. Then he pats it, lightly— like one would do to calm a puppy.

"Is this not okay?" she asks.

"Sure, it's fine. It's all good. There's no rush."

She sits back to take this in, squinting at him. "No rush?"

He grins, takes a swig of his beer. He's the kind of guy (a summer boy who belongs on a beach) it would be difficult to dislike for long, a pleasant shallowness about him that doesn't bear ill will against anyone, that only wants to have fun. A kind of fun Shady would tire of in about a week or two. He pats her shoulder again and she tells him she would rather he not do that anymore. This brings his grin into a broad smile, and he shrugs. He says: "You know, this beer has a high alcohol percentage in it, like eight percent or something. You have to be careful with this stuff." Then he stands up, and as though she had not just thrown herself at him or even mentioned so much as the weather, as if she is not sitting right there in the dying sun feeling humiliated and near to naked in her swimsuit and shorts, he tells her he shouldn't spend much time away from the rest of the class. Then, perhaps noting her wary disappointment, her sense of unbelief, he throws her a line of escape, saying, "I can't afford to be known as the instructor who hooks up with his youngest student. It's a small group, divers. Word gets round and a guy has to be careful. You coming down?"

She tells him she'll be down in a minute. "You go on ahead. They're probably *all talking about us right now*," and she rolls her eyes in a display of sarcastic fretting.

She feels the pout as soon as his back is turned. She's not sure how or what just happened, but the promise of the day that had begun with her early arrival at the quarry has vanished, and her pride is hurt. She thinks, I would never . . . , but immediately she recognizes she has done the same to boys before, not teasing them, exactly, but playing open to overtures, frolicking in their flirtations, and then backing out when the moment got too close.

What's going to become of me, she wonders.

She doesn't know. All she knows is that it won't be here. This leads her back to Cole, who had believed the same about himself, and she wonders again, did you do it, Cole? Are you living the life you hoped for—if not what you planned, close enough to claim you hoped for it? She thinks of that time just two years before when she had run into him at the Winn-Dixie and he had explained how he had returned to the lake to keep up on his mother, nobody had a clue to even wonder about Fleece then. After a few minutes in the cleaning supplies aisle he had asked if she wanted to hang out with him that night, and she had said yes. And how that night had ended at the seminary before it was torn down and there was that great thunderstorm and the transformer exploding not twenty feet away from her (a word that plied her mind, her imagination: *transformer*), it was like fireworks, or a brief act of war, and she had scurried back to the boys and found them on their backs and had called to them, come see, come see, and they did, they followed her up that dark corridor to where the transformer and the post it was attached to burned in the night, it pulsed with a fire like she had never seen before, and it was terrifying, it was beautiful, it was a miracle, and she did not say it then—she did not tell anyone ever— that it was like a promise to her, —when she reflected on this later she thought of it just like that, a promise from somewhere that miracles happen and that she is safe, the world was frightful but she is safe, she could ask what she wanted and she would be safe. And what is it she wants, that any of them wanted from this life? Life. Life and more life.

ABOUT THE AUTHOR

Kirby Gann is the author of the novels *The Barbarian Parade* and *Our Napoleon in Rags*, and co-editor (with poet Kristin Herbert) of the anthology *A Fine Excess: Contemporary Literature at Play*, which was a finalist for the *ForeWord Magazine* Book of the Year Award (Anthologies). He is Managing Editor at Sarabande Books, and teaches in the brief-residency MFA in Writing Program at Spalding University.